# THE KISS

*Lynne* Thompson

JANUS PUBLISHING COMPANY
London, England

First published in Great Britain 1996
by Janus Publishing Company
Edinburgh House, 19 Nassau Street
London W1N 7RE

**British Library Cataloguing-in-Publication Data.**
**A catalogue record for this book is available from the British Library.**

ISBN 1 85756 217 8

Cover design Optigraph Ltd

Phototypeset by Intype London Ltd
Printed & bound in England
by Antony Rowe Ltd,
Chippenham, Wiltshire

*For Steve, for believing in me*

# One

The grey, snow-laden January sky steadily spat out huge flakes all day, until the usually soot-covered rows of terraced houses were transformed into startling bright white lines, as if a new page had been turned in a book, waiting to be written on. It was the only time this town was ever clean, a quick lick behind the ears for a special occasion, knowing full well that by tomorrow it would be filthy again. The air was freezing and ice clung to the windows in myriad patterns. There was little chance that it would melt, for the temperature was as cold inside most of houses as it was outside.

Despite the arctic weather, Clara Johnson was sweating. She wiped away the trickles of water that dribbled along the wrinkles in her weather-beaten face and tried once again to ease the baby, whose head was firmly stuck, into the cold and uninviting world that waited. 'Elizabeth – push, you must 'elp, the baby's tired, push. Come on, you can do it,' she sighed, but it was hopeless.

Clara had been delivering babies for as long as she could remember, most of the children in this street, and now their children were encouraged into the world by her gentle hands. She prided herself that no one ever needed to go to the expense of calling out Doctor Pendleton unless it was a real emergency, and there was not much that Clara could not cope with. Never in all her years had she come across a

1

situation like this one, and for once she was unsure as to whether she would need help. For ten hours now she had soothed and encouraged, she had shouted and yelled, in fact done everything she could think of, but it was all to no avail. Elizabeth it seemed was lost, in a trance-like state, unable to hear or respond to the desperate urging. All her instincts told Clara that if this baby did not get some help soon it would die. For hours it had been stuck fast, just a crown of jet black hair visible, trying to force its way out, but held back by the vice grip of its mother. Each contraction had come and gone without any progress, almost unnoticed except for the wild dilation of Elizabeth's otherwise blank eyes.

Clara reached for the shiny blade that lay on a towel on the dresser. This was a last resort, but Clara felt she had no choice if Elizabeth would not help.

'Elizabeth, just one push, that's all yer need to do. One big push. Yer baby's dying 'ere.'

Her pleas fell on deaf ears. Expertly she nicked the taut skin that imprisoned the child and in a flurried gush the now blue baby slid unceremoniously into the world. Clara heaved a sigh of relief as it took its first hesitant breath and then whimpered, exhausted but nevertheless alive. She hated to lose them, especially at this stage; she could never rid herself of the memory of the tiny ghostly white faces, so perfect, yet so cold. She was furious with Elizabeth, and scooping up the little body she proceeded to wipe away the sticky mucus and dark blood that streaked its frail body, ignoring the fact that the afterbirth would come soon and she ought to be attending to the mother.

For her part, Elizabeth lay as she had done throughout the entire ordeal, rigidly still. Her only concession to the contractions that had racked her body, tearing it apart with cruel regularity, was to gouge her fingernails deeper into her palms, from which the blood now oozed in sticky scarlet rivulets. When the final contraction came, with such excruciating force that she could not bear the pain any longer, her mind, unable to exercise further control, plunged her into sheer panic and she let out her first and only scream of pure agony. Clara did not look up from her charge but continued to wrap the baby into a warm blanket. It was cold in the bedroom and the child must be kept warm at all costs; Elizabeth would just have to fend for herself.

Clara marched over to the bedroom door, behind which Edward had paced for hours wondering why there was no sound from within. In spite of his desperation he did not dare enter the room and face the wrath of Clara, who firmly believed that a birth was no place for the father. Flinging wide the door the midwife thrust the baby into his arms and; ignoring the astonished look on his face declared, 'You've a beautiful daughter, no thanks to yer wife.'

With that she slammed the door shut again in his face and proceeded to deal with Elizabeth as quickly and clinically as she could.

Some half an hour later, Elizabeth could hear the hum of muffled voices. She knew Edward and Clara were talking about her, but she did not care. Let them disapprove, she did not love this baby and she certainly was not going to pretend that she did. She had never wanted it. For one thing she felt she was far too old at thirty-eight to start caring for a child. She had never dreamt she would get pregnant again, it was all Edward's fault, forcing his body upon her. Even if she had heard Clara's words of encouragement throughout the birth she would have ignored them, for in truth she had switched off her mind, determined not to assist the brat any way. Throughout the whole torment of the pregnancy she had tried everything she could to miscarry, swallowing all sorts of pills and potions, heaving and hauling heavy weights, even throwing herself down the stairs. But the baby was as determined to survive as she was for it to die. That it was here at all stood as a triumphant and shining defiance of her wishes, and she hated its very existence.

The loud clumping of Edward's boots on the bare wooden stairs announced his arrival, Elizabeth sank deeper into the refuge of her bed.

3

'I thought we'd call 'er Annie,' Edward declared, placing his daughter into her arms.

Elizabeth disengaged herself from the red-faced crumpled infant, who was screaming incessantly as if to reinforce her presence on her reluctant mother.

'Call 'er what you like, I'm not interested. In fact I don't want to see 'er at all, I don't want 'er. Do yer understand, Edward?'

With that she flounced over onto her side, burying her face into the pillow to block out the vision of father and daughter that was so abhorrent to her.

Instinctively Edward scooped the baby up into his arms, hugging her to his chest, cradling the tiny body to try and give her some comfort. Inwardly he seethed, he just did not have time for all this nonsense, Elizabeth was his wife, this was her responsibility. Fighting back the rage that filled him, he gazed down at the helpless little bundle in his arms, still wrinkled and blotchy from her traumatic birth. Trails of black hair dripped from her head like muddy rivers, yet to Edward she looked quite beautiful and his heart stirred at the sight of her. A fierce protectiveness coursed through him taking him quite by surprise, so great was the impact she had upon him.

He knew he had to get back to work now, heaven knows he had wasted enough time already. Elizabeth he would have to deal with later, maybe she would feel differently once she had rested. Annie, oblivious to all the fuss and commotion she was causing, was carried back to the warmth of the kitchen, where a fire blazed in the stove and Clara's ever open arms waited.

Elizabeth stretched slowly in the bed. Her body ached but then she knew most of that was her own fault, for she had done nothing to help herself during the birth. She was clean now, all the horror and debris washed away. The sheets felt crisp against her skin, it was over, she smelt of lavender water and soap. She smiled to herself as she recalled her own mother giving her the tiny cask of perfume on her wedding day. She had worn it then to excite and arouse Edward, now

4

she had used the last few drops to drown out the smell of his offspring, and she certainly would never allow him to touch her again in that way. Her mind began to drift to her sons, her angels. She had felt such love and warmth when they had been born, such contentment as she had suckled them. First Jack and then two years later Luke, followed by the tragedy of her third son dying at birth and finally little Matthew consumed by cholera just before his second birthday. She had gained so much from her time with them even though it had been cut short with her youngest two. Here in contrast there was only a festering bitterness and indescribable anger at the unwanted intruder. The love for her remaining sons was all consuming, it left no room for anything or anybody else. Sleep began to drift over her in pulsating waves and gratefully Elizabeth sank into its beckoning depths, happy in the knowledge that she was free again, the parasite was gone from her body, her responsibility had finished.

'What am I going to do with 'er, Clara? She won't even hold the baby.' Edward dragged his fingers through his thick black hair in desperation.

'She'll come round in time, you'll see,' replied Clara, not entirely convinced of her words after the past few horrific hours. 'Meanwhile you leave the little one with me and get yourself back to the salt shed. Those boys of yours will wonder where on earth you've got to.'

'She says she doesn't want to see her, won't feed her either. What in God's name is wrong with 'er?' Edward shook his head wearily. Tending the salt pan in the shed was enough, more than enough, for any man, without all this as well.

Clara smiled reassuringly and squeezed his arm. 'I'll talk to 'er, and if she won't feed the baby, Sally Toscher at bottom of street is still feeding her latest. She'll wet nurse for you, I'm sure. Don't you fret, we won't let this little mite starve an' I'll be 'ere as long as she needs me.'

Edward was overcome with gratitude. Grabbing his thread-bare jacket he mumbled his thanks and backed out of the door into the cold street. The freezing afternoon air stabbed his chest viciously. Raising his eyes to the heavens beyond the falling snow, Edward said a silent prayer for Clara and Annie. As he scurried down the cobbled streets, trying to keep his balance on the slippery uneven surface, he buried his head deeper into his jacket, in a vain attempt to keep the frost from biting into his skin. He was comforted by the fact that no matter how cold it was outside, once he was in the wych shed he would soon be sweating.

The gloomy terraced houses of Lytwych leant against one another like a row of drunkards, each one unable to support itself. Some were sinking whilst others tried desperately to hold them up. Whole walls suddenly sagged and collapsed, windows and doors no longer fitted and here and there the gaping holes were stuffed with rags to try and keep out the winter draughts and rain. It was the legacy of the Cheshire salt towns that the more brine that was pumped from beneath them the more land sank. Whole streets and fields would suddenly disappear, swallowed up as if in revenge for the stolen brine. Wobbly houses, where bedrooms became parlours and parlours sank into cellars as the houses gradually slipped into the ground. Each building clinging valiantly to its neighbour until, eventually exhausted, it relinquished its hold and was devoured by the ever gaping mouth of the earth. Like most people living there Edward did not notice the crumbling landscape, nor the thick black soot that clung to everything like an inky blanket. It took a lot of coal to boil brine, so dozens of squat chimneys belched out poisonous smoke and noxious fumes. Houses, streets, grass, all scorched and blackened, for most of the year the Cheshire salt towns were shrouded in a perpetual dense fog. The salt sheds or wychs proudly lent their name to nearly every Cheshire town, declaring them to be salt towns, Middlewych, Nantwych, Northwych. Lytwych was no different – the wych sheds were the very lifeblood of its existence. Without them the town could not survive and they ruled the lives of all who lived there.

As Edward entered the wych shed the vapour took his breath away. For a second he could not see anything for it was far too steamy inside, but he knew where everything was by instinct. Grabbing the heavy wooden rake that hung on the wall, he flung it out over the bubbling brine and began to drag the bobbing crystals of salt to the side of the vat. As his eyes adjusted to the hazy light he could make out the shapes of his two sons stacking the salt bags in the far corner.

Jack the elder was fifteen, a tall strong lad. He towered over Luke, who was two years younger. Both boys had worked in the wych shed since they were eight or nine years old, and even before that they had been expected to help with the lighter jobs, like sewing the canvas salt bags. Every day from five-thirty in the morning until early evening they worked alongside their father. Sunday was their one day off, and then Edward tended the pan alone. The fire was allowed to die on Saturday evening and Edward spent the next day cleaning the pan ready for another week's production. He slept that night as best he could on the narrow wooden bench along the wall of the shed and tended the fire, stoking it through the night so that it would be ready for the morning.

Edward yelled across the thirty-five feet of bubbling liquid. 'You've got a sister, as nobody 'as bothered to ask.'

The boys greeted the news exactly as he would have expected.

'Told you it would be,' muttered Luke slyly.

'What use is she ever goin' to be in 'ere,' retorted Jack, equally unimpressed.

Edward sighed. Try as he might he could not fathom his sons. At their age he had been proud to work alongside his father. In this very shed they had sweated and toiled, driven by the knowledge that they were 'independents', free men. His sons could see no value in the fact they owned their own pan, passed down through the generations, cherished and slaved over unselfishly.

7

Jack and Luke were lazy and resentful, their heads were full of ideas of getting away and doing something different: ideas planted chiefly by Elizabeth, obsessed by the thought that her sons deserved better. Edward knew in reality that there was nothing better, they could slave away for someone else for a pittance of a wage or end up in the workhouse.

Most of the salt sheds in the small town belonged to John Ellis, a rich land and property owner, who resided in a large manor house. His home, situated north of the river that meandered through the town, was free from smog and filth and far from the slum houses where his impoverished workers lived. His estate was vast and most families in the area worked for him in some capacity and most hated him, for he was notoriously cruel and mean.

Edward was considered to be one of the lucky ones, and he only wished he could make his sons see that. He was one of only a handful of families that owned their own pan. Over the years John Ellis had tried every way he could to take these free pans; bribery, arson, threats and bullying were his tactics, but independents were proud men and not about to give up their birthrights easily.

To look at the sheds they hardly seemed worth fighting over; Edward's was typical, a low squat wooden hut crouching against the river bank. It was really no more than a shack, with a louvered roof to let out the steam and an open doorway in the side. Inside sat the huge vat underneath which burned the fires. At one end loomed the massive pump that sucked the precious brine up from the earth below, to feed the ever hungry vat. High in the rafters were long racks on which the salt was stacked in order to dry out before being sent to the barges and shipped to Liverpool and the markets beyond. Despite its bedraggled appearance the shed was Edward's only means of survival and he tended it lovingly, seven days a week, it was his whole life.

'Can we go 'ome an' see Ma?' Jack's voice broke the silence in the shed.

'Are all the sacks ready to go down to the barges? They sail on mornin' tide.'

8

'Yeah, everythin's done, fire's stoked, coal bins are full, salt's cleared from the floor . . .' Jack rattled off the list in a monotone voice, not wishing to disguise the boredom.

Luke hovered eagerly by the door, his jacket already slung around his shoulder. He was by far the more intelligent of the boys and therefore more manipulative. He sidled up to his father slyly. 'I can't wait to see the baby, it's not every day you get a sister. Besides, Ma might need some 'elp at 'ome. Best we try an' 'elp out, let 'er rest eh?'

Edward conceded, not taken in by his son's rhetoric yet too weary to argue. 'Get off 'ome then, and mind you're both back sharp in morning, these sacks 'ave to get to the barges.'

Before he had even finished speaking they had gone, racing off into the failing light outside, two prisoners released.

Edward shovelled some more coal under the boilers and sat on the bench to rest for ten minutes before he had to start raking again to prevent the crystals lumping together too much in the pan which made them twice as hard to lift out. He shuddered as a vision of his new daughter flashed before his eyes. It was frightening that such a tiny bundle could have such an effect on him, but he could clearly see her face, demanding his love and attention. She had, in a short space of time, changed his life and he felt powerless against these strange surges of emotion that she evoked. His mind raced to Elizabeth. He had no idea what was wrong with her, she had a perfect daughter and yet it was almost as if she hated her. She doted on the boys, too much for his liking, excluding him from everything until sometimes he felt an intruder in his own home. Surely she would take to Annie in the same way, given time. He dragged himself to his feet. She would have no choice. Tomorrow he would go home and put a stop to all this nonsense once and for all.

# Two

'**A**re you all right, Ma?' Jack perched anxiously on the edge of the bed in the cold sparse bedroom. He was shocked at the sight of his mother's pale face and the fact that she was so obviously exhausted, and yet another wave of resentment swept through him. This was all that baby's fault.

'I'm fine. Just a bit tired, that's all, son.' She pulled herself up in the bed so that she could see Jack more clearly. 'Where's Luke?' she asked, wanting both her children here with her.

'Clara sent him to get some wood from the yard to stoke the fire. She's got the baby down there, must keep it warm she says.' Jack paused, not sure how far he could go on displaying his dislike of the intruder; after all, his ma might have gone soft over it.

'What have you called it?' he enquired disdainfully.

'Yer father has called 'er Annie,' replied Elizabeth stiffly, and seeing that Jack too was not impressed with his sister she continued, 'Jack, I want yer to know that I'm not very 'appy about the baby, in fact I really don't want 'er at all.'

Relief flooded over his face and he leant forward to clasp his mother's hand. Just at that moment Luke burst into the room, cheeks burning bright red from the frosty air.

'It's all right, Ma don't want 'er either,' Jack blurted out, before his brother had even closed the door.

Both boys fell upon the bed, one each side of their

beloved mother, and she hugged them to her, kissing each head in turn.

'Nothing is going to spoil things between us, boys. You two are the most important things in the world to me. That baby is certainly not going to interfere at all.'

Elizabeth clasped them to her breast to reinforce her words. This was the picture that greeted Clara as she entered the bedroom a few minutes later, Annie in her arms, whimpering quietly.

'She's 'ungry, Elizabeth. I've brought 'er for a feed.' Matter-of-factly she bent to place Annie in her mother's arms.

'I'm not feeding 'er, I've already told Edward,' Elizabeth retorted, folding her arms to prevent Annie being placed in them.

Clara took a deep breath to control the anger she felt rising in her. 'She's yer daughter, yer responsibility. Just take 'old of 'er, you'll feel better then.'

She lowered Annie on to the bed but had to scoop her up again as Elizabeth recoiled in horror. Hissing now through gritted teeth, she viciously spat her words out at the startled old woman.

'You just don't listen do yer. I don't want 'er, I don't care what yer do with 'er, just take 'er out of me sight.'

'Elizabeth, yer don't know what yer saying. Yer tired, that's all,' Clara soothed.

'No Clara, I'm not tired, I'm 'appy. I've finally rid meself of that creature. Me only regret is that she survived.'

Elizabeth's eyes shone malevolently. Jack and Luke sat like two imbecile gargoyles on sentry duty beside her.

Clara enveloped little Annie in her ample bosom to shield her from all this unjustified hatred. 'You're wicked Elizabeth Hayes, quite wicked. Mark my words, God will punish yer for this.' Clara backed out of the room shaking her head in disbelief. 'Well, little Annie, it looks like we'll 'ave to take you elsewhere for yer supper.'

In grateful response the baby opened her large dark eyes and gurgled. Clara's heart turned, in just the same way as

11

Edward's had when he held his daughter. Wrapping her in a shawl and then inside her own coat, Clara hurried out into the freezing night air. She walked as fast as her legs would carry her to Sally Toscher's house, hoping that they wouldn't be turned away from there too.

Being the mother of eight and by her own admission dotty about babies, Sally soon had Annie suckling at her breast. Meanwhile she and Clara discussed the terrible situation and whether or not Elizabeth had gone quite mad, and more to the point, whether Edward would put up with it. Sally declared that her old man would give her a clout round the ear if she was so stupid, not that she ever would be, loving children as she did.

'Yer should've seen 'er, carrying on like that and with those two boys listenin', it's just not right,' Clara mused.

'If yer ask me, those lads are 'alf the problem. It's not natural, the way they 'ang round 'er. Even on a Sunday when my lot are all playing and getting into mischief in the woods, those two are always tied to 'er apron strings. It's not healthy.' Sally deftly swapped Annie from one nipple to the other, where she immediately sucked frantically.

'Nothing wrong with 'er appetite, anyway,' Sally laughed, feeling very satisfied in her rescuer role. 'Best leave 'er 'ere tonight. No point in taking 'er 'ome, and I expect that Edward's at the pan anyway.'

'Thanks, Sally, you're an angel.'

'Just doing what God made me for and what me old man says I'm best at,' Sally giggled, expertly throwing Annie over one shoulder to burp her.

As Clara stepped out once more into the hostile night, the snow had stopped at last and silver stars blinked in the navy sky. She scurried home to her cold and empty house, her breath making misty clouds in the air.

'You're getting too old for this, Clara Johnson,' she muttered to herself as she fumbled in the freezing scullery to light a candle. A few minutes later she lay huddled under the warm blankets on her bed, her mind drifting back to Annie. What a dreadful start in life the little mite had had.

Still, Clara had a good feeling about her; with those wonderful dark eyes she would have plenty of people to love her. One thing she was certain of, Elizabeth Hayes would live to regret today, oh yes, she thought, what goes round comes round, sure as fate.

Thin fragile streaks of light squeezed themselves down from the heavy sky and fell nervously upon the blanket of snow that covered the earth. It was still early morning and the strange yellow light hung in misty pockets, in a vain attempt to melt the frozen earth. Edward stretched his body wearily, trying to ignore the gnawing ache in his stiff limbs that reminded him, unwelcomely, that he was not as young as he used to be.

For once the air felt quite chilly in the wych shed, the fire beneath the boiler glowing with only dying embers. Edward knew he must get it stoked up soon or the boiler would cool altogether and a whole day of work would be lost while it re-heated. For a few seconds it seemed just like any other day and only as Edward pulled on his tired leather boots, worn almost away to the soles, did the realisation that things had changed hit him. Annie's angelic face appeared before him to reprimand him for his forgetfulness. It was a vision that refused to disappear for the next few hours as he shovelled the coal, cleaning out the dead ashes and replenishing the insatiable appetite of the furnace. Surely, he told himself, Clara would have talked some sense into Elizabeth by now. He tried to imagine Elizabeth cradling Annie in her arms, but somehow the vision would just not appear. He could not shake the feeling that things were far from all right. He couldn't just leave the salt pan, they were already behind him yesterday, yet all he wanted to do was run home. Angry with himself for being so disturbed by this baby he raked furiously, trying not to count the hours until Jack and Luke arrived and he could escape to see her. Chastising himself for going soft in his old age, he lugged the heavy salt bags onto the huge wooden barrow, ready to haul them down to the river later.

13

'Why can't we take the salt?' whined Jack, after Edward had told him and his brother that they had to tend the salt pan today instead.

Taking the salt to the river was the only enjoyable thing that the boys got to do. They were free down at the quayside, away from the steamy shed that imprisoned them every other day of the week. They both glared sulkily at their father.

'Well just today I'm taking it, and if yer don't put yer face straight I'll be taking it every week,' Edward barked sharply, 'I'll call at 'ome then and see the baby.'

Jack shuffled miserably. Unlike Luke, who knew when it was time to keep your opinions to yourself, Jack always had to have the last word; usually to his detriment. 'Suppose you 'ave to see the baby, Ma don't matter.'

The response was as always swift, and a sharp cuff landed across Jack's head. But not content to leave it there Jack continued to mutter under his breath. 'No point anyway. Ma got rid of it last night, and good riddance is what I say.'

Edward felt a rush of sheer panic sweep through his body, and grabbing his son by the collar he dragged the insolent face inches from his own.

'Got rid of 'er where, tell me, tell me now?'

Jack, enjoying the dismayed look on his father's face, smugly replied. 'Don't worry, our precious sister is safe. Clara took 'er away and Ma won't 'ave 'er back, don't matter what you say.'

Almost flinging Jack to the floor, Edward shouted some instructions to Luke, who had merely observed all the commotion, saying nothing but thinking a lot. Racing out of the shed Edward fled along the slippery river bank towards home, all thoughts of the loaded salt bags reaching the barges tomorrow gone from his head.

An hour later Edward knocked, somewhat sheepishly, on Sally Toscher's door, unsure exactly what he was going to say, knowing that he was completely at her mercy.

The sight that greeted him as he entered the tiny house was of utter chaos. There seemed to be children and clutter

14

everywhere. The noise was unbearable, a dog was barking, and there in the midst of all this stood Sally holding a small bundle that he assumed was Annie.

'Come in, if yer can. Come on, yer kids, out, out, go on, shoot,' and she shepherded the large brood out into the scullery, where the din continued but it was at least muffled now.

'Terrible row, but I love it when they're all here, makes the place alive, Lord just listen to it.' Edward could not fail to listen to it, but he was warmed by the fact that what he heard was laughter and she was right, the place was alive, with a warmth that he had never felt in his own home. Strangely, though, he had never noticed it was missing before today.

'I 'ave to thank yer so much for looking after Annie. I don't know . . .' he stammered.

'Don't say another word. She's a little princess. 'Ere,' and Sally placed Annie in her father's outstretched arms. The tiny face, no longer distorted by birth, shone up at him. Black hair curled on her head and two large eyes blinked out, owl like, from rosebud cheeks.

'She's bonny, isn't she,' grinned Sally, smiling at Edward's obvious admiration of his child.

'Yes, yes she is,' muttered Edward, embarrassed by the rush of emotions that had overtaken him once again as he cradled this child in his arms. This was overshadowed only by the glaring reality of his predicament.

'Sally, I really don't know what to do. Elizabeth just won't have 'er, I've just come from 'er now. It's hopeless, unnatural I know, but I'm afraid if I take Annie back she might just harm 'er.'

What he didn't tell Sally was that he and Elizabeth had just had a screaming row, during which he had had to use all his restraint to stop himself from striking her for the first time. Elizabeth had screamed that she wished Annie was dead, and had promised to kill the child if he brought her back into the house. He had never seen such wild insanity in her eyes before and he knew that although he could

15

force Elizabeth to take Annie back, he could not guarantee her safety. In his heart he knew that Annie would not be able to return to her home again. He was sick inside. Why should his child be denied her own home, when her only crime it seemed was to have been born?

Sally, being who she was, at least made it easy for him, and for that he was grateful.

'It's decided then, she will just 'ave to stay 'ere with me. Don't you fret, I'll love 'er just like me own, and you can come and see 'er whenever yer like.'

'But what about George, 'avin' someone else's child in 'is 'ouse? I don't want to cause yer any trouble.'

'You just leave me 'usband to me. Why, I can twist 'im around me little finger, if I treat 'im right,' she winked, her implication bringing a flush to Edward's cheeks.

'I'll give yer somethin' towards 'er keep and Clara will help out. Are yer sure yer can manage, yer 'ave so many of your own?' Edward asked, cradling Annie to his cheek, her own unique baby smell wafting up his nostrils, churning his emotions.

'Edward Hayes, I was born to be a mother, it's me talent. Now are yer goin' to stand there all day croonin' over that child or are yer goin' to earn yer livin' and let me get on with me job.'

Edward placed a kiss on Annie's rosy cheek and handed her back to Sally, who without hesitation exposed her full round breast and placed Annie to the succulent nipple. Unable to be shocked by behaviour that was so obviously natural to her, Edward planted a second kiss, this time on Sally's forehead, and left.

As he walked back to the wych shed he remembered the salt bags and the need to catch the barges. His walk turned into a run and soon he was heaving the heavy barrow to the river. He stared in dismay as he reached the quayside for it was empty, except for one dilapidated barge bobbing on the cold grey water.

He had missed the tide and the barges had already left for Liverpool docks. He sighed wearily. If he didn't meet the orders regularly there were plenty of other salt pans that would and the buyers would not hesitate to go elsewhere for their salt. He cursed under his breath, no salt on this trip meant a whole week without money, for he had no other way of transporting his cargo to the docks. Sitting down on the barrow he caught his breath, before he had to begin to haul the load back to the shed, to wait for the next lot of barges to return in a few days' time.

'You look like you lost a penny and found a farthing,' said a voice, making him jump, and jolting him back to reality.

Before him stood a woman he had never seen before, mid thirties, long blonde hair flowing to her waist. Her dress was that of a barge person, large serge baggy trousers, thick soled boots and a loose cord jacket tied round the waist with a piece of rope. Despite the unflattering dress, she still looked attractive, with high cheekbones and large blue eyes that twinkled mischievously.

'Not seen you here before, 'ave I?' she persisted when it was obvious that Edward was not going to communicate willingly.

'Usually me sons bring the salt down,' Edward replied gruffly, not wishing to further the conversation.

Ignoring the hostility, the woman perched herself next to him on the edge of the barrow.

'You missed yer barge then, 'ave you?' she continued.

'Yes,' Edward muttered, wishing she would go away and annoyed that she had sat down uninvited.

'I might just be able to help you there.' She waited for a reply but when none came she kept on talking unperturbed. 'The boat there, she's mine. It seems no one wanted me today, so I'll take yer salt for yer at the right price.'

If she was truthful people hardly ever seemed to want to use the services of the *Mary-Rose*, these days. Partly because she was manned single-handed by a woman and partly because she looked so old and dilapidated.

Edward peered at the sorry-looking vessel moored up to the quay. He was desperate though, so maybe it was worth considering.

17

'Me name is Sarah Carter. Pleased to meet you.'

She enthusiastically thrust out a small hand, grinning at him.

'Edward Hayes. The boat, she looks a bit old, are yer sure she's sound? The weather gets a bit rough out in the docks sometimes, especially at this time of the year.' Edward was feeling a little dubious about the whole thing.

'She'll be fine, don't you worry. Come on, let's get 'er loaded before I lose the tide altogether.'

Sarah leapt up from the barrow and strode off in the direction of the boat.

'Is yer 'usband aboard, then?' Edward called after her.

'No. Come on, I'll help you unload.' She laughed, and for the first time Edward really looked at her. He was struck by her beauty as she threw her head back and the wind sent her hair billowing out around her.

Between them they hauled the sacks off the barrow and down into the hold of the barge. Edward was amazed as she worked with him sack by sack. She never paused to rest or even seemed to struggle with the heavy weights.

'I'll be back Thursday then, and you can pay me when I bring back the papers. Which warehouse is it going to?'

Edward told her the name. This was the usual arrangement; the barges only got paid when the salt owners had papers showing delivery to the merchant.

Sarah immediately began to untie the ropes and started to expertly wind them in. Smoke puffed from the little chimney on top of the deck and Edward noticed a little white dog sitting bolt upright at the front bow.

'Right, see you Thursday,' she called breezily and turned to steer the barge out into the main channel of water.

'Where is yer 'usband, then?' yelled Edward, suddenly anxious about his precious salt.

'I haven't got one, I travel alone,' she laughed and blew him a cheeky kiss, as she chugged away into the distance, giggling to herself at the look of shock and disbelief on Edward's face. A face that she noted could have been quite

18

handsome, had it not looked so miserable. Well, she would see what she could do about that when she returned.

Edward, for his part, walked slowly toward the wych shed, doubting very much whether he would ever see the *Mary Rose* or her captain again. It really didn't seem to matter that much for Annie came into his mind and as always overshadowed everything else.

# Three

'Your ma 'ates yer, your ma 'ates yer, your ma 'ates yer.'
The chanting voices rang out again and again in
Annie's ears, as the half dozen or so bare-foot children
danced around her in ever decreasing circles, taunting her
with their high pitched cruel song. Annie sank to the pavement and pushed her fingers tightly into her ears to try to
block out the sound. Seeing their advantage the pack began
to pull her hair in sharp spiteful tugs, even kicking her every
now and then.

Annie sobbed, begging them to stop, her pleading only
fuelling their bravado. Unable to take any more, she
struggled to her feet and with all her strength forced her
way out of the circle and fled as fast as she could down the
cobbled streets to the safety of Clara's door, the jubilant
cries of her attackers ringing in her ears.

'Whatever's wrong, pet?' Clara said, anxiously hugging
the small shaking body to hers. ''Ave yer fallen over and
'urt yerself? 'Ere let Clara see.'

Annie shook her head, unable to speak as huge sobs
convulsed her body. Clara led her gently into the kitchen,
where the oven glowed as usual and warmed the room both
with its heat and the delicious smell of baking bread. Annie
immediately felt comforted by the familiarity and began to
calm a little.

''Ere, you drink this warm milk and tell your Clara all
about it,' soothed the old lady, tenderly wiping the strands

20

of dark hair back from the little girl's tear-stained face, now streaked with black where she had violently scrubbed it.

'They were teasing me again, pullin' me hair, and, and . . .' It seemed the effort of telling the tale renewed its horror and a fresh torrent of tears cascaded down her cheeks.

'Hush now, you take no notice. I've told yer they're only jealous 'cos you've lots of people to love an' care for yer, not like them.'

Annie looked dubious about this. At six years old the world seemed a very confusing place. Clara was right of course, she did have plenty of people to love her. First and most important was her pa and then there was Clara, and Sarah on the barge, Aunt Sally and all her children, who were just like brothers and sisters to her. But then there was that other part of her world that she could never understand. There were the two big brothers at the salt shed, they were horrid to her and Jack in particular was always teasing her and pinching her when no one was looking. She had overheard Aunt Sally say that they were her real brothers, but she didn't like that idea at all. Most difficult to understand was the fact that she didn't live with her pa but with Clara instead. Even though he came to see her every day or she went to the wych shed to see him, it wasn't the same. He told her it was because he slept in the salt shed, and that was no place for little girls, which she supposed was right.

Today the children had been yelling at her about her mother; strangely she had never questioned the fact before that she didn't seem to have one. She was perfectly happy with Clara, who loved and spoiled her, even though Annie knew that she wasn't her real mother. Now the children were saying that her own mother not only didn't love her but lived in this very street. Annie couldn't understand how this could be true when she had never seen her, and suddenly her whole safe world seemed threatened by this unknown person. She was too anxious to ask Clara about it, in case it upset her and made her go away thinking Annie didn't want her. She shivered involuntarily and squeezed herself up against the soft contours of Clara's undulating body, and hoped that none of what they had been saying was true, for she didn't want anybody else in the world.

'Now then young lady, yer pa is comin' to get yer soon an' take yer with 'im to the river. I expect you'll see Sarah. You'd like that, wouldn't yer?' Annie nodded furiously. 'So I think we'll 'ave to wipe away all those tears and get you tidied up or yer pa will wonder what I've been doin' to yer.' Clara planted a kiss on the upturned face that was hanging on her every word and sighed, wondering why life had to be so unkind sometimes, especially to those who least deserved it.

'You run along upstairs and change into yer clean pinafore an' you'd better put yer boots on. Brush that straggly hair, it looks like you've got a bird's nest in there.'

Annie giggled as she pictured tiny beaks poking out of her hair. Hugging Clara once more, she jumped down from the table and raced up the narrow stairs, all thoughts of her ordeal forgotten as the excitement of seeing her beloved pa filled her head.

'I love yer,' she yelled as she disappeared through the door.

'Love yer too, pet,' smiled Clara, glad that Annie's sunny nature soon wiped away the bad things in her life. She was such a loving child. Elizabeth would never know what a treasure she had thrown away.

Upstairs, Annie perched on the edge of her high wooden bed with the deep feather mattress that she loved to sink into cosily at night. She dragged the tortoiseshell comb through her long hair inch by inch, trying not to cry, as each snag caught in the teeth and had to be wrenched through. She gazed around her room and suddenly felt very safe and lucky. She didn't have to share her bed with two or three children like Aunt Sally's did, squashed in top to toe. She had her very own chest of drawers, made specially for her by her pa, with tiny leaves carved along the top edge. Unlike most of the other children in the street she had leather boots to put on her feet in the winter and three changes of clothes, sewn for her by Sarah. Her favourite was the dark blue pinafore dress with the smock top under which she wore the pale blue jumper, knitted by Clara. Maybe Clara was right, the others were jealous of her because she had more things than they did. Jumping off the bed she walked to the window and peered out from behind the curtain, down to the children playing in the middle of the dirty street. They were kicking a stone around in the gutter, bare foot and dressed in rags, despite the cold October wind that whistled along the street. Their faces were filthy, noses running from the cold, scratching frantically at lice-infested tangled hair. They didn't seem very happy and were arguing amongst themselves. Suddenly a fight broke out between two of the boys and instantly a jeering crowd surrounded them, egging them on with shouts and calls. The boys rolled around on the wet muddy cobbles, tearing hair and flinging wild punches, until one of the front doors opened and a woman's voice screamed at them to stop. The culprits scrambled to their feet and chased off down the street after the others, to escape the woman's wrath.

Annie knew, then and there, that it didn't matter what they said about her, she didn't want to be like them, and if being with Clara and not living with Pa or the woman who was her real mother meant they weren't her friends, she didn't care.

Down in the cramped kitchen Edward sat at Clara's table by the warm range and sipped a cup of strong sweet tea, as he listened miserably to the tale of Annie's plight.

'It's no use pretendin' that we didn't know this would 'appen, yer know what children are like. She were bound to find out sooner or later about Elizabeth.'

Edward nodded sadly. 'I suppose I just 'oped it would never 'appen, that Elizabeth would see sense, realise what she was doin'. It's as if Annie 'ad never been born, she never talks about 'er, 'ardly ever leaves the 'ouse any more. Spends all 'er time fussin' over those two boys, grown men really. They 'ave 'er on a fine lark. I 'ardly ever go 'ome now, there's no point really; far easier to stay at the pan.'

23

'What sort of way is that fer you to carry on, Edward? You deserve more. Is that pan really worth it? It rules your life.'

Clara already knew the answer: the pan drove him, gave him a purpose. A lesser man would have walked away from Elizabeth years ago. Despite the sham of his marriage he still provided for his dispersed family as best he could. Elizabeth lived in the house that was his, handed down from his father, whilst his daughter lived with Clara and he slept on an uncomfortable bench in a shed. The pan provided the money he needed to feed them all and without it none of them could survive. He worked day and night, and to make it worse Luke was leaving in a few days to join the army, which meant more work for him. Elizabeth of course blamed Edward for her son's departure and this had caused yet another rift between them. Despite the fact that she had been encouraging both her sons to get away for years and better themselves, she never thought they would really go.

When Edward thought about Elizabeth he was always struck by a deep sadness. He remembered the pretty young girl he had married. They were in love then. He wasn't quite sure where all that love went or when Elizabeth had turned into the icy creature who could extinguish the sun itself with her coldness. All he knew was that it had happened and now it was all too late to mend. He was a stranger in his own home, his sons treated him with contempt, his wife with disgust, there was only Annie who loved him. Annie was his angel and for her he stayed and endured the rest, providing for them all as best he could.

Then there was Sarah. His mind whirled when he thought of her. Beautiful, sensuous Sarah, in whose arms he could lose himself in endless ecstasy. A shameless passion fired them both and transported them to heights he had never known existed before she came. He wondered if Elizabeth was his punishment for Sarah, but he didn't care. If she was payment for his pleasure all the more reason to keep her, he would do anything to keep Sarah in his life. So he bore Elizabeth like a hair shirt, to ease his conscience and pay for his sins.

Annie walked along the river bank with one hand clasped in her father's. She kicked the deep bed of fallen leaves, enjoying the satisfying sound of rustling that they made beneath her feet. This was her favourite time, just her and her pa. But today she was quiet, preoccupied. After a long silence she asked quietly, 'Why don't I live with me mother then? Why doesn't she want me?'

Edward stopped. This was what he had been dreading. Falling to one knee he scooped Annie up, pressing his face close to hers.

'That's not easy to answer, Annie. I think she may be poorly in 'er 'ead, and we have to feel sorry for 'er an' try not to mind too much.'

Annie did mind, though. 'I want to see 'er,' she declared, and set off purposefully back in the direction of town. If that woman was her mother, she had to see her. Maybe then the other children would stop teasing her and maybe she could find out what she had done to make her mother not want her.

Edward broke out into a trot to catch her.

'Wait, Annie, you can't, not just like that. It wouldn't work,' he pleaded.

Her face was set into determined lines and she frowned crossly, not willing to give up yet. 'Will you ask if I can go and see her?'

Edward groaned inwardly. This daughter of his was so stubborn and he knew she would not give up on the idea easily.

'Yes, all right. I'll ask but I'm not promising that she will let you.'

Annie conceded but had already decided that one way or another she would see her mother, at least once.

They headed back towards the moored barge. Sarah saw them coming and came up on deck to greet them.

''Ello button, 'ow are you today?' she smiled, sweeping Annie off her feet and hugging her. A small white dog raced over and began furiously licking her all over.

'Get down Smudge, yes I've missed you too,' Annie laughed, cuddling the little dog.

Annie adored being on Sarah's barge, it was always so warm and cosy down in the tiny cabin. The little room was panelled with wood which Sarah had decorated by painting flowers and leaves in bright colours. The wooden bunks, which served as both beds and seats, were strewn with patchwork quilts and cushions. The open fire of the stove crackled with logs and blue flames leapt and danced within it. The room might have been small but it was homely and it always amazed Annie that Sarah seemed to have all her needs in such a small space without it looking untidy. Sarah often told her stories about the docks at Liverpool and all the huge cargo vessels from all over the world that sailed there. She had a way of telling stories so that Annie felt she had almost been there. If she was really good she was allowed to look at the two big books that stood on the wooden shelf by Sarah's bed. One was an atlas, the pages all yellowed and worn, and together they would find all the strange and exciting countries that the ships in the docks had come from. America, India, Australia, and lots of islands that Annie had never even heard of. The other book was her real favourite, bound in red leather that smelt delicious, with gold writing on the front. Sarah had taught her that this said, 'Peoples of the World'. Inside there were whole pages of writing that she couldn't understand, but also the most wonderful pictures of people such as she never imagined. Red Indians in full war head-dress, Eskimos muffled up in furs and skins, African tribes dancing with beads and feathers in their hair. Finally the page she always gasped in delight at, never tiring of its occupant. This was of an Indian Princess, clothed in a midnight blue flowing dress of silk and satin encrusted with jewels, rich red rubies and huge sparkling diamonds. Into her long black hair were plaited more precious stones that seemed to Annie like stars twinkling in the night. In the middle of her forehead was a deep red spot staining her sultry skin and beneath dark lashes her ebony eyes shone mysteriously. She was the most beautiful thing Annie had ever seen, and every time she looked at her she never failed to utter the same words.

'If only I could 'ave a dress like that, I'd be the happiest girl in the world.'

Sarah and her pa would always laugh and say, 'If wishes were horses then beggars would ride.'

'Can I take Smudge a walk?' Annie asked now, knowing that the little dog longed for her to come and run with him in the woods.

'Course yer can, but don't wander too close to the water,' laughed Sarah, lifting her deftly back up onto the cabin steps, Smudge in hot pursuit. 'And Smudge – no leaving Annie to go and chase rabbits.'

The little dog wagged its tail as if in reply and then in an instant both child and animal disappeared into the orange and red woodland, swallowed up amongst the swirling fall of autumnal leaves.

Once back inside the cabin, Sarah fell into her lover's arms, hungrily seeking his mouth with hers. In turn his fingers urgently roamed her body, never tiring of her, the excitement always intense. The time for talking would come later, these moments alone were too precious to waste on words.

# Four

**F**our weeks later, washed and dressed, her hair neatly plaited down her back, Annie stood on the doorstep of her mother's house. She nervously clutched the hem of her pinafore dress as Edward knocked loudly on the solid wooden door. The wait seemed endless and Annie had a sudden urge to turn and run away. Edward smiled down at her kindly, squeezing her hand for reassurance.

There was nobody more surprised than him that this meeting was taking place at all, for he never imagined that Elizabeth would agree to see her daughter after all this time. What he did know though, was that if she hadn't had done, Annie would have simply come and knocked on this door herself eventually, to satisfy her curiosity, and so perhaps it was better this way. In the back scullery, Elizabeth heard the knock and momentarily her heart flickered. She was not at all sure that this was a good idea but it seemed too late now to change her mind. She knew already that she had the advantage over Annie, in that she had watched her from the window many times over the years, never once feeling any emotion other than contempt. She had to concede, albeit grudgingly, that she was a pretty child, the image of her father with black hair and dark eyes. Elizabeth was pleased that there was no resemblance to herself. As the years had passed she had been quite able to detach herself and sometimes she even forgot that Annie existed at all. She was not resentful that because of her desertion of her daughter, nobody in the street spoke to her any more; she had learned to ignore the whisperings and pointing fingers. It had been her choice to tread this path and she did it unfalteringly.

When Edward had asked her if Annie could come and see her, her first reaction had been to forbid it. Then she thought about it for awhile. Perhaps the girl could be useful now she was older. After all she had not yet got over the shock of losing Luke to the army, and with him gone she would need an extra pair of hands around the place. The girl could collect her groceries and do simple chores for her. Elizabeth was beginning to panic a little about her future alone. Even though he sent money Edward rarely came home now, and who could tell how long Jack would stay now that his brother had left. Suddenly a lonely old age loomed, with no one to care for her if she needed help or when she could no longer manage. The prospect of having Annie around was seeming better and better the more she thought of it.

Straightening her apron she opened the door, and unsmiling and silent she stood to one side to allow the visitors to enter.

'Hello, I'm Annie,' stuttered the little girl, as she quickly tried to take in all the surroundings in this unfamiliar place that should have been her home.

'Yes, I know who you are. I'm yer mother.' The word 'mother' stuck in her throat awkwardly. 'You've certainly grown into a big girl now.'

'I'm six-nearly-seven,' said Annie proudly.

'Would yer like a drink an' a piece of cake?'

'Yes please,' Annie replied, eyes lighting up.

Edward followed his wife into the scullery suspiciously. He wasn't sure what he had been expecting, but it certainly wasn't this.

'Yer needn't look so worried, I'm not goin' to eat yer precious daughter,' smirked Elizabeth. 'She will be quite safe with me, so you can back to yer beloved pan.'

Edward hesitated. He did not want to cause any ill feeling

29

today, but something in Elizabeth's manner scared him, she was almost being too nice, too reasonable.

He hovered in the doorway while she made the drink and cut a generous slice of cake. They rejoined Annie in the parlour. 'Are yer going to tell yer father to go so that we can get to know each other? I think he thinks yer are not big enough to stay by yerself,' Elizabeth cooed, smiling sweetly. The effect was just as she planned.

'I'm fine,' huffed Annie indignantly. 'I can walk 'ome to Clara's from 'ere all right.'

Crestfallen, Edward kissed her goodbye, and told her not to stay too long and wear out her mother. He left the house with a heavy heart, a sick feeling that he might just have lost part of Annie and wondering what exactly Elizabeth was up to.

So began the visits that were to continue regularly, two or three times a week, uneventfully, for the next few years. Annie dutifully went to the shops and did chores for her mother and in return Elizabeth treated her not affectionately, but with a fair if somewhat serious manner. To Annie it was enough, it meant her mother did not hate her as the children said. True she did not hold her or kiss her, but then Annie had Clara for that, so it didn't seem to matter. The situation would probably have continued for years had fate not intervened and turned Annie's life upside down.

One day shortly after Annie's eleventh birthday was what she would remember as one of the worst days of her life. It was a Wednesday and she had just left her mother's house, having spent the morning helping with the washing. These were days that she actually enjoyed, for instead of simply doing chores alone, she worked alongside her mother. Sometimes she even got to talk to her, until Elizabeth could stand no more of her incessant chatter and would gruffly tell her to be quiet and get on with the jobs.

Together they would pour the hot water into the large metal tub and carefully add the soap until a creamy froth floated on the top. Annie would hold the scrubbing board whilst Elizabeth rubbed the clothes up and down. But the part that she loved best was catching the clean steaming washing as it was squeezed through the mangle and then hanging it out in long damp rows on the wooden rack that spanned the scullery ceiling.

By the time they finished Annie's hands were always wrinkled and soft, and she loved the smell of soap that lingered on her skin for hours afterwards. Today, because her mother had been in a particularly good mood, they had sat down after they had finished their work and eaten some warm scones, washed down with milky tea. As she left Annie had wanted to kiss her mother, but no physical contact ever took place between them, so Annie was left with an empty feeling, almost as if she had been cheated. It always left Annie feeling this way when things had gone particularly well.

Racing down the street back to Clara's house, she told herself not to be so sulky. After all, she had lots of people to love and cuddle her. Deep down though she longed for one of them to be her mother. She thundered into the hallway calling to Clara as she always did.

'Clara, I'm 'ome.'

Today however there was no reply. Annie quickly searched the parlour and scullery before bounding up the stairs, two at a time.

'Clara, where are yer? I'm 'ome,' she called.

Flinging open Clara's bedroom door, Annie froze to the spot. Her heart thumped wildly and her mind raced uncontrollably. There on the floor lay Clara, one arm partially covering her face, but Annie could still see her open eyes staring blankly upwards. She was perfectly still, and Annie knew she was dead.

Paralysed with fear, Annie pressed her back against the wall, her fist stuffed into her mouth, eyes wide with terror. She could feel the cry building up inside her like a volcano, slowly forcing its way up through her body until it flung her hand away from her mouth and escaped as a long hysterical scream.

31

Flinging herself prostrate on the lifeless body on the floor she sobbed, clutching at the old woman, begging her to wake. The unsmiling eyes that stared up at Annie's distraught face were cold and remote. Clara was no longer inside the shell that lay in an ungainly heap on the floor, and Annie backed away from the impostor. Dragging herself to her feet she stumbled out of the room, banging into the door frame yet not feeling the deep scrape to her shin. She had only one thought in her mind, and that was to get her pa as quickly as possible. Almost falling down the stairs, she rushed out into the street, leaving the door wide open, and ran as fast as her legs would carry her to the wych shed. Sally was just walking along and, almost knocking her over, Annie screamed out something garbled about Clara that Sally didn't quite catch, but Annie just kept running. She was so blinded by tears now that she could hardly see where she was going and she fell several times on her journey, cutting her knees until the blood ran in sticky trickles down her legs. In her mind only one thought: her Clara was gone forever.

'Annie, Annie, whatever's the matter?' gasped Edward, catching the body that flung itself into his arms.

His immediate thought was that Elizabeth had done something. He had been waiting for something like this to happen for a long time. Annie was so desperate to please her mother, so anxious for some scrap of kindness that it was pitiful to watch.

'Whatever it is she's done, we'll sort it out, just tell me what 'appened,' Edward soothed gently.

Annie fought hard to control her breath gasping in and out of her body. 'She's dead, Pa, she's dead on the floor, I tried to wake 'er up but she's dead.' The speech exhausted her and she buried her head against the warmth of her father's chest.

Dead. The word sounded so unreal and Edward repeated it in his head over and over as he fought to control the wild racing of his mind. Elizabeth . . . dead?

'Please come and see, Pa, please. We can't just leave 'er

there.' Annie whispered now, calmer in the safety of his arms.

They left the wych shed in silence and walked quickly, hand in hand, back to the smoky houses. Annie's mind whirled, a million questions raced through her head. Where would she live? She couldn't stay in the house alone. How would she survive without Clara to love her? No one to kiss her goodnight, no one to tell her stories and share secrets with. It was all too difficult to imagine, never hearing Clara's voice again, never seeing her smile, never hugging her warm cuddly body. Fresh tears washed her face as the reality of the whole nightmare became more and more clear to her. The very fabric of her world had been torn apart and Annie knew nothing was ever going to be the same again.

Edward too was in a state of shock. It was useless trying to get any sense out of Annie, she was far too upset. Worse still she was possibly involved somehow. His mind took him along all kinds of strange and fanciful pathways. Perhaps Elizabeth had tried to hurt Annie and, fighting back, Annie had caused some kind of freak accident to occur. Maybe Elizabeth had had an illness that no one was aware of and simply died of natural causes. Whatever the reason Edward knew that he felt no sorrow. His emotions were firstly to protect Annie from any consequences of the whole affair and secondly he felt a kind of relief to be rid of his wife. Elizabeth had become no more than a life-sucking burden, she was wicked and Edward had been constantly terrified that she might hurt Annie. Now she would be able to do no more harm and he felt lighter, as if a chain had been cut from him.

As they approached the street, they could see a small crowd of people gathered outside Clara's house. When they drew near a silence fell over the whispering faces. Sally Toscher rushed forward to hug Annie, her own tears mingling with the child's in fresh misery.

'Is Clara inside, Sally?' Edward quietly asked.

'Yes, yes, she's upstairs,' Sally mumbled through her sobs.

Edward was momentarily thrown, why on earth was Sally

so upset, and all these people? Everyone hated Elizabeth in the street, in fact no one had spoken to her for years, it just renewed his fears that Annie was somehow involved, somehow in trouble. Clara would no doubt have all the answers.

Silence hung unnaturally in the house and Edward bounded up the narrow stairs two at a time to Clara's room. The door was still ajar and Edward pushed his way in.

'Clara what on earth 'as 'appened, is Annie in . . .'

He stopped in his tracks, as Clara's prostrate body came into view. Sweat prickled his forehead and his blood began to pound around his body in complete disbelief of what his eyes were telling him. It was Clara, not Elizabeth. This could not be true. It was as if someone was playing a sick joke on him, it had to be Elizabeth, he was so sure that it was her, so relieved. Sickness swirled in his stomach, as he gently gathered up the old woman in his arms, tenderly laying her on the bed. He covered her stiff body with the thin thread-bare blanket that had kept her warm for years. Falling to his knees beside her, he let out a tortured cry that echoed poignantly in the silent room. Slowly he began to bang his head against the wooden frame of the bed, chanting to himself over and over, 'Why, why, why?' That was how Sally and Annie found him, the split in his forehead gaping bright red, spurting blood. Inch by inch they prised him away from the body and led him from the room. The three of them, united in common grief; though on reflection Edward's might well have been not just because Clara had gone, but because Elizabeth had not.

# Five

For three days Clara's body lay in the plain wooden coffin in her front parlour. A stiff white calico gown was tied beneath her chin and around her feet, leaving only the ghostly white face and hands exposed, folded as if in prayer. A procession of neighbours had called to pay their last respects, tears had been shed and heads shaken in sorrow and disbelief. Finally the day of the funeral had arrived.

It was very much like the day of Annie's birth, soft snow had laid a gentle blanket over all the smog and dirt, and freezing air bit into lungs and skin savagely. Annie was glad that it had snowed, for everywhere looked clean and special and Clara of all people deserved that. Annie had been into the parlour only once since Clara was put in there. She had crept quietly in when no one else was around for she wanted to say her goodbyes alone, without well-meaning arms holding her, or kind words of encouragement. No, saying farewell to Clara, was something she needed to do by herself. As she had peered down into the sea of white material that shrouded her friend, Annie had shivered. Clara's face looked shiny, almost like wax. The skin was tight and drawn back on her cheek bones, making the familiar face seem distorted, almost doll-like.

Tentatively she had reached out to touch the cheek, to stroke it, but her fingers recoiled at the hard cold feel. This was not her Clara, the warm loving Clara, that was always there with open arms to comfort her. Choking back her tears, Annie had fled from the alien body and had not returned. Wherever her Clara had gone, it wasn't in that coffin, so on the day of funeral Annie felt no sorrow that the wooden casket was going to be buried forever in the frozen soil.

Her pain was that of not understanding, not knowing where or why her beloved friend had gone. It was a desperation to see or hear her just once more, to be allowed one last chance to tell her how much she loved her and needed her. Strange feelings, that she did not begin to understand but that frightened her, especially in the long nights when the shadows closed in and she longed for the comforting smells and warmth that came only from a nearness to Clara.

Today all she felt was a kind of numbness, it was as if she wasn't really here at all, all the hustle and bustle went on around her and she stood mesmerised in the middle of it all. Everyone was so busy. Sally was organising food and drinks for after the service. Her pa was pacing anxiously in the hall, constantly checking his fob watch to see if the carriage was late and worrying that there were not enough bearers for the coffin. Annie, dressed in her best pinafore and starched blouse, her hair neatly plaited down her back, was overwhelmed by it all.

'Annie, will you 'elp Sally lay the table in the kitchen, please.'

Her pa's gentle voice penetrated the scary silences that kept flooding her mind, blocking out all the everyday noises and sending her to a lonely wilderness. Mechanically Annie obeyed, placing trays of sandwiches and pies on the long trestle table, Clara's table. It seemed so wrong to her that they were using Clara's plates and knives and forks. That strangers were opening drawers and cupboards and touching Clara's private things, but then what did it matter, what did anything matter now that Clara wasn't here.

'The carriage is 'ere,' her pa announced. His voice sounded strange, as if he were trying to swallow something to stop himself from choking.

Slowly the cumbersome coffin was manoeuvred out of the parlour and squeezed through the dark narrow hallway, out into the freezing January air. The two horses, with their black feather plumes, snorted impatiently, stamping their hooves on the slippery cobbles. A silent crowd gathered to watch Clara's final departure from Union Street, everyone it seemed; except Elizabeth of course.

Annie could see the beads of sweat on the men's faces as they heaved the coffin onto the back of the cart. The horses whinnied nervously, anxious to be off. The sombre procession, Annie and Edward at the front, followed the cart, as Clara was taken to her final resting place.

'Well, it were a decent send off,' Sally mumbled, as she handed out slabs of warm pie to the thankful frozen mourners.

'Clara would 'ave been pleased with the turn out,' someone replied.

'I expect the 'ouse will soon be taken, folks are always lookin' for houses to rent,' remarked one of the women.

'Yes, I told our Harold about it. If he and his intended get their name down quick they might be lucky, 'cos he needn't think he's livin' with me once he's wed. You can't swing a cat round in our 'ouse as it is.'

Annie listened in disbelief. How could Clara be forgotten so easily? Laughter from the parlour drew her instinctively, and poking her head around the door, she could see a group of people laughing and drinking merrily. They were telling stories and joking. It was just too much for Annie to bear, and the tears began to spill down her face. Racing upstairs to her room, she banged the door shut behind her and fell upon the bed weeping bitterly. Which was where Edward found her almost an hour later, blue with cold and shaking convulsively.

'Annie, Annie, this'll never do,' he cried, folding her into his arms.

'Pa, why is everyone so 'appy? Clara has gone and they're all laughin' and talkin' as if she never existed. I just want 'er back, it's not fair,' she sobbed. 'I want them all to go away.'

'They aren't 'appy pet. Everyone is sad, but they're try'in to remember the good things about Clara.'

He scooped her up into a sitting position, wiping the tears away with his hands.

'Clara wouldn't want yer to be sad, would she? Now come on, dry them tears. We have to hold on to all the good times with 'er. Clara may be gone but she'll always be in our hearts. No one can ever take away our memories Annie, they're ours to treasure.'

Annie sat up and looked around her little room, except it wasn't hers anymore. Since Clara had died she had slept at Sally's house and she hated it. She longed to be back in her own soft bed where she could stretch her legs without kicking someone else's or turn over without bumping into another body. She hungered for her own chest of drawers with the leafy pattern on and most of all for Clara's good-night kisses. She knew she could never have any of these things again and she was afraid.

'Please can I stay with yer tonight Pa, please, just tonight?' Annie pleaded. 'I promise I won't be a nuisance.'

Edward melted at the imploring face, he sighed and hugged her close. 'Yer can't sleep in the shed Annie, it's not right, but yer can stay with Sarah on the barge fer a night or two. You'd like that, wouldn't yer?'

Relief spread across Annie's face.

'Yes, please. It's not that I don't like stayin' at Sally's 'ouse, but it's not the same as bein' in me own bed.'

'I know it isn't pet. Come on, let's walk down to the river and find the *Mary-Rose*. I've 'ad enough of all these people too.'

Edward was already worrying about Annie's future. Sally was very kind but she had so many children of her own, there was simply not enough room in her tiny terrace house. It was out of the question that Annie should sleep in the wych shed, and as to Sarah having her, that had problems all of its own. The barge was so cramped and it would be no life for her to be continually sailing back and forth from Liverpool. Besides, Edward knew there would be no time for him and Sarah to be alone. He knew it was selfish, but he couldn't bear the thought of doing without her. He needed to caress her body and lose himself in her sensuality; without it life hardly seemed bearable.

There was only one other possibility, and he tried not to think about that: that Annie should live with Elizabeth.

In fact Elizabeth had already very astutely worked out this option, and the idea appealed greatly. Annie was homeless, Edward couldn't have her at the salt pan and he certainly wouldn't want her with his whore on the barge. Oh yes, she knew all about his fancy woman. Edward had been going to the tart for his pleasure for years, everyone knew that. But then what did she care, she had driven him from her bed, just the thought of him touching her sent shivers down her spine. No she didn't want him back, let the tart have him. It really didn't matter as long as Edward still looked after his responsibilities here, sent money to her, but she wondered how much longer he would. Whilst the boys were young he had willingly supported them, and he continued to do so for the moment. However, Luke had gone and Jack was so restless, hating the wych shed so much that he might just follow his brother's example and leave home. The thought terrified Elizabeth, for she had no means of supporting herself, nobody spoke to her, and nobody was likely to give her work. Besides she didn't want to have to go out to work. For years before Annie was born she had slaved in the wych shed, stripped to her petticoat, sweating, hauling the salt slabs around, breaking her back and her spirit day by day. Her freedom was Edward's price to pay for getting her pregnant again with that child. Annie was her guarantee of support and if the child lived with her, Edward would have no choice but to continue to feed and keep them.

Elizabeth smiled to herself, the nightmare visions of the workhouse began to fade and the future looked better already. She knew that Edward wouldn't be too keen on the idea but then she could soon persuade Annie and then the game would be won. The child was so sickeningly grateful for her attention it would be easy to sway her, and

Elizabeth was quite happy to play a few games if it got her what she wanted.

Annie and her father walked along the woodland paths, crunching the snow beneath their feet as they went, leaving footprints to mark their tracks. It was Saturday, and Edward had left Jack in charge of the pan, so that he could spend an hour or two with Annie. He was worried about her, for ever since Clara's death she had been quiet and withdrawn, she no longer skipped into the wych shed every day to see him, but crept in quietly. Nor did she sing to cheer him up as she sewed the bags for the salt, but huddled on the bench in the corner like a little mouse. The sunshine had gone from her life and it broke Edward's heart to see her so miserable.

The question of where she should live was still unresolved and for the past few weeks she had alternated between Sally's crowded home and Sarah's cramped barge. Edward knew that the situation had to be resolved soon for everyone's sake, mostly Annie's.

What he didn't know was that Elizabeth had already planted the idea of Annie living with her in his daughter's head, knowing full well that this was the simplest route to achieving what she wanted.

'Where are we goin'?' Annie piped up, slipping her hand into her father's.

'You'll see. It's a surprise,' he smiled. 'We're goin' to make somethin'.'

Annie was intrigued, but knowing he liked to tease her she feigned uninterest and picking up some powdery snow she threw a handful at him playfully. The snowball fight continued for some time as they danced in and out of the trees. To look at them together no one would have thought that they had a care in the world and for a short while they even forgot it themselves.

'Right young lady, if you want this surprise to work you'd better go and start collecting the things we need,' he laughed, scraping the wet melting snow from his collar.

Annie's face shone expectantly, as she awaited her instructions.

'We need some holly with red berries on, and some fir and some yew leaves. You find those and I'll find some twigs.'

'What are we making?' she asked casually, as if she couldn't have cared less.

'A kissing bush,' replied Edward, grinning at her.

'What's a kissing bush?'

'Ah, you asked what we were making, not what it was for, only one question allowed. You'll just have to wait.'

'I'm not a baby, don't tease me,' retorted Annie huffily.

'If we don't hurry up and gather the things it will be too dark and then you'll never know about the magic.'

'There's no such thing as magic,' tutted Annie in disgust.

Nevertheless it sounded exciting, so she rushed off to gather some holly, just to keep him happy of course. She loved being here, just the two of them, it was their special time. Once all the materials had been gathered, Edward made a cross out of the twigs and began wrapping the branches with greenery. Annie was soon choosing just the right piece of holly and strand of ivy to add the finishing touches.

'There, I think that about does it,' Edward smiled, lifting up the shining green cross to admire it. 'Now we add the magic.'

From deep within his pocket he pulled out a smooth round stone. It was clear like a diamond and it sparkled and glistened in the afternoon light. In the top of the crystal rock was a small hole through which he threaded a thin red cord. He tied it carefully and then hung it from the centre of the cross of leaves and berries. Slowly rising to his feet he started off through the trees until he came to a clearing in which stood a huge old oak tree. Annie followed in silence, afraid that the slightest noise might break the spell. Transfixed, she watched as Edward tied the kissing bush high above their heads, in the gnarled boughs of the tree. The sparkling stone danced for awhile, casting silver sparks

41

of light from its very heart, before it finally came to rest and hung shimmering like a star in the sky.

Edward took hold of his daughter's hand and drew her beneath the bush, pulling her gently to her knees beside him. He pressed his face close to hers until she could feel the warmth of his breath on her cold cheeks.

'The kissin' bush is very special, Annie, it can make yer wishes come true if yer believe in it and don't break the rules.'

Annie gasped. 'What do we 'ave to do?' she whispered.

'You 'ave to come to the bush with someone yer love very much, then yer hold hands and yer can both make a wish. But it must be fer whatever you want most in the whole world and yer must never tell anyone what it was or the magic will die.'

Annie's face radiated pure angelic innocence and Edward had to catch his breath as he looked at her. In solemn ritual they linked hands and with eyes tightly closed each made a wish. Annie leaned forward and kissed her father on the lips; he shuddered as the silk-like feeling wafted across his skin, so delicate yet so strong.

Annie's heart swelled with happiness as they walked, arms entwined, back to the town. She gazed at her father's handsome face, imagining that she would never love anyone as she did him. On reaching Union Street she tiptoed up and pecked his cheek affectionately.

'I've to go and see Mother now, I promised I would.'

It was almost an apology, for she knew he didn't like her being there. This she couldn't understand really, but she knew he thought that her mother wasn't fair to her and his protectiveness only made her love him more. If only there were something she could do to make Elizabeth love her she was sure everything would be all right. She stood and waved until he had disappeared from view before entering number thirty-four.

Things were getting better here, and last time she came her mother had hinted that it might be a good idea if Annie moved in permanently. Her heart had soared at that idea, for she knew if she could just prove to her mother how good she could be then Elizabeth would learn to like her. Excitement rose within her, as she imagined having a mother just like everyone else, a mother to say goodnight to her and even hold her if she cried. The problem of course was how to suggest this idea to her pa, for the last thing she wanted was to upset him. Then today her prayers had been answered, for her pa had made the kissing bush, and Annie just knew in her heart that it was going to solve all her problems and make her wishes come true.

Edward walked briskly down the river bank, his head swirling with the conversation he had just had with Sally Toscher. It was no shock, and she had obviously been upset at about it all but the simple truth was that there was no room for Annie in her tiny house. The stark reality of what he had to do hurt him, but what choice did he have? Annie had to live somewhere and Elizabeth seemed the only solution. He agonised over how he would tell his daughter that she would have to move in with the brother she hated and her mother who was so cold and unfeeling toward her. He already knew that Elizabeth would be quite happy to have Annie, it meant she would gain a personal servant and of course Edward would have to tip up more money. He knew exactly how Elizabeth's mind worked, and although it made him furious, he felt he would have no choice but to comply with her demands.

He quickened his step as he approached the barge. A tiny red light glowed out into the darkness, a small piece of comfort beckoning him in.

He sank wearily down onto the bed, and immediately two warm arms encircled him as he buried himself in an ample bosom. He unburdened his worries over Annie, but in truth he knew exactly what he must do. And so did Sarah.

'Edward you've no choice. She 'as to go to Elizabeth.'

She planted a kiss on his head and rose to her feet.

'Look I've finished the dress.' Holding up the finished product, Sarah smiled. It was a beautiful replica of the

43

Indian sari in Sarah's book that Annie always dreamt of wearing.

'Imagine the look on 'er face, Edward, when she sees this.'

The dress floated in the air, the beads sewn painstakingly on it shimmering like stars in a navy blue sky. Edward sighed, doubting whether fairy tale kissing bushes that produced longed-for dresses would go any way towards compensating his daughter for the sombre fact that she had to go and live with her mother. It certainly wasn't going to make him feel any less guilty for throwing his child into the lion's den.

Sarah hung the dress carefully by the cabin door where it fluttered in the draught mysteriously.

'You're right, she'll love it. I can't thank yer enough fer makin' it.'

'Oh, I think yer could if yer tried,' she smiled provocatively, moving towards him and running her tongue along his cheek. Edward felt the passion stir within him. She could always arouse him so easily. Gently he ran his hands along her body, kneading her breasts in his fingers and pushing her skirts higher until he exposed her thighs.

'Sarah, I'd die without yer,' he groaned and fell against her body to be transported once again to that delightful place that only she could take him to, all thoughts of Annie and Elizabeth temporarily forgotten.

# Six

It was six o'clock in the morning, and already the pale May sunshine was peeping shyly through the thin curtains that hung limply at the scullery window. Annie scrubbed her eyes and stretched out on the worn mattress that was thrown down each night in the corner. She didn't mind this arrangement for it was warm by the oven range even on the coldest nights. Besides there was nowhere else to sleep in her mother's house, as both bedrooms were already occupied by Jack and Elizabeth. She had lived here now for four months since the kissing bush had made her wish come true. She still marvelled at how its magic had known she was longing to live with her mother and even more that it had made her pa not mind at all. He had even given her the beautiful Indian dress as an extra treat and she felt as if she was the luckiest girl in the world.

Life was so busy now that between her work in the house and her work at the shed Annie never seemed to have two minutes to spare. Not that she minded, for she loved being with Edward and by spending time with her mother as well she almost felt she had a real family at last. Jack was the only bad part of her world. He frightened her with his cold grey eyes that seemed to look right through her and she tried to keep out of his way as much as possible.

Her days always started early. Her first job was to rake the ashes from the fire and stoke it up again ready to boil the big copper pan of water for breakfast. Jack would be down soon and he expected the tea to be mashed and the porridge ready. He never spoke much in the mornings, just the odd grunt here and there, moaning if the porridge had a lump or the tea was too cold. While he was eating Annie made sure his boots were clean and standing by the hearth ready to slip on and that his dinner was made up and wrapped in paper to take with him. She was always happy when the door slammed shut and he had left for the salt pan.

Next, Annie would brew a fresh pot of tea in the huge cracked pot for herself and Elizabeth. Her mother was 'indisposed' most mornings, which meant that she had to have breakfast in bed. Annie was not quite sure what 'indisposed' meant, but she eagerly deposited the breakfast tray each morning by the side of Elizabeth's bed. Her mother rarely spoke at this time, not being fully awake, and Annie tiptoed quietly out of the room so as not to disturb her too much and save herself a telling off for being too noisy.

This done she would set about her cleaning jobs. The kitchen had to be neat and tidy, pots washed, floor swept, so that it would all be straight for when her mother arose. The rest of the house she would clean later, for the mornings were spent in the wych shed. There she would sew the canvas salt sacks, sweep the floor and generally help where she could. Sometimes if it were a sailing day she would accompany her pa with the loaded barrow down to the barges. There she could see Sarah, and these were her favourite days.

Sarah always had something good to eat for them and she was glad, for her pa looked as if he needed a good meal in him. Annie would make stews and pies and take them down to the shed but she could never persuade her pa to come back and eat a proper meal at the house. If she tackled him about it he would only laugh and say he could live on love and fresh air. But she did worry about his thin face and pale complexion and the persistent hacking cough that doubled him over unable to catch his breath. At least on the barge Sarah made him sit down and eat until he was too full to move. When Annie prayed to God, which she did quite often, she would always ask him to look after her pa.

46

When her jobs in the shed were done Annie would return home to finish her household chores. The list was endless, washing, ironing, chopping the firewood, cleaning, cooking, and she was always exhausted at the end of a day. She never complained as she was so determined to show her mother what a good daughter she could be and then perhaps one day her mother might love her a little. Annie knew she had been given a chance and she wasn't going to waste it, so it didn't matter if Elizabeth made her re-clean the windows for the third time because they were streaked or tipped away the soup because it was too salty and made her start again; it didn't matter if it only meant she could please her mother, just once.

By the time ten o'clock at night came Annie could barely keep her eyes open but she couldn't go to bed until Jack came in, in case he wanted some supper. He spent most nights in the local public house until he was thrown out and then if Annie was lucky he was so drunk he would stagger straight up the stairs to bed. Sometimes, however, he would be hungry and come home demanding supper and Annie hated these times. He would grab her arms, pinching her and squeezing them or pull her hair until she screamed to be let go, all of which he found highly amusing. She never complained to her mother, after all her brother was the favourite and any criticism at all brought her mother's wrath cascading down upon her with venom. She knew she must tolerate Jack if she wanted to stay here, just as she had learnt never to mention Luke's name, for her runaway brother also seemed to cause Elizabeth such pain, so he was quietly forgotten.

This particular day in May was very special for it was a public holiday, and later in the afternoon all the local children were going to march through the town to a may-pole where they would sing and dance. It was the children from the Sunday school that were invited to parade and even though Annie did not have the time to go every week, she was so excited about it, that Mrs Caudle from the church had allowed her to join in too. She had to dress up in something pretty for the occasion and Annie knew exactly what she would wear. This was her chance to shine in her magnificent Indian dress, and she could hardly wait.

The dress was kept on Sarah's barge, for her pa had quite rightly said that her mother wouldn't like it cluttering up her house and it was best not to mention its existence, so she didn't. In fact Annie barely talked about Sarah at all as her mother always frowned at the mention of her and said, 'I'm not interested in her'. The tone in her voice soon taught Annie to be silent on the subject if she knew what was good for her. Tact and diplomacy were one of Annie's greatest assets in her bid to survive in her mother's regime.

Her pa had said that she needn't come to the wych shed at all today, so that when she had finished her chores at home she could go straight to the barge, where Sarah would help her get ready. He would stoke the fires up well at the pan so that he could come and watch her in the procession later and he promised to take her to the fair that had arrived by the river bank yesterday.

Annie could hardly contain the wonderful bubbling feeling inside her this morning and she hummed to herself as she mashed the tea in the stained brown pot. She had already asked her mother if she could stay out all day, trying hard not to show how desperate she was for her approval. She knew her mother wasn't interested in holidays and parades and she certainly wouldn't approve of Edward taking Annie to the fair. So she didn't actually mention that part, telling herself it wasn't really a lie as Elizabeth hadn't asked her about it.

To her sheer amazement Elizabeth had said yes, provided that all the chores were done and everything was prepared for the evening meal later. So this morning Annie was rushing around trying to make sure that everything was done and to ensure that she had forgotten nothing. By half past eight her mother had still not arisen from her bed and Annie was beginning to get anxious. Perhaps she was ill and would need looking after all day. Twice she crept up the stairs and pressed her ear against the bedroom door to listen for some sound within. Then just as she was about to pluck up courage to go and knock on the door and ask if she could leave, she heard footsteps above. She sighed in relief, she wouldn't be late after all.

Elizabeth slowly brushed her hair and smiled to herself, fully aware that downstairs Annie would be fidgeting around waiting to go. Let her wait, it would do her no harm, she thought slyly. Actually she was more than pleased the way things had turned out. Having Annie here was quite a stroke of genius on her part. Not only did she have her own personal skivvy but Edward regularly sent them money to keep them comfortable. They never went hungry, there was always coal for the fire and Annie was such a frugal little housekeeper that there was often enough left over from the shopping each week for Elizabeth to add a bottle of gin or brandy to the list. Annie fetched this without question, believing, as Elizabeth told her, that it was for medicinal purposes. It was really quite easy to tolerate the child under such circumstances and although she was firm, Elizabeth controlled her intense dislike for Annie, knowing she would only be spiting herself if she spoiled this arrangement.

However, on days like today she couldn't resist exercising her control and power, making Annie suffer for a while, it amused her, the girl was so naïve and easy to manipulate.

Tying her hair back into a severe bun, Elizabeth smiled at her own reflection in the mirror before gliding down the stairs to be met immediately by Annie at the door.

'Everythin's ready, Mother. The food's all prepared for tonight, the cleaning's finished, the fire's laid . . .' Annie rattled off the list, desperate to leave. She paused expectantly waiting for her mother's approval.

Elizabeth purposefully gazed around the room, inspecting the corners for lurking dust, deliberately prolonging her daughter's agony. ''Ave the brasses been cleaned in the parlour?'

Annie's face fell and her heart began to pound. It took hours to clean and polish the brass ornaments.

49

'It's not the day fer that, I usually do them on a Friday,' she whispered, afraid to meet her mother's eyes.

Elizabeth sighed, running critical eyes around the room as if seeking some other offending article to pounce on. 'Well, I suppose they can wait, but you mustn't have cleaned them properly last time or they wouldn't look so filthy now.'

'I will next time, I promise. Please can I go now?' Annie pleaded, twisting her fingers as she spoke.

Elizabeth gloated inwardly, she really enjoyed this.

'Well you'd best run along then. I don't expect I'll see anyone till you come 'ome but I'm used to bein' on me own,' she sighed dramatically. 'You go an' enjoy yerself.'

Annie's stomach churned with guilt. She was only thinking of herself, never imagining that her mother might be lonely all day and yet she was so excited about the parade, it all seemed so unfair. Sheepishly Annie backed out of the scullery, part of the pleasure of the day now ruined with self-reproach.

'I'll see yer later then,' she said quietly as she closed the door on silence.

As soon as the door had banged shut Elizabeth leapt for the cupboard where she kept her secret supplies of liquor and laughing wickedly to herself she poured a large brandy which she slurped down greedily.

Annie raced as fast as her legs would carry her down the grimy street, away from the dilapidated houses and out towards the river. Everyone she met today seemed in a lighter mood than usual the holiday spirit was infectious and laughter and cheery calls followed her on her journey. As she neared the river she slowed down to a jog and began to catch her breath. Before her the river was dotted with craft, the bank moored up solidly as far as she could see on both sides. The river people, determined to bring some excitement to their mundane lives, had strung the barges with brightly coloured bunting and flags, that buffeted gently in the May breeze. The sunlight sparkled on the water, reflecting the gay decorations, shouts could be heard

50

from one barge to another, as everyone prepared for a day of rest and enjoyment.

Annie smiled and chatted to everyone as she skipped along the towpath. The grass was already quite high for May and along the embankments bluebells tumbled down in waterfalls of colour toward the lapping river. Annie filled her lungs with the fresh air, for once not filled with the choking fumes from the wych shed chimneys, for most of the pans would only be smouldering quietly today, resting until things were back to normal tomorrow. Even the notorious Mr Ellis had allowed his workers a day off today. Huddled in between two larger barges the *Mary-Rose* lapped happily against the river bank. Having spotted her approach from some way down the towpath, Smudge had left his post on deck and leapt off to run yapping to meet her.

''Ello little one,' grinned Annie, bending to stroke the faithful dog that loved her so much. 'I've got no time for walks today, I've got to get ready,' and breaking out once more into a trot, she raced Smudge back to the barge.

Sarah was waiting, the wonderful dress was hanging in the doorway, fluttering in the breeze. She led Annie down into the cabin, where the tin bath waited, filled with hot steamy water. It smelt of aromatic herbs that wafted tantalisingly through the air.

'If you're going to be a princess, you'd better smell like one,' she giggled as Annie sank into the heavenly water, submerging her whole body in the luxury. Sarah washed Annie's long black hair gently and then left her to soak for ten minutes whilst she had the chance of such a treat.

An hour later Annie emerged from the barge into the world like a butterfly from the chrysalis. She walked serenely along the river bank with Sarah beaming proudly beside her. If anyone had asked Annie to describe how she felt, she probably would have been unable to express in words the joyous wonderful floating sensation she had as she glided along. She felt truly beautiful for the first time in her life. The midnight blue material of the dress undulated around her in billowing waves, each bead gleaming and

51

sparkling in the sunlight. Her gorgeous hair hung in wavy locks down her back and plaited into it were flowers and ribbons, but most breathtaking was her face. Sarah had drawn dark lines beneath her eyelids and painted her lips with a deep red colour; in the centre of her forehead she bore the blood red mark of the Indian princess, from beneath this flashed her ebony eyes. The girl had been transformed into a woman.

The effect on everyone who laid eyes on her was quite spectacular. For the first time in her life Annie found herself to be the centre of attention. The other girls in the parade sighed jealously over the dress and encouraged by their praise Annie twirled a pirouette on request, revealing layers of silky petticoat.

Only when one of the boys whistled at her did Annie blush and stop showing off, covering up her ankles modestly with her skirts, though inside she glowed excitedly at all the attention.

Later as Edward watched his daughter lead the parade through the streets, shining so brightly, he had to choke back tears that welled in his eyes and throat. For the first time he too saw the woman not the child, and it frightened him. The little-girl eyes looked at him from the beginnings of the woman's body, and a stunning one at that. The dress did not hang limply but clung to hips that were beginning to take shape and budding breasts that lifted the material into tiny but visible mounds. The realisation shocked him, she was no longer a baby and he knew that if he had noticed these changes in her then so would others. Sarah, seeing all these things tormenting his face, squeezed his arm.

'It 'ad to come, she's growin' up. Besides, she looks beautiful.'

'I know she does, I'm just scared fer 'er, she's almost too beautiful,' Edward sighed. Sarah dug him playfully in the ribs and pulled him off in the direction of the maypole. 'Come on, let's go an' watch 'er and stop bein' a misery just 'cos you've lost yer baby.'

Edward's stomach churned, much as it had the very first

time he held her as a baby. A feeling of acute loss ripped through him and he forced a smile as he forlornly followed Sarah toward the sound of music and laughter. In his head he told himself not to be so selfish, this was Annie's moment, let her have it. Another voice prayed that she wouldn't forget her father's love in this exciting world she was about to discover.

# Seven

Annie was dizzy, intoxicated by the atmosphere around her. Her pa and Sarah had watched her dancing around the maypole, skirt and hair flying with her spirit. She had soaked up the applause of the smiling crowd and allowed herself to be saturated by the compliments that were showered upon her. Never in her whole life, she thought, could there be another day like this one. Better still, it wasn't over yet and now the three of them were walking, arms linked, to the fair that was gathered on the river bank. To all intents they looked like a complete family and Annie liked that idea. Sarah was so kind and funny, she always made time for Annie, time to talk to her and she never laughed at the silly things she did. She tried to put the thought from her head that often crept in, and that was her wish: that Sarah was her real mother. Immediately a wave of guilt swept across her like a black cloud, she had a mother at home, it was wrong to think such things and she would surely be punished for her wicked thoughts.

Still she reasoned it was hard not to think that way when Sarah was so good to her, so perhaps it was only right that Annie should love her so much. She sighed and tried to put the unsmiling image of her mother's face from her mind. Today was not going to be spoilt at any price.

'Come on daydreamer, let's go an' see the side stalls. You're as bad as yer pa, in a world of yer own,' called Sarah, grabbing Annie's hand and half skipping, half running,

54

dragged her off towards the brightly coloured stalls lining the river bank.

Annie was soon distracted and gladly followed. She had never been to a fair before and was transfixed by the wondrous sights. Sights such as she had never imagined, men dressed as clowns balancing on tall stilts, dwarfs juggling balls, a fire eater swallowing flames and most fascinating of all a gypsy telling fortunes. Annie was drawn instinctively to the old woman sitting outside her tent, spellbound by her mysterious looks and weather-beaten face. As Annie approached she rose and disappeared into the tent, and in doing so allowed Annie a brief glimpse of the gloomy depths within. The walls were draped with red material and on a wooden table stood a silver crystal ball. For one second she was blinded by the reflection from it. She blinked and when she opened her eyes, the flap on the tent had fallen and everything was lost from view.

'Can I go an' 'ave me fortune told, Pa, please?' she gasped, still breathless from the brief sight into the tent.

'No, I don't hold with such nonsense. Gypsies – dirty thieves most of them,' Edward barked gruffly, dragging Annie away towards a coconut shy stall.

''Ere 'ave a go at this,' he smiled seeing her disappointed face and handing her a penny.

'Why can't I 'ave me fortune told?' she persisted, as was her way.

''Cos it's a waste of money an' you'll enjoy this more.' If he had been honest, he would have told Annie he was really quite afraid of Romany powers and be believed some things you were better not knowing, and the future was one of them.

Edward took the penny back from her open hand and gave it to the stall holder in exchange for five wooden balls. These he handed to his scowling daughter who refused to take her stubborn eyes from the gypsy tent.

'Come on, let's see 'ow good yer are.'

Reluctantly she gave up on her idea of fortune telling, for the time being any way, and turned to the coconuts instead, grinning triumphantly as she knocked four out of five from their perches.

All that afternoon the three of them strolled around the fair. They feasted on hot pies and cakes, played skittles, watched clown shows and finally collapsed exhausted with a bottle of cool lemonade on the grass. Annie loved the clear glass bottle and after it was emptied, she sat playing, tipping the bright marble in its neck back and forth. Sarah stretched out to soak up the last of the afternoon sun and Edward closed his eyes and drifted to sleep. Annie stayed alert, for although she was tired she didn't want this magical day to end or to miss out on any of the sights and sounds around her, so while the other two dozed she watched the world go by.

Her eyes were drawn by a group strolling by a cake stall. All of them were far too well dressed to have been salt workers. Two women in long gowns, each carrying a parasol, one older, one younger, whom Annie supposed were mother and daughter. There was also a man, whose attire was very sombre and his face even from a distance looked stern, almost forbidding. Some yards behind trailed a young man; he seemed to be dawdling and the older woman kept turning around, presumably to hurry him along to join them.

Annie stared unashamedly at him. He must have been sixteen or so she guessed, judging from his build and height. He was not strikingly good looking, with ordinary brown hair and a rather straight and large nose, but something about him held Annie's eye as he walked the full length of the field until he disappeared from view. She was still wondering who he was when a familiar and most unwelcome voice sounded in her ear.

''Ere with Pa and 'is whore then, are we?' Jack's face loomed above her.

Annie jumped, startled, she wasn't sure what a whore was but from the tone of his voice she assumed it was something unpleasant. Jumping to her feet she moved somewhat apart from the sleeping pair, hoping they had not heard Jack.

Along with him were two of his friends. They had all been

drinking for she could smell the ale on their breaths even from a distance.

'Who's this little beauty then?' leered one of the men, rubbing his hand across Annie's cheek.

She shivered involuntarily and Jack immediately saw her fear.

'Why this, gentlemen, is me little sister, though you can see, not so little any more,' he laughed raucously. 'In fact I'd say she's ripe, wouldn't you?'

He slid his arm around her waist, pulling her face close to his. Annie could feel her heart pounding in her chest and she fought with all her strength to push Jack away from her.

'A little fighter, eh, Jack, all the more fun if yer can 'andle 'er,' goaded one of the men, swaying back and forward, feeling quite sick from the ale he had consumed.

Taking this as a challenge Jack grabbed Annie closer to him with such force that the air was squeezed out from her lungs, causing her to cough and choke. The commotion woke Edward, who leapt to his feet instantly.

'What's goin' on, then?' he yelled, inches from Jack's face.

Jack smiled smugly, releasing Annie and reaching into his pocket to pull out two pennies which he pressed into her hands. 'Just givin' me sister a couple of pennies to spend at the fair, after all she looks pretty, don't she?'

Annie rushed to the safety of her father's arms. A silence hung in the air whilst father and son held each other's eyes. There was no love in either. After a few minutes of deadlock, Jack backed away, patting Annie's head purposefully.

'Come on lads, it's time we went. Bye Annie, 'ave a good time,' and with that he staggered off with his friends laughing coarsely.

'It's time we left too, Annie,' said Edward, stroking her head affectionately and nudging Sarah who had slept through the whole commotion. 'I'm goin' back to the shed to make sure the fire's still in. You go with Sarah an' get changed before yer go 'ome.' Picking Annie up, he hugged her to him and planted a kiss on her forehead. 'Yer looked

57

wonderful today, a real princess, don't you take any notice of what Jack says.'

Annie nodded and hugged him back, then she and Sarah walked hand-in-hand back to the barge. As they walked they went over the day's events excitedly and by the time Annie was sipping hot milk and admiring her dress one last time, the incident with Jack had gone from her mind.

'Will yer be all right walkin' 'ome by yerself?' asked Sarah for the third time as Annie was leaving.

'Course I will, it's no further than usual.'

'All right, straight 'ome though, it's gettin' late an' we don't want yer in trouble with yer mother.'

Annie skipped off into the night. Suddenly she remembered the two pennies that Jack had given her. Plunging her hand into her pocket she felt them, smooth and round and beckoning. Then the thought crept stealthily into her mind and once it was there she couldn't shift it: now she could go and have her fortune read and no one would ever know. She had to walk right past the fair on her way home and Jack had given her the money to spend, it wouldn't take her long, so what harm could it do. She pushed all thoughts of her father's disapproval from her mind and hurried on towards the sound of laughter and music ahead of her.

The fair at night was even more exciting than during the day, torches glowed in the darkness, lighting up the stalls and on a huge bonfire a pig was being roasted. The delicious smell wafted through the air making her mouth water. Crowds of people stood chatting in groups, eating and drinking, everyone happy, reluctant for the night to end. Picking her way through the crowd Annie made her way towards the gypsy tent. At first her heart sank for it was all closed up and in darkness and Annie thought she was too late. As she got closer she could make out the gypsy woman she had seen earlier, she was sitting by the closed flap in the darkness, her eyes were closed and Annie thought she must be asleep. It was pitch black, no lights or torches illuminated the tent and Annie was suddenly afraid to go any nearer. The old woman was wrapped in a long hooded cloak that she had pulled about her ears to keep her warm. As if she sensed Annie's presence she jerked her head up, allowing the hood to fall and revealing her long dark hair and wrinkled skin. She smiled and beckoned Annie to approach.

'I've been waiting fer you, come in,' croaked the ancient voice, holding open the tent. Torn for a second between walking forward or turning on her heel to run, Annie swallowed hard and taking a deep breath stepped into the tent. The flap fell shut behind her instantly, making her jump. At first she thought it was completely dark inside but then as her eyes focused she saw a tiny candle flickering on the table in front of her. The blue flame leapt in the chilly air, drawing strange shadows on the velvety walls.

'Sit down,' commanded the voice, though not harshly.

'I er . . . wanted to 'ave me fortune told,' stuttered Annie, feebly holding the two pennies in her sweaty palm.

The woman laughed a squeaky laugh, and it echoed around the tent eerily. 'Well, I usually charge a little more than this but as I was expecting yer and for yer cheek we'll see what we can do.'

Annie was mortified, she had never thought to ask the price and she was a little unnerved as the woman seemed to know she was coming. 'I'm really sorry, I didn't know 'ow much . . .'

'Hush child, the crystal's clearing. Look.'

Annie stared at the glass sphere in front of her, the gypsy moved her hands lovingly across its surface, chanting and moaning in words that Annie did not understand. At first she saw nothing except her own reflection in the shiny glass, but then slowly the image began to distort and an iridescent blue mist swirled within the ball. The gypsy stopped chanting and stared hard into the depths of the globe. Annie held her breath, terrified and yet fascinated all at once.

'I can see a girl dancin', dancin' in a beautiful blue dress, round an' round . . .'

'Yes, yes, that's me,' cried Annie excitedly.

'I can see tears in 'er life, an' many of 'em . . .' She paused to look at Annie and shook her head sorrowfully.

Annie frowned, maybe she meant losing Clara, for she had cried many tears then but she wanted to hear about the future not the past, and she urged the gypsy to go on.

'There's a woman, she's not kind to yer, but it doesn't matter. You don't need 'er in your life, you'll learn that. A child, a boy, he'll bring yer such joy an' heartache too. Then a man, yer 'usband. Beware 'im, he'll . . .' The gypsy gasped and, suddenly placed a golden cloth over the ball, sat forward to hold Annie's hands.

'Yer must always remember who yer are, believe in yerself. I can't tell yer any more, it wouldn't be right. But yer can change yer destiny, yer 'ave the power to do it. Go 'ome now. I can sense danger here fer you 'ere. Go on, yer mother's waiting.'

Annie rose to her feet, feeling bewildered. She hadn't understood most of what the gypsy had said and she was afraid, for the woman had obviously seen something terrible in the globe. Mumbling thanks she stumbled from the tent, intent only on getting home now, her mind churned up with so many questions. She told herself not to be silly, what could this woman know about her life, her pa was right, it was all a lot of nonsense and she wished she had never gone back to the fair.

Realising she would probably be in trouble for being so late, she started to run through the crowds of people milling around the stalls. As she was small it was difficult to get past people who pushed and shoved her aside roughly. She didn't even see Jack before she ran straight into his arms by the ale tent.

'Well, well, well, if it isn't our little runt,' he grimaced, even more drunk now than he had been earlier. 'And what are you doing here at this time, up to no good eh?'

He tightened his grip on her arm, pinching her skin.

'Let me go Jack please, I'm goin' 'ome,' Annie begged, afraid even more than usual of her drunken brother.

Dragging her away from the light of the tent and into the

60

shadows Jack pushed his face close to hers. His breath stank of stale ale and Annie recoiled in disgust.

'Not so fast princess, yer think yer can make a fool of me in front of me friends do yer? It's time I taught yer a lesson. I saw yer flaunting yerself in that dress today, face painted like a tart. Ma would like that, wouldn't she?'

'Please Jack, let me go. I'm sorry if I upset yer friends, please let me go.' Tears streamed down her face.

Jack pressed his wet lips against hers, slobbering as he did so.

'Yer dress like a tart so let's see if yer are one, let's see what's under that prim frock now.' Before she could wrench herself free Jack knocked her to the floor. He slid his hands under her skirt, lifting it high above her waist. One hand tore at her bloomers, while the other clutched at her tiny breasts, tearing her blouse to expose them crudely. His breathing was coming hard and fast and she could feel him pressing his body against her leg, it felt hard and rock-like.

Sheer panic swept through her, she was unsure of what he was doing but knowing it was wrong terrified her. With one hand she clawed at his face, feeling the blood she had drawn, sticky and wet in her fingers. In his shock Jack momentarily let go of her, just enough for her to roll away from him. But she was not quick enough and as she was halfway to her feet, he felled her again, sprawling his body across hers, forcing her legs apart with his. What happened next was so fast that she was barely aware of it all before it was over. She fought valiantly as he pushed himself against her, the excitement rising in his face. He grunted and beads of sweat appeared on his brow as he ripped off her bloomers. Tears choked her as she lay helpless under his weight, knowing that she had no power to stop this nightmare. Then as quickly as it began it ended, as she was aware of Jack's body being wrenched from hers. Fists were flying and two bodies fought in front of her. Within seconds Jack lay on the ground, knocked unconscious by his assailant. It was over.

Slowly Annie dragged herself to her feet, pulling down

61

her clothes to try and regain some dignity. The stranger gallantly turned away as she pulled up her torn underwear and covered her exposed breasts. Humiliated and full of shame Annie mumbled some thanks to her saviour before turning to flee. If she had stopped for a second she would have seen it was the very same young man she watched across the field earlier that day.

She had only one thought in her mind and that was to get to her pa. Dishevelled and sobbing she ran all the way to the wych shed only to find to her horror that it was deserted. The fire was banked up for the night and there was no sign of Edward. Her mind raced frantically, where else could he be? Then she realised he would be with Sarah on the barge, he had probably gone for his supper. Already panting from the exertion, Annie broke out into a run again, determined to find him, knowing she would be safe then.

The barge seemed to be all in darkness as she approached, and trying to control her sobs, Annie climbed quietly aboard. Smudge was asleep in his usual position on deck and he lazily opened one eye, saw it was only Annie, and closed it again.

Annie paused just before she entered the cabin, a strange moaning noise made her hesitate and she very gently eased open the door. Her heart thumped in her chest at what she saw. In the semi-light she could quite clearly see the two naked bodies of her pa and Sarah. They were intertwined, Sarah's legs spread wide apart with her pa in between them, just as Jack had been with her. Sweat prickled on her brow and her stomach churned with nausea. She could feel her face burning in the darkness. Horrified yet fascinated Annie watched the rhythmical movements as her pa pushed that hard part of his body, the same part Jack had tried but failed to force into her, in and out of Sarah. She in turn arched her back in pleasure, moaning and crying. Shock and disbelief raced through Annie's mind, now she knew what being a whore was, it was doing this terrible thing that Sarah was doing with her father.

62

Groping her way out onto the river bank Annie fell to her knees and vomited. Now it all made sense, everything Jack had said to her. She would never be able to look at Sarah again without thinking of tonight. She felt dirty for she too was a tart, a whore, for Jack, her own brother had touched her body in that way.

Distraught, Annie somehow managed to find her way home, praying that Jack would not be waiting for her. The house was in darkness and she gratefully collapsed onto her mattress and wept bitterly, it was all spoiled, the whole day, her whole life. The best day of her life had turned into the worst and she wished she could fall asleep and never wake up again.

# Eight

'You're very quiet today. Cat got yer tongue, 'as it?'
Edward playfully ruffled the top of Annie's head, as
she sat cross-legged on the wych shed floor, sewing the
rough bags.

The material was coarse and her fingers were red and
sore from pulling the big needle through the stiff cloth.
Occasionally she pricked herself and drew blood. Her face
was very serious and she kept her head down as she worked,
too miserable with herself since that terrible day last week,
to want to talk to anyone.

'I'm fine,' she lied unconvincingly, not wishing to prolong
the conversation with her pa.

'I'm about ready to take the barrow down to the river,
d'yer want to come?'

Annie was in a dilemma. She just could not face the
thought of seeing Sarah yet, but she was afraid to be left
alone with Jack in the shed. Ever since that dreadful night
at the fair, Jack, still sporting a black eye and bruised face,
had been using every opportunity he had to scare her. He
never actually said anything, but the evil gleam in his eye
told her that he was waiting for an opportunity to get her
alone. She knew there would have to be some sort of punishment, for Jack was not prone to forgiveness, but it was what
he might do that terrified her most. Maybe he would try to
touch her body again and she found herself praying that he
would simply beat her instead.

She had not told anyone what had happened, how could

she. She had already been in trouble with her mother for being home so late, she couldn't talk to her pa or Sarah, not after what she had seen them doing. She had thought about talking to Sally, but she was just too ashamed and so she decided that it would have to be her secret, and it was a secret that was lying very heavily indeed.

'I've got to get back early today, Mother wants me to go to the shops fer 'er, if that's all right?' She avoided meeting her pa's eyes, for she hated lying to him.

Edward frowned. It wasn't like Annie not to want to come to the barge, especially when Sarah had been away all week and she hadn't seen her. Still as Sarah kept reminding him, she was growing up, changing, so perhaps it was only natural that she was moody sometimes. He shrugged his shoulders and smiled at her.

'See yer tomorrow then.'

'Yes, tomorrow,' muttered Annie, as she scrambled to get her cotton jacket and disappear out of the shed before her father had time to reach down and kiss her. She wished she could make the sordid pictures in her head go away, for until they did she could not bring herself to kiss her beloved pa; seeing him with Sarah had spoiled everything. She was so angry with him and Sarah but mostly with herself, nothing seemed as if it would ever be the same again.

It had not been a complete lie that she had told her father, for she did have to run some errands for her mother, but she could have gone later in the day. Today was market day and all the shops and stalls stayed open until eight o'clock or so. Now of course she would have to lie to her mother as well and explain why she was home so early.

She sighed and crossly kicked the pebbles as she walked, everything was so complicated at the moment. The sun shone warmly and even though it was only May the grass was lush and tall, the trees all danced in their emerald finery. Annie gazed behind her, across the fields beyond the wych shed. Woodland stretched away into the horizon, spoiled only by the squat sheds, dotted about, billowing out steam. Before her lay the town in total contrast, a grimy blot

65

on the landscape. It looked just as Annie felt, soiled, unloved and very miserable. Suddenly she knew she couldn't go back there just yet, she wanted to run until she could no longer see the dilapidated houses or pitiful streets. Filling her lungs with air she turned her back on the grime and broke out into a jog, she began to climb up into the woods away from the river in the exact opposite direction to the one she should have been going in.

She had no idea where she was going or how long she had been running but she knew that she couldn't stop until she felt her heart bursting and pounding in her ears. The sweat pricked her back, as she pushed herself harder and harder. Driven by despair and the desire to rid herself of the devil within, she kept up her relentless pace until there was no breath left in her aching body. Eventually she collapsed, exhausted, beneath a tree in a shady dell. Closing her eyes Annie listened to the relentless pounding of her own heart, it was somehow comforting and she felt better.

'Hello. Are you all right?'

The voice intruding her private silence made Annie shoot up, startled, cross to be disturbed just as she was feeling peaceful. Opening her eyes, Annie squinted at the figure before her. He was standing directly in front of the sun and she had to raise her hand above her eyes to shade them before she could see him properly. She recognised him instantly as the boy she had been watching at the fair and his dress confirmed her thoughts then, that neither he nor his acquaintances were ordinary townsfolk but in fact gentry. His attire today was riding jodhpurs, shiny leather boots and a blue velvet jacket to match the hat on his head. By his side his horse whinnied impatiently and he stroked her muzzle softly, whispering soothingly before he tied her to the nearest tree.

'I'm sorry, am I trespassing?' Annie uttered, all too aware of her inferior position and the fact that she had no idea whose land she was on.

He smiled kindly and extended a hand to help her to her feet, which she sheepishly accepted.

'Yes, you are, but it does not matter, as it's my father's land. So you need not worry, we won't have you shot.'

Annie backed away from him nervously and, seeing the frightened expression on her face, he laughed.

'I'm only teasing, you are welcome to walk here any time,' he grinned. 'I am Richard Ellis, and you . . .?'

Annie was momentarily taken aback, this was John Ellis's son. It didn't seem possible, this boy seemed so friendly, not like his ogre father.

'Annie, Annie Hayes. Me pa owns one of the salt sheds by the river,' she said proudly. She wanted him to know that she was not just someone whose family worked for his father.

'Aah, an independent. I think that my father would not approve of me talking to you.'

'Then don't,' retorted Annie huffily, seeing what she thought was a display of the famous Ellis arrogance.

'But then I rarely do what my father approves of, so if you could stop being prickly, perhaps I could walk with you for a while.'

His smile was infectious and Annie despite herself grinned back and nodded. There was something about him, something she could not label, that drew her eyes as it had the first time she had seen him. It was not an obviously handsome face, more rugged than distinguished, but the way his lips curled as he laughed and the two dimples that appeared on each side of his cheeks, caused Annie's heart to flicker, much to her horror and she hoped fervently that he had not noticed her staring.

'So Annie, what are you doing wandering all alone in my woods?' His tone was teasing but she could not bring herself to be cross.

'I think that the trees an' fields an' rivers are free things that belong to no one but themselves, an' so we should all be able to walk where we want an' enjoy them.' She knew she was being impudent but he made her feel reckless.

'That's an interesting theory, not one I feel my father would uphold,' he laughed, picking a strand of tall grass as he strolled, and placing it in his mouth to chew.

'From what I 'ear yer father's only interested in makin' money, which leaves no time fer enjoyin' beautiful things.'

Richard's face hardened and Annie cringed inside, realising how rude she sounded. 'I'm sorry, I shouldn't 'ave said that . . .' she whispered, her face crimson with embarrassment.

'No, it's all right, actually I quite agree with you. Sometimes I try to pretend to myself that he's not as bad as people say, but then when I talk to you or someone like you, I know he is. I may be his son but that doesn't mean I have to be like him,' he looked pleadingly at her for approval and Annie suddenly felt quite sorry for him. 'I can't wait to get away from here. I'm going to medical school in London in the autumn.'

'Oh yer going to be a doctor, yer must be very clever,' Annie sighed enviously, thinking of Sarah's atlas and how she would love to get away from here too. 'I'd love to be able to travel to other countries, see all over the world.' Her voice was wistful and yet resigned that it was just a dream.

Richard watched her dark eyes shining as she spoke and he realised what a beauty she was going to be in a few years' time.

'Then do it if you want to,' he said so matter of factly, as if it were perfectly feasible.

Annie laughed, it was ridiculous, but still it made her feel good that he should imagine her capable of it.

'Why I can 'ardly read, I've never been to school. I think the furthest I'll ever get is Liverpool docks, if I'm lucky.'

He knew she was right of course, but her destiny seemed so bland for someone so alive and beautiful. A future of hard work, childbearing and poverty was probably the best she could hope for. Such drudgery seemed inevitably cruel. This was just the kind of injustice that made Richard so angry inside, and he despised his privileged existence in such an unbalanced world.

They walked for a while in silence, the huge chasm between their worlds mocking them both. Richard guided his horse behind him and the plodding rhythm of its hooves

68

marked time. As they reached the lane that led back towards town, Annie paused to say goodbye, before he should risk the embarrassment of being seen with her.

'Thanks fer walkin' me to 'ere. I've got to go to the market fer me mother.'

Richard suddenly felt himself overrun with panic, what if he did not see her again? He told himself not to be ridiculous, she was just a child, nevertheless the feeling persisted.

'If you could meet me here next week, I would enjoy another walk with you.' He knew he sounded stupid and he mounted his horse, angry for making a fool of himself.

Annie stood gazing up at him, her face shining like an angel, her dark tousled hair enhancing her beauty. 'I'd like that very much. Next week, then.'

Annie felt her heart swell with excitement and smiling at him one last time she turned and fled, leaving him spellbound as he watched her disappear.

As she skipped along the pathway, she kept the image of Richard's face in her mind and even though she knew it was wrong she was already longing for next week to come. She felt so different in his company. He certainly didn't treat her like a child, and she realised she was smiling again. As with the ever changing moods of adolescence, the nightmares of last week paled into insignificance, as new feeling swept through her blossoming body. She was happy again, for now there was Richard to think about, and she could forgive the rest of the world anything as long as this wonderful feeling filled her senses.

'Where've yer been? It's late.' Elizabeth's gruff voice met Annie as she entered the house. She was laden down with the shopping and the handle of the basket cut cruelly into her skin, still nothing could dampen her spirit as Richard still filled her head.

'I went to the market, remember,' Annie called as she lugged the heavy load into the scullery.

Elizabeth hovered around her as she unpacked the

groceries. Her mouth was dry and she longed for a taste of brandy; her last bottle had run out two days ago.

'Did yer remember the brandy, me stomach pains 'ave been awful bad today,' she badgered. Unable to wait any longer she began to rummage through the bag in search of the golden bottle.

Annie's heart sank, she had forgotten in her daydreaming.

'I'm sorry, I forgot all about it. I 'ad so much to carry today an' I thought I'd brought you some last week.'

It was true, but Elizabeth was drinking more and more these days, sometimes starting first thing in the morning after her breakfast.

'I don't need yer to keep a check on me, lady, in future you just do as yer told,' Elizabeth snapped, her mouth twisted in anger. 'Yer can go straight back to that shop now, yer don't know the pain I suffer without it.'

Annie stared at her mother's contorted face, she really looked very ugly, her eyes filled with such venom, almost like a mad woman. It made Annie shudder and grabbing her purse she fled from the house, to the grocer's, at the end of the next street. Her mother must be more ill than she imagined.

'Please Mr Greaves, can I 'ave a bottle of brandy,' she puffed out breathlessly.

'Your old ma at it again, is she?' he smirked, handing over the liquor.

Not understanding the implications, Annie nodded, adding that her mother's pains seemed to be worse than usual. Mr Greaves smiled sardonically as he handed her the change and as she closed the shop door she clearly heard him mutter, 'Stomach pains my foot, the old soak.' Annie did not run back with the bottle, for Mr Greaves's words were preying on her mind. Perhaps he was right, perhaps there was nothing wrong with her and the drinking had nothing to do with medical reasons. It was true she got through more and more gin and brandy lately, although Annie never actually saw her drinking it. When she took a new bottle home it simply vanished; what Annie didn't realise was that the bottles were not even lasting from one shopping trip to the next.

What she did know was that her mother's moods were becoming more and more erratic and unpredictable. She had to do something to help her mother, but what? Then it came to her. She would dilute the liquor, it was simple if she tipped half away and filled it up with water. Elizabeth would never know, perhaps she could cure her of her weakness and then she would be forever grateful to her daughter.

Feeling very saintly for her good intentions, Annie breezed back into the house, where Jack and his mother were talking together in the front parlour. The walls were so thin that every word could be clearly heard. What she heard horrified her.

"'E's been coughin' an' chokin' up blood again today, 'e can 'ardly lift the rake now without restin' every few minutes, it's pitiful.' Jack's voice sounded mocking.

'Well, when he's gone it'll all be yours, son,' Elizabeth crooned.

'I've told 'im we need to take on someone else, he can't do much an' Annie's useless except fer sweepin' or sewin'. Besides, all he's interested in is seein' that tart when she's 'ere. She'll 'ave a shock when he's gone, 'cos I won't be usin' her barge for transportin' me salt that's fer sure.' Annie's head reeled. Was her pa really so ill, how could this be happening and she hadn't noticed? It was true she had seen him coughing, but all salt workers coughed, it came with the job.

'Anyway, I've found a lad, smart boy, fourteen years old, desperate fer work. He'll be just right fer doin' all the stokin' and rakin'. I've got 'im comin' down to the shed tomorrow,' Jack continued.

'What if yer father says no?' put in Elizabeth slyly.

'You just leave 'im to me. Besides, if we're lucky he won't be around much longer to say no to anythin'.'

The pair laughed wickedly like two conspirators and Annie pushed her hands over her ears to try to block out the dreadful sound. She was filled with unusual venom and

71

marching to the sink she began to pour the bottle of brandy away. The door opened as she was halfway through and Elizabeth and Jack entered the room.

'What d'yer think yer doing?' cried Elizabeth, rushing forward to save some of her golden nectar before it disappeared down the hole.

Annie stood rigidly still, tears coursed down her cheeks in torrents and intermittent sobs shook her body. ''Ow can yer talk about Pa like that, 'ow could yer?' Her accusations fell on deaf ears.

Elizabeth, almost beside herself now with the loss of her liquor, quivered uncontrollably. Her eyes were wide with rage as she moved forward to strike her daughter, but before she could, Jack stepped in between them.

'Let me deal with this, Ma.'

Forcibly he dragged the now screaming Annie into the parlour, slamming the door closed behind him. Laughing hysterically he placed her over his knee, and exposing her buttocks, he proceeded to beat her mercilessly. Unable to struggle free, Annie collapsed and hung limply across his legs. Once she had stopped crying out and fighting Jack lost interest in his game and he flung her to one side, striking her brutally across the face before he stamped from the room.

Annie crawled into the corner, exhausted and sore. Gingerly she felt her face with her fingers, the huge weal was already swollen and she winced as she touched it. There were no more tears left in her body. She had been expecting something like this from Jack anyway. Today had simply given him the excuse he was looking for. She was almost relieved; at least he might leave her alone now.

Her mind centred on her pa, how could she not have noticed how ill he was. Guilt swept through her again, she hadn't even kissed him goodbye today. The incident she had witnessed with Sarah suddenly did not seem important and if that was how her mother thought of him no wonder he wanted to be with someone else. All that mattered now was that Pa was all right. Annie closed her eyes tightly and prayed, begging God please not to take him away from her, as he had Clara. It was a desperate prayer, a prayer in which she offered willingly to take any punishment God saw fit to make her endure, in exchange for her pa's life.

Dragging herself to her feet, she straightened her clothes and scrubbed her eyes with the back of her hands. She knew she had to go into the scullery and prepare tea or she would be in trouble again. She was relieved to find the room empty. Her mother had gone upstairs with the last saved dregs of the bottle and Jack had disappeared for a sleep before he went out to the public house after his tea.

Slowly Annie began to prepare the food, trying not to bend too much, for her bottom was stiff and sore. Her mind went to Richard and she hoped her bruised face would be healed by next week. The thought of seeing him again was a bright flame, shining in an otherwise miserable world, and she longed for the days to pass quickly.

# Nine

Edward struggled to lift the slippery, cumbersome block of salt, and he wheezed in the steamy atmosphere of the shed. Cursing to himself, he dropped the heavy slab on the floor. The tightening band in his chest crippled him for a moment. He knew he was getting worse. It was not just the agonising pains in his chest any more, but at night cold sweats awoke him from his sleep, drenching his skin until he shook uncontrollably. Damn, damn, damn, he repeated under his breath, forcing himself to straighten up; he had no time for this, there was still too much to do.

He hated to admit it but Jack had been quite right to take Joe on, they did need extra help now and the boy was very willing and helpful. Although he was only fourteen he already worked far harder than Jack and despite being quiet and shy his presence did seem to have cheered Annie up.

That was one thing at least to be happy about, she seemed less withdrawn these days and had even begun to sing again in the shed. Edward's main worry was what she would do when he had gone; the thought terrified him that she would be left to the mercies of Elizabeth and Jack. He knew he was dying, despite Sarah's insistence that he would be better in the warmer weather next spring. It was only September now and Edward knew in his heart he would be very lucky to see the next year arrive. Strangely he was not bitter. Even though he was only fifty-four years old, his life seemed to have been long. Perhaps it was just that he had become so exhausted, that the very effort of living was becoming too much of a burden for him. He had reflected a lot lately about his life, all the good and bad things, successes and failures, and he had come to the conclusion that this illness might be part of his punishment for his illicit love affair with Sarah. If it was it didn't matter, it had all been worth while and given another chance he would do it all again. His only regret was that he hadn't been able to give Sarah more, for she deserved that. She had never once complained that she had to work alone, hauling the loads back and forth to Liverpool, nor that she hated the lonely nights away from him. When she returned her welcomes were always loving rather than reproachful and she never asked for more than he was able to give, giving all of herself to him in exchange. He knew he had been truly blessed with her love and with Annie, the sunshine of his life. For her too, he felt remorse, that he could never make up for the things she lacked in her life but she too gave him all her devotion, never blaming him or burdening him with guilt. His heart was torn not so much with his impending death but by what he would leave behind.

Sarah was independent and proud, he knew she would survive, but what of Annie, so young still and vulnerable? That was why he had decided to make a will and why, despite his fading health, he had struggled to Manchester last week, to ensure with the solicitor that all things were legal and proper. He could ill afford the expense but it was the only way he knew to protect Annie. The precious document now lay signed and sealed in the parson's desk with instructions that it be opened on his death. Its contents declared that the pan belonged to Annie and her alone, it was the only gift he could impart and he prayed it would somehow give her a chance in a life where the odds seemed so heavily stacked against her.

Joe's voice interrupted Edward's thoughts. 'I'll stack these for you, Mr Hayes.'

The boy was only trying to be helpful but Edward was angry enough with his inadequacies without being reminded of them. He snapped back irritably.

'You've got yer own jobs to do without worryin' about mine.'

The boy's face fell and Edward immediately regretted his short temper. 'Sorry Joe, I know yer only trying to 'elp, but let me do it while I can, eh.'

'Yes, course, I shouldn't have . . .' Joe's face flushed. He felt very awkward about Edward's illness, as if it was something he shouldn't talk about.

To Edward to it seemed sometimes as if he must already be dead, the way everyone whispered and smiled patronisingly at him.

A difficult silence prevailed, until a few moments later Annie skipped into the shed, bringing with her the warm rays of September sunshine and lighting the whole place up instantly. ''Ello Pa, 'ave yer seen the weather today, it's beautiful and far too nice to be cooped up in 'ere all day. I've brought you some nice warm meat pie fer yer dinner, come an' sit in the field with me to eat it.' She reached up to peck his cheek and began leading him by the hand, before he could protest. 'Joe can manage perfectly well for 'alf an 'our, can't yer Joe?' Joe nodded, before burying his head against his chest, in an attempt to slow down the rush of colour that always flooded his face whenever Annie spoke to him. She grinned at him knowing full well that he was sweet on her and enjoying the attention.

Edward linked his daughter's arm and they strolled out of the gloomy shed into the bright sunshine. Finding a dry spot on the grass they sat down to enjoy the picnic. Edward too was quite aware of the effect his daughter had on Joe and he mistakenly believed that this was the reason for her recent happiness. The idea pleased him for although Joe was shy and reserved he was reliable and Annie was going to need someone she could trust when he had gone.

If he had been aware of the real source of Annie's joy he certainly would not have approved, which was why Annie had kept it a secret for the past five months. She knew her father was desperately ill now, there was no point in upsetting him unnecessarily.

76

She hadn't quite given up hope yet that he would recover, for his death was so unthinkable to her. Steadfastly she prayed each night to her God, with whom she felt she had a special relationship. She didn't so much pray as hold a conversation with him, albeit a one-way conversation. She never actually heard his replies, but the answers would somehow seep into her head gradually. At the moment though this was not happening and the thoughts in her head were not what she wanted to hear. God was in fact telling her that no matter how much she wanted her pa to live, it was no good, when someone's life was over, that was the end. Annie was persistently refusing to acknowledge this and continued to plead and bargain for his life, even though it was falling on deaf ears. She was doing everything in her power to help, working harder at the Wych shed, cooking him stews and nourishing foods, and trying to make him rest as much as possible. She only wished she could stop him sleeping in the draughty shed, especially now that winter was coming. But he was stubborn and insisted that he had slept there for years and would continue to do so. Besides where else could he go apart from his occasional night with Sarah on the barge. He certainly would never go back to the house, he never mentioned Elizabeth's name, nor she his any more. Annie knew she simply had to try and do her best for him, and she did.

The source of her smiling face and happy disposition was at that very moment waiting for her in the woods that stretched away from the river below. Richard Ellis sat beneath the beech trees, his arms folded behind his head, enjoying the autumn sunshine on his face and counting the minutes until Annie arrived. They had been meeting regularly, twice or three times a week now, ever since that first encounter, and neither of them could wait each time until the next rendezvous. They talked and walked and he brought her books to look at and helped her with her reading and writing. She was quick to learn and was soon competent with most text.

Sometimes he would take her on the back of his horse and she would snuggle close into him her arms wrapped tightly around his chest. These were the moments he loved best and yet dreaded most, for he longed to hold her and kiss her. He wanted to stroke her hair and caress her angel lips but he knew it was wrong. She was after all still a child, and yet she was so much more than that. That he loved her was without doubt, what she felt for him he wasn't sure, but unless he was mistaken those huge eyes were filled with passion too, though perhaps a more innocent one. He had asked himself a million times what it was that bewitched him so about her, but there was no clear answer. There were plenty of more suitable girls his own age, that his father constantly paired him off with, but they were all so bland in comparison to her. Their ambitions lay no further than securing a good marriage and following their mothers into lives of indulgent complacency. Annie had a fire, a thirst for knowledge and a gentle wisdom way beyond her years. These secret meetings between them had fuelled a passion that ran so deep within him, he knew it would never die, no matter what distances and obstacles fate threw in their path.

The effect Annie had on him was only equal to that he had on her, though she understood its implications less. To Annie he was the most wonderful person she had ever met, he stirred strange passions within her that scared yet excited her. Her desires were not as physical as his for she was much younger, but she did long for his company, to be simply near him, and in her mind she knew she was in love for the very first time. It was a fierce and powerful love that made her tingle when she thought of him, that filled her head day and night with longings and needs, that made her adamant that he was the only person she would ever fall in love with. She was so lost in her dreams that she did not think about the future, about the differences in their worlds and the impossibility of them being together. Love and inexperience made her blind to the dangers and heartaches and she threw herself into it trustingly, never imagining the joy would end.

But today reality took its first hungry bite at their precious secret world. Richard knew he had to tell her he was leaving for London, it was time for medical school, for he had other dreams and ambitions to fulfil and becoming a doctor was one of them.

He heard Annie singing long before he spotted her coming through the trees. She looked as breathtaking as ever, her long black hair loose and floating around her. Her dress, which was a little too small, hugged her small breasts, emphasising them. Richard felt his body stir at the sight of her, and part of him thought it was a very good thing that he was going away soon, for the urge to caress her was becoming too strong for him to control. The last thing he wanted to do was frighten her away, and so fighting to gain control he leapt to his feet to greet her.

'Hello, my Annie and how are we today?' he grinned and stooped low to kiss her hand. Annie giggled, these were the things she loved about him, he always made her feel so special.

'I am just fine, but I can't stay long today, I've got to get back to the house. I can't be late again this week.'

It was a miracle to Annie that nobody had ever found out about the secret meetings. Perhaps that was what made them so exciting. Actually Annie found it quite easy to tell her pa that she had to go home early sometimes, or her mother that she had to work later at the shed. As her parents never met it was simple to keep up the deceit and it allowed her a few free hours to spend with her beloved Richard uninterrupted. Today however her mother had made a point of asking her to be home early to catch the grocer before he closed, for things she needed desperately. Annie already knew what that meant but she had given up worrying about that particular problem as it was beyond her control.

Of course Elizabeth was quite capable of walking the few yards to the shop herself but she never left the house now, shutting herself off as a total recluse.

'I have something to tell you,' Richard began, anxious now to get this over with.

Annie linked her arm with his and smiled up at him. 'This sounds like a confession, 'ave yer done somethin' really wicked?' she teased.

Richard's heart turned, he had practised this speech a dozen times but there was really no easy way to say it. 'It's time for me to leave for London.' He hung his head, as the full impact of his words took their toll.

For a second she stood quite still, and then allowing her arm to slide down his, she entwined her fingers into his.

'Annie, you knew I would be going soon, it's not for ever.' Her silence was unbearable and Richard turned and held her to him, his emotions swirling as his arms folded her into his body. 'I will come back, Annie, I promise. When I do you will be older, we will be able to be together, please understand I have to do this.'

Annie understood perfectly, he was going away for years, leaving her. She brought her huge black eyes, brimming with tears, up to meet his. The vision took his breath away, choking him with sorrow.

'I think we should say goodbye now, then,' she said stiffly, trying to keep her voice steady. 'Good luck. I'm sure you'll make a brilliant doctor.'

'Please don't be like this. I can't bear you to be angry with me.'

'I'm not angry, Richard. I just pretended to myself that today would never come and now it 'as. I don't expect yer to come back, one day you will be rich doctor and I will always just be Annie Hayes.'

She pulled away from him, not wanting him to see her pain, her pride was too fierce for that. In spite of all her brave words about knowing that today was inevitable, she had allowed herself to dream impossible dreams, in which Richard loved her too much to ever leave her. She felt very silly and childlike now, this was Richard Ellis before her, not some lad from the town, how could she possibly have imagined that he would care about her.

Annie tip-toed up to kiss his cheek before she left, but as she did he pulled her to him, covering her lips with his.

80

Annie felt every nerve in her body tingle as she melted against him, her body moulded into his in intimate embrace. Then, as they were both shocked by their reactions, they sprang apart. Annie, face flushed, gently pressed her fingers to her lips and blowing him a kiss she turned and fled. It was an image Richard would hold in his head for many years to come, for she was to remain the most beautiful girl he would ever know and her face would always haunt him.

Annie did not turn around, for she did not want him to see her face that was sodden with tears. In her chest her heart ached and she felt desolate as she had never done before. Once she was out of his sight completely, she allowed herself to fall to the ground where she wept bitterly, until her ribs were sore with sobbing and her eyes bright red.

Eventually she stopped and sitting up she gazed at the sky hoping for some comfort from the white billowy clouds that whisked across it, but none was offered. At that precise moment nothing could comfort her, for she knew that she loved Richard and that she would probably never see him again. Although she had fooled herself with daydreams over the past few months, at heart she was a realist, and common sense as always prevailed with her. Richard was from another world, he was six years older than her, his life was just beginning. It was a life that could take him anywhere in the world. She began to get cross with herself for being so stupid, how could she have ever fooled herself that she could be part of that? Why, he was probably laughing about her this very minute, she could see it clearly now, she was nothing more than an amusement for him.

She groaned in humiliation and vowed never to let Richard see how he had hurt her or how much pain he had caused her. Her determination made her feel better, and getting to her feet she began to walk back down to the town. It seemed gloomier than ever as it coughed out its dirt and smog, matching her mood perfectly. She talked to herself sternly. She knew she must put Richard from her mind, he was just a dream, nothing more, he could not be part of her life, ever. Gently she rubbed her fingers across her lips, picturing for one second the kiss they had shared, and the magical shudder ran through her again. That was her memory to treasure, no one could take that away and she truly believed, for that one brief second that their lips had joined, that Richard had loved her too. When over the next few years, he would creep into her head, as he often did, she would imagine that kiss, before dismissing his image and banishing his smiling face from her mind. Desolately, that day she collected the shopping but as she left the grocer's shop the bucket filled with flowers caught her eye. Huge golden chrysanthemums, heads heavy, hung amongst the green foliage. Annie thought they looked beautiful, shimmering golden suns reflecting the afternoon light. Suddenly she wanted to do something to cheer herself up. Having a few pennies left, she went back into the shop and bought a bunch as a surprise for her mother. She imagined the gift might stir some dormant emotion in her, that maybe just once they could find some fragment to share. She knew that there must be something very wrong with her, something lacking, that stopped her mother from feeling any emotion for her. Maybe she was waiting for Annie to make the first move and once the ice barrier had been melted everything would be all right. She knew her mother was capable of such emotion for she hung on Jack's every word. Annie had seen her hug and kiss him with such fervour that she had been stung with jealousy. Today of all days Annie needed her mother's arms. If Clara had been alive she knew she could have run to her for comfort. Why, oh why, she thought can't my own mother give it.

As she entered the house she heard movement in the scullery and sure enough Elizabeth was sitting by the oven range, rocking back and forth on the wooden chair that squeaked piteously.

''Ave yer got all the shopping?' Her mother's voice sounded monotone as usual.

'Yes an' I've brought these to cheer yer up,' said Annie proudly placing the flowers in her mother's lap, smiling sweetly.

82

Elizabeth rose to her feet and for one second Annie thought she was going to bend forward and hold her. Instead her face contorted into anger and she threw the flowers onto the floor.

'What d'yer think yer are doin' wasting money on flowers, 'ave yer gone mad?'

'I just thought . . .' wailed Annie, devastated that her gift should be shunned in this way.

'Yer never think, that's yer problem. I 'ate flowers anyway, specially these, they're funeral flowers. Get rid of them before Jack sees them or you'll be in fer another beatin'. Yer probably deserve one, anyway.'

Annie's crestfallen face exuding such obvious pain made Elizabeth smile inwardly. She loved to twist the knife and so she couldn't resist a final cruel comment, to wound her daughter further. 'Better still save them fer yer father, I 'ear he'll be needing them soon.'

Annie never spoke a word as she gathered up the torn petals that were strewn everywhere, but at that very moment a seed of hatred was sown, as Annie began to drive out any yearning for her mother's love. Her heart had been broken twice in the space of a few hours, today she knew she had grown up.

# Ten

The week before Edward Hayes passed away, he suddenly decided that he would like to sail with Sarah into Liverpool, for he knew in his heart that this would be his last cargo of salt. He had been much weaker these last few weeks and he coughed up so much blood now that he wondered if he had any left. However, the prospect of the journey seemed to have given him a new lease of life and today he felt more sprightly than he had for months. He felt no sadness as he left the wych shed in Jack's care, for his son was quite capable of running the pan alone. Besides, Joe was there to do all the hard work, so it didn't really matter how lazy Jack was, the jobs were completed. Actually it amused Edward to see how hard Jack found it to hide his delight at his father's departure, imagining as he did that the pan would soon belong to him.

Edward laughed to himself as he imagined Jack and Elizabeth's faces when it was discovered that he had left the pan to Annie. Served them right, he had no guilty feelings at his decision, he only wished he could be there to witness their disappointment.

His mind rambled as he struggled down to the river, stopping every few steps, gasping to catch his breath. Clara had been right, she had always said, what goes round comes round, and sure as fate Elizabeth would get her just deserts. The sweat began to form on his brow and he wiped it away crossly, he didn't want to arrive at the barge exhausted. Sheer determination drove the pain from his body into his

84

mind, where with steel will he held it, refusing to allow his last journey to be marred. In the distance he could see the barge and his heart leapt, as it had done each time he had come to her over the years. It was his sanctuary, and there seemed no more fitting place for him to come to die. He was at peace with himself, now all he needed was those he loved around him to bid him farewell.

Sarah and Annie rushed off the barge to meet him and they each linked an arm, gently leading him onto the rocking boat. It beckoned like a cradle, swaying in rhythm to the river's swell. At that precise moment nothing else mattered in the world for the three of them, except to be together and to cherish these last hours.

Annie knew that her father was dying. She had stopped pleading with her God, for the answer had never changed and she knew it was inevitable. She wasn't angry, nor did she feel cheated, for in her many prayers he had never given her false hope, but allowed her time to get used to the terrible truth and for that she was grateful. She didn't think about the future without her pa, that she could not imagine yet, but instead she concentrated on making the most of every last moment. She had not even asked her mother's permission to go on this trip, but had simply announced that she would be away for a few days with her pa. She didn't care what she thought, or if she would be punished, that she would deal with later. In reality her mother had been so shocked by her forthrightness that she had not uttered a word.

Jack had been secretly pleased, for he had already decided that once his father was gone, he would make sure Annie was no longer welcome in his house. Jack had already planned out his future very nicely, and he had no intention of slaving away forever in the wych shed. Once Edward was out of the way he would sell the pan to John Ellis, and move away to start a new life, it didn't matter where just so long as it was away from the smog and salt. Time was on his side and he wouldn't have to wait much longer before he was free. He had no thoughts of caring for his mother, she would have to sort something out for herself, there was no room for sloppy sentiment in his world.

Only Elizabeth appeared unaffected by Edward's impending death. But then why should she care, they hadn't spoken for years, he was almost like a stranger to her now, all those feelings of intense anger she had carried had been somehow diluted over the years into apathy, frozen beyond reach. Elizabeth possessed an ice-maiden ability to simply dismiss anyone she did not care for, she had no compassion, no gentler side, only a frigid coldness that exuded from her. Like a snow queen she remained impregnable, incapable of feeling emotion for anyone save her remaining son. She was quite sure that her future was secure, after all Jack would look after her, of that she was certain.

The mood on the *Mary-Rose* was cheerful, and for all intents it might have seemed to a stranger that the three occupants of the cabin were embarking on a holiday rather than a last crusade. Sarah had cooked a mouth-watering meal, and the little room was filled with delicious smells of stews and cakes. Smudge lay contentedly at Edward's feet, groaning in pleasure as he relished his ears being rubbed tenderly. Annie sat at her father's side, chatting just as if it were any other day.

The three of them laughed and joked as they ate, all trying to forget that this would all be over too soon. Later that night Edward slept fitfully in the narrow bunk, disturbed every now and then as he wheezed. Sarah and Annie sat silently by the fire that glowed in the stove and watched him sadly, both their hearts torn with sorrow. Tomorrow they would leave for Liverpool. Normally Annie would have been excited at the prospect of seeing somewhere new, tonight it hardly seemed to matter at all. Laying some blankets on the floor, the two of them, with Smudge pushing his way in the middle, huddled together to try and get some sleep. It was impossible, for through the night, Edward's cries of pain kept them both awake, racked with helplessness at being unable to ease his suffering. The next few days Edward sat out on the deck of the barge, wrapped in blankets, and watched the countryside float by. He seemed content and called cheery hello's to passing barges, managing to laugh and joke as if everything was normal. Slowly the landscape began to change as they approached Liverpool, the fields disappeared, and everything became gloomier and desperate. If Annie had thought her home town Lytwych was desolate, nothing could have prepared her for what she saw now.

Miles and miles of terraced slums spilled down onto the river bank, filthy children scraped around like animals on the muddy banks, begging the passing boats for scraps of food. Annie was horrified as the tiny toddlers cried, freezing cold and alone on the soil, hardly dressed in ripped rags. It was hard to tell whether they were boys or girls as their long hair hung matted and filthy around thin black faces.

'Yer get used to it,' Sarah squeezed her arm reassuringly, as she saw the distress in Annie's face.

'Can't we do anythin'?' she cried, in total disbelief that so much poverty existed.

'What can we do? If we feed one, we'll be swamped by hundreds. It's no good Annie, yer just 'ave to close yer eyes to it or it'll drive yer crazy,' Sarah said sadly. 'It's even worse than this in the town.'

Annie could not imagine that anything would be worse and she was starting to dread the rest of the journey. All the years Sarah had been making this trip she had never once heard her mention these appalling conditions, yet it must have affected her every time she came. Annie realised what a strong and independent person she was, and how much she admired her.

The docks loomed ahead of them for Annie could see the tall masts of the cargo ships, willowy waving fingers, stretching skyward. Despite her feelings of sorrow at the sights she had just witnessed, Annie could not stop the stir of excitement she felt at the view ahead. For years she had longed to see this, she had imagined a million times how it would look, but now seeing it all for the first time she was overwhelmed. The sheer size of the vessels looming up above them was breathtaking. Annie was fascinated by the names of the ships and all the different country flags they flew so proudly. She heard strange languages being spoken by foreign men, some with skin jet black and shiny, others so blond that their hair seemed bleached.

Slowly the *Mary-Rose* inched her way between the sea giants and moored up against the wharf beside a huge warehouse. The quayside was awash with people, everyone rushing around, carrying crates and boxes, shouting and calling instructions to one another, a mass of activity. Annie stood mesmerised on the deck, as Sarah expertly began to throw off sacks of salt to a man standing by the barge and he in turn tossed them effortlessly into a cart. Once finished he produced a ticket, which he stamped and without a word handed it to Sarah. Edward managed to come and stand on deck and father and daughter stood in admiration as Sarah skilfully guided the barge down the narrow channels of water between other vessels, until finding a space on the quayside she moored up. Lighter now for her lack of cargo, the *Mary-Rose* was tossed back and forth by the swell of tidal water, crashing her wooden sides against the green algae duck boards.

'Why don't yer take Annie fer a look around while you're 'ere?' Edward suggested, seeing the curiosity burning in Annie's face at everything around her.

'We can't leave yer alone,' Annie cried, suddenly ashamed of her inquisitiveness.

'Don't be silly. Yer can't come all this way an' not at least go an' explore. Besides I'm tired, I'll 'ave a sleep while yer go.'

Edward kissed his adventuresome daughter on the forehead and hugging Sarah for one second he shuffled slowly to the cabin, for his weary body felt he could not stand a minute longer. Hiding the agony of each and every step he called a cheery goodbye and sank gratefully down onto the bunk. His eyes were heavy and he knew he would be asleep in no time. With his mind firmly fixed on the image of the two people he loved most in the world, Edward allowed himself to drift away. Though if he had realised that he was never going to wake up again, he might well have fought the relentless march of exhaustion that seeped through his broken body and tempted him away to everlasting peace.

Annie's dark eyes were like two saucers as she tried to take in all the wondrous sights around her. She had never dreamt that the place would be so huge, or that there would be so many people from all over the world. It was almost as if Sarah's book had come to life in front of her eyes. Hungrily she drank in the sights and smells, anxious not to miss anything. They walked through rows and rows of warehouses all teeming with people and activity and then turned away from the docks towards the town itself. Huge buildings rose before her, extravagantly carved and decorated with forbidding faces and exotic creatures, grimacing down at her severely. Well-dressed gentlemen hurried in and out of doors, alighting from carriages and chatting together as they did. They all looked very important and Annie wondered if she and Sarah should be walking along these streets. But as she looked around she realised that this was a jumble of all kinds of folks, rich and poor, gentlemen and beggars all rubbed shoulders together, a veritable stew of mankind.

She began to feel less nervous and realised that nobody was taking any notice of either of them. Sarah took her along rows of shops, not tiny grocery stores like she was used to, but huge stores, teeming with treasures of every sort. She drooled as Sarah dragged her past the dress shops, fantastic gowns in silks and satins caught her widening eyes. Even the food shops delighted her, stalls selling fruits and vegetables that she had never seen before, brought into the maritime centre from all four corners of the world. By the time they came to the end of the shops Annie was intoxicated and floated dreamily on the visions she had seen.

They bought a hot pie from the street seller and a bottle of lemonade and, finding an upturned crate by the side of the road, sat to enjoy their lunch and rest their aching feet.

'This is so wonderful, 'ow could yer ever bear to keep coming back to Lytwych,' Annie swooned as she savoured the delicious juices that dripped from her pie.

'Don't be fooled by all this. By day it's full of busy people, all working. At night Annie it's something quite different,' Sarah warned, seeing the intoxication in Annie's face. 'Then it's full of sadness and loneliness, of cold hungry people with nowhere to go. It's a dangerous place, and no one is safe to walk around alone.'

Annie found this hard to believe, especially as she was surrounded by such delights. All the men and women looked happy as they went about their business, it seemed a magical place. Seeing her doubts, Sarah took Annie's hand and led her away from the noise towards the streets that stretched away in every direction. The further away from the docks they walked, the more desolate the surroundings became. The streets seemed to shrink and the houses leant menacingly towards each other as if they were quarrelling. Even the daylight seemed to disappear, squeezed out fearfully. Open sewers ran the full length of each street and even though it was late September and not high summer, the smell rose in noxious waves, killing any clean air that might have filtered down into the gloom. Annie retched as she saw children sitting and playing in the filth. Dogs ran, yapping and fighting with each other and women stood watching, oblivious to the disgusting mess that their children paddled in. A sadness hung drearily over each street like a black cloak, as if all the occupants had given up hope and were simply reconciled to their miserable fate. Pitiful voices begged for food or a spare penny, some older children clutched at Annie's skirts, their faces haunted and defeated by life already.

'Please Sarah, let's go, I can't bear it,' cried Annie, dragging her friend back in the direction they had come.

As they neared the shops again they passed a public house, teeming with people in spite of the fact that it was only early evening. Mostly sailors from the ships, making the most of a few free hours before embarking on another horrendous

90

sea journey and determined to enjoy themselves. A group of them, drunk and finding it difficult to stand on their feet, lurched out towards Sarah and Annie as they passed. One grabbed Sarah by the hair, forced her back against the wall, and pushed his slobbering lips on hers.

Her screams only served to excite him more and cheered on by his mates he ripped at her bodice, exposing her voluptuous breasts, much to the delight of the onlookers who shouted lurid encouragement. Annie did not think, but suddenly remembering her awful nightmare with Jack at the fair, flung herself at the attacker, gouging his skin with her nails. He was startled enough to release Sarah, who grabbed Annie's hand and began to run.

'Don't stop, Annie, just keep goin',' she panted breathlessly, afraid to look behind to see if they were being pursued. In fact the men were so drunk, they had already forgotten the women's existence and had moved on to look for some more fun.

Only when the harbour was in sight did Sarah slow down the pace. She hurriedly tied together her ripped blouse to cover her naked breasts. She certainly didn't want Edward to see her like this, and she chastised herself for putting Annie in such danger.

'I'm so sorry, I should never have taken yer there, it were stupid. But now yer see what it's really like.'

'Don't tell Pa, he'd only worry,' gasped Annie, trying to get her breath back before she boarded the boat.

She need not have worried, for as they entered the cabin, the silence was broken only by Smudge's whimpering. The little dog was frantically licking Edward's limp cold hand in a vain attempt to wake him up.

The pain of realisation shot through Annie's body like lightning, and then burst from her lips in a haunting cry that filled the tiny cabin with poignant echoes. She fell to her knees unable to support herself as the stark truth that her pa was dead sank in. Then a swirling darkness overtook her and she passed out.

# Eleven

On the 14th January 1876, Annie Hayes made a decision that would change her entire life. It was her sixteenth birthday. Five years had passed since she had watched her beloved Pa disappear into the blackness of the earth, five long and miserable years. The pain of his loss still cut deeply into her, the yearning ache to hear his voice or touch his hand still gnawed inside her. On dark nights she still wept bitterly, when it seemed only his presence could ease her pain, her dreams remained filled with him. When she first awoke, just for a split second she sometimes believed he was still alive and her heart would leap, until she realised it had been just another dream. Her distress was not eased by the fact that she carried it alone, she had not only lost him, but also Sarah, the one person who could understand her grief. She had fled too, unable to remain in the place that reminded her of Edward so much. Sarah had said her tearful farewells and disappeared in her barge, to try and somehow come to terms with the loss of her true love and attempt to live out the remains of her shattered life the best way she could.

Abandoned and lost, Annie was faced with a hostile world, where nobody loved or cared for her, where her only hope was to somehow draw on the strength left in her, instilled first by Clara and then her pa, and only this determination not to be beaten kept her going.

After Edward's death when it had become known that the salt pan now belonged to her and not Jack, several changes had taken place. The hatred her mother and brother felt for her only deepened, yet ultimately they were now dependent on her for their survival. Being too lazy to leave and have to work properly for someone else, Jack realised that he was far better off to simply stay put. After all he had a home to live in, meals cooked for him and enough money to spend every evening in the local public house. The fact that Annie actually owned the pan did not alter the everyday running of events and once the initial disappointment of not being able to sell the wych shed had worn off, Jack lazily carried on just the same as before. As for Elizabeth, her resentment of Annie for depriving her son of his birthright ate into her daily, but she too knew that she relied on Annie and so the bitterness festered away inside her, just waiting for the opportunity to spill out. Like a witch she plotted and schemed, waiting for the day of revenge. The more alcohol she drank, the wilder her imaginings became and in her twisted mind only the demise of Annie would right the wrongs she felt had been done.

The practicalities of running the salt pan had been Annie's saviour, for at least it occupied her mind and brought some sanity to her world. Many times she said a silent thank you to Richard, for without his help with her reading and writing she would not have been able to deal with the running of the business. She found that she enjoyed the power her new position brought and although she had quivered inside the first time she had to find a new barge owner to transport her salt and negotiate a price with the buyers in Liverpool, she soon found her confidence. The dealers, albeit out of respect for her dead father and pity for her, mostly treated her fairly. At least here she had control, she was important and she poured her energy into the running of the pan as her father had done before her. She found a kind of peace and contentment, and at what point she stopped doing it for her pa and began to do it for herself she wasn't sure, but she knew the pan was her life as much as it had been his.

Throughout all her misery one person had always been

there, a reliable rock on which she could depend. Never demanding anything from her, Joe worked diligently, never complaining and she knew she need never worry about the work being done. And it was about Joe that she had made the decision today that was to shape her future. She had decided to marry him.

Joseph Arnold Jenkins was nineteen years old and for the past five years he had worked every day from five thirty in the morning until six or seven at night, depending on the work load, in the Hayes wych shed. He was happy in his own quiet way, in fact he felt he had really fallen on his feet working for an independent, rather than Ellis, who treated his workers so badly. Coming from a family of eight children, Joe knew all there was to know about hardship. In their house there was never enough food to go around the ever-hungry mouths, clothes were handed down until they fell apart, never mind if they fitted or not, and ten bodies squashed into a two-bedroom freezing terrace slum was not a comfortable way to exist. Joe was the eldest and as only two of the younger ones worked, this job was a godsend, for it paid regular wages and that put bread into mouths. The work had been fine when Edward was alive, for he saw to it that Jack did his fair share and there was always the bonus of seeing Annie.

Annie had captivated his heart from the very first day. As she breezed into the shed it was as if the sunshine always came in with her. Joe hated the way that Jack treated her, for the moment that Edward was not around he always teased and pinched her, but what Joe hated most was the way he looked at her, his own sister. He knew very well what those looks meant for they were the same ones that his own father gave him, the ones that led to all that black part of his life that he tried to forget.

When Joe knew that Edward had finally passed away he was mortified, assuming that he would now lose his job, but then by some miracle it seemed that Annie was now the pan owner and she wanted him to stay. Since then he had worked his hardest for her, and he now slept in the shed, as Edward had done, to keep the pan stoked. He much preferred this to going home, for he had his own safe little world now where it was easy to forget the horrors that awaited in his father's house. He returned only once a week, on a Sunday afternoon, to give his mam some money. He usually played with the little ones a while and sometimes talked with his father. This was the hardest part for it seemed he could never do anything to please the man, the money he brought was never enough and there was always a long list of jobs that needed doing and not enough time to do them. It would always be Joe's torment that part of him hated his father and yet he was drawn irresistibly to him like a magnet. He knew if he failed to go home each week he would be racked with overpowering guilt, for despite his father's terrifying manner, he knew he was still the favourite. the special one and the burden of that and all the responsibility that it implied lay heavily on Joe's heart.

Now there was an even worse guilt to carry, for since he had left the house he had seen the change in his younger brother, the telltale dark circles beneath the eyes, the furtive and silent behaviour of a once rowdy and vocal boy. He knew that the secret was being shared again and it was his fault for if he had remained at home the others would have been safe. Joe's anger was more often directed at his mam than his father for allowing her children to suffer at her husband's hands, but then when Joe really looked at her what he saw was a broken spirit. He had lost count of the number of beatings he had seen her endure and now there was no fight left in her, just an empty shell that survived as best it could, along with the rest of them.

Today was special because it was Annie's birthday, and Joe could not wait for her to come into the shed so that he could give her the present he had for her. He had bought it weeks ago from some travellers who were selling all kinds of craft. The minute he had seen it he knew Annie would love it and so even though it took more money than he could spare, he bought it and had kept it hidden in the old wooden box in the corner of the shed. What was even better was that

Jack was down at the river loading the barge so Joe would have her all to himself.

'Good mornin' Joe,' the familiar sweet voice made him tingle inside as usual.

''Appy Birthday, Annie, come an' sit yerself down on the bench,' he began eagerly, steering her to the seat.

Annie laughed at his unusual boldness, enjoying the attention.

'Close yer eyes and hold out your 'ands,' he commanded.

Annie giggled, obeying meekly while Joe placed the brown paper parcel in her hands. 'This is me first an' only present, I thought everyone 'ad forgotten. I might have known as you wouldn't.' She paused and teasingly opening one eye said, 'Well, can I open it or do I just have to sit 'ere all day?'

'Yes, yes open it,' Joe flushed, his normal self-consciousness returning as he suddenly wondered whether she would like it or not.

Excitedly Annie ripped off the paper and then gasped in delight at the contents. Inside lay a small shiny mirror enclosed in a wicker plaited frame, along which had been painted tiny pink rosebuds, encircled with curling green leaves. Annie's face lit up in delight as she held the delicate treasure in her hand.

'Joe, it's beautiful, thank you,' and leaning forward she pecked his cheek.

Annie gazed at her reflection in the glass and was struck as always by her likeness to her pa. For a second it sent a pain through her heart. Then she remembered her decision, of which Joe knew nothing as yet. She had to smile as she looked at him, so eager to please her, thriving on every bit of attention she gave him.

'Joe, I wondered if a could ask a favour of yer, as it's my birthday.'

'Course yer can,' he replied, excited at the prospect of doing anything for her.

'It's a bit cheeky really, so I want yer to say no if yer don't want to do it,' she continued teasingly. Joe waited, wide eyed like a puppy wanting to please its master and Annie knew

96

full well that no request would be too much. 'Next month there's a meetin' in Liverpool of all the salt suppliers and buyers, to talk about prices an' trading an' afterwards there's goin' to be 'ot food and dancin'. I really need to go, but it just wouldn't be right to go on me own, so I wondered if you'd come with me.'

Before she could even finish the sentence Joe had enthusiastically nodded his agreement. His body visibly swelled in pride that she should ask him of all people.

'Oh Annie, I'd love to,' he stuttered, face bright red now.

Annie smiled, this was going to be easier than she thought. 'Well you'll need some decent clothes, so I'll give yer an advance on yer wages. Mrs Slade from the dress shop is makin' me a new dress. We don't want anyone thinkin' we're paupers.'

'Don't you worry, I won't show yer up.'

'I'm sure yer won't, Joe,' she smiled kindly and squeezed his arm. 'Oh an' not a word to Jack, or he'll want to go instead. We won't tell 'im until the last minute, eh.' She laughed, winking at him and, picking up her present, she breezed out of the shed.

Joe was floating somewhere between the floor and the sky, he just could not believe his luck. Firstly that she should actually ask him, as if he could refuse her anything, and secondly that he was to accompany her to such an important event. His head raced with excitement, he had never been to Liverpool, in fact he had never been out of this town. He was already planning in his mind the clothes he would buy to wear. Suddenly the money did not matter, even if it meant not paying out as much at home. He would go hungry, starve, anything, but he would do her proud whatever it took. The sombre image of his father flashed before his eyes, he knew that he would certainly not approve, probably even forbid his son to go. Joe knew that it did not matter; at this moment he could take on the world, for nothing and nobody was as important as Annie. He never usually sang, but today the notes burst from him as he shovelled the salt crystals as if they were made of feathery snow. He did not

97

feel the sweat pouring from him or the aches in his muscles. Today he thought he could conquer the world.

Annie meandered slowly down from the wych shed to the river. She did not want to go home today, nor could she have faced staying in the shed any longer even though there was work that she could have been doing. Part of her was sad, not just because Joe had been the only one to remember her birthday, for who else was there, but because even though she was only sixteen she felt as if her life was ending not beginning. Inside her spirit still ached to fly, to find new places, explore and learn and yet she knew her life was here. That was why she had decided to marry Joe. She certainly did not love him, actually she felt nothing for him at all, but he was suitable. He was reliable and hard working, he would make her a good husband, provide for her and be on her side. That was what Annie craved for most, a friend and ally. She was tired of fighting her mother and Jack. She longed for a face that would smile on her return, a voice that sounded loving not hostile, a place where she could live in peace and safety and Joe seemed to be the only answer to these things. She argued fiercely with the voice in her head that reminded her of passion and love, those things she had felt for Richard, but she was no fool, he had not come back and Annie knew that he wouldn't. She resigned herself to the fact that she was not meant to have those joys, so she would take the next best thing, Joe. She had tried to imagine herself in his arms and kissing his lips, but somehow the image refused to appear. She felt no tremors of excitement in his company, but then there was no real repulsion either. So she convinced herself that a kind of love might grow between them in time. The arguments in his favour were strong. Firstly they could find a house away from her mother, secondly she would have the added status of having a husband, for even though she did not like it, some of the traders still refused to deal with her because of her age and sex, which was unfair as it did not allow her to secure the best price for her salt. As a married woman she would hold a completely different position. Mostly though she was tired of being alone, of making each decision by herself; with Joe, at least there would be someone that belonged to her.

Standing on the river's edge, Annie watched the cold dark water lapping on the muddy banks. She gathered up some pebbles and threw them into the waves, watching each ripple until it disappeared. The dispersing circles, like the things in her life that she treasured, slipped away forever. First Clara, then Richard, her pa and even Sarah; perhaps it would be better not to love Joe, that way at least he might remain in her life.

Sighing deeply, Annie inhaled the freezing air and told herself that now the decision was made she must do it and quickly in case she lost her resolve. Turning determinedly into the wind she set out with a striding step back towards the salt pan; there was plenty of work to be done and no time to stand around feeling sorry for herself all day. As if to confirm her thoughts Joe greeted her with a smiling face and she was able to throw herself enthusiastically into her new role, chatting brightly to Joe as if it was the most natural thing in the world that they should be together from now on.

Three weeks later Annie excitedly collected her dress from Mrs Slade. She could hardly wait to get it home to try on, for it was the first proper dress that she had owned, apart of course, from the Indian sari. That she kept hidden away with her treasure collection, which included a dried flower that Richard had given her, her pa's cloth cap and the *People of the World* book that Sarah had given her before she left.

She had tried to be sensible in her choice of material, even though she had longed for a dress in silks and taffetas. So taking the dressmaker's advice, she had chosen a deep blue heavy cotton to be trimmed with a red braid on the waist, collars and cuffs. The neckline was high and the bodice fitted, the full skirt fell to the floor gathered into a small discreet bustle at the back. Stylish and practical Mrs Slade had said, and she was right. Curbing her disappointment at not having a chic ball gown, Annie had thrown herself into practicality instead and now this too seemed exciting, she could hardly wait to get home and try the dress on with the other accessories she had purchased. For once spending money on herself instead of on her mother or Jack, she had allowed herself to be indulgent. She had a pair of new leather shoes with small buckles, a pair of long blue gloves and her favourite, a long swirling red cloak with hood. The cloak she had not been able to resist and, telling herself that she had been sensible with the dress, she splashed out on it instead. She bubbled with excitement at the thought of wearing them all.

Racing into the house, Annie quickly checked to see if her mother was upstairs. She was as usual asleep, taking her afternoon nap. Jack she knew was at the shed and so she would be safe to go into his room, where there was a full length mirror in which she could see herself. Flinging the clothes on the bed, she quickly stripped out of her working skirt and blouse and put on the new dress. She could hardly believe the transformation. The dress hugged her slim figure, emphasising her waist and breasts and when she piled her black hair onto her head, she could have easily passed for a woman of twenty or so. Amazed at her own reflection, she stared at the strange vision before her. Suddenly Joe seemed very unsuitable and she pictured herself on Richard's arm being led into a ballroom full of important people, all smiling and laughing with her. If she closed her eyes she could see his handsome face close to hers, hear his voice and feel the caress of his lips. She knew in her heart that things would never be this way with Joe. He seemed so ordinary, compared to Richard.

Her daydreaming was interrupted by the sound of footsteps on the landing. Thinking it was her mother, Annie quickly took off the dress and hurriedly began to fold it up, with the other things on the bed.

When Jack opened his bedroom door, the sight that greeted him made his heart pound. Annie, dressed only in her shift, backed away from the bed clutching at her clothes to cover herself, but not before he had seen the shapely legs and small waist.

'I'm sorry, I thought you were at the shed.' Annie moved hesitatingly towards the doorway which he was blocking.

The strange smile on his face scared her, and her mind flew back to the night at the fair. Fear pounded through her body and she could feel the sweat on her back.

'Please let me out, Jack.'

'Not in such a hurry. I'd forgotten what a beauty me sister was,' he leered, moving towards her, his breath coming fast and heavy. Pulling her close, he forced his wet lips down against hers, so hard that she tasted her blood as it spurted from her lip.

Panic took over her mind, as she struggled to free herself from his iron grip. Pushing her roughly backwards on the bed, Jack was about to fall on top of her when their mother's voice called from her room.

'Jack, is that you? Jack?'

Muttering curses under his breath, Jack pulled himself up and stamped out of the room.

Annie knew that she would not be so lucky again, and it made her all the more determined that her marriage to Joe should be as soon as possible.

# Twelve

When Annie gazed around the room full of people, she could hardly believe she was here. Surrounded by land owners and business men, shipping company directors and salt buyers, all here like her to protect and promote their livelihood. If she felt overawed by their presence she did not show it, but watched excitedly as the speakers discussed the new tax laws and legislation that was affecting their industry. She listened intently, learning from their knowledge, picking up ideas here and there. She even plucked up courage to speak to one or two of the buyers and realised for the first time what a powerful position she had as an independent. As soon as she said that she owned her own pan, traders were eager to offer her prices for her salt, knowing that she could undercut the estate owners. She even had a couple of offers to purchase the pan itself from her for more money than she ever dreamt possible. But this only made her realise how precious it was. By the end of the afternoon she had secured a new deal for her salt cargoes, more regular payments for the loads and learnt many things that she hadn't understood before about managing her business. She was thoroughly enjoying herself, so much so that she almost forgot about Joe who had trailed around loyally after her, saying nothing.

'I'm sorry Joe, yer must be really bored now, let's go an' get a cup of tea from the stall,' she said apologetically and led the way through the crowds to join the queue.

If she had recognised the figure before her she would

have turned and walked away, but before she knew it she found herself face to face with John Ellis.

'Well, well, if it isn't our little independent neighbour,' he smiled graciously but failed to disguise the sarcasm in his voice.

'Good afternoon, Mr Ellis.' Her reply was curt and she let her eyes drop, not wishing to prolong the conversation. He however had different ideas and proceeded in a loud voice, ensuring that everyone standing near them could hear.

'It must be very difficult for you running the salt pan all alone.'

'I'm not alone, I've me brother an' Joe, but thanks fer yer concern.'

'Still, it's no life for a young lady, stuck in that shed day and night, and it must be hard for you to get the traders to take you seriously. No disrespect but they hardly want to deal with a girl – young woman, I mean.' His tone became more and more snide as he continued.

'I can assure yer that I manage very well an' the traders yer talkin' about are all quite 'appy to deal with,' and here she emphasised the words, 'a girl, as yer put it.'

John Ellis smiled sardonically at her, and then in a manner which could only be described as patronising he added, 'If you ever find it too much, you know that I will be quite happy to take the pan off your hands, at a fair price of course.'

'Mr Ellis, the pan has been 'anded down fer three generations in me family and I can assure you that selling it is the furthest thing from me mind. Extendin' it is more likely.' Annie was enjoying herself now and in particular the astonished look on his face as she continued. 'I'm sure that yer offer is made in good faith an' had nothing' to do with the fact that not only is my salt of a purer quality, but I can sell at a cheaper price. I only 'ope that my growing business doesn't affect yours too much.'

She knew that she was being over bold, but John Ellis was not a new adversary and his reputation for terrorising anyone who stood in his way went before him. Annie had

103

learnt to get in first before the enemy had time to attack and she had certainly taken him by surprise.

Turning on his heel Ellis stalked off across the room, but not before making some comment about young upstarts and pride coming before a fall.

'That certainly put him in his place.' The stranger's voice made Annie swing around, still smiling from her victory.

The tall young man grinned back, extending his hand in a friendly gesture.

'Peter Smith, engineer and representative of Hunters Machinery.'

''Ello, Annie Hayes. An' this is Joe.'

'Did I hear you say that you were considering expanding?'

Annie laughed. She had never considered any such thing until the words had slipped from her mouth. 'Not really. I just like to give Mr Ellis somethin' to think about.'

'Maybe you should think about it. I am sure I could give you some advice.'

'I really have nowhere to expand to, and besides I've no money fer such things.'

'You own the land and the shed, don't you?' Annie nodded. 'Well in that case you have nothing to worry about. Most brine pits extend for miles and can be pumped from several points, and as for money, you own the land, any bank in the country will lend you money on that.'

Seeing Annie pondering on his words, Peter Smith continued, 'I'll be here all day and quite happy to give you advice. You can find me in the far corner with the display of one of our pumps. Come and have a talk when you're ready.'

With that he left her, having set her mind whirling excitedly.

Some minutes later as she sat with Joe sipping the much needed tea, Annie spoke.

'D'yer think we could really do it, Joe?' He stared at her blankly and so she continued excitedly. 'Expand, expand the salt pan. Maybe that Mr Smith's right. Now that I think about it, the deed papers that Pa left me don't just show the shed but quite an area of the field around it.' Her eyes shone brightly as she chattered and Joe was transfixed by them, rather than listening to what she was saying, he smiled encouragingly though and she babbled on. 'I must go an' talk to him, ask his opinion, maybe we could sink another brine pump an' run another pan alongside ours. Joe, just think what this means, more brine, more salt, more money, what a chance this could be.'

'We could never manage another pan though, could we,' he put in, imagining all the extra work.

'Then we'd employ some else. Don't you see, we would be able to afford it.'

She was not going to listen to any negative thoughts, for now her imagination was running wild. At this moment she felt she could do anything.

'You finish yer tea an' I'll go an' talk to Mr Smith.' Anxious now to share her ideas with someone equally willing to dream, she certainly didn't want Joe putting a damper on her enthusiasm. She knew Joe was no risk-taker, but that didn't matter. He had other qualities, as well as his loyalty and strength, and secretly she knew that she had more than enough ideas for the future for both of them.

She scurried across the hall to find the display from Hunters Machinery. She soon picked out Peter Smith's voice from amidst a crowd huddled around a huge pump that was slowly moving up and down, whilst he described its workings. His voice was so alive and bursting with excitement that the crowd stood fascinated, hanging on his every word. He was a good salesman and enjoyed every minute of his job. Annie joined the throng of people all pressing forward to get a better view of the wonderful new machine that could so effortlessly suck their precious brine up from the earth. She too was drawn into the web of his rhetoric, and by the time he had finished she too desperately wanted one of the magnificent machines that, as he had put it, could transform her life. The crowd eventually began to disperse, allowing Annie the opportunity to speak with him alone.

''Ello again,' she began, 'we met a little while ago.'

105

Her reminder was unnecessary as he knew her instantly, such was his training, always ready to recall a potential customer.

'Annie of course, how could I forget.' His smile was wide, engulfing. 'How do you like our little wonder?' He patted the machine affectionately almost as if it were human.

'Oh it's marvellous, wonderful. I've been thinkin' about what yer were sayin' about expandin' my salt pan. If yer aren't too busy I'd be glad of some advice.'

'I'm never too busy for a pan owner, especially a pretty one.' His laugh was infectious and Annie was not offended by his obvious flirting, rather she was flattered. 'Where is this pan of yours?'

'In Cheshire, a small town called Lytwych. I don't expect you've heard of it.'

'On the contrary, I know exactly where it is, I've done business with your friend and neighbour Mr Ellis, much to my shame now that I have seen the way he treats you.'

'Please don't feel badly. John Ellis treats everyone with the same contempt.'

'Then he is a very stupid and arrogant man. Anyway enough of him, what of you? Tell me about this pan of yours.'

'It has been passed down in me family for three generations and when my pa died it was left to me. I realised when yer said about expandin' that the plans of the shed do show the surroundin' land as belongin' to me. I've never taken much notice of 'ow much or where the boundaries lie, it's always just been part of the river bank. But now you've set me mind thinkin' that perhaps there is room to sink another brine pump.'

Peter Smith grinned, this was going to be such an easy sale, she was so enthusiastic and good luck to her. 'I think I should come and have a look for myself. That way I can see the land and really be able to give you the best advice.'

Annie beamed delightedly. 'Would yer really do that fer me?'

'Of course I will, and there is no charge or obligation. If

you decided to use one of my pumps so be it. If not, I will consider it a privilege to have helped you.'

'You're very kind, Mr Smith. But believe me, I'm really serious and yer won't just be wastin' yer time.'

It was settled that the very next week Peter Smith would visit the shed and Annie would have the deeds ready to show him.

Annie was bursting with the news as she found Joe sitting patiently waiting for her. She failed to notice his lack of excitement as she was so lost in her own thoughts for the future. For the first time since her pa had died she felt she *had* a future and she knew if he were there he would be just as carried away with this idea as she was.

The afternoon was coming to an end and most of the crowds had begun to disperse back to their hotel rooms to change for the evening, when in this very same hall there was to be dancing and hot buffet. Already a stage was being erected for the musicians and wooden tables were being laid at the far end. Annie and Joe did not have a hotel to return too, being unable to afford such luxuries. They had travelled here on the morning train from Manchester, having already journeyed there at six a.m. on the stage coach that also delivered the mail. Their route home was the same, but though there was a train back to Manchester at ten p.m., they were not guaranteed a horse carriage home once there. Still Annie had decided to worry about that later, there was usually someone willing to give them a lift.

So they now had to fill in the time until the evening commenced, and Annie decided that they could walk around the shops while they waited. She was a little upset at not having a gown to change into for the evening, but this was overridden by the sheer excitement of simply being here.

For Joe too this was a wonderful experience. Never having left his home town before, he followed Annie along the rows of brightly lit shops wide-eyed and incredulous. Today he was in heaven, he had Annie to himself and he was seeing all this. His chest had swelled with pride as she had held her own amongst all those men, her dreams and plans were so far-fetched and yet she made it all seem possible. She was truly wonderful and he knew that whatever she suggested he would willingly do just to remain close to her. As they walked he spotted a stall selling ribbons and finding unknown courage he grabbed her small hand and ran towards it.

'Come on, let's find a ribbon fer yer hair tonight.'

Willingly Annie followed, this was the Joe she wanted, someone to take charge of her every now and then, surprise her.

The stall was a mass of brightly coloured ribbons and bows of every colour of silk and satin imaginable. 'We want a ribbon fer the lady's hair, please,' Joe demanded.

'What colour?' asked the woman on the stall.

'It's to wear tonight, at a dance with this dress,' put in Annie grateful for any advice the lady could offer.

'I've got just the one, look here,' and she produced a long scarlet silk ribbon that matched the cuffs and collar of the dress exactly.

Seeing Annie's eyes shining, the woman kindly offered to braid it into her hair, at no extra cost.

'Yes please, if yer could,' cried Annie delightedly.

Before she knew it the job was done and Annie had been transformed into a beauty fit for any ball. The woman secretly thought that it did not matter what dress this girl wore. She would turn a few heads tonight anyway.

As they reached the hall, Joe paused to buy her a flower to pin on her dress and as he fastened the pin carefully to her, he stooped and brushed her lips with a kiss.

'You're really beautiful, Annie,' he uttered breathlessly.

'Thank you, Joe.' And she squeezed his arm affectionately, a little disappointed that his kiss had produced no feelings of excitement within her, in fact the wetness of his lips had made her shudder. She banished the thoughts from her mind and linking his arm they entered the hall as proud as any other that they were there.

The hall was heaving with people standing around in

small groups or seated at the tables, and music filled the air. Annie shivered with excitement as she drank in the scene. Although some of the women wore fine ball gowns, some like her were still dressed in their day clothes and she did not feel too dreary. Joe too had done her proud today and he almost looked handsome in his tweed jacket and trousers. She was determined to enjoy herself tonight; heavens knew when she would ever go to another evening like this.

'Come on, let's dance, Joe,' she cried, grabbing his hand and dragging him onto the already crowded floor. Annie had always loved dancing. As a little girl her Sunday school teacher, who shared a similar passion, had taught the interested girls the basic steps to the accompaniment of the out-of-tune piano in the Church hall – after lessons, of course, Annie had practised for hours, sometimes swirling by herself, sometimes dragging Sarah along the river bank with her until they were both breathlessly giddy with pirouetting.

'I can't, I mean I don't know how,' he stammered, embarrassed.

'Of course yer can, everyone can dance, it's easy. Look, you just let me lead and I'll show yer.'

Oblivious to the rest of the crowd, Annie gracefully helped Joe's clumsy feet around the floor, until a few bruised toes later he had finally got the hang of the waltz. They laughed and giggled at each mistake, falling into one another's arms until, too exhausted to carry on, they decided to have a rest and get some food. Annie could not remember the last time she had enjoyed herself so much. Joe, she thought, might not be any great scholar or even that handsome, but he was fun and that was what she needed more than anything in the world.

She sat watching him as he ate his pie and rolls, considering that having Joe as a husband might not be such a bad thing after all.

'What are yer dreamin' about, Annie Hayes?'

His voice interrupted her thoughts.

109

'No let me guess. I bet it has somethin' to do with pumps an' salt. You're buildin' yer very own empire.'

She blushed. He was teasing her but still she was glad that he couldn't read her thoughts.

'No, wrong actually. I were thinkin' that just as soon as you have finished feedin' yer face yer can take me back on that dance floor, 'cos I'm goin' to get me money's worth out of you tonight.'

They laughed and chatted together and both were completely content in one another's company. As the evening drew on Joe realised that if they didn't leave soon they would miss the train.

'We have to go, Annie, or we'll never make it to the station.'

She scowled sulkily. 'Just one more dance, please?'

'No we can't, unless yer want to walk 'ome.'

Annie smiled her sweetest smile and gazed up into Joe's eyes pleadingly. 'Please, just one more. Then I promise I'll go.'

Joe melted; how could he refuse her anything? 'One, an' only one, promise.'

'I promise,' she cried joyfully and almost ran back onto the dance floor.

Joe whirled her around almost expertly now, as they enjoyed their last waltz. She looked stunning, a point which had not escaped the notice of several gentlemen in the room, who looked on enviously at Joe.

It was just as the dance was coming to an end that Annie was brought back to reality with a jolt and wished with all her heart that she had listened to Joe and left previously. On one of her pirouettes, she twirled around and came face-to-face with Richard.

It was as if her heart stopped beating for a second, and then she felt the blood rush through her. His face was inches from hers, and for a split second they saw no one but each other. He looked as shocked as her. Regaining her composure Annie glanced away and then when she looked back she saw that the lady in his arms was draped across him with obvious intimacy.

'Come on Joe, it's time to go,' she said hastily and before the music had even stopped she began to make her way to collect her cloak.

Her mind was whirling and she found she could not even speak to Joe as they walked the length of the hallway. Hurriedly swinging her cloak around her shoulders she half dragged him towards the exit.

'Slow down, what's the sudden rush? A minute ago I couldn't get yer to leave.'

'I just don't want us to miss the train,' she lied, not wishing to look to right or left in case she saw *him* again.

As they came to the exit door her heart sank, for standing right by the doorway was John Ellis and his party. Richard, with his companion hanging on his arm, was with them. Annie knew she had no choice but walk straight past them, and taking a deep breath she quickened her pace.

'Well, Annie Hayes going home already. Too late a night for you is it?' John Ellis spat the words out spitefully, quite apparently a little worse for wear with drink.

Annie smiled sheepishly and tried to ease past his portly figure, but he was having none of it.

'Don't be in such a rush. I want to introduce you to my friends and family, it's the neighbourly thing to do.' He placed his arm around her shoulder, pulling her close to him until she could smell the wine on his breath. 'Now then everyone, this is Annie Hayes, independent and neighbour. Who apparently is going to expand her salt pan and take some of my business and that's not a very neighbourly thing to do, is it?'

His voice became higher and higher as his agitation rose and Richard stepped forward to check him.

'That's enough Father, let the young lady pass.'

'Ah Annie, let me introduce you to my son, Richard, and his beautiful fiancée.' Ellis's speech was slurred and he swayed precariously from side to side.

111

'We've already met, now if you'll please let us pass we've a train to catch.'

Not waiting for him to stand aside Annie pushed her way through with Joe in her wake. Tears were stinging her eyes now and she could not trust herself to look backwards.

The sound of Ellis shouting and jeering after them lingered in her ears and somewhere in the midst of the jumble of noise she could have sworn she heard Richard's voice sadly saying, 'Annie, I'm so sorry.' But then she could have been mistaken.

All the way home she feigned sleep so that she did not have to speak to Joe, her mind churning Richard's name over and over again. She knew he was never coming back for her, how could he, he was a doctor now, she was nothing. But she loved him, she loved him so much that the pain of seeing him holding someone else in his arms was just too much for her to bear. This was love then, this agonising ache in her chest and head, this wild longing for someone she could never have. She knew she must somehow put him from her mind, though at this moment it was impossible. She told herself that tomorrow she would begin to banish him, but for tonight she could only wallow in this self-pity and mourn her loss. Tonight she could not bear to look at Joe or even talk to him, tomorrow she would make him the centre of her world from then on and try to forget Richard Ellis and love and all such nonsense. The future was Joe and the salt pan, that was her destiny.

# Thirteen

True to his word, a week later Peter Smith arrived at the salt pan, enthusiasm still oozing from him in every word and gesture. Annie was delighted to see him, as she had thought of little else since they had met. With determined effort she had forced all thoughts of Richard from her mind. She had run headlong into each day not allowing herself time to pause and think, but filled every second and in abject desperation focused all her energy on her new dream.

'These are the plans that Pa left. Yer see that although they show a boundary which is quite a way from the shed, there's no measurements, so I'm not sure how we know exactly which land's mine and which isn't.'

He studied the tattered pieces of precious paper.

'The clues are here. We just have to look carefully, that's all. Let's go and walk around the area and then I can see for myself.'

The March wind was bitter, creeping into every nook and cranny with its icy breath. Snow, still lying in thin patches on the brown earth, made it look like a patchwork quilt. Both of them huddled into their collars, sniffling in the biting air. At first sight it seemed hopeless to Annie; the open ground around the shed was simply that, open ground. Behind the shed it sloped up gently towards the woods and in front the land meandered down to the river bank.

She watched as Peter turned first this way and then that, considering each view and every angle. She had no idea what it was that he could apparently see that she was unable to, but it must have been something for every now and then he would smile or exclaim, 'Ah, yes', or 'I see.' Whatever it was though, it evaded her.

'Right, now it's all clear,' he suddenly announced.

'It is?'

'Yes. Your land extends from the line of the river, to the edge of those first oak trees to the north and then as far as the stone wall on one side and the stream that cuts down to the river on the other,' he proclaimed triumphantly.

'How d'yer know?'

'It's quite easy really, it's all on the map if you know how to read it.' He positively bubbled with excitement. 'But that's not important. What *is* important is that you own a considerable area of land here. You could easily sink one or more pumps.'

Annie, reluctant to get too carried away, tried to remain cautious but he was having none of it. He scoffed at her idea that there was no more brine beneath the land, laughed at her fears of subsidence and would not even listen to her doubts about raising the money for this venture. By the time he had finished Annie too was swept along on the tide of this beckoning adventure that he had shown her.

It all seemed so simple. All she had to do was borrow the money, buy the pumps, Peter's company would come and sink the shafts, install the pumps and vats and there it was, done. It all seemed too good to be true, but then he had a way of making anything seem possible. By the time he left it was no longer a mere idea in her head but definite plans for her future. Annie was going to expand.

'Expand, expand, have yer gone mad?' Jack thumped his fist down on to the kitchen table making the pots leap into the air.

'No I haven't gone mad. It'll work, you'll see.' Annie tried to keep her voice even as she faced the two angry and hostile glares.

'Yer'll end up ruinin' us, that's what yer'll do. Just 'cos Pa left the pan to you, don't give yer no rights to do just as yer please. We're still family.'

'Family.' Annie choked on the word. 'Since when have I ever been treated as family 'ere? But now when it suits yer both, suddenly I'm family. Well it's too late, it's my pan whether yer like it or not an' tomorrow I have an appointment in Manchester with the bank manager an' if he'll lend me the money then I'll extend the pan and neither of yer can stop me.'

A crashing silence hung in the room, whilst Annie stared defiantly at her mother and brother. Jack eventually flung back his chair, scraping it across the quarry tiled floor, and stamped out of the room, slamming the door behind him.

'He only worries about yer,' Elizabeth whined, knowing full well that she could not win an argument with her daughter at this point, so best to try a different tack.

'Don't, just don't start, Mother, we both know that Jack has 'ated me all me life. Just for once I'm goin' to do somethin' that I believe in an' quite 'onestly I don't care whether you two agree or not.'

Elizabeth bit back the words that were itching to pour forth from her; she knew that she had to be a little careful now, this was no longer the girl that she could manipulate and use. The new Annie disturbed her greatly, mostly because what she could see was Edward's stubbornness and independence shining through.

Deep down, Elizabeth's main concern was still for herself. It did not matter what she really felt just as long as she had a roof over her head and food in her belly, she was clever enough to play any game that was necessary to survive. She knew that Annie had stopped trying to win her affections and though that did not concern her, it did mean that her daughter was less easy to manipulate, maybe it was time to stir a few emotions in Annie and reawaken some guilt. What Elizabeth needed was for Annie to be an ally not an enemy, at least that way she could be more sure of her regular supply of gin.

Elizabeth's small blue-grey eyes glistened and producing

115

her most pathetic face, she forced unwilling tears from her dry eyes, interspersed with a sob or two just for good measure.

'Annie, 'ow can yer say such things, all the years that I had to watch yer playin' in the street, me own daughter not even knowing who 'er real mother were. D'yer know 'ow precious yer are to me? And now yer treat me like this.'

Annie had heard Elizabeth's version of her disjointed childhood many times, and it was certainly not how she remembered it. As far as she was aware her mother had abandoned her at birth and it was only her own curiosity and persistence that prompted a meeting of the two of them in the first place. Her mother conveniently chose to see it differently and she was so convincing that Annie sometimes wondered whether her own memories were distorted with childhood fantasy.

Elizabeth, seeing that her distress was beginning to take effect, continued. 'Yer don't know all the years of torment I had, never knowin' where yer were or seein' yer grow up. Yer childhood was stolen from me, Annie, all I want is fer yer 'appiness. If that means expandin' the salt pan, well so be it. I couldn't bear it if you or Jack went away. I've already lost Luke and if you drive Jack away I'll die of a broken 'eart.'

'Don't cry, Mother, please.' Annie felt her resolve weaken, even if she found it hard to imagine that her mother had a heart. Her mother was just an old woman really, and who did she have if not her daughter. The old familiar guilt feeling swirled in her stomach, the one that made her feel she had somehow failed her mother, been a bad daughter. She sighed, her instincts were to place her arms around the huddled figure before her and try to bring some comfort, but it had never been possible to touch her mother in any way. Between them stood an impenetrable barrier, years of coldness and frigidity that could never be warmed.

Awkwardly Annie brushed her hands down her dress, and shuffled in her uncomfortableness. 'I'll make things right with Jack, you'll see.' Though she wasn't quite sure how, so

116

she said the first thing that came into her head. 'I'll put him in charge of the sheds an' that way he'll be important an' he won't want to leave. I'll go to the grocer's now and get you some gin. That'll warm yer up, won't it?'

Elizabeth's face immediately brightened, and she gave a small smile, which was almost a smirk, but which Annie chose to ignore as she left for the shop. Elizabeth had won again, and already Annie was doubting the wisdom of her promise. She didn't want to give Jack any position of power, in fact her intention was that Joe would be in charge of the new pans. Oh well, it was done now and she was still the owner and perhaps it wouldn't do any harm to have Jack on her side instead of fighting her every move.

She smiled to herself as she rounded the street corner. Nothing was going to spoil this wonderful feeling she had right now. Suddenly the whole world seemed different, suddenly she wasn't just Annie Hayes. She was somebody, someone with power and dreams. She was going to change her life to make things happen and the people around her would just have to get used to the idea.

To her sheer amazement it was not too difficult to persuade the bank to lend her the money she required for her plans. Although she had been nervous when his prim secretary had ushered her into the manager's gloomy office, she had soon recovered her composure and as the excitement of relating her plans took over she forgot that the austere gentleman before her could smash all her dreams if he chose with a refusal. Fortunately for her his only concern was that she was so young and unmarried but her attributes outweighed these things, especially as she told him that she was to be married in the near future. As they shook hands on her leaving, he was left with the impression of a very ambitious and capable young woman and he had no doubts at all on his decision to lend her the money she required. As for Annie herself, she did not feel too badly about saying that she was to be married for it was not strictly a lie; all she had to do now was tell Joe.

117

Four weeks later, the Wych shed was the talk of the town. Men had arrived from Hunters Machinery and huge shafts were being dug into the ground, other men brought pumps and materials to build new sheds, and two huge new shiny vats had been delivered ready for brine to be pumped into. Rumour had it that Annie Hayes was sinking not one, but two new shafts, and what's more that she was looking to hire at least three if not four men to work for her. Bargemen were already offering their services for transporting her salt and she had secured a very good price with her buyer for all the salt she could produce. In the local shops and pubs Annie was a much talked-about subject. There were those who prophesied her doom, saying she was just a young upstart and how could a woman survive in a man's business. But mostly she was admired and respected, especially by those who knew her. But not by John Ellis. He was far from pleased.

It was no surprise to Annie that today two of his men had been snooping around the site to see exactly what she was doing. Actually it rather pleased her that John Ellis saw her as a threat and she did nothing to dispel the rumours and speculation that this was merely the start of a growing empire.

Torrential rain had turned the area into a swamp and the diggers were finding it increasingly difficult to work. As fast as soil was hauled out of the pits it was sliding back in muddy waterfalls. The April sky laden with heavy black clouds showed no sign of relenting its onslaught. Annie stood in the doorway of the shed watching the dismal scene. It was not only the weather that was irritating her, but also Joe.

Ever since the work had begun he had been in a mood. He showed little if any interest in the progress and huffily slammed and banged around in the shed, grunting that he was too busy to watch other people work. Annie was hurt; she had wanted to share this dream with him, she wanted him to feel as thrilled as she did. Instead he was behaving like a sulky little boy who wasn't getting all the attention. She knew part of it was because of Peter Smith, for every

118

time she spoke to him Joe would glare ferociously at her. In a way it was flattering that he was so obviously jealous, but surely he could see that she needed Peter here at the moment and that there was nothing between them. This behaviour had gone on for days now and Annie was truly weary of it. Part of her wanted to take Joe by the scruff of the neck and give him a good shaking for being so silly, but the hostile look in his eyes scared her. It hadn't helped matters that Jack was now officially foreman and that he had the job of hiring the new men. Jack of course, being Jack, soon fell into the role of being in charge and took full advantage of his uplifted status, and unfortunately Joe, at present the only other employee, had to bear the brunt of his unbearable arrogance.

Annie was in a quandary. Perhaps now was the time to talk to Joe about marriage, but after all he was supposed to ask her and despite being given many opportunities to take their relationship further he had never bothered. This too was beginning to agitate her greatly. Last Sunday she had suggested that they take a walk by the river. It was the perfect opportunity for him to discuss his intentions. Instead he had stiffly walked by her side, making no improper moves, just polite conversation, until Annie had become so annoyed that she had feigned a headache and returned home. She knew that he loved her, in fact that he had loved her for years. What she didn't guess, was that he now felt so inferior to her that he assumed she would never be interested in him, especially with men like Peter Smith around who were so much cleverer and richer than he was. The situation would probably have continued for months had not an incident occurred to dispel Joe's misunderstandings and her frustrations. It was another whole week before the driving rain abated, by this time the whole area was an unworkable swamp, men tramped around knee deep in sticky mud trying to erect the sheds and fit the pumps and machinery. Annie could not simply stop the work because of the weather, she needed to get the pans working and some salt sold. The first payment at the bank was due and she didn't want to get off to a bad start. Peter Smith who had left last week was returning today to test out the pump which was installed. Temporary sheeting had been fixed to the new shed roofs to keep the precious machinery dry inside, until the roofing materials, which were over a week late, finally arrived.

Today the old sheeting, which had been loosened in the high winds and was flapping dangerously about, had to be replaced. The morale of the workers was probably at its lowest, toiling in such hostile conditions did not help anyone's patience and petty squabbling had been going on all day. The men who worked for Peter knew that he was arriving later that day and that there would be hell to pay if the job was not finished. Black faces matched the black skies and Annie trudged in the sticky mud trying to encourage the men and keep them supplied with warm drinks. By midday the wind had changed from a breeze to a stiff wind with occasional gusts that almost knocked Annie off her feet. The men struggled with the roof of the sheds, desperate to secure them down before the next deluge of rain started.

By two o'clock one of the sheds was finished and inside some of the men were busily adjusting the machinery, ready for Peter's arrival. The second shed was proving more difficult. Annie watched in frustration as the wind tossed aside the wood and slates as though they were made of paper. One man slipped from his ladder crashing down onto the wet ground, winded though fortunately not injured. It was enough though, and helped to his feet by an anxious Annie he declared that it was just too windy and that he was doing no more. His workmate was quick to agree, and shouting to make themselves heard above the now gale force winds, they ignored Annie's pleading and gathering their tools stomped off in the direction of the town. The rain began again and was soon driving across the open ground in sheets. Annie gazed in dismay at the gaping hole where a roof should have been, exposing the precious machinery. The rain stung in her eyes as she struggled to the shed and once inside tried as best she could to cover up the machinery with

120

tarpaulin sheets. It was hopeless, for as fast as she secured one end, the wind would free the other and send it billowing up into the air like a deranged kite. Annie's fingers were blue with cold and tears of frustration spurted from her eyes. She knew that she needed help and facing the elements again she stumbled her way across the field towards the shed to get Joe.

When she fell into the shed, the heat from the pan made her gasp for air. It was just as steamy inside here as it was misty outside, and at first she could see nothing.

'Joe, Joe are yer 'ere?' Her voice was a tiny cry in the vapoury shed.

'Annie, are yer all right?' He was instantly by her side and, exhausted from her efforts, she collapsed against him. It was the closest they had been and Joe felt a surge of passion flood through his body.

'Joe, we have to fix the roof, the men have gone, an' the water's pourin' in, everythin' is gettin' ruined. Please 'elp me.' Her voice was filled with desperation and as she pulled away from his arms her dark eyes melted him.

Within minutes they were both outside. It was impossible to see the shed, in fact they could hardly see one step in front of them. The wind howled and swirled the icy rain in torrents that lashed against their skin cruelly. Having reached the shed, the best they could hope to do was somehow secure the old sheeting and try to keep out as much rain as possible. Joe managed to capture one end and with all his strength drag it to the floor. Pushing Annie down, he yelled at her to lie on the edge until he could find something to secure it with.

After what seemed like an eternity to Annie, who lay shaking with cold on the floor, he reappeared with some boulders which he placed at intervals along the ground. Indicating for Annie to get up, he gave her one corner of the end of the sheet, whilst he took the other end and they tried to cover the machinery over. The wind was vicious and four or five times it savagely ripped the sheet from Annie's frozen fingers, sending it careering through the air, with a

121

terrifying howling sound. Finally they managed to pull it over and down to the floor on the other side and Joe secured his end under the heavy wheels of a salt truck, and then racing to Annie he grabbed the final corner from her.

'We need somethin' to 'old it down,' he yelled at the top of his voice.

Frantically they searched around with their eyes. Annie spotted some wooden beams that were going to be used in the proper roofing and she tried to drag one from the corner of the shed. It proved impossibly heavy and seeing that she could not manage it he shouted for her to come and hold the sheet down while he tried. Dragging them over one by one he weighted down the sheet until it was safe, and they collapsed to the floor, sweating and shivering.

What happened next was so quick that when Annie looked back she hardly remembered blinking and it was done. The wind whipped up in a crescendo and gusts ripped through the tiny building, shaking its very foundations. The slates piled in the corner ready to be placed on the new roof wobbled precariously and then slid, crashing down in a splintering torrent. One caught by the wind flew through the air and sliced into the side of Joe's head. In an instant rain was mixed with blood and he collapsed to the floor, where the remaining slates rained down on his prostrate body, pinning his legs down. Annie sat stunned for a minute and then frantically tore at the grey slabs to release his trapped limbs. Joe was lying perfectly still, blood not only oozing from his head but pumping from a gaping hole in his thigh.

'Please don't die, yer mustn't die Joe,' she begged. She fled from the shed to get help.

Jack was now the only other person around and on seeing her blood-streaked face and hearing the orders she screamed for him to get a doctor, for once he didn't argue but raced off into the filthy weather to get help. Sobbing uncontrollably Annie stumbled back to Joe and wrapping him as best she could in her shawl she crooned softly to him, praying as she had not done since she had begged God for her pa's life.

It took over an hour for help to arrive, and when it did it seemed as though both Joe and Annie were dead. He was lying in a congealed pool of blood, she was bent over him to try and protect him from the onslaught of the freezing rain, seemingly frozen solid herself in the effort. The rain continued to pound unmercifully and the offending sheet flapped defiantly, jubilant at its escape. Only when Annie uttered a tiny moan did the rescuers realise she was still alive.

# Fourteen

For a while, Annie too was unsure as to whether she was alive or dead. At first she had talked to Joe, quietly pleading with him to hold on, not to leave her. She had tried to stem the oozing blood from his head with strips torn from her skirt. She had tied a tourniquet around his mutilated leg but the blood continued to pump out in bright red spurts. She crooned to him, resting his broken head against her thigh, and tried to ignore the creeping cold that was overtaking her shaking body. Her fingers and toes became quite numb, and slowly the painful freezing dampness crept up her legs and arms, finally sweeping over her whole body. She shook convulsively, teeth chattering, lips blue, still aware that she must try and shelter Joe from the pouring rain and howling wind.

Some time later her mind began to play tricks on her. She imagined that her pa was here, talking to her, telling her he loved her, and then images of Clara, brushing her long hair and cuddling her on her knee. Clara was speaking too, reassuring her that it didn't matter if her mother didn't want her, other people loved her. Then there was Sarah holding out the Indian dress as it floated in the wind. Annie could see herself dancing, the beautiful skirt swirling out around her in billowy blue waves. A light appeared ahead of her, it was pulling her towards its white beams, faster and faster she flew. The nearer she got to the light the warmer she became, she knew she was dying but the irresistible

124

comfort of that light was too much and she longed to get there.

Suddenly she heard a voice, it could have been her pa, but she wasn't sure. The voice was sending her back, even though she didn't want to go. Over and over it repeated the same words.

'It's not time Annie, it's not time.'

The warmth of the light died and then she was aware of the penetrating cold again ripping her apart, and voices swirling in the background.

'She's alive, quickly over here, get a blanket.'

Opening her eyes, Annie saw Richard's face before her, and imagining that she must be dreaming she tightly closed them again. Still it sounded like Richard's voice, calling her name, demanding that she look at him. Slowly allowing her eyelids to open, she focused on the face she knew so well, every detail of it stored in her memory. And now she really saw that it was him.

Richard gently rubbed his fingers along her cheek and then shouted instructions to the two men he had with him. Annie was very carefully lifted up and carried out to a carriage waiting on the field.

'Don't worry Annie, my men will take you home and I will see you later. I have to see this other man now.' With that, Doctor Richard Ellis set about trying to save the mutilated leg of the man before him.

Annie must have drifted from consciousness, for the next thing she remembered was waking up in an unfamiliar room. The first thing she was aware of was that she was warm and dry, her body no longer shook or teeth chattered. Then as she looked around her at the luxurious room she remembered Richard. A warm feeling of comfort flooded over her and then just as quickly as it came it was replaced by the horror of remembering the accident. Joe's blood-stained face flashed before her and the whole nightmare relived itself in a second.

Struggling to sit up, she swung her legs over the edge of the huge double bed. She noticed that she was dressed in a beautiful white embroidered gown, which under normal circumstances she would have been overawed with. Her only thoughts now were to find out where she was and see if Joe was all right. Her movements alerted the housemaid who had been stationed in a chair by the fire.

'You mustn't get up, Miss. Doctor Ellis gave strict instructions that you was to stay in bed till he came.'

The girl hurriedly tried to push Annie's legs back into the bed, before she got into trouble for not doing her job properly.

Annie, however, was not one to be pushed and, forcing the girl to one side, she slid out of the covers and rushed to the window to look outside. Pulling back the heavy drapes she could see nothing but pitch darkness.

'How long have I been 'ere. Where am I? Where are me clothes? I have to leave at once,' she demanded of the astonished girl.

'You've been here for a few hours now, out to it as well, fast asleep. You're at the Ellis manor. Rest is the best thing, Doctor Ellis says. As for your clothes, what's left of them is drying down in the kitchen.'

'Go and get them for me, please.'

'Doctor Ellis won't like . . .' stammered the girl.

'I don't care what Doctor Ellis would or wouldn't like, just get me me clothes,' raged Annie, furious that Richard had brought her here of all places, his father's home.

The girl scurried out of the room, muttering as she went about folk being so ungrateful. She obviously went straight to her master for a few minutes later, following a brief tap on the door, Richard strode into the room.

'You are feeling better, I hear. Good.' He grinned in the way that usually made her heart turn, but at the moment it only fuelled her anger.

'How dare yer bring me 'ere, why didn't yer just send me 'ome. I don't need yer father's charity, thank you. Now please tell yer maid to bring me clothes an' I won't trouble yer further.'

' "It was very nice of you to save me Richard, thank you

126

so much, Richard, oh yes, and to save my worker's leg and stick his head back together," ' Richard paraded before her mocking. 'Don't mention it, Annie, it's all in a day's work,' he continued.

Annie immediately felt humbled and she knew how ungracious she sounded. 'I'm sorry, I'm being very rude. Of course I'm grateful fer yer 'elp,' she whispered. 'How is Joe? I must see 'im.'

'Joe, if that is his name, is fine, he is resting, just two rooms away from you and that is where he is staying, as my patient at least for the next day or two, before you get any ideas of rushing for his clothes too.' Richard sounded wounded by her abruptness.

Annie was sorry for her quick temper. 'Please can I see 'im?' she asked meekly.

Richard passed her a warm red velvet gown to put on over her nightgown. She had forgotten that that was all she was wearing and blushed as she realised it. Without a word she followed him from her room along a magnificently decorated hallway, lined with oak panelling and strewn with wonderful pictures of vivid hunting scenes. Her bare feet sank into the deep piled rugs as she gasped at the beautiful surroundings. She had never imagined that the Ellises owned such wealth as this. No wonder Richard had never come back for her; to him she must just be another poor ignorant patient, a commoner in comparison with the rich ladies he must know now. She knew then that she had to get away from here as soon as possible. She could probably never afford to pay Richard for his services but she certainly could ensure that she did not embarrass him by remaining here longer than necessary.

Joe was propped up in the comfortable bed, a bandage around his head and one leg on top of the covers, also strapped tightly. On seeing Annie his face broke out into a huge grin and only when he tried to lean forward did the pain in his head cause him to grimace and lie back against the soft pillows again.

'Joe, Joe are yer all right?' Annie rushed forward and

sitting on the edge of the bed she clasped his hand within hers.

Richard Ellis was slightly taken aback by this rush of apparent affection and coughed uneasily to remind her of his presence.

'You need not worry, Joe here will be just fine. He's had some stitches in the gash in his head and hopefully that leg will be fine if we keep it strapped for a week or two. Rest is the most important thing and I don't think that he should be moved at least for a few days.'

'I feel fine, Annie 'onest, don't worry. I'll be back at the shed before yer know it.' Joe smiled reassuringly.

'I'm so sorry, Joe. It was all my fault, pushin' to get the roof finished in such terrible conditions. If anythin' 'ad 'appened to yer I . . .' Annie felt a sob rise in her throat and she swallowed hard, not wishing to cry in front of Richard.

'Well I'm fine, so stop worrying,' Joe shifted in the bed, shooting pains in his leg causing him to groan quietly.

Richard nodded to Annie to leave quietly and let the patient sleep. Stooping to kiss Joe's already closed eyelids, Annie brushed her lips tenderly across his skin and silently left the room. The action caused a surge of jealousy to race through Richard's body, a million questions begging to be asked, but he knew he had no right to ask them. In silence they returned to the room in which Annie had slept, and only when they were inside did she turn to speak to him.

'If yer could have me clothes sent I'll trouble yer no further.'

'Annie, you're welcome to stay, why not wait and rest, and in a couple of days you will be feeling so much better.' Richard tried to hide the desperation he felt at her departure.

'It's very kind of yer to keep Joe, an' I'll always be grateful fer what yer've done fer 'im. I'll send a carriage to collect 'im the day after tomorrow, an' if you let me have yer bill . . .'

'Annie, Annie, stop. There will be no bill, is our friendship forgotten?'

For a split second she had the urge to run to him and

fling her arms around his neck, to tell him that she still loved him and even after all this time she still dreamed only of his arms around her, his lips on hers. But reality rushed in like an icy wind and she remembered her position, so lowly compared to his, he was probably teasing her, laughing at her naïvety right now. After all he had a fiancée, so why should he have any interest in her?

'I'd rather pay me way, but if yer don't feel it's right to charge me because of our past acquaintance then I'll be very grateful to yer. I don't wish to offend yer generosity.'

Her words were stiff and the effect was crushing. Sadly Richard bowed his head defeated and backed out of the room, informing her she would have her clothes directly.

His heart might have been less heavy had he seen the single tear that trickled down her face before she brushed it away angrily, cursing her stupidity.

Two months later, with the June sunshine pouring down from a friendly sky, Annie smiled as she surveyed her completed wych sheds. The three stood, solid and sturdy against the shooting green grass and blue skyline. The two new sheds were up and running now and she had three new men working for her. Her salt yield was beyond even Peter Smith's expectations and every day sacks of salt left for Liverpool marked with the Hayes trademark. Annie felt content that her dream was coming true and her only wish was that her pa could see this, for she knew he would be so proud of her.

She was glad that she had been so very busy since the night of the accident, for it had helped her to put Richard from the forefront of her mind, back into the special box in her heart where she was safe from him, but where her memories were still treasured. Joe had not recovered fully from the accident and his smashed leg, although healed, had left him with a pronounced limp. Blinding headaches would strike him and sometimes she still saw him grimace in pain if he tried to do too much, and for this she felt very guilty. If she had any doubts about making him her husband this dismissed them all; after all, it had been her fault. She could never leave him now, for he needed her. She knew that he would have difficulty finding work elsewhere, there were too many able-bodied men all too willing to work. So she concentrated on looking after him, making him meals and even bringing a mattress for him to sleep on in the shed instead of the hard bench he had endured for years. Although her mind was made up, no matter how hard she tried to deny it her heart was heavy, she didn't love him and she couldn't make herself; but she did care for him and she certainly felt responsible and that, she thought, would just have to be enough.

When Joe had left the Manor house, to his dismay he had then had to spend a further week at his parents' home, convalescing. It should have been longer but he could bear it no longer and so hobbled on his stick back to the wych shed, which he considered home.

When Annie had asked him why he had come back so soon, he had muttered something about being bored, not wanting to tell her of the black oppressive mood that swamped him as soon as he was confined for any length of time with his father. Even though he was now a grown man Joe could not cope with the diverse feelings that tore him apart over the man he hated and yet loved so much. The only time he felt safe was when he was away from him, safe from the evil power that he wielded, the cruel manipulation. Yet despite that he could never break the cord entirely, and every now and then he was drawn back by some invisible hand which toyed with him and having destroyed him again tossed him aside. Only Annie could save him, with her he felt safe and clean and sometimes he could imagine that he was just like everybody else. He knew that she must never know about his past, for it would destroy her trust of him. She was good and pure, not soiled as he had been, and he knew that all he wanted in life was to be near her. He never dreamt of her plans to marry him, for he considered himself far too unworthy of that, he was content to simply be near her, his only nightmare that she should find another man.

When that thought crept into his mind he was filled with a jealous rage, and he knew he would probably kill any man who tried to come between them. He had had to work very hard to control himself when that Peter Smith had been here. He had seen him sniffing around his Annie, that look in his eye, the one he knew only too well from his father. Fortunately the man had gone now and things seemed safe again in his world, a world that revolved entirely around Annie.

It was on the same bright June day, just when Annie was feeling so at ease with everything, that Richard appeared and once again set her emotions in turmoil. She had spent the afternoon in the shed with Joe; he was finding it difficult throwing the heavy wooden rake out over the brine for it made him lose his balance and so Annie had taken over the job of raking the crystals to the side of the bubbling vat and Joe was scooping them out on the huge shovels. It was work that Annie was well used to, although today was particularly hot and she had stripped to her shift in the intense heat. Sweat was pouring from her and her face was streaked with dirt and grime. The brine was bubbling noisily in the huge vat and neither Joe nor Annie heard the footsteps approaching the shed. If they had they would have thought nothing of it assuming it would be Jack. Since his promotion to foreman Jack spent most of his day walking from one shed to the other checking on his workers but actually doing very little himself. This infuriated Annie but she was weary of constantly arguing with her brother and she chose to ignore him most of the time.

The footsteps actually belonged to Richard. He was in the area visiting patients and decided to go and see how Joe was faring with his leg. At least, that was the reason he told himself, in truth he would never have gone to see a patient, especially a non-paying one, without being called out. But since seeing Annie again he had thought of nothing else and he was desperate to see her again. Her apparent hostility had done nothing to dampen his feelings, on the contrary he only wanted her more and though he wasn't sure what he was going to say to her he knew he had to speak to her. If she would just listen to how he felt then maybe she would come to him and leave these dreadful wych sheds behind. She was worth so much more than this and he could give her a life of comfort. Of course he realised the wrath of his father would have to be faced, he would have to break the engagement to that simpering Dorothy Mountjoy that his father had arranged, but none of that mattered. It was worth sacrificing it all for Annie.

As he entered the shed he was horrified. Annie, standing almost naked in her shift, was hauling the wooden rake back and forth over the brine. She seemed oblivious of the fact that each throw of the rake almost exposed her breasts beneath the flimsy material that clung to her. His horror was momentarily replaced with desire as he drank in the sight of her body and then disgust again as he saw Joe scooping out the salt crystals a little further along the vat, and the realisation that this worker was appreciating the same view as he was.

'Annie, Annie, what are you doing?' he cried, unable to contain himself.

Annie, startled by his shout, almost dropped the rake in the swirling liquid and cursing him she dragged it to the side.

'D'yer know 'ow much a rake costs to replace?' she yelled angrily. 'What d'yer mean, scaring me like that.'

She was suddenly aware of his eyes on her body and hurriedly she pulled her blouse on, despite the fierce heat in the shed.

Richard felt quite silly and was not sure what to say, he had no rights to come in here shouting at her, she probably thought he was quite mad.

'I came to see if Joe was all right,' he said feebly.

Joe nodded his head to confirm that he was indeed fine and then carried on shovelling the crystals. An awkward silence prevailed.

'Well that's good news, then. I'll be on my way.' Richard moved towards the doorway.

Annie stood silently watching him as stepped outside into the sunlight. Instinct told her not to follow him, she was angry at his intrusion on her property, but she could not resist the chance to talk to him and so ran to catch him up. Anger was her best defence and so she launched into him.

'I don't take kindly to people bursting into my shed shouting at me.'

'I'm sorry. I was just shocked to see you like that.'

'Shocked? Shocked by what, Richard? The fact that I was working?'

'No – that you were half naked in front of that man. Annie, you are worth so much more than this.' He turned to face her. Clasping her hands in his, his face distraught, he continued, 'I hate to think of you slaving away in that dirty shed, it's not right. I could change all that for you if you would just let me.'

Anger flooded through her body, flushing her face bright red with indignation. She could stand no more of his patronising attitude and ripping her hands away from him she took a step backwards, before letting her emotions spill out.

''Ow dare yer, 'ow dare yer come 'ere pityin' me. I don't want yer 'elp or charity. Though yer may find it 'ard to believe I love these sheds, they're me life an' yes I 'ave to work 'ard. That's the joy of it, I can't run 'ome to a pampered lifestyle, I 'ave to toil fer every penny, but that brings me riches that you'd not even begin to understand. Go an' live in yer shallow world Richard, with yer spoilt fiancée, but never imagine it's what the rest of us want. What were yer goin' to offer me, a clean job as a chamber maid or a nanny? There's nothin' yer can give me Richard that would compare with what I 'ave 'ere.'

'Of course I don't want you to be a chamber maid, if you would just listen to me for a minute . . .'

'I don't 'ave to listen to yer at all, an' as fer the worker that I were stripped off in front of, not that it's any of your business, but it might help yer morality to know that he's me future 'usband. Now get off me land, Richard, and don't ever come back patronisin' me again.'

133

With that she turned on her heel and stamped back into the shed. Joe, having heard all this conversation, stood mouth wide open and incredulous.

'Well, is it such a terrible idea to be me 'usband?' Annie snapped.

'No, not if yer mean it,' Joe stuttered.

'I do, so yer'd better arrange fer the banns to be read at the church.'

Joe hobbled forward and clasped Annie to him, overcome now with emotion.

'Oh Annie, me love,' he babbled.

Annie prised herself from his arms, trying to dismiss the repulsion she felt at being so close to him. 'We've a load to get ready fer the barges.'

With renewed venom she slapped the rake against the brine, while in her head she repeated the same words over and over, 'Damn you Richard Ellis, damn you.'

# Fifteen

In 1884 the Cheshire salt industry was booming. Despite years of decline and the constant uncertainty of wildly fluctuating salt prices, vast new trade opportunities had opened up in the new Eastern and Indian markets and the large proprietors, independents and newcomers all prospered. This sudden growth and expansion was unfortunately short-lived, as overproduction quickly reduced prices drastically. However, at this very moment Annie was enjoying the rewards of hard work and a very favourable market for her salt. At twenty-five years old she had achieved what many had failed to find in a lifetime, a very profitable business which was growing steadily. Not only did she own the three original pans but also another four that she had purchased from bankrupt owners and now rented out to families who worked them independently. Her bank loan was repaid and she was living in her own small stone cottage which nestled beneath her wych sheds on the river bank.

Annie reflected all these things as she sat by the open window of her parlour, from where she could see the river. She loved to watch the boats sailing up and down. Steamships were now replacing the horsedrawn barges and the river was congested with traffic, so much activity and hustle and bustle, it always made her feel restless, anxious to be going somewhere though she didn't know where. The river was alive and it reminded her that she was too, replenishing her weary spirit and driving out the creeping apathy that wore her out constantly.

She knew she was ungrateful. She must be. With all this, what more could she hope for? She was never hungry or cold, she always had a clean bed to sleep in and warm water to wash with, so many things to be thankful for. Yet she could not shake the gnawing loneliness that seeped through her body, the yearning for some love and comfort and the unbearable feeling that she was to be cheated of these things for the rest of her life. She craved for some excitement, something to make her heart race or stomach flutter, and sometimes desires that she could not even put a name or description to burned within her with such ferocity that she wanted to burst. Today was one of those days. She could settle at nothing and so had placed herself in her favourite spot, watching the river, hoping its ebbing water could somehow soothe her ragged nerves.

She had been married to Joe for five years and she knew that it had been the biggest mistake of her life, something she had realised from their very first night together as man and wife. She did not love him, though she had known that much when she married him. She had stupidly believed that she could learn to feel those things for him, but she could not. On their wedding night she had cringed as his hands had run over her body, his wet lips repelled her as they closed over hers, and when he had finally finished with her rigid body she had felt only relief. Nothing had changed in all the following years; even Joe's tears and pleading for her to love him, though moving her to cry with him, altered nothing. She never refused him his pleasure, she considered it her duty, but she never experienced any joy from it, dreading it when his clammy hands groped her in the darkness of their bed. She knew that he loved her, more than that idolised her, jealous of anyone she spoke to or anything that took her away from him, and like a child he demanded complete attention. Without it he sulked unbearably or worse still flew into uncontrollable rages that usually resulted in her receiving a beating. She knew he was sorry afterwards and she had begun to dread the moods and sulking more than the beatings. At least the pain from the

136

bruises healed quickly, the mental torture was far worse and so sometimes she would deliberately provoke him, until she knew he could contain his fury no longer, and the whole miserable cycle would end at least for a while.

At this point in time Annie did not really blame Joe too much, she considered that the fault lay with herself. She had married him knowing she did not love him and so in her mind had cheated him, this was her punishment. Adding to her guilt of being a bad daughter she also considered herself a bad wife, in fact at times she believed that she must be truly wicked and this was God's punishment which she must bear.

All this she could have endured if her mind would just stop tormenting her. She yearned for her freedom, for passion, for anything that would take her away from this colourless life she had. Now she understood why her pa had cherished Sarah all his life. In total contrast with her frigid mother, Sarah had exuded love in all its glory, unashamedly and with no regrets. Annie was no longer clear what the elusive butterfly she chased even was. Her first thought was always Richard, her one love. But Richard was lost to her forever, he was married now and lived just two towns away. She winced as she recalled reading about his society wedding and all its splendour, she had cried all that day and the misery had lasted for weeks. But he was happy now with his prim and suitable wife and his comfortable living, and probably never gave her a thought.

This thing that she chased, then, was not him, but something unknown, a desire for some magic to soothe the ache within her, to put back that something which was missing from her life.

She had thought that a child might fill this gaping hole for her and had yearned for a baby, someone she could love and care for, devote herself to unselfishly. But that too was not meant to be. Joe did not want children, in fact his vehemence on the subject shocked her. When she had suggested it to him, she thought that he would be pleased, but instead he flew into one of his uncontrollable rages, saying

137

that he must never father a child under any circumstances. He refused to elaborate and when she pressed for some reason, he simply said that there were things in his past that must never be passed on. She assumed that he must mean some kind of illness but he refused to discuss it further and retreated into one of his black moods that lasted for days, until Annie wished that she had never broached the subject in the first place. Secretly she prayed that she might fall pregnant anyway, being sure Joe would change his mind then, but what she didn't realise was that Joe was careful never to ejaculate inside her body. Never having slept with another man she knew no different and cursed her body every month on the appearance of her period.

She knew nothing of his past, he never spoke of his family and as far as she knew he had not seen any of them since just before the wedding. It was a taboo subject and she knew better than to pry for the consequences were never worth it. Before they had married, she had asked him if his parents would be coming to the wedding and he had returned home to ask them. Later that day, when he had come back, sporting a black eye and split lip, he had coldly said that they would not be attending and that she was not to mention them again.

The wedding had been a sparse occasion, her own mother had not come, showing no interest in her daughter's big day. Annie bitterly recalled how she had tried to talk to her about making a dress to wear, only to be told that it was a waste of money when she had a perfectly good dress already. On the day of her marriage Annie had dressed alone into the simple white dress she had sewn and plaited some flowers with great difficulty into her hair. Without even a goodbye from her mother she had walked down to the little church alone. Jack had stood as witness even though he showed no interest in the ceremony and Mrs Grenale who cleaned the church and arranged the flowers was also present. After the service Joe had returned to the shed and Annie had walked home to change back into her working shift and then returned to the shed to help load the barrows with salt.

For the next two years Annie and her new husband turned the front parlour into a bedroom in the tiny terrace house in Union street. This was a time of agony for her. Not only did she have to endure Joe's lovemaking in the same house where her mother and brother were quite able to hear every move, but it seemed to increase Jack's desire for her and at every opportunity he would burst into the room when she was half naked, or leer knowingly at her the morning after Joe had been particularly noisy the night before. Annie was still afraid of Jack, even though it was he who was dependent on her for his livelihood. He had a sinister ability to chill her to the bone with his lurid looks and stares. At least now she had her own home, space that belonged to her, that Jack could not invade or her mother poison with her spiteful tongue.

For a while it had made things better, she had fussed around her little home, making things how she wanted them. Joe never had any opinion about household matters and so she was given a free hand in furnishing and decorating the cottage. But the novelty of white-washing walls and sewing curtains had died and the rooms now all seemed to reflect the barrenness that she felt within.

Annie shifted on the seat by the window. Tomorrow she was going to Liverpool to see her buyers and her solicitor. Joe hated her going anywhere and so was already giving her the silent punishment, ignoring her if she spoke and scowling at her constantly. But she was past caring about this and she promised herself no matter how big a row it caused he would not ruin her day. She had already booked her train ticket and decided that once the business was over she would have time to look around at some of the clothes stores and that always cheered her up.

The day dawned with drizzly rain that stuck to everything with sticky fingers. It was not cold and even though it was only April the breeze was warm as it caressed the drenched trees. Annie walked a little stiffly to the station. Joe's fury had culminated in him taking her body with unusual ferocity last night and her thighs were bruised and sore; this, he had told her, was to remind her who she belonged to. In his twisted mind he constantly accused her of affairs. He had no justification for such thoughts. Annie was used to it though and besides she considered it worth it for a day's freedom, the soreness would pass and when she returned home Joe would be remorseful and hopefully leave her alone for a day or two.

As the train steamed into Liverpool station, Annie felt the excitement rushing through her body. So many people and such noise and smells, she failed to see how anyone could not be exhilarated by it all. A smile seeped across her face quite involuntarily as she pushed her way through the throngs of people on the busy platform, she was free for a whole day and that freedom held such power for her that she buzzed inside.

She knew exactly where she was going, for she had visited her buyer's office many times. Today she was going to sign a new contract for supplying her salt out to East India; the prices were good and Annie meant to take full advantage of the current world market. She had a new project in mind and increasing her sales would help her to pay for it. That was the reason for her appointment with the solicitor later in the morning. Annie had developed quite a thirst for business and when she had heard of a small company just a few miles from Lytwych going out of business, she had immediately been interested. It was quite a run down and dilapidated shed and the machinery old and out of date but the brine field was vast and Annie had both the resources and enthusiasm to modernise it. Added to this she knew full well that John Ellis was also looking to add this particular pan to his empire, and this gave Annie all the more reason to want it herself. She knew that he had put in a bid for the company and she to had offered her best price, and this morning the solicitor would tell her if she had been success-ful. Already her stomach was in a turmoil over it. Realistically it would be no great loss to her if she had failed to secure the deal, but this was the only excitement her life had to offer and so it seemed far more important than it probably was. She also had to admit that anything that put John Ellis's nose out of joint was worthwhile anyway, not that she was particularly malicious but over the years he had done everything in his power to be obstructive to her and she found his treatment of people so obnoxious that it served him right not to always get his own way. Her mind was whirling all these thoughts around as she picked her way through the busy streets of Liverpool's dockside. In front of her stretched the harbour crowded with bobbing masts of the huge sea ships and behind her the tall majestic buildings with their elaborate carvings reached skyward as if in thankful prayer. It was a sight that never failed to move her, as she scurried ant-like below them.

So lost was she in her daydreams and wonder that she failed to see the well-dressed man also rushing along the pavement towards her. Seemingly oblivious to the rest of the population neither was aware of the other until they crashed together.

'I'm terribly sorry,' stuttered the man apologetically, not really looking at the woman but continuing on his way. He was late already for a meeting which explained his abruptness and as the lady seemed unharmed he had no wish to delay himself any further.

'It was my fault, I was daydreaming,' Annie smiled sheepishly.

Her voice was familiar and it caused him to stop and look at her properly.

'Annie, Annie Hayes?' His voice was surprised, not just that he should see her again but that the attractive young girl he once knew was now a quite beautiful lady.

'Yes. Have we met?'

'It's Peter, Peter Smith, Hunters Machinery.'

Now it was Annie's turn to be amazed. She gazed at his face and beneath the beard and moustache she instantly recognised him. He looked much older and from his dress she realised that his success had obviously continued, no

141

longer dressed in the casual cords of a sales representative but now sporting a stylish suit and carrying a leather briefcase.

'I really must rush. I'm already late for a meeting, but if you are here for the day perhaps we could meet later for afternoon tea?'

'Yes I'd like that very much. I've a few people to see, but this afternoon would be fine. Three o'clock?' Annie smiled, hoping that she didn't sound too forward, but she liked Peter and impulse had made her agree readily to his suggestion.

'Fine, three it is then. The Palace Hotel serves a very acceptable afternoon tea, unless you know anywhere better?'

'The Palace would be lovely.'

With that agreed they parted, Annie feeling very daring and cosmopolitan for embarking on such a venture and Peter reflecting what a stunning beauty she had turned into.

The morning went well for Annie, in fact she almost felt like singing as she skipped along the pavement towards the Palace Hotel. The buyers agreed to higher prices than she anticipated for the salt and the solicitor gave her the good news that she had secured the bid for the pan. Things she thought were certainly looking up; she wallowed in the feelings of achievement and, dispelling any thoughts of Joe's disapproval, she breezed into the foyer of the hotel looking for all the world a confident businesswoman, without a care in the world. This was freedom, this was what she craved, to be herself and having shaken off the oppressiveness of Joe's presence she shone, if only temporarily.

She spotted Peter instantly where he sat at a table by the window, and smiling in genuine pleasure at the sight of him she glided serenely across to join him. She was oblivious of her attractiveness and failed to notice the turn of appreciative heads as she passed, intent only on enjoying a pleasant drink of tea with an old acquaintance.

Instantly a waitress hovered expectantly to take the order.

'Afternoon tea for two, I think,' Peter ordered. 'Unless you prefer something else, Annie?'

142

'No, tea's fine, thanks.' Annie blushed suddenly feeling vulnerable. It was obvious that Peter was well used to this and she felt inadequate, afraid to do something wrong. She had never taken tea in such an upmarket hotel before and her real position in the world flooded back in stark reality, accompanied by Joe's mocking voice, reminding her just who she belonged to. She bowed her head hoping the colour would fade from her cheeks before she made too much of a fool of herself and cursing her impetuousness for allowing herself to get into this situation.

Peter, oblivious to her internal torment, saw only a very pretty face before him and found it quite charming that she flushed with colour so easily.

'So tell me all your news. What of the salt pans? I hear trade is booming at the moment, world-wide.'

Annie embarked on her tale, relaying to him all that had happened over the previous six years, her success and expansion. By the time she got around to her latest acquisition this morning, she had become so engrossed in conversation she had completely forgotten all her inhibitions. Peter was so easy to talk to, he laughed a lot and she had forgotten how refreshing it was to be with someone enthusiastic and ambitious. Joe was so narrow in his thoughts and views, his world so small and rigid, stifling her.

Peter too had been successful. He was now a director of Hunters Machinery, the company had grown beyond all his expectations and now employed some six hundred men in the factory in Manchester and engineers out in the field.

They talked so incessantly that the tea went cold before they had time to drink it and so they ordered another pot and some extra scones and jam, and before they realised it it was six thirty and the anxious waitress was hovering again, to collect the tray and politely inform them that the tea room was closing in ten minutes. Annie could not remember the last time she had enjoyed herself so much, and her sides ached from laughing at Peter's hilarious tales. Joe had not entered her head once in the last three hours and it was

143

such a relief to be rid of his presence for a while, that she felt totally refreshed.

Peter offered to accompany her to her train. His voice was sad too for he had enjoyed her company immensely.

'Really there's no need. It's only five minutes from the station. I'll be fine,' Annie replied though in not too convincing a voice, for she quite liked the idea of being escorted to her train.

'Nonsense, I couldn't possibly let you walk alone.' And linking her arm firmly into his, he led her from the hotel in the direction of Lime Street station.

As they walked Annie did not remove her arm but actually enjoyed the feel of it resting on his. They laughed and talked all the way and on reaching the entrance Annie felt a twinge of sadness that her exciting day was almost over.

'Thank you, Annie, thank you for your lovely company, we must do this again.'

His eyes held hers and for a split second something more than politeness flickered in each. 'Yes I'd love that, an' once the papers have been signed on the new pan I 'ope that your company will come an' fit the new pumps an' vats fer me.' Annie smiled, stepping backwards and putting a more acceptable distance between them, one with which she felt more comfortable.

'Of course. Here, take one of my cards and as soon as you need me drop me a line and I will be delighted to come out and take a look.' Peter raised her hand to his lips, and brushing the skin with a kiss he smiled and turned to leave her.

Annie stood for a moment transfixed, and then brushing her hands down the sides of her dress in embarrassment and irritation with herself she scurried along the platform to catch the departing train. Scolding herself for being so childish, after all she was sure Peter Smith always kissed ladies' hands out of etiquette and politeness.

As the train rattled its way along the track, Annie stared out of the window into the growing darkness of the night. Her heart was heavy again as each turn of the wheel sped

144

her back towards Joe and his evil moods. The nearer she got to Lytwych the more her spirits sank with impending doom, slowly she turned the gold edged card bearing Peter's name over and over in her hand. She knew that she would have to hide it for if Joe found it he would immediately accuse her of having an affair and then any future trips to Liverpool would be even more difficult to arrange. She pushed it deep into her bag intending to hide as soon as possible when she got home. She had no reason to feel guilty, for in essence she had done nothing more than have tea with an old acquaintance, but inside a voice nagged her that it wasn't really proper, especially as in all the three hours of non-stop talking, Annie had never mentioned once the fact that she was married.

Closing her eyes she let the rhythm of the train rock her and tried to savour the last moments of freedom before returning to the prison she called home.

# Sixteen

'Why 'im?' Joe had asked the same question at least five times now over the past half hour, each time becoming more agitated at Annie's reply.

She sighed, knowing full well exactly where this conversation was going to lead but powerless to stop it. It was all a game with Joe, and one that she always lost.

'Yer know why Peter Smith is comin', to look at the new pan an' see what machinery I need to get it up an' runnin'. Joe please stop gettin' so wound up about it.' She tried to keep her voice level, to do nothing to aggravate him more, but it was pointless.

'Wound up, don't tell me not to get wound up. Yer think I don't know what's goin' on, yer think I'm stupid, me own wife carryin' on right under me nose.' Joe's face began to contort with rage.

'Nothin's going on Joe, nothin'. If you'd rather go an' meet Peter tomorrow, you go. I really don't care. I'm just sick of this.' Annie felt the anger rise within her and her eyes blazed in defiance. She knew that she was dangerously close to Joe losing control, but it was true, she was sick of all the accusations every time she so much as spoke to another man.

'Yer know I can't go, it's not my pan or my money, is it?' His voice was bitter and more and more now he would let this spill out into their rows. Bringing his face within inches of hers Joe spat out his words with venom. 'But yer are my

146

wife and I'll kill any man that touches yer, so you just remember that in case yer tempted to lead 'im on.'

Normally Annie would have backed down at this point, she had long since learnt when to quit; but today, possibly because she was looking forward to seeing Peter, the injustice of Joe's behaviour seemed all the more infuriating.

'Who'd blame me, Joe? I get accused of it all the time anyway. Why not do it? At least it would make all this worthwhile.'

Grabbing her long hair viciously, Joe yanked her face towards him with one hand whilst bringing the other down in a crashing blow against the side of her head. Only his grip on her hair kept her from falling to the floor. Annie winced as the pain shot through her and then cowered waiting for the next impact. Surprisingly it didn't come.

'I swear I'll kill yer, Annie, if yer so much as smile at that man, so yer just remember.'

In truth Joe was a little taken aback at Annie's defiance, it frightened him to think she might just do something. She was obviously not so afraid of him as before and he was not quite sure how to handle her new confidence. What he did know was that he would have to stamp on this new streak in her, and now, before it got out of hand. It was no bluff that he would kill any man that tried to take her from him, she was his possession and no one else could ever have her.

Inside, Joe knew he was wrong to constantly accuse her of things that she was not doing but he loved her so much that the jealousy ate away at him and left no room for reason. He knew that he was not worthy of her, but he would die without her, she was the only pure thing in his life and he would fight for that no matter what. His distorted mind did not see that he was driving her away, for he believed that the tighter he held her, the less likely she was to escape. He wished he could encase her in a glass box so that no one could touch her or talk to her but just envy him for his prize. Now he was sorry again, sorry for hurting her, he was always sorry afterwards. He decided to be especially nice to her later and then she would see that he only did these things because he loved her so much. Annie was everything, his life, his reason for living. Besides only Annie could calm the worm that lived in his head, the one his father had planted, that threatened to come alive each time he lost control of himself. She could never leave him, never in her life.

Annie sat savagely dragging the brush through her hair, tears trickling down her cheeks in salty rivers until they dripped from her chin, making a damp patch on her skirt. They were not tears of pain but frustration, as she asked herself over and over again why Joe had to be like this. She had lost count of the number of times this situation had occurred, always without reason, always ending in the same way.

Only this time was different, this time she wanted to fight back. She wanted to tell Joe that this was an attractive man, a man that she liked and admired, a man who listened to her and yes, excited her. And still she had done nothing wrong, because she was *his* wife, because she had made a promise to *him*, because despite all her unhappiness she believed that she owed him her loyalty. It was still not enough for Joe, and that was the thing that really hurt her now. He simply did not realise the sacrifice she was prepared to make for him and it was never enough. She was right when she said she might as well be unfaithful to him, what difference would it make, he believed it of her anyway and, if she was truthful, for the first time she was tempted. Over and over she asked herself why she put up with all this misery for a man that she did not love, and the answer was always the same, guilt. She knew she was responsible for his injuries, it was not his fault that she was unable to love him. When she had married him, she had lied to him and herself, so how could she ever leave him when he loved her so devotedly. This was her payment, but for the first time she wanted something for herself, her needs were overpowering now and in all this turmoil she despaired of her conscience or will power. Joe's unreasonable behaviour was all the excuse she needed to justify her own desires.

148

In truth she had thought of little other than Peter since their meeting in Liverpool. She had felt so exhilarated that day, so alive. Peter had made her feel like a woman, an attractive, intelligent human being. He took her opinions seriously, he listened to her, laughed with her, made her feel important and special and all the things that she had not felt since her walks in the woods with Richard, when he too had believed in her fire and ambition. The power was intoxicating and better still it stifled the imprisoning feeling she had with Joe, she wanted more of it, not just wanted, desired, needed.

She had written a very businesslike note to Peter asking him at his convenience to call on her and discuss the new pan. She had been careful not to give away her excitement at the prospect of seeing him or her impatience that he should reply quickly. Within days his reply had reached her, and tomorrow was the day. Annie could hardly wait. Despite strict conversations with herself that Peter Smith was far too busy and important a man to be interested in her, she could not quell the growing excitement within her as the day approached. Joe made it so easy for her to bury her conscience, but deep down she knew that she was only feigning anger at him to make things simpler for herself.

She was only human, she told herself, everyone needed excitement in their life, and so she buried the nagging voices in her head and thought only of seeing Peter tomorrow. That night she did not lie rigidly still as Joe took her body but pretended to join in, a sigh here and a groan there. She told herself that he would never know the difference and if it made him feel better, that he was somehow making up to her, why not keep him happy. Her mind was miles away – it was simply an empty shell of a body that he took.

The day dawned bright and it matched her mood. Joe had been gone for hours now and having the place to herself Annie sang as she got ready to go and meet Peter. Carefully she brushed her hair until it shone ebony black and choosing her newest gown she smiled at her own reflection in the mirror. It was nearly time to leave and the butter-flies in her stomach refused to stop their dancing. From out of nowhere her pa appeared in her mind and his face was smiling, adding his approval that his beloved daughter should have some sunshine in her life. As she left for her new pan Annie positively floated and all that zest shone from her face, making her more beautiful than ever.

The effect on Peter Smith was immediate and he could not hold back the pleasure from his smile as he greeted Annie. Together they toured the new pan and discussed the requirements and limitations. On the face of it, it was all very innocent but both knew that something more was simmering beneath the politeness and formality and when they had finished the business of the day Peter readily accepted Annie's invitation to eat lunch with her at a local café before he left for Manchester.

Billy's Café as it was called was hardly the same as tea at the Palace Hotel, but the surroundings did not seem to matter. The small room set out with tables and chairs was clean if not expensive. Each table sported a red checked cloth and matching salt and pepper pots and a single flower in a tiny glass vase. The place was popular with local office and shop workers and Annie and Peter were lucky to find one table free at the back of the shop. After studying the menu and deciding that they were both hungrier than they first imagined, especially now that they had smelt the food cooking, they ordered the home-made steak pie and potatoes. When the waitress had gone and they were once more alone, they fell easily into conversation again. Annie smiled to herself, with Peter she felt like a completely different person, and she liked the change it produced.

'Three weeks and I think we can have you in production.' Peter was rambling on still about work and Annie tried hard to concentrate on his words rather than watch his face. 'Do you have anyone in mind to run the place for you? Annie? Are you listening?'

He laughed and Annie noticed that two small dimples appeared on each cheek as his face screwed up.

'Yes, yes, I mean no I don't have anyone yet an' yes I was listenin',' she blushed at being caught out daydreaming.

Peter's face softened as he gazed at her. 'What were you thinking about?'

Momentarily she was thrown, hoping fervently that he could not read her thoughts. She felt her breath quicken as her eyes met his knowing eyes that seemed to reach into her. 'I was thinkin' that I 'ad a lovely time with yer again today,' she managed to stutter, unsure of her boldness.

'Oh Annie so have I, I love being with you.' He reached across the table and enclosed her fingers within his tenderly. 'You are very beautiful, Annie and . . .'

The waitress arrived with their lunches and Peter hastily removed his hand while Annie flushed in embarrassment unsure of what the girl had heard.

The blood pounded in Annie's ears as she tried to eat her meal calmly. But she didn't feel calm, she felt excited and scared. It was obvious now that Peter had feelings for her too, but what now? It was almost too much for her to bear. They ate silently, both of them with minds in turmoil, a fever burning inside them.

'Let's go somewhere for a walk and we can talk,' Peter suggested.

Hurriedly paying the bill, they left like two children about to commence an adventure into the unknown.

Silently they walked away from the shops towards the park, Peter linking her arm into his as he had in Liverpool. Annie felt the same tingle of excitement as she felt the strength of his muscles through his sleeve. Inside her head Joe's face kept floating round and round and guilt began to seep through her, drowning the new, exciting feelings that bubbled. Finding an empty seat Peter drew Annie down next to him and as if in a dream she found her lips pressed against him. The sensation was delicious and Annie melted against his body unashamedly for a second, forgetting everything but the moment.

Joe's voice crept ominously in to spoil the dream reminding her she was his wife, and abruptly Annie pulled away.

'What's wrong, Annie?' Peter's voice was hurt at her sudden rejection of him.

'This is wrong. Oh Peter there's something I haven't told yer.' Annie bowed her head in shame and continued, 'I'm married, I'm a married woman. I'm so sorry Peter, I should never have encouraged yer, please forgive me.'

Desperately she searched his face for a reaction.

'Why didn't you tell me?' His voice was level, not angry or sad, just monotone and it added to Annie's misery.

'I couldn't. I knew you'd probably not have come today an' I wanted to see yer. I love bein' with yer an' I enjoyed our tea in Liverpool so much I just wanted to do it again.' Annie hung her head dejectedly. 'I've spoiled everythin'.'

She was right, the day was spoiled and a strained silence hung between them, both feeling awkward and unsure what to do next. Peter did not feel any different about her but he assumed that she now wanted to stop this before it went any further and so he must respect her wishes. Annie was thrown into confusion and was sure that he must now have no respect for her and could probably not wait to leave.

'If yer don't want to do the work fer me I'll quite understand,' she said quietly.

'Don't be silly, of course I'll do the work. My men will be here first thing next week. We are still friends aren't we?' He smiled kindly. The relief was enormous and Annie gratefully smiled back. 'Let's just start again and forget any of this happened, that way no harm's done.'

'Can we do that, Peter, are yer sure?' She felt like a child being given a second chance and she grasped at it.

'I really should leave now, let's just part friends.' Peter knew he was being slightly pompous but strange feelings of disappointment swirled around inside him and this was as gracious as he could manage to be.

Stiffly kissing her hand with nothing more than courteous etiquette he left her and strode off in the direction of the railway station.

Annie made no attempt to accompany him, but stayed alone on the bench whilst she tried to regain her composure. There it was gone, she thought bitterly, a few hours of tantalising enjoyment, one kiss and a lot of daydreaming for nothing. Well, what did she expect, nothing could ever have come of it, she began to chastise herself for being a very stupid woman, for chasing impossible rainbows. All she had achieved was to embarrass Peter and make a complete fool of herself. Now she was back to the reality of her life, back to Joe. The thought of Joe made her shudder, she knew he would interrogate her the minute she got home, wanting to know every detail of the day, trying to somehow catch her out. Only this time she would have to lie, this time she really had done something wrong and all for nothing. She turned her head skywards and misery washed over her.

Would God forgive her? She began one of her conversations with him, her words spoken silently in her head. No replies came and so she knew she had angered him too. Her soul cried for his help, begged for some guidance, some pity. Her prayers fell on deaf ears and she concluded that was all she deserved, God would speak to her when he was ready and not before. Resolutely Annie dragged herself to her feet and stumbled blindly in the direction of home, she could have caught the tram but she didn't want to speed the journey up and so decided to walk the whole distance and give herself time to calm down before facing her husband.

'All sorted out?' Joe's voice greeted her as she entered the cottage door.

Annie sighed, here we go, she thought.

'Yes, the work's bein' started next week, the pan should be workin' inside a month,' she chirped in her most cheery voice.

'No more meetings, then?'

'No, no more meetings, Joe.'

'Good. 'Ow about some tea then? It's past six.'

She pulled her apron around her waist. She wasn't hungry at all but Joe liked tea on the table at six o'clock and any deviation usually caused a row, or worse if he was feeling particularly bad tempered. As she stood at the stone sink preparing the potatoes, she sensed Joe creeping up behind her and immediately assumed that some kind of blow would rain down on her at any second. Her mind raced. Perhaps he had followed her today and seen her with Peter, or someone else had seen them and rushed to tell him. Her guilty conscience consumed her and turning on her heel to try and prevent what she thought was an inevitable punishment, she cried out to him.

'Please Joe, don't.'

His look was one of astonishment, for far from punishing her for some crime he knew nothing about, he was going to hug her and tell her how sorry he was for not trusting her. Her reaction humbled him further and the fear in her eyes melted him.

'Oh Annie love, don't look so afraid. I'm just a big ignorant lump who doesn't deserve yer,' and clasping her to his chest he buried his face in her hair.

A tortured cry ripped through Annie's body which she barely managed to stifle before it escaped from her guilt-ridden lips. Holding Joe to her she gently rocked him back and forth, none of this was his fault she thought, it's all mine. It seemed all the more ironic that the one time she would have felt she deserved a beating she didn't get one and she was almost sorry. Later that night as Joe grunted and groaned his sweaty body against her, she tried with all her might not to give in to the feelings of disgust and repulsion. Her intentions were as usual overridden by her horror and she chanted over and over in her head the same words to block out the ordeal of Joe's lovemaking. 'Please finish, please finish, please finish.' And when he finally did she said a silent thank-you prayer and turned her face away from him so that his hot breath no longer touched her skin. She drifted into fitful sleep, the monsters of guilt and desire rampaging through her dreams giving her no release or rest.

The next day in his plush office in Manchester, Peter

Smith sat at his desk thinking of Annie. He was angry, not with Annie but with himself. He had, even by his standards, handled the whole situation badly, but then Annie was no ordinary run of the mill lady, and therefore this problem required some delicate manoeuvres. He had desired Annie the minute he had laid eyes on her in Liverpool, and he was a man used to getting what he wanted. But this was not like one of his usual affairs, where he would meet some pretty girl, and a few drinks later seduce her and then probably never see her again. No, Annie was different, he could talk to her and enjoy her company, in fact he couldn't get her out of his mind which was irritating him immensely. Any other woman he would have written off now as a bad idea, but not Annie.

He smiled to himself at her naïvety. Perhaps that was part of her charm. Did she seriously think that being married would stop his desire for her? In fact it had the reverse effect, making her more elusive and therefore more enchanting. He had not told her that he was married himself, with three children; what would have been the point? it had borne no part in affecting his affairs before, why should it this time?

He drummed his fingers impatiently on the table whilst considering what to do next. Annie obviously had a conscience, but that only made her more of a challenge. He decided he would leave it for a few weeks, let her stew on it all and then he would surprise her with a visit to inspect the new pan. That would be the time he would make another move. He licked his lips in anticipation. One thing was sure: if Peter Smith set his sights on a woman, he got her, and he was determined that Annie would be no exception.

# Seventeen

'**D**ecided to come an' see yer mother, then?' Elizabeth sat hunched by the oven range in the draughty kitchen of her home. Her face was contorted with bitterness as she spoke. Life seemed to have dealt her with a very raw deal, one to which in her mind her daughter contributed.

'I was 'ere yesterday, just like I'm 'ere every day to see if yer all right.' Annie sighed trying very hard not to become irritated by this woman who seemed to do nothing but complain.

'The fire needs stokin' an' I need some things from the grocer, if you've time,' Elizabeth whined pitifully.

Annie ignored her and busied herself tidying the kitchen, clearing the dirty pots that Jack had simply left in the sink. Glancing at her mother she was struck by how old she looked. This wasn't helped by her continual drinking, for her skin had taken on a yellow dullness, her eyes were a colourless grey. She did no more these days than rise from her bed each day to sit by the kitchen range and drink throughout the day before returning to bed again. Annie thought she looked dirty and wondered how long it had been since she had washed. Her mother was becoming more and more of a problem. Occasionally now she would have bruises on her face and legs where she had fallen in her drunken states. The whole thing was a huge sick game, for even though it was Annie who brought the brandy or gin for her mother, Elizabeth would hide the bottles, drinking furtively when she thought no one was looking. Many times

156

Annie had tried to deny her mother alcohol but then she would fly into terrible rages, abusing her daughter and flinging herself into hysterical fits, demanding that she needed the drink for medical reasons and that Annie was killing her. Annie would always give in and go to the shop for the liquor, telling herself it was too late to do anything, her mother was an alcoholic and she would just have to accept that. Now, looking at the wizened face and hunched shoulders, she could see quite clearly that her mother was simply drinking herself to death. She tried her to feel pity or sympathy but she could feel nothing. All her life her mother had driven her away, denied her any love or affection, and having systematically destroyed that love it could never be replaced. What Annie felt was an obligation, a duty, nothing more. She could not bring herself to even touch Elizabeth and had never kissed her once in her entire life.

Every day she came and fulfilled what was necessary for her, hating every minute she had to spend in the tiny house. She had nothing but bad memories of her time spent there and the moment she walked through the door she was counting the minutes until she left. The future brought only worse nightmares, for Annie could see that soon Elizabeth would not be fit to be left alone, she was already trying to make Annie feel so guilty that she would take her back to live with her in the cottage. Jack was never in, only using the place as somewhere to eat and sleep, and even in her befuddled state Elizabeth was astute enough to constantly bring pressure on Annie reminding her of her duty and responsibility as a daughter.

'Jack says that you've bought another salt pan,' Elizabeth commented as Annie cleaned around her.

'Yes, over at Lowerwych,' Annie replied curtly, knowing some snide remark was bound to follow. Elizabeth could never forgive Annie that Edward had left her the pan and every success that Annie achieved after that only seemed to deepen the injustice of her son's denied birthright.

'You'll end up with nothin' if you keep gettin' greedier

an' greedier. Jack says this one's a real run down place an' you must want your 'ead feeling.'

'Yes Mother, if yer say so,' Annie sighed. It was not worth arguing about, her mother only ever saw one point of view and that was never Annie's.

'It's not just you to think of, Jack's entitled to a say in things as well.'

'Yes, Mother.' Annie's head buzzed, the same old arguments went round and around. 'Jack's foreman, he does have a say an' I pay 'im well, you're not short of anythin' are yer?'

'That's not the point, he has rights, rights that you've taken away.' This was Elizabeth's favourite subject and she never tired of rowing about it.

Annie remained silent, knowing nothing she said would stop her mother's ranting.

'Drive 'im away yer will, just like Edward drove away my Luke an' then what will I have?' Tears of self-pity slid down the wrinkled cheeks.

Annie was unmoved, she had heard it all before, until she was sick of hearing it. 'I'm off now, dinner's in the oven, I'll call later with yer shopping.'

She knew she sounded hard and unfeeling but it was the only way to deal with Elizabeth. As she closed the door Elizabeth muttered a comment that she was just like her father. Thank God for that, Annie thought as she walked down the street, and that familiar ache she had never lost over not having Edward in her life anymore sent a stabbing pain through her heart. If only he were still here this would all be so much easier to bear.

Annie's deep unhappiness weighed her body down with unbearable persistence and she could see no escape from her dreary life. It was ironical, she thought, that even though she could not bear spending time with her mother, she was sometimes so desperate to be away from Joe that she couldn't wait to escape from the cottage, using her mother as the excuse. No sooner had she got there than she couldn't wait to leave. It seemed the only enjoyable part was the walk from one house to the other, a walk she prolonged as much as she could.

She had tried to drive Peter Smith from her mind ever since that dreadful day in the park, but it was not easy. She longed for his smile, for the light-heartedness of his company. He shone like a light for her in an otherwise very black world. She knew nothing could ever happen, but just the memory of the possibilities excited her. He had shown her another world, and that tantalising bite of freedom was hard to shake off.

She knew also that she would probably never see him again; in a couple of days his men would have finished work in the new shed, and then once she had paid her bill she would have no excuse to contact him further. That left her with Joe, and she was beginning to despise him completely, she couldn't bear him touching her and now even his voice and mannerisms agitated her so much that sitting in the same room as him drove her crazy. As she walked along the pavement she asked herself over and over what she was going to do, but no answers came, the pain only deepened, as the realisation dawned that she was totally trapped in her narrow world.

There were no escapes, no happy endings here; she knew she would somehow have to make the best of it.

Four days later Annie stood in her new shed and watched with satisfaction as the steam rose from the bubbling vat. She had employed four men to work the pan for her and if it yielded as much salt as she hoped, she had already decided that she could afford to look for a larger house to live in. At least she reasoned that would give her a renewed interest for a while; and there were other reasons. If she lived a little further away from the pans it would not be so simple for Joe to keep popping home unexpectedly. She felt like a prisoner when he constantly came checking up on her, timing how long she was at her mother's, watching her every move. If she was late returning from town for some reason there were always rows about where she had been and what she had been doing. This way she might at least gain a little freedom. Even her visiting the new pan today had caused a row for Joe could not bear for her to be out of his sight and control. Every new situation was a threat to him and his reactions were as always violent and uncontrolled.

Despite that, Annie was here, and enjoying every minute of her new acquisition. She relished the sense of her achievement, here she had really done something and it felt wonderful. To an outsider Annie's position would have seemed quite ludicrous. She was a successful businesswoman, with a thriving company. She had the means and resources to simply leave Joe and support herself completely, and yet she stayed. She stayed in that misery because she couldn't see that she had a choice, bound by unbreakable ties of guilt and duty, of insecurity and fear. Annie was as good as a prisoner, she could not see any feasible route of escape. It was unthinkable to her that she would be strong enough to stand alone against Joe and her mother and Jack. After all she was only Annie Hayes. They all owned a piece of her and she didn't have the courage to fight that all alone.

'Well, you did it, then.'

Peter's voice jolted her from her daydreaming, and the familiar sound of him sent shivers of excitement up her spine. She spun around to face him, trepidation in her heart. She wasn't sure how he would feel about her now and his appearance was a total surprise. The smile on his face reassured her and she beamed back.

'What are you doing here?' she cried unable to contain her delight.

'I had to come and check that everything was fine,' he lied, smiling warmly at her.

'Well as yer can see it is, everythin's just fine.'

'Perhaps I can take a look around and check that the men have done all that they should have.'

'Of course.' Annie felt an awkwardness come over her, she knew she was being silly to imagine that Peter could be here for any other reason than business, especially after what had happened. 'I'll leave yer to it, then,' she said and backed into the doorway that led into a small room that she planned to use as an office.

'I'll give you a call when I've finished.' His voice was light and cheery and Annie closed the door hurriedly as the colour washed over her face.

Sitting behind the table in the room she tried to control her quickened breathing, chastising herself for her reactions, after all she had already made enough of a fool of herself over Peter. There was a tiny window, streaked with dust and grime, that looked out from the room over the rest of the shed and through the grime Annie watched Peter as he went about his checking. She could hear her heart beating loudly in her chest when he removed his jacket and rolling up his sleeves in the fierce heat, revealed his large muscled arms. Annie remembered the sensation of her hand resting on his sleeve and she shivered involuntarily. She was drawn to him like a magnet, studying his every feature, he exuded strength and a physical force that left her breathless. The voices in her head kept telling her to stop this nonsense, but the rest of her body ignored them and she sat mesmerised.

When he eventually finished he strode jauntily towards the office door, wiping the sweat from his brow. Annie hurriedly picked up some papers in front of her, she certainly didn't want him to think she had been staring at him all this time. He knocked and entered before she had time to speak, breezing into the room and perching himself on the edge of the table.

'It all seems to be in order.'

'Good. I'm sure you needn't have gone to all the trouble of comin' 'ere.' Annie hoped her voice wasn't betraying the horde of butterflies that danced in her stomach.

'Of course I had to come, I couldn't keep away from you.' Peter moved closer towards her. Aware that the men working in the shed were all watching and listening to this conversation Annie blushed and moved towards the door to close it.

161

'I think yer teasin' me, which I probably deserve,' she almost whispered, her heart pounding.

Peter's boyish smile spread across his face and taking her hand he bowed, kissing it in mock reverence. 'Would I tease you, my most beautiful customer?' His laugh was deep and throaty.

Annie knew he was flirting outrageously but it made her feel so good she could not help but join in the game. 'Well, I suppose yer treat all yer customers like this until they've paid, but yer needn't worry, I can afford your services,' she giggled.

'I haven't even given you a bill yet, and when I do there are certain provisions with it that will affect the price.' His face was inches from her now and his warm breath caressed her cheek making her feel heady.

'Really? an' what conditions would they be?'

'Well, in order to get the full discount you have to come to Manchester to pay me in person. Over lunch, of course.'

Annie jolted herself away from him, what did she think she was doing, playing such dangerous games. 'I can't Peter, yer know why,' her voice was soft, almost apologetic.

But Peter Smith had done his homework on Annie. It hadn't taken long to find out that she was married to one of her workers, better still it was common knowledge that she had only married him out of sympathy, for some accident she thought was her fault. He smiled to himself, that was typical of her, always putting herself last. Even better, the gossip reliably said that she was unhappy, and that was all he needed to know. She was as good as his. This, he thought, was going to be easy.

Taking her hands in his, Peter gazed into her eyes, deep black pools that fascinated and excited him. Mentally he chastised himself, he mustn't go too fast here and scare her away but it was impossible to be so close to her and not feel the excitement flood through his groin.

'Annie, tell me something, truthfully. Do you love your husband, are you really happy?' He did not let her answer but placed his finger against her lips and continued. 'I know

162

you're not, Annie, I can see it written in those beautiful eyes. I'm just asking you to lunch, that's all. We get along fine, don't we, enjoy being together, what harm is there in that? You are entitled to a little enjoyment in life and as long as no one gets hurt, why not? Life is too short to be miserable.'

He knew he was winning, her face had softened and she did not try to take her hands from his but let them lie limply enclosed. Nearly there he thought, the adrenalin buzzing in his blood, this was the part he loved most, the chase. 'Who will know? You can quite easily go to town on business, and you will be, partly. You are a good customer and I extend the courtesy of lunch to my best customers. There, does that ease your conscience?'

She smiled, he made it sound so easy and innocent.

'Go on, for once do something you want to do, and you do, don't you?'

She nodded in child-like fascination.

'That's settled, then. Next Friday, nice and early and we can really enjoy the day.'

On that winning note he breezed out of the office, as he had come in. Annie felt as if a whirlwind had stirred her insides up and she watched him walk away spellbound. The voices in her head had already won. He was right – why shouldn't she have some enjoyment, what harm would it do, it was just lunch. Joe owned most of her life and she stayed with him, despite the things he did to her. Just once she would have some freedom, some fun. She felt full of excitement and hope that she could have done anything. She smiled broadly as she left the shed and made her way home, at last there was some sunshine in her life. She wallowed in its power and warmth, feeling indestructible.

All afternoon Annie rehearsed the speech in her head, she knew exactly what she was going to say to Joe, she had answers prepared for every question and explanations for every difficulty he would invent. She actually sang as she cooked the stew, it was his favourite; it was worth it getting him in a good mood before she broke the news about her

163

Friday excursion. Nothing was going to stop her doing this, she had already decided that. She liked this new strength and determination she felt. She had forgotten that this was really just being herself, the person she used to be, before Joe had suffocated her.

By the time Joe returned home the table was set with a clean white cloth, a vase of flowers nestled in the centre and the smell of rich dark bubbling stew wafted through the warm cottage kitchen.

'I'm starvin'. What's fer tea?' His face was clouded with irritation.

'Get a wash then, it's all ready. It's stew.' Annie smiled, ignoring his frowning glare.

'Again? Is that all we live on?'

She sighed, aware now that this was going to be difficult after all. 'It's yer favourite, that's why I made it.' Joe grunted and rinsed his hands under the cold tap. At the table he held his head in his hands and then angrily jolted himself upright.

'Yer got a bad head again, I'll make yer a warm herb drink, that'll make yer feel better.'

'I don't want one, I'm fine. Just get me tea on the table,' he snapped, picking up his knife and fork in readiness.

Annie stood with her back to him serving up the stew on his plate. She bit her lip. Should she say something now or wait till he'd eaten? Maybe better to get it over and done with and then the food would take his mind off it. Swallowing hard, she swung around and producing her sweetest smile placed the plate before him and then sat opposite with her own meal.

Her stomach tangled in knots as she watched him start to eat. Nervously she pushed her meat around the plate trying to form the right words in her mouth, and taking a deep breath she blurted out as casually as she could manage, that she needed to go into Manchester next Friday to see the bank manager. Silence hung on the air deafeningly when she had stopped speaking and she dared not raise her eyes to meet his. For what seemed like a lifetime Joe said nothing, and then, scraping his chair across the floor in screeching sound that jangled Annie's nerves, he rose to his feet.

'This stew's got gristle in it.'

Annie was startled, this was not what she had expected. 'It's the best meat, I bought it especially.'

'It's shit, like everythin' yer give me. I am not eating shit.' Holding the plate high in the air Joe swung it around his head and flung it with all his might against the wall. The stew stuck momentarily before sliding down in brown lumpy blobs.

Annie sat rigidly in her chair, fear mixed with rage, pounding through her.

'Don't just sit there, get me somethin' else, woman.' Joe's eyes were almost bulging out of his head and as he spoke saliva spat from his lips.

Slowly and deliberately Annie rose to her feet and made her way to the stove and a pan half full of soup left over from yesterday. Placing the pan over the heat she began to slice off some large chunks of bread. She was silent; the only thing in her mind was that she was going to Manchester whatever it took.

Joe watched her, drumming his fingers impatiently on the table, his agitation clearly rising as each minute passed.

Without meeting his eyes Annie placed the steaming bowl of soup before him and waited.

'Is this it?' Joe slapped the spoon into the liquid, slopping it all over the table.

Gritting her teeth to contain her anger Annie answered quietly, 'It's soup, Joe, an' there's nothin' wrong with it.'

'Nothin' wrong! I've been at work all day an' I come 'ome to shit an' soup.' He was on his feet again leaning across the table toward her. 'If you'd been here all day where yer should've been, instead of out at that shed doin' who knows what, I'd have a decent tea.'

Annie's temper got the better of her and she did just what she knew she shouldn't, she shouted back. 'We're back to this are we. I go out to work, to our shed, that will make us money and yer just can't stand it, can yer, Joe. Yer sick, yer know that, sick.'

He reached for the soup and before Annie could duck out of the way the boiling liquid splattered her bare arm as the bowl flew through the air, crashing just behind her to join the remains of the stew congealing on the floor. She screamed as her burnt skin stung in the air and racing to the tap she pushed her arm under the cold water.

'When yer've cleaned up in 'ere I'll have somethin' proper for me tea an' maybe yer'll learn to do as yer told, an' then I wouldn't need to punish yer.' There was no remorse in Joe's voice as he stared at her with a look of sheer contempt on his face. 'An' forget goin' to Manchester next week, yer place is here where I can keep an eye on yer.'

Inside Annie seethed, she knew if she carried this argument on she would only end up with a beating, but injustice bubbled within her. After all, she had done nothing wrong. She almost began to believe that she really was only going to see the bank manager, for in truth, if she had been, Joe's reaction would have been no different.

'I don't care what yer do to me Joe, hit me, beat me, what does it matter. But I am goin' to Manchester an' what's more you can't stop me.' Tears coursed down her cheeks as she sobbed out the words.

The look of shock on Joe's face at her defiance was soon drowned out by rage and his hand crashed down through the air, sending her flying against the table. She collapsed on the floor, weeping.

'Don't yer ever talk to me like that again or I swear I'll kill yer.'

Kicking his boot into her ribs just for good measure he stamped out of the door and left her alone. Annie dragged herself to her feet, the burn on her arm had now risen into an angry red weal that stung unbearably. Soaking a tea towel in water, she wrapped it tightly around, to try and bring some relief. Crying with anger and humiliation she slammed and banged the pots as she cleared up all the mess and as

166

she did she kept repeating in her head, 'I 'ate yer, Joe, I 'ate yer.'

It made her feel no better, she knew he would be back in an hour or so, and once he had calmed down he would be sorry again, but what did that mean or matter. One thing was certain, come hell or high water she was going to see Peter and if it cost her a beating so be it; it would be worth it.

Three hours later, Joe crawled sheepishly into bed beside her, once again full of remorse for his temper. Reaching out he slid his fingers along her thigh and felt her shudder at his touch. He knew she hated this, but he needed her body and he believed if she would only learn to relax and enjoy him, things would be so much better. As he climbed on top of her and entered her unwilling body, she turned her face sharply into the pillow, making it impossible for him to kiss her. It didn't matter. She excited him enough that even when she lay rigidly still, he could climax easily, and within minutes he withdrew quickly from her making sure his seed would not impregnate her, totally oblivious to her groan of disgust as the warm slime slid down her stomach onto the bed.

# Eighteen

During the whole of the next week Annie's excursion to Manchester was not spoken about once. Joe presumed that she had forgotten the whole idea and Annie had decided the best thing was simply not to mention it, but just go anyway and face Joe's wrath afterwards. Nor were the burns or bruises referred to. Joe always chose to ignore the things he did to her and that way they seemed less significant, it was almost as if in his mind they had never happened.

However, just because they did not talk about it did not mean that Annie had forgotten it all. A festering bitterness was growing within her and she found each bout of violence against her more difficult to accept. She was far less willing to shoulder the blame now, less ready to always be the guilty wife, and instead of trying desperately to make up with Joe each time they argued, just to break the terrible silences he punished her with, she now ignored him. Surprisingly, his tantrums rather than lasting longer, actually started to subside more quickly when he found he was having no effect on her.

It was not until Thursday night when they had gone to bed that the subject reared its head again, much to Annie's distress. Joe had lain quietly by her side for some minutes and she was just sighing in relief that he did not want her body, when he suddenly spoke.

'I think yer should come down to the shed tomorrow an'

check the batch of salt ready fer shippin'. The gradin's not as good, but see what yer think.'

Her heart jolted. Normally it would have been quite in order for her to do just that. Joe never questioned her superiority at work, even though he was sometimes bitter about the fact that she was the owner and he was merely a worker. It was a silent agreement between them that where work was concerned Annie was the boss, but none of this spilt into their private life.

'I can't tomorrow. Have yer forgotten, I'm goin' to Manchester.' Despite fighting to keep her voice steady Annie trembled inside.

'I thought we'd agreed yer weren't goin',' Joe replied, his voice taking on an icy edge.

'No Joe. You agreed. I didn't. I've an appointment an' I have to go. Please don't let's argue about it.'

She rolled towards him and squeezed his arm, hoping to cajole him out of rapidly approaching temper.

Joe, far from being soothed, snatched his arm away angrily. 'Don't think that yer can get round me like that. I've forbidden yer to go an' that's an end to it.'

Annie lay silently for a moment whilst she considered what to do. She could simply ignore him and when he had left for work in the morning go, without telling him. But she knew him too well, there was no way he would let her out of his sight for a minute. He would probably insist that she went to work with him and then she would never be able to escape. No, she knew she had to make her stand now whatever the consequences.

'It's no good, whatever yer say I'm goin'.' Her voice sounded far more in control than she felt.

'I've said . . .' His voice had real menace in it.

'Yer just bein' silly, yer know I've to see people, bank managers, solicitors, buyers. Please try to be reasonable, please, Joe.' She knew she had lost, for the moment she began to plead, Joe thought he had won and it was signal for him to reinforce his power.

In one swift move he had her pinned to the bed, his hands

cutting down into her wrists stopping the blood supply. She wriggled helplessly beneath him, trying to free her hands, which throbbed painfully.

'Yer'll do as yer told Annie, or I'll just have to teach yer to be a good girl.'

His eyes shone malevolently and Annie knew he enjoyed this, this was his supreme moment, to control and humiliate her. Normally she would have submitted to save herself a beating but tonight the laughter in his eyes stirred a new defiance in her.

'It doesn't matter what yer do or say, I'm goin'. Go on hit me, I don't care.' Her voice rose higher and higher and she laughed hysterically.

Thunder crossed his enraged face and he crashed an arm down against her face. Annie was not for submitting, not this time, and she fought cat-like with her free arm scratching her nails across his cheek. For minutes they struggled, Annie biting and kicking whilst Joe tried to hold down the thrashing creature beneath him. Only when he placed his hands around her throat and squeezed until the breath was forced from her did Annie relent. Coughing and choking, she allowed her arms to drop, and lay perfectly still.

The sweat was pouring from Joe's face and he licked his lips to moisten them. He never knew Annie could be such a wild cat and her resistance had evoked a new anger in him that had taken him aback. As he had tightened his fingers around her small white throat, for a split second he had lost all control and the desire to kill her had washed over him. This had been just as quickly replaced by a feeling of panic that he could think such things.

Annie's eyes held his, shining, unblinking, and a look of sheer hatred and contempt swept across her face. 'I will go, an' short of killin' me yer can't stop me.'

For a second they were locked in a battle of eye contact before Joe relented and pushed himself to his feet to tower over her. 'Very well, go an' I'll come with yer.' With that he stamped out of the room.

Annie heard the front door slam. She knew he wouldn't

170

return for hours for he often took himself off for solitary walks if he couldn't just get his own way. She dragged herself to a sitting position on the bed and rubbed her throat, it was sore already and no doubt tomorrow would be bruised. Inside she was shaking, for with all her bravado Joe had frightened her. Never before had he tried to strangle her and for a split second, she had seen that strange look in his eye, and wondered if he were going to stop squeezing his fingers together.

She was cold, and wrapped herself in the blanket, rocking back and forth like a child to give herself some comfort. She groaned as she recalled his parting words. Now what should she do? She would have to go. What if he insisted on coming into the bank with her, worse, what if Peter was waiting at the station to meet her? The stark and terrible possibilities raced through her mind, until she lost all control and scenes of Joe strangling Peter flashed before her eyes. This was all her fault, why couldn't she just have said no to Peter, why did she always want what she couldn't have?

She wanted to pray but it wasn't worth it, how could God help her, when she had brought this all on herself. She wanted her pa to be there to comfort her and tell her what to do but what could he have said? No one could put this right and she allowed herself half an hour of indulging in self-pity before the Annie Hayes practicality took over and she began to make a plan of just what to do.

If she could persuade Joe to wait outside the bank for her, it would be easy. She would simply go in and ask if she could speak to the manager; if she was lucky he would see her and she could discuss the buying of a new property with him and no one would be any the wiser. It would probably be quite easy as Joe felt intimidated in official buildings and he certainly could not cope with talking to a bank manager. He would be quite happy to stand guard outside. If she could not see the manager, she would just have to try and loiter around in the bank foyer until sufficient time had passed to fool Joe. The worst possibility was if they bumped into Peter. But she knew if that happened she would simply

171

have to pretend it was a coincidence and hope that once she had introduced Peter to her husband, he would join in the charade of an accidental meeting.

She sighed as she lay down pulling the covers up to her ears. What a mess this all was. She told herself that if by some miracle she managed to get away with this she would never do anything wrong again. She knew the best thing she could do was to try and get some sleep, but it was impossible and she tossed and restlessly turned for hours.

Some time in the middle of the night she was aware of Joe sliding into bed next to her. She immediately lay rigidly still until she heard his breathing slow down and fall into rhythmical snoring, before she dared move again, and then she counted the hours until dawn.

She dressed in silence, being careful not to look too dressed up but smart enough for the business she was supposed to be on. Automatically she made the breakfast for Joe, serving it up to him without looking directly at his face or making any conversation. There was no point in further arguments this morning, everything that needed to be said had been said. After he had finished eating, she cleared and washed the pots and then without a word gathered up her cloak to leave the house.

The walk to the station seemed endless. She kept going straight ahead, never turning back though she was perfectly aware that some ten yards behind her trailed a very dejected-looking Joe.

As she paid for her ticket her stomach churned and sheepishly she stood on the platform willing the train to hurry up. Eventually she heard the familiar chuffing in the distance and she breathed a sigh of relief. Joe stood by her side, his face dark and grim, staring at the track as if he could somehow make it disappear. Only when the smoke from the oncoming train could be seen whisking across the sky did he speak and so quietly that it was almost a whisper.

'Don't go, Annie.'

His eyes were pleading and for a second she felt that he knew exactly what she was doing today. Guilt swept through

172

her and his pathetic face moved her to pity, she was almost swayed, until the bruises on her neck reminded her of what Joe really was.

She didn't answer him and he took this as a denial. Instantly the sadness left his face to be replaced with that fearful arrogance that Annie hated. 'If yer go I'll kill yer,' he spat.

The train pulled to a standstill on the platform, steam and smoke gushing from it, whilst it took its momentary rest before pulling off again. Annie boarded the train and looked around expecting to see Joe behind her, he wasn't there and only when she sat down did she spot him on the platform, staring after her, his face distorted with rage.

Her heart skipped a beat as she realised that he wasn't going to board the train. She had won, she was free and her spirit soared. As the train pulled away, she held the image of him in her head, and suddenly he seemed quite insignificant. After all he hadn't stopped her, he couldn't stop her, she could do just as she pleased. When she got home she knew there would be a row, maybe a black eye or worse, but at this moment none of that mattered, for she was free. Leaning back on her seat she closed her eyes. This was just her first victory and it felt very sweet.

'There's a lady in reception to see you Mr Smith, an Annie Hayes.'

'Ah send her in. Thank you.'

The secretary smiled. She was well used to a long stream of women passing through the office, and from the gleam in Peter Smith's eye this was obviously the latest one. Still, none of her business, as long as he didn't try it on with her. If he did she'd give him what for, boss or no boss.

'You can go in, Mrs Hayes.' Miss Stot smiled sweetly, holding open the office door while Annie nervously stepped through to be greeted by Peter's grinning face. She didn't know why she had called herself Hayes, rather than Jenkins which was her married name. Somehow it just didn't seem right to use that name today.

173

'Annie, come in and sit down.'

'Coffee, Mr Smith?' Miss Stot hovered in the doorway.

'No thank you, we will be leaving shortly.'

Miss Stot smiled knowingly and closed the door, pausing on the other side to see if she could catch any of the conversation, but it was too muffled and so disappointed she returned to her desk.

'It's a little early for lunch, isn't it?' Annie asked.

'Ah, well, we're not exactly going for lunch just yet,' Peter smiled, melting Annie with his charm.

'What exactly are we doin', then?' She just could not help this wonderful floating feeling she felt every time she was with him.

'It's a surprise. Come on, let's go.'

Before she knew it he had her hand in his and was whisking her from the office and into a carriage outside.

'Platt Fields, driver,' he called and sat grinning like a schoolboy next to her.

'Have you been brave, Annie?' His blue eyes pierced into her.

'Yes I have,' she laughed, 'and you'll never know 'ow brave comin' 'ere today.'

'Good. In that case you deserve a treat and today you're going to have one. We're going to the fair. Would you like that?'

Annie felt like a little girl and excitement stirred within her.

'The fair,' she repeated, eyes like saucers.

'Yes, today is the Manchester Show and we are going to have a good time and you are going to smile that beautiful smile all day long.'

Reaching across he kissed her cheek and on touching her skin felt that familiar rush of excitement run through him again.

Annie shuddered too, there was no feeling of revulsion as there was when Joe kissed her, rather tremors of excitement that tingled through her. Inside she glowed and instead of moving away from Peter's body that leaned against

174

hers, she allowed herself to relax against him. Today, she thought, is my day and I'm going to enjoy it.

As they approached Platt Fields Annie could see the rows and rows of marquees, flags flying in the August breeze, carriages queued up to enter the gateway and already there was a faint sound of a band practising in the distance. The place buzzed with activity, people stood in lines waiting for the gates to open, families with children in their Sunday best jumping up and down excitedly, lovers arm in arm, everyone laughing and joyous, anticipating their great day out.

The Manchester Show was a big event, farmers, traders, merchants, all travelled from miles around to exhibit their goods. There were cattle prizes and dog shows, sheepdog trials and sheep shearing competitions. All around the ground the noise of penned animals wafted through the air. The shire horses were being combed and groomed before having their brasses and head dresses attached and being put through their paces to practise for the display. Men laughed and joked with one another as they put the final touches to their displays of tools and machinery, huge threshing machines coughed and chugged into action, potato pickers and hay balers worked away. The massive traction engines, gleaming and winking in their polished paintwork, blew their whistles and puffed out billowy smoke to signal the start of the show.

Into this intoxicating atmosphere Peter and Annie submerged themselves, drinking in all the sights and sounds and smells, racing from one attraction to the next like children afraid to slow down or miss anything. By lunch time the whole five acres of field was heaving with people. Peter held Annie's hand so that they did not get separated in the crowd and as it felt the most natural thing in the world she did not try to retract it from his grip.

'Come on, let's find a tea tent and have some lunch,' he yelled above the sound of the band that was playing in the arena in front of them.

Annie dragged her eyes away from the troupe of dancers

175

that performed to the music, marching perfectly throwing their batons with precision in the air. They fascinated her and she was daydreaming of herself in the Indian dress floating to the beautiful melody.

'Come on, you can't stand there all day.' He laughed and as he did, his eyes twinkling, she was suddenly struck with just how handsome he was. She blushed at her thoughts and as if he could read them he squeezed her hand gently. The food in the tent smelt delectable and they feasted on fresh crusty bread, still warm and delicious, huge chunks of crumbly white Cheshire cheese, with pickles and gherkins, scones dripping with fresh strawberry jam and cream and mugs of steaming tea. Annie was amazed to find how easy it was to relax and be herself with him. He respected her ideas and views, he treated her as an equal, not a creature to be yelled at and controlled. He was like a breath of fresh air to her and she blossomed before him, unafraid to express herself and her opinions.

By the time the afternoon came and they were strolling amongst the flowers in the horticultural tent, she had been transformed before his eyes from the nervous unsure creature that had crept into his office that morning, to the beautiful intelligent woman he knew she was. He was captivated by her and she in turn felt she was adrift on some magical carpet. They found a seat amongst the roses, the heady smell hung on the warm air inside the humid tent, and they sat drinking in the nectar silently. Annie closed her eyes and throwing her head back she allowed her hair to cascade down in black undulating waves, creating a startling contrast to the delicate pink blossoms that brushed against her. The vision stirred passion within Peter and, unable to resist her any longer, he leant across and gently caressed her lips with his. Within seconds she was enfolded in his arms, her body moulded against his; she abandoned herself fully to his lips, frantically returning his kisses with passion she had never felt before.

'Annie, you are so beautiful, I just can't resist you.' Peter's voice was deep and husky. Placing her fingers to his lips, she wrapped her arms around him and held him to her, emotions flooding over her.

'Let's go for a walk, there's a wood over to the far side of the field, at least we can be alone.' Hand in hand they walked, away from the crowds, no words passed between them, they were simply lost in each other's presence.

The August sun shone down brightly, the ground was hard and dry, and finding a grassy bank among the trees they sank to the floor. They were out of sight of the crowds, secluded in the leafy dell. As they fell to the floor Peter gently pushed Annie beneath him, his lips sought hers and soon they were lost again. Annie trembled at his touch, her body ached for him to explore her and as his fingers deftly undid the buttons on her blouse, she did not push him away but pulled him to her breasts, which he caressed with his tongue. She shuddered as he pushed up her skirt and expertly removed her undergarments before raising himself on top of her body. As he entered her she cried out with a pleasure she had never felt before, a desire she had never known existed.

She watched his face, so handsome, a face alive with passion. He kissed and stroked her gently encouraging her body to respond with his, until they moved together in perfect rhythmical harmony. She felt his pushing becoming more urgent and waited for him to withdraw from her body as Joe always did. A feeling of disappointment swept through her, she didn't want him to move away from her, not while these wonderful warm waves pulsated across her stomach and thighs. Then the most astonishing thing occurred. He did not pull out from her but pushed deeper and harder into her body until they both exploded in a crescendo of electrical spasms that caused Annie to cry out with shock.

Peter groaned with satisfaction and, relaxing against her, he fell into a instant sleep leaving Annie completely bemused. She held his warm body against hers, enjoying the comforting feeling it brought and stared at the canopy of leaves above. The sunlight played hide and seek among the foliage and every now and then a warm splash of light would fall on her upturned face. She hugged his body to her and sighed, as she thought about what had happened.

This is love then, she thought, so different from the crude act that Joe performed, this was gentle and sensitive and yet strong and passionate as well. She hadn't realised that her body was capable of this; at last she felt contented, warm, safe. This was the most precious thing and so special she knew she could not live without it now.

Peter stirred and opening his eyes a tender smile lit up his face.

'Thank you for sharing yourself with me, it was wonderful.'

He pulled himself from her and kneeling beside her, straightened his clothing before standing and extending a hand to help her up.

Quickly she tidied herself up, knowing her face was still flushed and her hair dishevelled. She didn't care, at this moment she was the happiest person in the world and Peter was the most important. Arms wrapped around each other, they strolled back to the hustle and bustle of the show. Peter shook out his fob watch and sadly shaking his head announced that it was really time that they went. Disappointment flooded Annie's face and he bent to kiss her again to dispel it.

'No long faces, Annie Hayes, we have had a wonderful day and there are plenty more to come.'

'Yes, yes, please,' she cried, already feeling the impending doom of saying goodbye to him today.

'Now I have a meeting to go to, so I'll have to drop you straight at the station for your train.'

'When will I see yer again?' her voice was eager, almost pleading.

'Whenever you want I'm here, just come whenever you can. I don't want to cause you any problems with your husband, Annie, I told you that.' He sounded businesslike now and almost in a rush to get rid of her.

Annie's stomach churned at the mention of Joe, but her desperation not to let Peter go overruled everything and she failed to see the change in him. Clinging to his arm, she pressed her lips to his, as the carriage drew up at the station.

'I'll come as soon as I can, I promise,' she whispered, and with eyes moist with love and a sense of missing him already, she alighted from his carriage, blowing him kisses until he pulled out of sight.

Floating on a cloud of happiness and blinded by her emotions Annie stood on the platform waiting for her train. Nothing, she thought, was ever going to be the same again, for she loved Peter and he loved her.

As the horse and carriage made its way steadily back towards the town Peter leant forward and instructed the driver to change direction. He had changed his mind about going back into work, he had no meeting to go to and he asked to be dropped at the Liberal Club instead. He needed a drink and besides some of his friends were bound to be in there and he could have a good laugh whilst he related the tale of his latest conquest. Women, he thought, they were so stupid, he could see it already in Annie's eyes, that love-sick gaze. Well, he would enjoy her for a while longer but the minute it began to get too complicated she would have to go; a pity really for she was quite something.

# Nineteen

Joe had not spoken one word to Annie for a week and a half now, ever since her return from Manchester. She was grateful for the silence as it allowed her two things: firstly she did not have to lie to Joe about what she had been doing, and secondly she could spend all her time thinking about Peter undisturbed. Little else entered her head, she had relived their precious day over and over, every kiss and touch was recorded in her memory in perfect detail. If she closed her eyes, he appeared before her like a vision, always smiling, his eyes shining with love and longing. Her body ached for his touch and sometimes she felt as if she would explode if she couldn't see him soon. All night her dreams were filled with him and the second she awoke he leapt into her thoughts. She longed to write to him, to pour out her feelings, to tell him how she would move heaven and earth to be with him, that without him everything seemed meaningless, but it was too dangerous. Every day she schemed of ways of getting to see him without creating too much suspicion. She knew she had to be careful just yet, in the long term it wouldn't matter for she knew that all she wanted was to be with him. She pictured them together, living in a beautiful house, sharing their work and leisure time, completely happy in one life. It was a dream come true for her, at last all the love she had craved was here and it was hers.

The problem of course was Joe, how and when to tell him. She was not sure what he was capable of, her fears were for Peter, not herself. What if he tried to kill Peter? It didn't bear thinking about. That was why she had to work all this out so carefully, Joe must not get the slightest idea that she was leaving him until she had found a safe way to do it. She couldn't simply disappear because of the salt pans, they were hers, she couldn't just abandon them. But then if it meant she and Peter could live in safety, would it matter? Peter was obviously successful in his business, they wouldn't need the money, so why not leave them. She'd give one to Joe and the rest to Jack, that way at least Joe would have his livelihood and she would make her mother happy at last.

All this benevolence was beginning to make her feel very pious, and she almost began to feel justified in her actions. She would not be leaving Joe high and dry and it eased her conscience considerably. Perhaps it was not so impossible after all, but it was imperative that she speak to Peter soon so they could make their plans and settle everything, before Joe found out. Actually his silence was making this easy and she decided that she would go to Manchester the next day and see Peter; if Joe wasn't talking to her she wouldn't have to tell him anything. I'm in control here, she told herself, I can make this happen and I will.

At ten thirty the next day Annie stood in front of Peter's secretary's desk, smiling calmly and asking if he was available. Miss Stot recognised her instantly, but knowing her boss as she did she knew he would not be pleased that Annie was here unannounced. He didn't like surprises.

'I'll just check if he is free, if you would like to take a seat,' she replied efficiently. Gesturing Annie towards a chair, she swept from the room being careful to close the door behind her in case Mr Smith decided that this visit was not convenient, and so save him the embarrassment of a face-to-face meeting.

As she had expected, he grimaced at the news.

'Shall I tell her you are busy?' She suggested in her matter-of-fact voice.

Peter considered for a moment, he certainly did not want to encourage Annie into impromptu visits, but then he reflected he had told her to call any time and the thought of her was tempting, and besides he had nothing else pressing today.

'No that's fine, show her in.'

Annie could hardly wait for the door to close before she flung herself in to Peter's arms. Raining kisses upon his face, she hugged him close as if she had not seen him for months rather than days.

Momentarily taken aback by her forwardness, Peter stepped backwards and then, overcome once again with the sheer physical aura of her, he returned her kisses with fervour. This, he thought, was what made Annie so rare, he did not have to coax her with games, her passion was honest and the naïvity of it was what excited him so much. She was like an unspoilt flower, delicate and precious and yet so earthy and sensual, quite breathtaking.

'I've missed yer so much, Peter. I've thought of nothin' else but being' 'ere with yer.' Her eyes shone with the sheer joy of being with him.

'Well, you are here, so let's make the most of it.'

Picking up his coat he led Annie from the room, telling Miss Stot in passing that he would be out for a few hours. She smiled knowingly and as soon as he shut the office door she took the book she was reading from the bottom drawer of her desk and opened it at the bookmark. She settled herself down to an hour or so of undisturbed reading until Mr Smith returned, and thanked her lucky stars yet again that she was very fortunate in her job.

Annie did not question their destination but gazed longingly into Peter's face as he ordered the carriage to Oxford Street. During the short journey they did not talk, but kissed and caressed each other, stopping only when the carriage jolted to a standstill and the driver coughed loudly to get their attention. Alighting to the pavement Peter instructed Annie to wait a moment and he disappeared into the foyer of the very grand hotel before them. Within minutes he was beckoning her to the door and she followed him in a dream-like trance up the flight of golden stairway, along the richly

182

carpeted corridors until he stopped outside a door with the number 32 on it. She giggled as he flung her against the sumptuous bed and was soon breathless with longing as he removed her clothes until she lay naked before him, watching him in fascination, as he revealed his body to her.

Their lovemaking was intense and furious the first time, and then slower and gentler when they had got over the initial fever of each other. To Annie there was nothing sordid about any of this, she was here with the man she loved, the man she wanted to spend the rest of her life with. This was only right, this was how it should be as far as she knew, this was love. Peter fell into a short sleep again and she lovingly watched him in slumber, tracing every feature of his face with her eyes, drinking in his beauty. Her body was warm and satisfied and she was so happy she felt she could burst. Gently she brushed his forehead with her lips and whispered 'I love yer' into his ear.

He stirred, groaning with pleasure as he remembered her presence. Sliding his arm around her body he caressed her breasts and pulled her body tight in to his so that they fitted snugly together. It was good with her, he had to admit it, what a pity it could not last. Still, he reasoned, why not enjoy it while he could, and he nuzzled against her neck running his tongue into her ear until she wriggled seductively.

Some half an hour later Peter laughed as he unwound her arms from his neck. 'I have to go and so do you.' He slapped her thigh playfully and threw her dress at her. 'Come on, get dressed before I need you all over again.'

She pouted and feigning a sulk she pulled on her clothes, refusing to smile until he gave in and kissed her passionately.

'Peter, we haven't talked and there's so much we have to decide.'

He frowned. He knew what was coming, it was always the same with women – a couple of times of sleeping together, they wanted your soul forever.

'Annie, don't let's spoil this, let's not hurt anyone, we are enjoying ourselves so let's just keep it that way.'

'I don't want to spoil anythin'. I just want to be with yer. I love yer.' Annie clasped his hands, her voice full of emotion.

Peter's heart sank, there it was already, the I-love-you line. He shook his head. 'Annie, you are married. I knew that all along. I can't take another man's wife, you don't belong to me, you told me that.'

'But I don't love 'im, I don't even care fer 'im. You an' I should be together, we love each other.' She was beginning to feel sick in her stomach, this was not how it was supposed to be.

He turned away from her and dramatically ran his fingers through his hair. 'I couldn't live with myself knowing I'd stolen another man's wife. I don't want to lose you, Annie, but I can only see you like this, nothing more, it just wouldn't be right. If you can't bear that then I will understand that we must say goodbye.'

Fear raced through her body. Say goodbye? What was he talking about? All her dreams and plans were suddenly being smashed right in front of her.

'No Peter, please don't say that.' Her brain was frantically trying to find a solution before the situation got out of control. She knew she would agree to anything just as long as she did not lose him, maybe what he needed was time. Time for her to prove to him that she really did not love Joe and wanted only him. Well, if that was what it took, so be it, she could play by his rules for a while and soon he would realise as she did, that they belonged together.

'You're right of course, we shouldn't rush into things. I'll just come to see yer when I can and we'll let time work it all out.' She was keeping her voice steady and trying not to allow her desperation to be reflected in her face.

Peter's face softened and she relaxed. He smiled kindly at her and drawing her to him hugged her tightly. 'It's not practical for you to just arrive out of the blue, Annie. I might have clients with me or even not be here.'

184

'I don't mind. I'd just wait, or try again another day,' her voice begged.

'How long do you think it would be before Joe began to suspect so many trips away?'

She felt like a child being reprimanded. She wanted to scream that she didn't care if Joe knew, that it made no difference anyway as he always suspected the worst of her even if she was doing nothing. But she was afraid that Peter might send her away for good and she just couldn't bear it. She raised her huge eyes appealingly to him, and he couldn't help but be swayed by them.

'What if we make a definite arrangement,' he suggested. 'Then I can make sure I will be here and you can organise yourself properly.' She nodded eagerly, her heart soaring again. 'Right. How about every third Friday in the month? I will be at the office waiting and if you cannot come I will understand that things are too difficult at home and I will simply wait for the next time.'

'Yes, yes that's fine, but yer needn't worry I'll be there I promise, nothing could keep me away from you,' Annie cried, hugging him to her.

Peter sighed inwardly. At least things were under his control now and if he could keep it that way it might be quite a treat to look forward to once a month, for he could not deny that she was tantalising.

Down in the street he ushered her into a carriage to take her to the station. 'Aren't yer comin' with me?' she asked, disappointed that he did not climb in beside her.

'No, no I have things to do.' He reached in and kissed her hand. 'Off you go and I will see you soon.'

Annie smiled but inwardly she felt wounded, the passionate man who held her in his arms seemed to disappear so quickly afterwards. Still she reasoned at least they had an arrangement, she could now count the days until she saw him again.

The carriage pulled away and Annie watched Peter's tall figure weaving through the crowd of people until he vanished. She sighed, knowing that she now had to face Joe and somehow get through three weeks of misery and heartache, whilst all she would be longing to do was see her true love. But the sweet memory of him would keep her going and so she resolved to stay brave for Peter.

Joe flung the sacks of salt on to the cart as if they were filled with feathers. He was angry, but not just angry, scared too. He thought he was losing Annie and it terrified him.

He had returned home at dinner time today to find the house empty. He wasn't unduly worried – she was probably at her mother's – but then unable to ignore the nagging voices in his head that wove such fantastic tales in his imagination, he returned later in the afternoon to check if she had returned. To his horror the cottage still stood empty. Like a madman he had searched for clues to her whereabouts, her best dress was not in the wardrobe nor her red cloak and he knew she would wear neither of those to visit her mother. His mind took him on wild and tormenting adventure, where he pictured her in some man's arms and worse, her leaving him altogether. Unable to settle in the house he returned to the wych shed and took his frustrations out on the salt bags. The other two workers in the shed, knowing of his fierce temper, said nothing, and continued on their tasks of raking and loading, exchanging knowing looks between each other, but remaining silent.

Joe's first instincts were of course all based on rage, he wanted to kill her and him whoever he was, but time calmed him and reason began to filter through into his tormented mind. The last thing he wanted was to lose Annie, for what was he without her. He knew he treated her unfairly but she never understood that that was just because he loved her so dearly. He reasoned that it was not her fault that she was so beautiful, that other men forced themselves upon her, and that what she needed was protecting from herself. That was why he could not allow her any freedom, it was too dangerous. He decided then and there that he would show her just how much she meant to him, he would shower her with love and then she would not be tempted elsewhere.

Meanwhile he would find out who this latest man was who was annoying her, for he was convinced that there was someone and he would deal with him. The fat worm his father had planted in his head stirred and wriggled, despite his frantic efforts to make it lie still. He needed Annie, only she could quieten it. The more he thought about his idea the more he liked it and by five o'clock he had decided to leave the shed and go home to initiate his plans. He walked into town and stopping at the grocer's he bought a large bunch of flowers and some fresh vegetables. Then he visited the butcher's for some of their delicious home-made sausages.

The cottage was still empty when he arrived and Joe immediately set his plans into action. He laid the table with a fresh white cloth and placed the fragrant flowers in the centre and then set about preparing the meal. He actually began to feel quite jubilant, this, he told himself, was the husband that Annie wanted and deserved. The worm slept. By the time Annie arrived home from the station some hours later, the kitchen was warm with delicious cooking smells and Joe, washed and changed into a clean shirt, was tending the stove.

Annie stopped in her tracks as she entered the kitchen, a look of amazement on her face. All the way home she had been rehearsing her speech as to where she had been, bracing herself for blazing rows and physical abuse. Instead she was met with a smiling face and a cheerful greeting.

Joe mustered all his resolve and did not ask her where she had been, but directed her to her chair and served her with the meal he had prepared. She was speechless, never in the whole time she had known him had he so much as offered to pour her a glass of water. He didn't see it as his place; and suddenly all this. He made conversation about the salt yield and day-to-day activities and after they had eaten suggested that they could take a stroll by the river. Annie was too dumbfounded to do anything but agree and so she found herself strolling along the river bank, Joe clasping her hand in his. Her mind was in turmoil, guilt swamped over her for her deceit and fear also that something was about to happen, that this was all some kind of trick.

Later when they went to bed Joe placed his arms around her, gently, ignoring her shudder at his touch. To her relief he did no more than that, and fell asleep cradling her against him like some precious doll. Annie lay awake for hours. She longed for Peter, she felt so guilty. This was not Joe's fault, she was wronging him and his crime was simply that he loved her. She knew God would not want to talk to her tonight, no one would and despite all the love she had found, she had never felt so alone as she did at this moment. I am wicked, she thought, but I can't help it, I love him, I am sorry Joe, I truly am, and with those thoughts she drifted into a fitful sleep.

# Twenty

On a warm September day in 1885, just over two months since her affair had begun with Peter, Annie sat high up on the hill, in the woods that stretched away from the meandering river below. It seemed to her that she had been running to the comfort of these trees for as long as she could remember. She liked the feeling of being dwarfed by their magnificence, it made her humble, almost as if she were in a church and God was looking down on her sins, reprimanding her. She deserved that today. The leaves were beginning to die and the ground was carpeted with orange and gold, reds and browns. Annie sank down into the soft inviting leaves and wished she could simply disappear amongst them for ever. Her head ached with thinking and her body with lack of sleep. Lying back she closed her eyes and let the fragile, soothing autumn sun warm her face. Richard suddenly flashed through her mind. This was exactly how she had met him, whilst she was hiding in the woods venting her emotions. If only he had come back for her none of this would be happening now. She chastised herself for her stupidity, Richard was an impossible dream, he had probably forgotten her existence entirely. Squeezing her eyes together tightly as if that would somehow expel him from her mind, she sighed miserably. What a mess her life had become.

Her head was as always filled with Peter, he dominated her thoughts completely and constantly, until she longed for him with such an intensity that her chest ached from her burning heart. She had been to see him twice now since their last time together, firstly three weeks ago and then yesterday. How long those first three weeks of waiting had been, every day, every hour counted, the longing growing more and more. She had been so excited as she travelled to Manchester, all her senses tingling and alive. She could not describe the disappointment when she arrived to be told that he was not in the office that day and he was not expected in, and she had stood rooted to the spot for a moment, dumbstruck. It had never occurred to her for one moment that Peter might not be there, she had pictured him waiting for her, arms open, as desperate for her as she was for him.

Her misery had given way to anger as she walked aimlessly from his office. How could he do this to her, when she was risking everything to be there? The anger too had been short-lived and by the time she boarded the train to return home, her heart was heavy again with the sheer agony of not seeing him. She had tried to make excuses in her mind. Perhaps he had been called to an unexpected meeting; but then he could have left her a message. Or maybe he had forgotten, worse still he might be avoiding her. She had dismissed these negative ideas and had begun to plan the next visit she could make.

Added to the pain of not seeing him was her new nightmare, one that would also not go away, no matter how she tried to deny it: she was pregnant. The first period she missed was due the day she had spent with Peter. She wasn't worried when it didn't happen for she thought her body was simply reacting to this new found joy she had, but then last week the next period failed to appear as well. Every day since then Annie had waited anxiously for some sign of it, but none came and for the past three mornings she had been violently sick when she awoke. No one had to tell her, she knew she was pregnant, she could feel it. The full impact of this and all its terrible implications had swirled around in her head constantly. She was pregnant with Peter's baby; there was no doubt that it was his. Suddenly the reality of

Joe withdrawing himself from her when he took her body was obvious. She couldn't believe that she had been so stupid, of course that was why she had never fallen pregnant by him. All these years she had thought that perhaps there was something wrong with her, that she was unable to bear children. Now that Peter had made love to her properly and allowed his seed to stay within her, of course she had fallen with his child.

After the initial horror of her discovery, Annie had been filled with joy, she had tenderly held her stomach, cherishing Peter's offspring within her. Now she thought all her dreams could come true, now Peter would understand that they had to be together and she would be able to leave Joe and this miserable life for ever. She had travelled to see him again yesterday full of hopes and plans and imagining the scene of joy when she told him the news.

She sat up suddenly, and holding her head in her hands she recalled the events of yesterday. The reliving of it did not ease the nightmare, and the sound of her crying echoed around the trees eerily. A blackbird disturbed by the sound chattered a noisy warning to its friends, in case this haunting cry was a danger of some kind. There was no one other than the creatures who lived here to witness her torment, and for that she was grateful, for there was nobody who could have comforted her.

Her mind went over and over her meeting yesterday morning with Peter but she could resolve nothing. There were no gentle answers, only brutal reality.

When she had arrived at his office she had been delighted to find him waiting for her this time. She had eagerly fled to his arms and surrendered herself to his kisses, bursting with impatience to share the news with him.

'Annie, I'm so sorry I wasn't here last time, I got held up in a meeting and couldn't get a message to you.' His lies were convincing, in truth he had been occupied with a lady friend in the self-same hotel that he had taken Annie to, where he was in fact quite a regular customer.

'It doesn't matter, you're 'ere now an' we must talk.'

She could forgive him anything and her eyes shone with anticipation.

'Talk, talk, that's all you want to do. Let's not waste our time together, we can talk later.' He drew her to him, tracing her breasts with his fingers, his voice deep and husky with desire.

'No, we have to talk first. It's important.' Pulling away from him, she sat down in the chair by his desk.

Peter laughed, her obstinacy was very attractive. He perched himself on the edge of his desk, telling himself there was plenty of time for his pleasure. 'So what is so important that the world must stop while we discuss it, then?'

Annie took a deep breath and then she blurted out her joyous news.

'I'm pregnant, we're goin' to have a baby.'

The impact of her words took a few seconds to sink in but as they did Annie saw Peter's face fall and then distort with rage.

'Pregnant? But you can't be,' he stuttered unable to regain his composure.

'Yes, isn't it wonderful? Don't yer see, now we can be together.' In her enthusiasm she refused to see his horror.

'No Annie, it's not wonderful. We can't be together, not now, not ever. You are married to Joe.' He began to pace along the floor, agitated and angry.

'But I love you, not Joe. We love each other,' she cried, desperate for him to see things as she did.

'No, I don't love you, I enjoyed you and you wanted me, that's all.' He spat the words out cruelly, not caring that each was a vicious wound.

'No Peter, don't say that, it's not true.' Tears crept from her eyes, as she struggled to come to terms with this unfolding nightmare.

'Grow up, Annie. This is the real world. We were lovers, nothing more. Go back to Joe, that's where you belong. And I will go back to my wife and children.' He turned his back on her in dismissive manner.

Annie sat for a minute as his words sank in, and then as

if in a trance, she rose to her feet. Her voice felt as if it no longer belonged to her.

'Yer wife? Yer married?'

'Yes I'm married, Annie, and you were just a bit of fun.' He turned to face her, and she hardly recognised the unfeeling cold eyes that bore into her. 'Don't even think of trying to blame this baby on me, I'll deny it, in court if necessary. Save yourself the pain, Annie. I'm a very nasty enemy, just get out of my life and don't ever come back. As far as I'm concerned you don't exist.'

She couldn't remember how she had got herself back to the station or the journey home but she had somehow found her way back to the cottage and, feigning illness to Joe, she had gone to bed and stayed there until today, when she had escaped to the woods to try and make some sense of it all before she went completely mad.

It was difficult to separate the pain of facing the truth about Peter and what she should do about her future, but she knew she must do just that. She knew no matter how much she ached inside, no matter how much she longed for him, she had to put aside the agony of rejection, the dreadful realisation that she had been used, that she was nothing more to him than a 'good time'. It ripped her apart that this love she thought was so rare and precious, was no more than a cheap toy to him. She could not hate him, not yet, though she knew it would probably be better if she did, but how could she despise someone that she adored. She knew she had been a fool, a stupid lovesick fool, he had told her to grow up, maybe he was right. She was still a little girl believing in kissing bushes and dreams, happy-ever-afters. Well, not any more. She vowed never to give her heart again, to have her trust destroyed and brutally held up for ridicule. Memories flashed through her head of children dancing around her in the street, chanting on and on. 'Everybody hates you, everybody hates you'. It was never-ending, and all she wanted to do was run and run until no one could find her. That was how she felt now. She wanted to flee from the mocking faces, to block out the cruel voices, mostly to stop hearing Peter saying 'I don't love you'.

In the midst of all this misery and dejection Annie prayed to her God, not her usual conversations where she reasoned and bargained, but just a simple plea. Over and over she repeated, 'Please help me, please help me.' and as he always was, when she really needed him, today God was listening. He gave her no miracle answers, no instant remedies but he conveyed to her in soothing tones his support and bit by bit Annie calmed down, until the tears stopped and reason began to creep back into her mind.

Once this was done and she was once more in control, he disappeared and left her to work out for herself what was the best thing to do. She expected no more of him, and silently, said her thank-you prayer.

Locking Peter firmly into a compartment in her mind where she could control her emotion, she focused on the future, her future, the one without him but with his baby. It seemed at first like a huge gaping black hole, sucking her in, swallowing her. But then images of the child in her womb played in her head, she held her hands to her stomach, it seemed so marvellous that deep inside her lay a life, a growing life that belonged to her. She might not ever have Peter but she would have his child, created in love and passion, no one could take that from her. Emotions flooded through her, this baby would be hers to love and it would love her, an unconditional love that no one could destroy. She hadn't lost everything, she had gained this wonderful miracle of life and this was all that mattered now. For the first time in her life something would be truly hers. Rocking back and forth, her knees hugged to her chest, Annie felt a warmth within, it was a start.

Then suddenly she remembered Joe, poor stupid Joe. She groaned at the thought of him, since that night he had cooked her meal, he had never mentioned her excursions, burying his head, not wishing to see the painful truth. There had been no rowing, no shouting, no violence for weeks.

He had not forced his body upon her, he had systematically torn Annie apart with guilt, though he did not realise it.

She knew she would destroy him if she left, that he was not capable of surviving without her, and she cursed her conscience. As much as he was abhorrent to her, she could not shake the feelings of responsibility. She could understand now how her pa had felt for Elizabeth. He had never been able to sever the cord completely, unable to appease his guilty feelings. She carried Joe like a weight in just the same way.

The only way she could stay was to convince Joe that this was his baby and even if she could, what then? He was so adamant that they should not have children who could tell what he would do? Perhaps she reasoned that he might feel differently when he knew she was really pregnant, he might even like the idea of bonding the two of them closer together, it might convince him that she wasn't going to leave him. The more she mused over the idea, the more convinced she became that it could work. Joe would be happy, the baby would have a father and a family and wouldn't have the disgrace of being labelled illegitimate. She knew all about the pain of growing up without a mother and father, she had had to endure the teasing and heartache that it brought. She didn't want that for her baby.

The sun had slipped away behind the oncoming clouds, and Annie shivered as she realised that she must have been sitting here for hours. Her eyes were sore from crying and her legs stiff and aching. Dragging herself to her feet she stretched, taking in gulps of air to revive herself, she raised her face to heaven and cried out loud as a final release of her pain. Then she straightened her clothes and set off determinedly down through the trees. Every step of the way she talked to herself, convincing her reluctant mind that she could do this, she would manage, she would find a way, she could survive or her name wasn't Annie Hayes. By the time she reached the cottage her mind was weaving plans and schemes, and forcing a smile to her bedraggled face she breezed into the cottage to prepare her husband's tea.

195

When Joe returned that evening he found a very different Annie from the one he had left ill in bed that morning. He had been worried about her, she was never ill usually, but tonight seemed to have brought a miraculous recovery. She still looked red and swollen around her eyes but he supposed she was just tired. Tea was ready on the table and instead of the sad face opposite him at the table, he was met with a smile and conversation about the pan and his day's work. Silently he congratulated himself, it was working, he knew he could win her round and he had. This was the wife he wanted, obedient and pleasant, not wilful and sulky. Tonight, he thought, I will have her, I've waited long enough.

Annie played her role to perfection, she cooed and fussed around him, she flirted and teased and when he finally climbed onto her in their bed, she gritted her teeth together and allowed his wet lips to slobber over her. She forced her repulsion of his sweaty body deep down inside her and instead of laying statue-like, she enfolded her arms around him and feigned pleasure at his touch. The effect was amazing and Joe grunted with ecstasy. Holding on to him with all her might, Annie tried desperately to prevent him from withdrawing from her body. He groaned and Annie silently prayed that he was so overcome with this new her that he would lose all control. At the last minute he wrenched himself from her, and she felt the hot liquid spurting up her belly.

Damn, damn, damn, she repeated, over and over. Joe rolled off her and instantly began snoring loudly. Angrily she dug him in the ribs, making him jump before turning over on his side fast asleep.

She lay staring at the ceiling. I can do this, she told herself, I will do this. She knew she had limited time, she had to convince Joe that he had made her pregnant before the baby started to show. Tomorrow, I'll do it then, gently she rubbed her hands over her stomach wiping off all traces of Joe, swallowing hard as she did so to prevent herself from retching. He was so repulsive to her, just the slightest brush of his skin made her shudder. Rolling to the very edge of the bed she pulled the covers up around her ears. Sleep began to beckon her and as she drifted away, exhausted now, both mentally and physically, she focused on her baby. I am doing this for you she told it, I love you and that's why I'm doing this.

# Twenty-One

**A**nnie was tired. No, more than tired. When she awoke in the morning all she wanted to do was roll over again and go back to sleep. Everything was an effort, getting dressed, cooking breakfast, walking to the wych shed, sometimes she felt even breathing was hard work. This baby was draining every ounce of her strength, sapping her from within, day by day. Not that she minded, she would happily sacrifice anything for it. She felt a wonderful warm contentment as it blossomed, a sense of satisfaction,. It was still her secret. Despite being over five months pregnant she was the only one who knew of her condition. She had been very sick for the first four months and she had lost so much weight that no one would have guessed that she was pregnant. It was only during this last month that her waist had begun to thicken and her belly swell.

She had never seen or heard from Peter. She did not expect to, he had made his views perfectly clear to her. The pain of losing him still hurt her, but the sharpness of it had dulled with time. She realised what a fool she had been, how naïve to have fallen for his charms, she could see quite clearly now that she was just one of his many women, yet despite that she knew that what she had felt for him was love. It seemed such a waste of a precious thing, but she had her compensation, she had her baby.

Her life had fallen back into its miserable regime. Joe was all-powerful now and she survived as best she could under the tyranny of his rule. The more she submitted to him in

198

bed, the stronger he became out of it, and he had turned her into a virtual prisoner so obsessed was he that no one or nothing would ever take her away from him. She was allowed no free time, he accompanied her to and from work and even to her mother's, though he never spoke when he got there, but sat stiffly in the parlour whilst she did her jobs. Each month when she went to the bank to pay in the money, he would go with her, watching her every move in the pretence of caring. Sometimes Annie felt as if she could no longer breathe he suffocated her so much, but she knew she had no choice but to play this game by his rules. Nearly every night he took her body, she had learned to tune herself out totally from what he was doing, letting her mind take her far away whilst at the same time her body performed with practised enthusiasm. She had waited patiently for him to ejaculate inside her just once, but no matter how frenzied he became in his passion, he never totally lost control. Annie was beginning to get desperate, she would have to tell him soon before her condition became obvious, but she just didn't dare, not yet, not until she felt she could convince him the child was his. She knew it wouldn't be long before he began to notice her growing waist line and she shuddered with fear for her unborn child, terrified that he might harm it.

Today, despite being totally exhausted, she worked side by side with her husband loading the salt sacks on to the huge carts ready for the barges. Even though she had ten men working for her now between the sheds, there was still plenty of work and she and Joe worked her pa's pan between them. She no longer had an afternoon to herself every now and then for Joe wanted her with him all the time and so constantly found work for her to do at the pan. She did not argue. She certainly didn't want to risk a beating that might harm the child.

Actually she quite enjoyed being in the shed, there was a kind of freedom there. She could lose herself amidst the steam, she did not have to look at Joe or talk to him, she could submerge herself in those private dreams she had locked in her mind and Joe could not invade them. The lapping of the rakes on the brine had a soothing rhythm and Annie almost felt tranquil whilst she could hide in the warm vapours.

Today she wallowed in its safety and let her mind drift, taking her away form the harsh reality of her life. It was Jack's voice that invaded her privacy and irritably she jolted herself back to her surroundings, resentful of the intrusion.

'You better go 'ome, Ma's ill,' Jack yelled at her across the bubbling vat of brine.

Annie sighed, there was always something wrong with her mother, mostly it was just for attention.

'What's wrong now?' she replied, uninterested.

''Ow should I know, I'm not 'er nurse maid. She were whimpering this morning about pains, told me to fetch you.'

Again, thought Annie. Her mother had cried wolf so often that Annie never believed her any more. She had lost count of the number of times she had rushed over there simply to find her mother had run out of gin or just wanted some attention.

'I'll go as soon as we've finished loadin',' Annie replied wiping away the sweat from her brow with her forearm.

Jack leant against the bench, watching his sister struggle with the cumbersome sacks. He could have offered to help or even to finish the job for her but it never entered his head, and she in turn would never have expected him to.

Unexpectedly Joe put down the sack he was heaving into the cart to speak to Annie. 'You'd best go if she's ill, I'll call later when I've finished 'ere.'

Annie tried to disguise the obvious pleasure she felt at being allowed the freedom to go alone, and not waiting until Joe changed his mind she hurriedly pulled on her coat and escaped into the fresh air outside.

She felt like a prisoner released, and taking huge gulps of air as if they were her first she wandered slowly down from the sheds and towards the town. She was in no hurry to hasten the journey, and as she strolled she hummed a little tune to herself and hoped that Joe didn't arrive too soon and spoil this.

She was still singing to herself and in good spirits as she entered the house. The place looked as always in a tip. Jack never made any attempt to clean up after himself and very often her mother would not rise from her bed at all. Annie hated Elizabeth's bedroom, it smelt of gin and stale urine. Her mother had a brown earthenware chamber pot under the bed and this was left for Annie to empty, sometimes being so full it was impossible not to spill some of the putrid contents. Since she had been pregnant Annie heaved every time she had to perform this job and she tried to hold her breath so that the vile aroma did not cause her to retch too much. She steeled herself today as she mounted the stairs, knowing that would be her first task.

''Ello Mother, it's only me,' she always called out before she entered the room for her mother hated being surprised, and this warning gave her time to hide the gin bottle under the covers.

Today there was no answer and as Annie pushed open the door her first thought was that Elizabeth was dead. Only when she heard the muffled whimper did she realise she was not. Her mother was slumped over to one side in the bed, her face ashen and her eyes wide and rolled backwards in her head. Saliva trickled down the side of her chin from her twisted mouth and brown sticky vomit was stuck to her nightdress.

Annie rushed forward and lifted her mother into a more upright position, propping her in place with the pillows.

'Mother, can yer 'ear me?'

Elizabeth stared blankly ahead, her body limp like a rag doll. Annie realised that she had had some kind of seizure, and ran from the house to the doctor's surgery, hoping against hope that she would catch him before he left to do his rounds. The lady assistant behind her frosted glass screen was sour and unsympathetic. 'Please can Doctor Bradley come, it's me mother,' Annie sank onto a hard wooden bench.

201

'An emergency?' she snorted.

The little pig-like eyes narrowed and her face hardened. 'The doctor will call as soon as he is able.'

Fuming silently, Annie forced a polite smile from her lips and walked from the surgery, waiting until she was out of sight before she broke out once more into a run.

Elizabeth had not moved since Annie had left her, her eyes stared blankly ahead and her arms hung limply on the bed covers. The whole of the left side of her face looked as if it had dropped, and her mouth was twisted into a distorted line. Annie was shocked at how ugly she looked, it was as if all the bitterness and hatred she felt for her daughter was painted on her face now, displayed for Annie's benefit to emphasise her contempt. Annie shuddered suddenly, feeling afraid not just for herself but for her baby. Wickedness seemed to ooze from Elizabeth and Annie automatically placed her hands on her belly protectively.

Quietly she sat by the side of the bed and waited for the doctor. She felt helpless. The only thing she could have done was give her mother some comfort, held her hand or stroked her brow, but these were impossible tasks for her and so she simply sat staring into space, counting the minutes.

An hour later the doctor had still not arrived. Elizabeth had not uttered a word but her breathing was noisy and laboured now, though she still lay rigidly still, corpse-like. Annie walked around the bedroom to stretch her legs. In her head she was telling herself that her mother was probably dying, but the thought brought neither pain nor gladness, just a numbness that washed over her; the whole thing seemed so unreal, undramatic, inevitable.

Joe's voice penetrated the silence and for once Annie was glad to hear it. She did not want to be alone here any longer.

His heavy boots crashed up the stairs, shattering the ethereal spell that had hung in the air. 'What's wrong with 'er, then?' His voice sounded suspicious as usual. Annie had been gone for hours and he was rankled already.

'Look fer yerself, I don't know,' Annie sighed. 'The doctor's comin', though heaven knows when.'

Joe shifted uneasily, he didn't like illness and he never felt comfortable with Elizabeth anyway. Her cold eyes seemed to be boring into him and it unnerved him.

'Well, I don't suppose I can do anythin'. I'd better go back to the shed.' He reasoned that Annie could get up to no mischief and it was not his place to be here.

Annie's heart sank. She spent all her time wishing he would leave her in peace and now when he was doing just that she wanted him to stay. 'D'yer have to go just yet? I mean Jack's at the shed isn't he?'

Joe laughed sardonically. 'Jack? What use is he? He'll just sit there an' watch the salt lump until we can't lift it from the vat at all. You stay as long as yer need to and I'll call back later.'

As quickly as he had arrived he had gone again and once more Annie was plunged into the oppressive silence of the room. She laughed inwardly to herself, did he really think he was doing her such a favour by allowing her to stay? If she didn't know him as well as she did, she would have said he sounded almost compassionate, but she did know him and there would be a price to pay, even for this short time away from him.

A pungent smell wafted from the bed until it filled her nostrils and made her screw her face up. Crossing to the bed Annie drew back the covers and as she did the sight and smell caused her to clasp her hand to her mouth as she heaved violently, for Elizabeth had soiled herself. She knew she would have to clean the mess up but she wasn't sure how she'd manage without vomiting herself. That was not the only problem. Annie could not bear physical contact with Elizabeth, she had certainly never seen any part of her body and now not only was she going to have to touch her but also see her mother naked. The blood began to pound in her head and sweat prickled in her back; her only consolation was that Elizabeth would despise this as much as she did.

203

Fetching some water, clean sheets and a gown for Elizabeth, Annie began her unpleasant task. She had to keep stopping to turn away and let her nostrils clear and her stomach settle from the putrid smell. Apart from the distress of nausea, she struggled with the sheer weight of Elizabeth. Although she was not a heavy woman she was a dead weight and Annie puffed and panted as she heaved the unyielding limbs back and forth.

She had just finished dressing Elizabeth when there was a hammering on the front door. Annie bounded down the stairs. This must be the doctor at last.

It was, but not the doctor she expected.

'Richard!' Her voice was incredulous. 'I don't understand, Doctor Bradley is supposed to be comin'.'

'Hello Annie. I'm sorry, but Doctor Bradley is away. I'm standing in for him for a few weeks.'

She fought to regain her composure, angry with herself that Richard always managed to churn her up inside.

'It's me mother,' she said matter-of-factly. 'Please come up.'

The mixed aroma of faeces and vomit hung noxiously in the bedroom and Annie hurriedly scooped up the dirty linen, and opening Jack's bedroom door hastily pushed it in there, ashamed of the vile smell.

Richard sat next to Elizabeth on the bed, seemingly oblivious to everything except the patient. Carefully he listened to her heart and pulse and only when he had finished his examination did he turn his attention to Annie.

'Your mother has had a stroke, a kind of seizure.'

'Will she die?' Annie knew she sounded cold but she could not feign sorrow that wasn't there.'

'She might. The next forty-eight hours are critical. If she survives those then she is in with a chance.' Richard rose from the bed and moved closer to Annie. She automatically stepped backwards from him, and he noticed immediately and felt the pain of her reaction deep within him.

'I have to warn you though she might never fully recover. She could be bedridden, unable to speak or move, it's impossible to tell. On the other hand she could recover quite normally. All you can do is try to get some water down her and keep her warm and clean.' He shook his head apologetically, wishing he could give her a better prognosis.

Annie's heart sank. Her mother could be an invalid for years, need constant care and attention, how on earth would she be able to manage with a baby *and* her mother. Pushing the horrific thoughts from her head, she silently followed Richard down the stairs.

'I'll call tomorrow to see her. There's nothing I can really do to help you, Annie, it's just a matter of time.'

'Thank you,' she replied in a monotone voice. This was a nightmare unfolding before her and she was finding it difficult not to scream out that she didn't want this, this was not her fault but she knew that sounded both spoilt and pathetic and Richard was the last person in the world in front of whom she wanted to break down.

'Will you be all right here on your own?' Richard's voice was full of concern, this staring silent creature in front of him was not the Annie he knew.

'Yes I'm fine, thank you,' she answered and before he could say another word she closed the door in his face and sinking to the floor in the hallway she buried her head in her hands and cursed herself for being such a wicked selfish daughter. She prayed that she might find the compassion to care for Elizabeth and that her baby would not be punished for her wickedness. She tried to push the thought from her head that it would be much simpler if Elizabeth simply passed away.

When Joe returned that evening he found her washing sheets out in the back yard, viciously slapping the material against the washboard, her arms bright red from the cold wind that was chapping her skin.

'She's not better, then.' It was not a question.

'No. I'll have to stay 'ere with 'er, Joe. The doctor says the next two days will decide things.'

Joe's face temporarily blackened. He didn't want her away

205

from home, but then he reasoned it was her mother and she had been good lately.

'I'll stay an' eat 'ere then,' he mused resentfully and sat himself on the step of the scullery watching her working.

Annie seethed, knowing that he was now waiting for her to produce a meal out of nowhere and if it didn't come soon there would be trouble, whether her mother was dying or not. Squeezing as much of the now cold water out of the sheets as she could, she hurriedly threaded them through the mangle before hanging them on the kitchen rack to dry. In silence she busied herself around the warm oven range. Fortunately she had shopped yesterday for Jack and Elizabeth and there was liver and onions and potatoes to make a meal with. Every so often she would pop upstairs to look at Elizabeth, who still sat statue-like in bed. Joe sat watching her, offering neither conversation or assistance but simply making her feel uncomfortable as usual, as though she were on trial.

Much as she despised Joe – and normally she would have relished the idea of a night or two away from him – today she was in a dilemma. She knew she would have to stay here but the thought of being alone with Jack for a whole night also terrified her, especially as he would probably come home drunk as usual.

'Are yer goin' to stay overnight, Joe?' she enquired quietly.

'No there's no need. I'll have to be at the shed at dawn an' you've yer mother to see to.'

Annie knew that what he meant was that if her body wasn't going to be available to him he could see no point in staying.

'I'd really like yer to stay,' she ventured. 'I just don't fancy bein' 'ere alone.'

'Yer won't be. Jack'll be 'ome. 'Ow long's tea goin' to be? I'm starvin'.'

Annie wanted to say, Jack is the reason I don't want to be here, but she did not dare, Joe was so possessive over her that if he thought for one moment that her own brother had designs on her, who could tell what he might do. She served the thick liver and onion gravy onto the plate and silently placed it before her husband.

He raised his eyes as if to make some comment about the food but then seeing how exhausted she looked for once he decided not to. True he didn't like her staying here without him, but it looked as if Elizabeth might not pull through and for Joe that could only be a good thing, for then Annie would have one less reason to leave his side. Hopefully this whole thing would be over soon and Annie would be at home where she belonged. He shovelled the warm food down as if he had not been fed for weeks, even though he didn't like liver very much.

Without a word of thanks or concern he scraped the last of the gravy from his plate and then reaching for his jacket left the scullery.

'I'll call tomorrow,' were his parting words and then he was gone, leaving Annie to clear the table and wash the pots.

The next few hours were the longest of her entire life. Feeling uncomfortable at the thought of being alone anywhere in the house with Jack, she decided the best thing to do was to sleep in the chair next to her mother's bed. She found a blanket in the linen box on the landing and although it was thin and smelly it was better than nothing. No sooner had she settled herself into a reasonably comfortable position than her mother stirred, causing Annie to jump out of her skin with the suddenness of it. The noise that came from the almost blue lips was an eerie wail, followed by what Annie could only liken to a fox's cry. Seconds later this was accompanied by huge quantities of frothy vomit that spurted out across the bed. Annie groaned; now she would have to struggle and clean her mother all over again. Elizabeth's little grey eyes held her accusingly as she hauled and heaved with the dead weight of limp body. It seemed to Annie that no sooner had she settled her Mother than the whole cycle began again and if it wasn't vomit it was faeces. Elizabeth never uttered one word nor did she try to help by moving her body, but the look in her eyes told Annie that she had no intention of trying.

By dawn the whole of the bedroom floor was piled up with dirty linen and bowls of cold water, the smell was overpowering and Annie knew that if she did not start washing that there would be no clean bedding left. She could hardly keep her eyes open and would have given anything at that moment to simply lie down and drift away into sleep. Jack had not been into the bedroom once to see how Elizabeth was, though Annie had heard him moving around the house. At one of her lowest moments in the middle of the night she had cried out to her mother that her favourite son could not even be bothered to look into the room to see if she were alive or dead, that it was Annie the daughter she despised who was here. Immediately she had felt guilty, for perhaps her mother could understand what she was saying and there was little excuse to be cruel, even if she had good reason.

As daylight filtered into the dark little room, Annie sat watching her mother's blank face. It was almost as if Elizabeth were a stranger. Annie could not remember one occasion when her mother had ever shown her any compassion or love, she had never held her hand or kissed her goodnight, never tried to be understanding or to give advice. Annie still longed to have been loved just once. Coming to terms with her mother's hatred was impossible and even here at her death, Elizabeth was managing to hurt Annie and make her feel totally useless. The steel barrier stood intact.

Annie could not say at what point her mother actually died, but she became aware that something was missing in the room, and the something was Elizabeth's rasping breathing. The face never changed expression nor did the body move, but the thin blue lines on her mother's lips spread until all her skin took on a cold purple hue. She still stared at Annie accusingly, and Annie sat and stared back for a while unable to move. No tears rushed from her eyes, no stabbing pain of sorrow ripped her apart as it had when

208

her pa had died, in fact she felt nothing at all. Matter-of-factly she began to clear the bedroom of all the dirty clothes and carrying them downstairs she put on the huge cast iron pan to boil so that she could begin washing them. She did not move or touch her; she simply closed the door and left her as if it were any other day.

She drove all thoughts of her mother from her brain and threw herself into the cleaning, and that is how Richard found her an hour later.

'I let myself in, the door was open,' he called as he entered the scullery. 'How's your mother this morning?'

Annie turned, wet through from the effort of washing, soap and water soaking her dress against her. The material stuck to her growing belly making it seem much larger than it already was. Richard gasped as he looked at her. She was still beautiful even when she was so exhausted and bedraggled and his heart turned.

'Annie, you're pregnant, you shouldn't be hauling these heavy things or lifting your mother. Where's Joe or Jack?'

His concern and the gentleness of his voice penetrated Annie's resolve and she burst into uncharacteristic tears, flinging herself in his arms. She clung to him and sobbed out her words, gasping for breath.

'Mother's dead, Richard, and yer mustn't tell Joe about the baby, promise me, promise me yer won't tell anyone.'

She was so distraught that Richard had no choice but to nod his consent, but one thing he did know was that this time she would not send him away and like it or not she would accept his help. Cradling her to his breast he let her cry gently, assuming her grief was for her mother, although actually she was so touched by this unusual concern for her that she had simply let go of years of misery and sorrow.

As Joe entered the door his hackles rose as he saw Annie enfolded in the doctor's arms. Richard, seeing the black face, spoke firmly.

'Elizabeth's dead.'

'Then it's a good job I'm here to look after me wife,' Joe

retorted and snatching Annie from Richard's arms, he glared with obvious hostility.

Richard stood for a moment taking in the situation before he spoke. It was apparent that Annie was terrified of this man for she cowered now by his side, eyes cast down to the floor. Best not to make the situation worse now.

'I'll just go up and see Elizabeth,' he said in a matter-of-fact tone, 'then I'll be able to issue the death certificate.'

By the time he came back down the stairs Annie had disappeared, no doubt on the orders of Joe, and nodding his farewells Richard left with fear in his heart for Annie's well-being.

# Twenty-Two

Annie felt it was ironic that her mother should be buried in January, the very same month she herself was born in. She knew Elizabeth would have hated that and somehow she felt it served her mother right. There had only been two people at the graveside today apart from the preacher and the gravedigger, and that was herself and Jack. Neither had cried or shown any emotion as their mother had been lowered into the frozen ground in her plain wooden coffin and the preacher had hurried through his words, seemingly eager to be out of the freezing air. It appeared to Annie that Elizabeth's life had been a complete waste, nobody would miss or mourn her, soon nobody would even remember her. She had made no mark in life, left no treasured memories or special moments. If Annie and Jack had not been here today it would almost have been as if she had never existed.

As soon as they had said their thanks to the preacher, Jack had left and she was abandoned in the cold afternoon trying to make some sense or reason out of her mother's existence. She stood by the mound of freshly dug earth; it was hard to imagine her mother was in there, that she would never see or speak to her again. It was a kind of release, the years of guilt and torment when she tried so hard to please Elizabeth flashed before her, then the resentment and jealousy she had felt for the attention Jack received, and finally the realisation that no matter what she did her mother never felt anything but contempt for her. It all slipped away now,

211

poured out from her and slipped down into the frozen soil in front of her. What she was left with was pity. Pity for a sad woman, whose sons did not return the love she had given them, for Jack it seemed cared nothing and as for Luke no one had heard of him for years. Elizabeth's life was like an empty shell with nothing to fill it except bitterness and resentment.

There was nothing here for Annie, no sorrow or love and as she turned to walk away she spoke to her own baby within her, telling it that no matter what else it did or didn't have in life, she would always make sure it knew of its mother's love. The child had begun to move now and Annie loved the feel of the new life as it wriggled inside her. This was hers to treasure and love, someone that would not judge her, but simply love her in return for what she was. She could hardly wait to see and hold and caress this miracle of hers. The dismal afternoon light began to fail and an icy mist hung over the graveyard; the tall poplar trees; naked and thin, stood sentry-like at its entrance. As Annie passed through the gate she did not look back, there was no point, what she was leaving behind was not something to mourn but almost a joyous release of her tormented feelings.

She pulled her cloak protectively around her belly, as if to shield her baby from the freezing wind that bit through her skin. The roads did not have the benefit of a frosty white cloak, which might at least have made the dreary streets look prettier, instead a dull black wetness clung to everything enhancing the ugliness of the dirty houses, reminding Annie what a miserable place this was. She shuddered and quickened her step, her desire to get home increased by the knowledge that at least there would be a warm fire in the grate and with any luck Joe would not be home for an hour or two yet, so she could sit by the flames and sip a warm drink in peace.

She heard the steady clip-clop of horses' hooves on the cobbles behind her but that was not unusual, for despite the new trams in the town plenty of people still preferred to travel by horse and carriage, not trusting the new ideas yet. Only as the noise slowed by her side did she raise her head from deep within her cloak where she was huddled against the approaching night air. She recognised the figure instantly as he dismounted by her side.

'Annie, I wanted to see you, I knew the funeral was today. Are you all right?' Richard's voice as always was full of concern for her and she could not help but be moved by him.

'Yes, I'm well, thank you. I am sorry about Joe the other day, he was rude to you, please take no notice of him.'

'I don't care about Joe. I was just concerned for you. Have you seen a doctor since you have been pregnant?'

'No, but I'm fine, really.' She felt embarrassed now, knowing he was bound to ask her why her own husband was unaware of the baby.

As if reading her thoughts Richard chose his words carefully, he knew this was not his concern but anything to do with Annie always seemed as if it were. Ever since their early days he had thought about her, wondering how she was, what she was doing, and fate kindly kept crossing their paths. If that was all he could have, he was grateful. He certainly did not want to upset her now by prying, for having gained this precious contact with her the last thing he wanted to do was chase her away.

'Annie, I'm not asking you your business, but please come into the surgery let me examine you, for the baby's sake if not yours. I promised I wouldn't tell Joe or anyone you are pregnant but you know you can't keep hiding it, even if you have your reasons.'

She knew he was right, she was almost six months pregnant now, her belly was rounded and her breasts enlarged and swollen. Even Joe in his ignorance would soon realise what the changes in her body meant.

'I feel healthy an' the baby moves and kicks, really I'm well, Richard. You're right, I 'ave to tell Joe soon an' I will. Thanks for yer concern. I mean that.'

Suddenly filled with compassion she gently squeezed his arm, and the shock of her touch made him recoil. Assuming

213

she was being too familiar she pulled her hand away apologetically.

'I must get 'ome,' she muttered and leaving him spellbound by her presence she hurried off. Richard stood watching her until she was swallowed up by the descending darkness before remounting his horse and turning towards home, his heart both soaring from the meeting and aching from the brevity of it.

She sat in front of the crackling logs watching the dancing blue flames. She sipped her hot sweet tea, savouring the milky liquid as it slid warmly down to her stomach and warming her fingers on the hot mug. The clock ticked steadily; she loved the solid sound of it breaking the silence with its even and precise movement, it helped her to think. She knew that she must think, for Richard was quite right, she could not keep her baby a secret any longer. The problem was just how to tell Joe, firstly because she knew that he was going to be furious and secondly she realised that she had probably left it too long now, for the baby was due in twelve weeks and that would make him suspicious anyway. But tell him she must and tonight was the night. Hopefully he would be mellowed by the fact that her mother had been buried today and that would at least curb his reaction. Inside Annie was afraid not for herself but for her child, she knew she was exposing it to danger but she had little choice and so she steeled herself for the fray.

By the time Joe returned home some two hours later, the cottage glowed warmly and the inviting aroma of food wafted through the air tantalising his taste buds as he entered the kitchen.

''Ello, somethin' smells good.' He smiled, something he did more often these days since things seemed to be more and more under his control.

'Get yerself washed, an' I'll serve it up.' Annie made herself sound cheerful and returned his smile, best to get off on the right footing.

'Did the funeral go off all right?'

214

'Yes, only me and Jack, but I didn't expect anyone else.'

'Well, it's over now, things can get back to normal.' Joe was actually delighted at the way things were turning out. With Elizabeth out of the way Annie had no distractions.

Carefully Annie served up the piping hot food before her husband and then sat opposite to him at the small wooden table. She toyed with her fork, knowing that now was probably as good a time as any, but the words seemed to be refusing to come out of her mouth. She took a deep breath and told herself she must go through with this.

'I were thinking today it's funny 'ow life is,' she began nervously.

Joe raised his head from his plate wondering what on earth she was talking about, his eyes looked expectantly at her.

'Well, yer know when one life ends another starts somewhere,' she stuttered; she knew she was doing this badly.

'Yeah I suppose so,' Joe muttered, uninterested, and turned his attention back to his dish.

'That's why it's so wonderful that we should have started a new life now, as Mother's has ended.'

The words tumbled from her lips in their desperation to escape and having done just that, Annie wished she could swallow them back.

'What d'yer mean?' Joe's voice barked. Annie recognised the familiar prelude to uncontrolled anger that would surely follow.

'I mean we're havin' a baby, I'm pregnant Joe, isn't that marvellous?'

Try as she might even Annie failed to make this sound at all marvellous and she anxiously watched as the dark cloud descended across Joe's face.

'Yer can't be.' It was not a question but a statement, and Annie trembled inside.

'I am, Joe. I wasn't sure but now I am, an' soon you're goin' to be a father. Just think, a child of our own, someone to work alongside yer, someone to pass the sheds on to, it will be wonderful.'

215

'No children, we agreed no children. Have yer any idea what yer've done now?' Joe sounded distraught as he tried to take in the magnitude of the news. His emotions swirled, how could she be pregnant. He was so careful, and yet they had done it so much lately maybe he had slipped up one time. It certainly wasn't impossible.

Strangely, Annie's worst fear was unfounded. For once Joe did not think she had been with someone else, in fact the thought never entered his head. Instead his brain fought frantically for a solution, there had to be a way out of this. And then it came to him. Surely Annie must only just be pregnant, it would be easy to get rid of the child, there were doctors in Liverpool or Manchester who for the right money could perform operations to dispose of unwanted babies. He never stopped to consider for one moment that this might be dangerous for Annie or even that she might have a choice in the subject, he had told her a long time ago that she wasn't allowed children and she would not disobey him now.

Leaping to his feet Joe paced the floor, his agitation growing. Annie sat pale faced, waiting for the explosion.

'I'll find a doctor an' we'll sort it out, straight away. Tomorrow I'll go into Manchester. There must be somebody there who'll get rid of it.'

Annie felt the baby kick within her almost as if it had heard the words and reacted accordingly. Her stomach churned.

'Joe, yer can't kill yer baby. I won't let yer, it's alive, we can't kill it.'

'Yer'll do as yer told. I said no babies an' I meant it.' Joe flushed red.

'But why, yer never told me why?' Annie pleaded.

'It doesn't matter, I just don't want children, ever,' he yelled back.

'Well you've got one now. No doctor will get rid of it, Joe. I'm six months pregnant. It's too late.'

Joe stopped pacing and turned to face her. His hand flew

216

through the air and as it crashed against her face Annie stumbled to the floor.

'Yer bitch, yer little bitch, yer didn't tell me purposely till it were too late. Yer've known for six months an' hidden it from me, well it won't work, I'll still find someone who'll do it fer the right price.'

'Please Joe, stop, the baby is here, yer can't just destroy it. I won't let yer, it's my baby too.'

She dragged herself to her feet, rubbing her stinging face. Her eyes were defiant and she held Joe's glare refusing to be intimidated.

'I'll leave yer, so 'elp me, I'll go away till the baby's born.'

Joe knew too well that stubborn look in her eyes, he knew that as much as it tore him apart to have this child it would be a million times worse to lose her. For a long moment they stood locked in visual combat and then, knowing he was defeated, he grabbed his jacket.

'Very well, have it. But I tell yer now, yer keep the brat well way from me, or I won't be responsible fer what I'll do.' With that he left as he always did, when she had defeated him, to lick his wounds and retrieve his pride.

Ever since Annie had given him the terrible news Joe had struggled to come to terms with it. For three weeks now he had thought of nothing else, his head churned and even at night his dreams had turned into nightmares. That whole dark part of his life that he had managed to bury burst out again to torment him. The worm began to wriggle hungrily in his brain. He relived the nightmare of lying in his bed at home, listening for his father's footsteps on the stairs. He could almost feel his heart pounding in his chest as the sound got nearer and nearer, knowing that the handle on the door would squeak as it was turned. He felt again the sweat on his face as the lumbering bulk of his father slid into the bed next to him, he could smell the stale breath as the thick lips slobbered against his skin. He recalled that his worst fear was that one of the two younger boys who shared the bed with him would awaken, and witness the horror that followed but strangely they never did, though that was partly because he never cried out for fear of disturbing them. He tried to block out the next part but he couldn't do it any more, and the cruel memories danced before his eyes, over and over again. His father would turn him over so that his face was buried in the pillow and then pinning him to the mattress he would lower his full weight on to Joe's body, squeezing out the air from his lungs as he thrust himself into his son's body. It was not the pain that Joe remembered hating most but the feeling of helplessness, the inability to stop the grunting noises in his ear, or get away from his father's stinking aroma. He felt again the slithering worm slide into him and then hide itself within his innocent body waiting for the chance to reappear. It lived in his head now, waiting.

When it was over, his father would always whisper that he loved Joe, that he was so special and then withdrawing himself he would slip from the room, leaving Joe feeling soiled and dirty.

For years Joe had managed to make these things disappear, Annie had done that for him, now the wound was reopened and it was all the fault of that baby. He was plunged back to that swirling abyss from which he could see no escape and from where he could see his new nightmare about to begin. This was the hardest part for Joe, his old life was past, gone; he could control that, but not the new one. The disease that his father had begun had not died but was lying in wait, a taste and desire planted so long ago, which would surely reappear. Joe despised this part of himself most, for after being abused for years by his father he too had been infected with terrible longings and needs. He had tried to deny them to himself for years but he knew they were there. That was part of the reason he had been so desperate to leave home, to get away from his younger brothers, whose firm bodies excited him so much. He was disgusted and tormented by his yearning but try as he might he could not deny them, and every time he had seen his brothers naked or brushed against their smooth skin in the bed they shared he had become aroused and he had to use all his strength to fight the urge to reach out and caress them. He knew it was wrong and wicked but still those feelings lurked in the dark corners of his mind.

With Annie he felt normal and safe, he took her body with force and each time the power he felt buried his demons a little bit more, proving to himself that he was all right, he was just like everyone else. All that security had now gone, and he was afraid. This child was a devil sent to test and torment him, growing before his very eyes, tempting him with its innocent sweet body. It would not matter whether it was a boy or girl, the desire would be the same and all Joe saw ahead was years of torture whilst he tried to control himself, or worse, years of abuse whilst he took his pleasure. He felt he was sinking, drowning in a putrid swamp of corruption and all the while he could hear his father's voice telling him what a good boy he was, a very special boy. He began to think he was going mad, he avoided Annie for he could not bear to look at her growing belly. He stayed most of the time in the wych shed, hoping that he would find a way to control the monster that grappled within him before the child was born, unable to share this terrible burden with anyone, such was his shame.

Annie was relieved. The secret was out, and she had won the battle. Joe was angry and sulking but she didn't mind that, in fact she was enjoying the fact that he hardly came home now. She began to feel more in control, that she was shaping her own destiny, that perhaps Joe was not all-powerful after all. He had not beaten her, as she had expected and that was at least something for it meant her baby was safe. She felt very smug now about her rising belly; this was her achievement and she no longer tried to hide beneath huge dresses and loose cloaks but proudly showed off her pregnancy. A growing feeling of excitement filled her and she tried to imagine what her baby would look like. She enjoyed people congratulating her and asking her when the baby was due, and she began to prepare for the child's arrival. Last week she had bought a second-hand cradle and begun to sew and knit clothes and sheets and blankets.

As for Joe, he would come round, he always did. Once the child was born things would be different, it might even mellow him a little. She rarely thought of Peter Smith now, in fact it didn't seem like his baby at all, after all he would have no part in its life. She was almost grateful to him for he had given her this opportunity to bear a child, to have something to love and cherish of her own. She thanked her God in her prayers for this gift and fully believed that she had his approval, in fact he was instrumental in bringing her and Peter together for this very purpose. If anyone had asked her how she felt, which they didn't for she had neither family nor friends to share her feelings with, she would have said she was happier than she had ever been for she had a future to look forward too and the future was her baby.

# Twenty-Three

It was cold for March and a thin scattering of snow had iced the landscape with powder puffs of sugary white, through which the golden crowns of daffodils poked up, dancing precariously on willowy emerald legs in the biting wind, jumping the gusts to prevent being snapped. Today the sky was brilliant blue and the snow sparkled, dazzling the eye in a blatant attempt to deceive that it was warmer than it really was. Its trickery had worked, for Annie looking out of her window earlier that morning, had seen what she perceived to be a sunny spring day and had dressed accordingly. Now, however, as she struggled back from the shops with her parcels, the wind savagely bit her face making her eyes stream and her lips sting.

She huffed and puffed as she walked, not just because of the cold but because her baby was so heavy now it pushed her ribs into her lungs and she found it hard to breathe. Only three weeks to go and Annie was counting the days. Her belly was huge and she hadn't seen her toes for weeks. She waddled along the road with duck-like gait as her back attempted to compensate for the lump ahead, and it ached mercilessly in the process until she couldn't wait to get home and sit down. As she left the streets behind her, she was suddenly overcome by the delightful vision of the trees decorated in silver finery and the river winking in the sunlight. Emotion seemed to have overtaken her senses these days and she found herself smiling. She felt at one with everything and an inner glow warmed her body, driving out the freezing wind that buffeted her.

Her feet crunched the ice crystals on the path, reminding her of her precious salt. She had not been down to the sheds as much recently, partly because there was little she could do in her condition and partly because Joe made it quite clear he did not want her there. She reasoned that he was quite capable of running the sheds; and Jack too was always around, not doing much, although his experience was vital should something go wrong. Also she thought it was good for Joe to take charge, to give him more responsibility and perhaps he would snap out of the never ending sulk he seemed to be in. She even let him bank the money these days and pay the workers, which he managed perfectly well. The business was still doing well and Annie had no fears for the welfare of the baby for it would be well provided for. As for Joe, his opinions seemed less and less important and she had become dangerously complacent about his temper, believing nothing could harm her now.

As she rounded the corner, the sheds and her cottage came into view, standing solidly on the river bank; she felt her pride swell, it was a good feeling knowing that she had achieved all that. It all seemed so indestructible that she felt nothing could go wrong and it would all be made perfect when her little one was born. Quickening her step she scurried inside to the warmth of her kitchen, eager to unwrap her shopping and look again at the things she had been buying for the baby, for she wanted to make sure that she had everything she needed.

She spent the rest of the day rearranging the drawers of tiny clothes, folding and re-folding the shawls and blankets and gazing longingly at the cradle which she had placed at the side of her bed in readiness. She hummed and sang to herself as she pottered around, every now and then stroking her belly affectionately and talking to her baby as she did. This was the contented mood that Joe found her in when he returned from the shed later that night.

That Annie was so beautiful in her pregnant state irritated

Joe greatly, for it somehow made him feel more inadequate. He reasoned that in all their years together he had never seen Annie so contented or attractive, and it was not him but a child that was doing this to her and he was jealous. She spent all her time now knitting, sewing or ironing baby clothes, she seemed oblivious to the rest of the world and Joe wondered if she noticed he was there at all. She was no longer upset by his silence, she did not try to cajole him from his sulks nor did she seem afraid of his wrath. He felt he was losing her and losing control of the situation and he was beginning to panic. He had still not come to terms with the baby; his future seemed so unsure and Annie was the only solid thing he could see to hold on to.

Tonight once again she was ignoring him because of the brat, for having placed his meal in front of him as a matter of duty, she had disappeared back to her sewing in front of the fire. He shovelled the food into his mouth, irritated that she had not sat with him at the table, so agitated that he couldn't swallow the meat. Slamming the plate to one side, he yelled through to the living room, determined to get her attention.

'Am I supposed to eat this?'

Annie sighed, put down her needle and waddled through to her husband.

'It's full of fat. I can't even chew it,' Joe spluttered like a spoilt child.

'Then leave it an' eat the potatoes instead. There's a rice pudding in the oven, yer can fill up on that.' Annie voice sounded patronising, though in fact she was simply unconcerned.

Joe shifted on his chair. The old Annie would have been scared now and rushed to make him something else to eat, even though they both knew that the meat was perfectly good. His fears were reinforced. She didn't care any more. It was time he taught her a lesson.

He sat silently fuming, plotting his revenge. Once his mind was set on this dogmatic course it was as if he were being sucked down a narrowing spiral, all reason and logic disappearing until Annie became the enemy. Normally she would have seen all the danger signs and would avert a potentially dangerous situation by giving in to Joe's ridiculous demands. But her forthcoming motherhood seemed to have coloured her judgement and lulled her into a false sense of security. Today she chose to ignore him, to her detriment.

All evening he sat glaring at her, never speaking a word. His sick mind was now weaving itself into ridiculous knots and strange flights of fantasy, so that he had begun to lose all sight of reason. The baby was the enemy, stealing Annie away from him, and she was betraying him. As he studied her face he could have sworn that she was laughing at him, mocking his weakness. He knew she had never thought he was good enough for her, just the stupid worker, whilst she was the boss. Well, he'd show her who was boss in this house. He began to drum his fingers on the edge of the chair, the veins in his neck bulging.

Suddenly Annie yawned and folding up her sewing she rose to go to bed. She had been so engrossed in what she was doing she had failed to notice Joe all evening.

'I'm going up, then,' she announced and without waiting for a reply she left him. Joe leapt from his chair the minute she had closed the door, and began pacing the floor.

Normally she would have offered him supper but not tonight, his needs just did not matter at all these days. Of course he could quite easily have made himself a drink and cut a slice of cake, but that was her job. Besides if he were truthful he didn't really want anything, but she should have asked anyway. This was the catalyst he needed and he bounded up the stairs, two at a time, ready to attack.

As he pushed open the bedroom door Annie was just about to climb into bed, dressed only in her night-dress, which clung to her huge stomach, incensing him even more. Then he spotted it, the cradle, by the side of the bed and he totally lost control.

''Ow dare you put that thing in my bedroom, I told yer I didn't want to have that baby near me.' Grabbing the cradle in his hands he flung it out of the door and it crashed one by one down the stairs.

Annie jumped out of bed and ran to try to rescue her treasured possession, but by the time she reached the stairs it lay shattered at the bottom.

'What's wrong with yer?' she screamed.

Joe proceeded to drag all the baby clothes out from the drawers and systematically ripped each one before flinging it into the air. Annie threw herself on his back trying to get him to stop. She was shouting and crying, but it was as if he couldn't even hear her. Once the clothes were ruined he turned his onslaught to the lovingly sewn blankets and sheets. Annie by now was hysterical, as she tried to save some of her baby's things, but everything she picked up Joe dragged savagely from her grasp, his eyes wild and insane.

Soon the whole floor was covered in debris and he turned his attention to Annie, wrenching her to her feet and pushing his face inches from hers.

'The baby has to die, don't yer see it's spoilin' everythin'.'

She backed away from him, tears cascading down her cheeks now. She shook her head in disbelief. 'No, no Joe, please don't hurt me, please.'

The first blows were to her face, punches in her mouth and cheeks and when she fell to the floor he began the assault on her body, kicking her ribs and stomach, whilst she tried to curl into a ball to protect the baby.

'Tell Joe that yer love him,' he laughed like a madman. 'Tell 'm, Annie, be a good girl an' I won't have to punish yer.'

Annie raised her bruised and blood-stained face to his. She had never seen him look like this before and she knew he was quite capable of killing her. The pause was enough for him to begin his next attack, and yanking her to her feet by the throat he proceeded to squeeze his fingers together.

'Yer bitch, yer betrayed me didn't you, admit it.' He spat the words at her.

Her mind was whirling, what did he mean, had he found out about Peter, but how?

225

'No Joe, I haven't,' she gasped, hardly able to speak as he choked her.

His fingers tightened. He was intoxicated by the power as she started to choke. He squeezed harder until her eyes began to bulge and her face burned scarlet.

'Yes yer did, no children that's what we agreed an' now it has to die, 'cos you're a wicked girl.' He laughed in hysteria as he felt his fingers gouge deeper into her neck.

Annie imagined her end had come, thoughts flashed through her brain, firstly that she would never see her child and secondly if she had a knife at that moment she would have been quite capable of murder herself. She prayed, begged and pleaded with God in her head to save her for the sake of her baby. The voices told her to stop struggling and lie still, which she did and it worked, for Joe immediately slackened his iron grip. Annie remained statue-like, her eyes closed, trying to keep her breathing shallow.

If she had opened them she would have seen a look of sheer horror on Joe's face, for he thought he had killed her. Her face was smashed into a bloody pulp and the marks around her neck clearly defined his fingers, her body was limp and she remained screwed up in the unnatural position into which she had fallen when he dropped her in panic. He fell against her, weeping and sobbing until she felt the salt from his tears washing over her lips. Instinct told her still not to move and she remained corpse-like.

'Oh God, Annie I'm so sorry, so sorry, Annie my love, please wake up, please.'

He shook her body as if trying to inject some life back into it, but she fell back onto the floor as he released her. Even as he walked round and round the room wailing and hitting his head against the walls, she managed not to move a muscle.

After what seemed to Annie like hours of his remorse and self-pity, he left and silence fell on the room. Cautiously she opened one eye and then remained still, waiting and listening. For a while he banged around downstairs and then she heard the door slam. He had gone out.

Her mind raced. She knew she had to get away from here, for he was sure to come back soon. He had probably gone to get something to put her in, maybe he was going to hide, or bury, her body.

Wiping her hands across her bloody face she tried to drag herself to her feet but her body too was broken and it was agony to move. The voices were telling her she must hurry, she must find the strength, and so using every ounce of courage she had left, she staggered down the stairs to the front door. She had no idea where she was going, all she knew was that she must get away before that madman returned. She began to run. She realised that he had probably gone to the wych shed, so she headed in the opposite direction. The night air was freezing and she was still dressed only in her thin night-gown, but she felt neither the cold nor the sharp stones that cut into her bare feet. In her desperation she ran to the protection of the woods, the place she always ran to, where she felt safe and she could think.

By the time she sank to the frozen ground some fifteen minutes later, she gasped for breath as she collapsed. She knew she could not manage another step; not only were her lungs bursting but the blood pounded in her ears and her heart thumped loudly. Crying and sobbing she held her belly, telling her baby to hold on, that it was all right, they were safe now. Shooting pains ripped across her stomach and she feared she was about to give birth. She knew she must get help and soon.

Her thoughts flew automatically to Richard, he would help her, and she knew she must get to him. Struggling to her feet she turned round and round, desperate to find some landmark which would give her a clue to the direction she had run in. It was pitch black in the trees, the only light a silvery glow from the moon that shone in a starlit clear sky.

Panic began to race through her mind, she had no idea where she was, she could be lost in the frozen woods all night. She knew that her baby, let alone herself, would

227

probably not survive that. The cold had begun to seep into her now she had stopped running, the sweat on her skin turned to ice particles, she shook and her teeth chattered. Spinning round on her sore and bleeding feet she put herself in the hands of God and set off in the direction that felt right. As she walked she talked constantly to her baby, telling it how much she loved it, describing the walks they would have together in these very woods, gathering the bluebells in spring and the holly in winter. She told it about the wych sheds and the town, the boats on the river and how they would go to Liverpool to see the ocean ships, with their tall masts. She looked neither right nor left but plodded on oblivious to where she was going. For hours she continued until the navy sky gave way to red as the sun's dye washed over the horizon, painting out the stars one by one. By dawn her whole body was numb, her face covered in dried blood interspersed with purple bruising, and her feet shredded in ribbons by the ground. Her steps were faltering now and her mind becoming delirious, she squinted against the sunlight as she forced her legs to keep going. Over and over in her mind she kept repeating Richard's name, she must not sit down even though all her body was telling her to do just that, for she knew if she did, she would never get up again.

The trees had thinned out and ahead she could see hedges and fields, she blinked, unsure whether it was a building in the distance. It was easier to walk on the soil of the field for it squashed softly beneath her toes, the birds were singing cheerfully and that encouraged her steps onward. The building she could see grew and grew, it was a large Georgian residence, set back behind rolling tree-lined lawns. The white blinds at the tall windows reflected the morning sun, blinding her as she approached the driveway.

She had no notion of her whereabouts, having wandered for miles, but she really did not care, the house meant she could stop walking, she could sit and sleep and her baby was safe. The last few yards were the worst, but she made it, collapsing in the front door step, managing to ring the bell as she sank to the ground and passed out.

The sight that met the butler as he opened the door was horrific, a girl heavily pregnant and yet dressed only in a night-gown. Her face was swollen and beaten and her feet and legs too streaming with blood. Annie was carried into the hallway and then on the orders of the lady of the house wrapped in a blanket, on a sofa by the fire in the drawing room, while a footman was dispatched to fetch Doctor Ellis straight away.

Annie vaguely remembered waking and seeing a kindly and anxious face hovering above her and feeling the warmth of a fire. She called out for Richard but he was not there, and she wondered if she was dead. Then blackness enveloped her again and in her dreams she thought she was being carried in Richard's arms. His voice was whispering her name and his words were smooth and comforting. She felt herself sink into deep soft sheets and Richard's gentle fingers bathed away the dried blood from her wounds and told her to sleep and she did, for three whole days.

# Twenty-Four

On the fourth day Annie awoke and realised she wasn't dead at all but in fact lying in a very warm soft bed, the smell of fresh cotton sheets and flowers filled the room. Instinctively her hands flew to her stomach and she heaved a sigh of relief when she felt the hard lump that was her baby. As if to reassure her it kicked and she felt the outline of a tiny foot push her hand away. Tears of relief and joy filled her eyes and she said a dozen or so thank-yous to the voices in her head that had helped her survive.

Gingerly reaching up, her fingers tentatively explored her battered face. She could feel the lumps and weals across her cheeks and the swollen lids of her eyes. Her lips were drawn tight where the ripped skin was beginning to heal and her throat, so badly bruised, was sore and stiff. As she moved she winced in pain and she was reminded that her ribs too were battered and her feet lacerated and torn. She closed her eyes again as the memory of that night replayed before her, making her realise what a miracle it was that she had survived not only Joe's frenzied attack but her escape afterwards.

She could see again Joe's wild-eyed madness, and she could not believe that he had actually tried to kill her. Of course he would now realise that she hadn't died at all and the terrifying thought that he might well be looking for her rushed into her mind. She must find out where she was and then find somewhere to go and hide, at least until the baby was born. Struggling to sit up, she gritted her teeth against the pain and swung her legs over the edge of the bed. Her mind was filled with only one thought, and that was find some safety for her child, somewhere Joe would never find them. As her feet touched the floor it seemed as if the carpet flew up to meet her and the next thing she knew she was lying full length on the rug with Richard standing over her.

'Where are you trying to run off to now?' His voice was gentle as always, and he carefully lifted her back onto the bed.

'What happened?' Annie muttered in a daze from her fall.

'You passed out, that's all. You are far too weak to get up yet, you have to rest.'

Annie groaned and let her head sink into the pillow, and as she did so Richard tenderly pulled a blanket over her to keep her warm.

'Yer don't understand. I have to get away from here in case Joe finds me.'

'Joe did this to you?' He had thought as much. There were a million questions he wanted to ask her, but not yet. First she had to rest, get better and gather her strength for the birth of her baby. It was a miracle that the child had survived this attack, and having done so, had not been born prematurely. In any case the birth would be soon, and Annie was going to need all her strength for it.

'Joe won't find you here, Annie, you are safe. But you must rest for your baby's sake.' He stroked her hair affectionately and had to blink back the tears as he gazed on her beautiful, broken face. 'I promise you I will look after you, no one will find you, trust me.'

Annie, like a lost child, soaked up his words gratefully, she did not have the energy to fight, her head and body ached and all she wanted to do was sleep again. The feel of his hands on her head was comforting and she moved against him, so glad that he had not asked her what had happened. She wasn't ready to talk about it yet, but then Richard always understood her so well. She allowed her eyes

231

to close and with the rhythmical feel of his hand on her skin drifted away, peacefully.

Richard did not move but sat for the hour or so while she slept, watching her steady breathing. Inside he was a turmoil of emotion, his rage at Joe was intense and his first impulse when he had laid eyes on his precious Annie was to rush around and kill the animal himself. However once he had calmed down his rationality returned, better to let the law deal with the matter and his resolve had been to report the incident immediately. Now, though, seeing all that fear in Annie's eyes he knew he must wait, he had no idea what had really happened and it was Annie's decision as to how she wanted to deal with the matter, so he knew he must wait until she felt well enough to talk about it. He had been truthful when he said she would be safe here, for he had brought her to a remote cottage on the edge of his father's vast estate. It was some thirty or so miles from Lytwych and Joe would certainly have no idea where to begin looking for her. Besides he might not be looking for her at all but lying low in case someone was looking for him in connection with his assault; he might well believe he had killed Annie and that, thought Richard, was probably for the best.

When he had been called out to Alferston Manor four mornings ago, he had never dreamt of the sight that was about to meet him. The servant had indicated that some poor peasant girl, pregnant, had been attacked, and he went along on a duty call. Imagine his horror when he recognised the brutally beaten face before him. Not knowing the circumstances he had considered it prudent not to acknowledge that he knew the girl and declaring that she had probably been thrown out of the poorhouse, he had ordered a carriage to take her to his surgery, where he could patch her up and send her back with instructions that she must be allowed to stay.

The story seemed acceptable to the lady of the house, who although feigning shock at such a dreadful situation, was actually quite enjoying the commotion and thinking what a wonderful and exciting tale this would be to tell at her ladies' morning.

Richard carried Annie out of the Manor, before too many more prying eyes had taken a look at her. Once in the carriage and away from view of the house, he had instructed the driver to change direction and head for his father's estates instead. He knew that the cottage was empty, for the gamekeeper who lived there had died recently. On arrival he tipped the driver generously, asking him not to repeat to anyone where he had dropped his passengers off. For the next three days whilst Annie had slept, he had cleaned the cottage, lighting the fires and filling the rooms with flowers to take away the musty smells, returning to his own home each morning to hold his daily surgery and deal with any important matters. Nobody noticed his disappearances, his wife Dorothy was away in London with her mother and wouldn't be back for weeks. All that mattered was Annie, he would have risked anything for her and all he wanted to do was sit by her and care for her until she recovered. And then ... well, he tried not to think that far ahead, but sometimes in an unguarded moment he dared to imagine that his dreams might have come true.

When she awoke for the second time Annie felt much better, she had the security of knowing Richard was there to care for her and that she was safe, for he had said so. She managed a smile followed by a grimace as it pulled her sore skin, and then with Richard to help her she sat up propped on the feathery pillows and sipped a warm drink. With slow and steady progress her bruises began to fade and cuts heal. As each day passed her body ached less, and she stayed awake for longer periods of time. Eventually she got up each day for some exercise and fresh air and by the time three weeks had passed she was almost looking like her old self again.

Through those days Richard helped and supported her, he never asked her about what had happened, never pressed her for reasons or explanations but was simply there with the loyal and rock-like support she so desperately needed.

She could not begin to tell him how grateful she was, but then he didn't expect her to. She knew that he went to his surgery each day, but she never questioned him about this private life. A silent pact had developed between them and they both enjoyed this secret world they shared while they could. Both knew it was removed from all reality, but somehow that didn't seem to matter.

On the third day of April 1886 Annie went into labour. It started suddenly as she strolled in the garden of the cottage enjoying the warm sunshine. Richard was not back from his surgery yet and Annie knew she would have to cope alone. She was not afraid, she and Richard had already discussed the birth and she felt well prepared. When her first contraction had passed she went to prepare the bed, stripping off the good sheets and getting towels and bowls prepared. She filled the huge cauldron with water and placed it on the oven to boil, resting each time a wave swept across her body with increasing intensity. When Richard arrived back two hours later he found her squatting in a corner of the kitchen, sweat pouring from her face as she tried to cope with the increasing pain.

She grinned, to reassure him, rising unsteadily to her feet. 'It's the baby, I'm fine, that was just a comfortable position to be in. I'm so glad you're here though,' and she fell against him.

He placed his arm around her shoulders and smiled. 'You do just what you want. If you want to walk around do, if you want to go to bed that's fine.'

'Could we stand in the garden for a little in the sunshine?'

'Of course we can. You'll be fine. I'll look after you.'

They stood beneath the trees watching the dappled sunlight playing on the ground until Annie's contractions became so intense that Richard found it hard to support her and then he gently led her into the house and bathed her forehead. Sitting her on the edge of the bed he massaged her shoulders and back, comforting her through the pain.

Though the birth was not easy or fast Annie was not

234

frightened. Richard supported her with such obvious love and devotion, she knew she could have survived anything. At six o'clock that evening, her son made his appearance in the world and as Richard handed the wet bundle to her, tears of joy fell down both their faces. They sat, the three of them huddled together on the bed, bonded by the miracle of the moment, for all the world like a complete family. James Edward Hayes, for Annie thought of herself as Hayes still, was a healthy bouncing boy. He had his mother's dark hair yet his eyes were a bright blue and the contrasting effect was startling. Annie immediately saw Peter in this child. She could not help a sorrow passing through her, she had loved Peter so desperately, her heart could still turn at the thought of him and now this product of that emotion was here as a reminder. She would never forget him and she would never let anyone hurt her again in that way. It seemed so sad that James would never see or know his real father.

Richard saw the dark shadow cross her face and assuming that she was thinking about Joe he kissed her cheek, telling her not to worry, Joe would never find her here. In truth she had thought very little of Joe since she had been here, her mind blocking out the horror of the real world that she knew she would have to face at some point, for even in her emotional state Annie knew this was just a dream time and it could not last for ever. For the moment though she chose to enjoy it before the bubble burst.

For Joe, the last few weeks had been a living hell, tormented with nightmares. His mind was ripped apart with guilt and remorse. Every waking minute his head was filled with pictures of Annie, he could think of nothing else, she consumed him totally. At night he cried to the heavens for forgiveness and by day he searched for her endlessly.

When he had returned to the cottage that dreadful night, it was relief that had first swept over him when he found she had gone. As always when the swirling beast had settled in his head he had been mortified by his behaviour, and now his heart had soared, she was alive, he hadn't killed her. But as the night wore on his misery returned.

He managed somehow to mechanically take himself to the wych shed each day, telling Jack that Annie was resting as the baby could be born any day now. Jack, uninterested in his sister at the best of times, thought nothing of her absence. As soon as he could leave each day he continued his search, though not knowing really where to begin. He tried the midwife and old Mrs Toscher who used to look after her as a child. He asked at the railway station if anyone of her description had bought a ticket. Had she died after running off into the night, and been discovered, an unknown body . . . been taken to some hospital to recover until the child had been born? It was if she had simply vanished into thin air. His life without her seemed a meaningless existence, he couldn't be bothered to wash or shave or even eat most of the time. He had stopped going back to the cottage for the emptiness only reminded him of her loss, and so he slept in the shed finding warmth from the boilers. There was not one minute of any day that she did not fill his head, she was his protector, his inspiration and she owned his very soul.

Deep down he knew that if she was alive she would come back for the pans if nothing else. They were her life, her pa's gift to her and she could not just leave them for ever and that was the only thing that kept him going.

The pans were the only thing she would return for and so he tended them devotedly as if they were Annie herself. This was the only way he could show her he loved her, by keeping her sheds safe, ready for her return. He knew when she came back he would never let her go again, she was his wife, his possession, and he would build a fortress so high she would never escape from it. All he needed was the chance to tell her how much he loved her, he would even put up with the baby if that made her happy, anything would be worth it to stop this living hell without her. While he waited he tried to ignore the demons in his head that tortured him, mocking him and reminding him of who he really was. Only Annie could stop the pain, and he would wait for her for ever.

Jamie was three weeks old when Richard told Annie that he could no longer sleep at the cottage every night, but that his wife had returned from London and for the sake of appearances he must go home. He assured her that he would still come every day and soon Dorothy would be off again on one of her extended trips and everything would be fine. He had never really spoken much about her before but it seemed that they lived very separate lives and Annie did not feel it was her place to pry.

She would have been surprised to learn that Richard considered his marriage the worst mistake of his life. His father in his usual bombastic manner had coerced him into a loveless match. But it had been suitable even though he and Dorothy were completely incompatible. From John Ellis's point of view it was socially right that Richard should have a wife, and for Dorothy's mother Richard was sent from heaven. Dorothy was no great beauty and at twenty-six almost considered a life-long spinster; the Ellis's were rich and a doctor's wife was very respectable.

Richard reasoned that it was not Dorothy's fault that he could not find her the least bit attractive and so it was only right that he present himself with her at functions when she required him and leave her to go off to her mother's as she wished; he owed her that at least. For Dorothy being a country doctor's wife was no fun at all and she craved for the excitement of London and the great social scene, and other than when her mother sent her home as a matter of prudence she was quite happy to reside away from Richard as much as possible.

'Yer father is bound to find out sooner or later that I'm 'ere, Richard,' Annie mused as they strolled in the woods behind the cottage.

Richard carried Jamie wrapped in the cream woollen shawl which he had bought. 'My father has no idea what goes on on his estate. He's usually too drunk to care. Beside

I've already had a word with the manager and told him that I am using this cottage for now. He was quite happy to keep quiet about it especially when I slipped him a guinea and the promise of more. He thinks I bring my women friends here.'

Richard laughed at Annie's shocked face.

'Richard, that makes me . . .'

'It makes you a very beautiful woman that I am looking after. You are safe here Annie, both you and Jamie. Don't worry, things will work out fine in time.'

They continued walking in silence, both their heads swirling with the future. Richard was planning how best to deal with the problem of Dorothy. The humiliation of a divorce seemed so unfair for her, but maybe she would be happy simply to lead her own life somewhere if he supported her financially; she might well even be relieved to be free. He did not hate Dorothy or even really dislike her, but he could only love Annie. But not yet. Annie needed time to regain her strength before he began to even suggest such plans; he had waited all his life for her, a few more weeks would make no difference.

She watched him carrying her son so tenderly in his arms and was saddened by the realisation that this dream must end. She had to face the past, she had no right to jeopardise Richard's marriage by expecting him to come here. He was a good friend, the best she had ever had, but that was all. She crossly checked herself for imagining there could be anything more. She had told herself that after Peter no man would ever get close to her heart again, she never wanted to feel the pain that she had experienced then. So she denied the fact to herself that Richard was already in her heart and had been for as long as she could remember. It was just her and Jamie now, that was what she had to concentrate on. Thoughts of Jamie drew her back to her salt pans, they were his future, she could not simply leave them behind. She knew that no matter how frightening it would be she had to go back and face her past for Jamie's sake.

As they neared the cottage, Richard handed the baby back

238

to Annie, kissing his cheek first. She hugged him to her breast, his warm milky smell comforting her, as Richard turned to go home. At that moment if both of them could have made a wish they would have asked for the same thing, and that was that this idyllic private world they had created could last for ever. But they both knew that was impossible.

# Twenty-Five

**A**ll that night Annie tossed and turned, her mind plagued with thoughts of her uncertain future. She had resolved that she could not stay here much longer, it simply would not be fair to Richard. After all he had risked so much already, his reputation, to say nothing of his marriage. It would only be a matter of time before someone found out she was here and then he would be branded for keeping a woman and suspected lovechild on his father's estate. His life could be ruined, and for nothing. He deserved far more than that. When he had given her so much unselfishly the least she could do was remove herself from his life. Thoughts of leaving here hurt her so, she felt so secure and safe, and though she hated to admit it she had grown to depend on Richard already. She loved his calm and reassuring ways, they talked so easily and laughed all the time. She knew that she would miss him terribly, he was a very special man and she felt so privileged to have known him.

Try as she might, sleep continued to evade her and already the light was beginning to soak up the night. Annie gazed lovingly at the small bundle that slept so peacefully beside her, his steady breathing punctuating the silence. The love she felt for Jamie was all-powerful; every time she looked at his perfect little face or stroked his smooth white limbs she was startled by the intensity of her emotion. She found she could sit quite happily for hours at a time gazing at him and trying to take in the wonder of his very being. As he suckled her breast, his bright blue eyes would hold hers, full of such trust and devotion, that sometimes she would have to blink back her tears. He was truly a miracle and she knew she could do anything for him, for he was the most important thing in the whole world and from now on her life would revolve only around him and his needs.

The birds had begun their dawn chorus and Annie shivered, for she had been so lost in thought, she had failed to notice the blanket slip from her shoulders. Pulling it up now she snuggled back into the warmth of the bed relishing the comfort and the uninterrupted moment with her son. He whimpered in his sleep and instinctively she drew him to her, the contact of her body reassuring him back to his slumbers.

She sighed and spoke to herself in hushed whispers. 'Oh Jamie, Jamie, what are we to do?'

She knew the answer, but it seemed so harsh and terrifying that facing it was almost impossible, but face it she must. Focusing all her strength she allowed her mind to wander to that dark area she had so successfully shut out over these past few weeks.

Joe appeared in her mind. To try to keep things in perspective, she first imagined the shy introverted young boy who came to work for her father. He had been besotted with her from the beginning, she knew that, such a dark horse, never talking much or mixing with anyone. After her pa had gone she had relied on him, and he was always there willing to do whatever she wanted, almost a slave to her. So much so that he had put his own life in danger and almost died on the night of his accident. He must feel resentful that because of her he was disabled, but she reasoned that that would not make him want to kill her. She knew that she had done an unforgivable thing by marrying him, she had lied not only to him but to herself, she did not love him. She knew that she had systematically rejected his love for her, been ice-cold to his passion, rejected him in the worst possible way. The more she considered these things the more she began to think that his attack was an explosion at the end of years of frustration. She could not excuse his behaviour but she could begin to see a reason for it and she began to believe that she was the cause.

She knew that however abhorrent, she had to go back, to face Joe and try to make some kind of future for herself and Jamie. Her fears were for Jamie's safety but she also knew Joe; after the storm always came calm and he would now be full of remorse. Whatever his reason, the pans were hers and she had no intention of letting go of them, so Joe would simply have to be faced. The sooner the better.

Later that day when Richard arrived at the cottage he found Annie in the sitting room. By her side was a small bag, packed with the few clothes that Richard had provided for her and Jamie. A cloak lay on the chair next to her and Jamie was wrapped up tightly ready for an outdoor excursion.

'Richard, sit down. I have to talk to you,' she said fidgeting her hair around her fingers. 'I have to go back.' Her words fell like stones, crashing in the air.

For minute he stood, too shocked to move. Then, as the impact of her words struck, he laughed nervously.

'Don't be ridiculous, you can't possibly go back.'

'I have to, for Jamie if nothing else. The salt pans are 'is, it's all I have to give 'im for the future. Besides I can't stay 'ere forever, it's not fair . . .'

Richard rushed to her, silencing her words and holding her hands in his. 'Annie, you can't go back. For one thing it's not safe, and besides, what would I do without you and Jamie now.'

'We'll miss you too, but you 'ave yer own life, Richard. We don't belong 'ere.'

His mind was in turmoil, he had to stop her from leaving, he had to tell her that *she* was his life, that he loved her. He had loved her ever since he had rescued her from Jack's clutches that night at the fair all those years ago. He had never told her it was he who had dragged Jack from her, not wanting to embarrass her. Her dark flashing eyes, so full of indignation as she covered up her nakedness that night, had captivated his heart. He had loved her ever since and

242

now just when he finally thought she had come back to him, she was talking of leaving. She was such a contradiction. There was the woman Annie, strong and ambitious needing no one in her stubborn path; but then there was the lost child desperately needing love, putting everybody else's needs first and letting others walk over her. This was what Richard could see now. She was, unbelievable as it was, considering Joe, and then Jamie and finally what she thought Richard needed. Her own desires did not count, almost as if she were a puppet in others' lives. The two parts of her in total contrast warred within, creating turmoil and confusion.

Falling to his knees before her, he clasped her fingers within his, to begin to pour out his heart. At that very second a loud hammering on the cottage door made them both jump out of their skins. Richard instantly leapt to his feet and Annie grabbed her bag ready to take flight.

'I told yer it would 'appen. Quick, let me go out of the back door, it might not be too late.' She swept Jamie up into her arms and made towards the rear door.

The voice calling her name stopped her dead in her tracks. It was Joe.

'Annie, Annie, I know you're in there, please open the door.' His voice sounded desperate.

She stood rooted to the spot, unsure of what to do. If she ran he would only follow her. Reason told her she had to face him.

'Annie please, just talk to me, I won't hurt yer, I promise. Please, Annie.'

She knew he was crying, and to Richard's horror and disbelief she laid Jamie on the couch and walked slowly to the door to open it.

The sight that met her made her gasp, for Joe looked so old. His face was haggard and worn from weeks of not sleeping, covered in stubble, and his hair dirty and dishevelled, he looked thinner and completely exhausted. As her eyes met his what she saw a lost soul, desperate and distraught, and guilt swept through her as she thought, I have done this to him.

'Annie, oh God Annie, please forgive me.' The words tumbled from his lips, interspersed with giant sobs, as he collapsed against her.

Richard cut in, his voice high-pitched in anger. 'How dare you, how could you come here after what you have done to her.'

Joe brushed his presence aside. 'Annie, please come home, I'm begging' yer. It will never 'appen again I swear. I can't live without you. I'll do anythin', but please come 'ome.' He pleaded now, pulling at her cloak.

'Come home to you? She won't ever come back to you. Do you understand? You're lucky that you're not up before the magistrate,' Richard spluttered, wrenching Joe's hands from his beloved.

'Please Annie, the cottage is warm an' ready, the pans are all up an' running. It's yer 'ome, Annie, yer belong there, yer belong with me.' Tears washed down Joe's face in torrents and his eyes never left Annie's for one second.

'Annie, don't listen to him, stay here with me, you're safe here.' Richard tried to push his way between them, but Annie put up her hand to stop him.

'What about the baby Joe? Our son, what of 'im if I come 'ome?' Her voice was steady, not betraying her torment within.

'I swear I'll look after both of yer. No more trouble, Annie, I promise, never again.'

She knew what she must do, she had to set Richard free, she had to go back to Joe. Joe needed her, she owed him that, she had created the monster, now she must care for it. There was no escape, this was her destiny, she had to make the best of it.

Annie turned to Richard. In his face she saw sheer disbelief but in the long run he would be grateful, she couldn't ruin his life, she owed him so much more than that. She took his hand and pulled it to her cheek, gently rubbing her skin on his. 'Richard, I have so much to thank yer for,

244

I can never repay yer for yer kindness. But this is your world, not mine. You have a wife and whole different life. I don't belong here, yer know that. Joe's right, I belong with the sheds, in me own 'ouse. I'll never forget what yer've done fer me, but you'll see it's fer the best.'

Richard was dumbstruck. That Annie could even consider going back to the maniac who so savagely beat her was beyond his comprehension. He watched incredulously as she picked up her bag and with Jamie slung under one arm, walked calmly out of the door behind Joe. She did not look back but silently followed her husband along the path, almost in dream-like state. If she had turned around not only might her step have faltered but Richard would have seen the tears streaming down her face. As she disappeared from view and from his life he fell to his knees and placing his head in his hands he let out a cry from his very soul. He called into the air, 'Annie I never told you that I love you,' but she could no longer hear him, for his words were lost in the breeze.

They walked in silence, Annie a few steps behind, Jamie in her arms fast asleep and totally unaware that the world he had known so far in his short life was about to change so drastically. Joe's heart was soaring, she was coming home, his Annie was coming home, now everything would be all right again.

''Ow did you find me?' she asked quietly, wondering who was responsible for the betrayal.

'I asked everywhere, I've never stopped searching fer yer Annie. The manager of the estate told me that Doctor Ellis had someone staying in a cottage that might be you. When I paid 'im he told me where yer were. But I'd never have given up, Annie, not all me life till I found yer.'

Annie's stomach churned. The same estate manager that Richard was paying to keep quiet. She could only pray that she had left in time and that he would not think of selling the information on to Richard's wife or father.

'The pans are all at full production, I've banked all the

money, yer'll see I've taken care of it all fer yer Annie, until yer came home.'

His tone was gleeful, like a child who has done a good deed and waiting for a reward.

'Joe, what yer did was wrong . . .' she began. It couldn't just be forgotten.

'That's over now, it won't 'appen again. Everythin' will be fine now that yer 'ome.' His voice was dismissive and carefree. Nothing mattered now, and he continued to chat about the salt and prices as if this were any other day.

Annie groaned inwardly, he was always the same whenever he had behaved badly, whenever he had hurt her, he would simply pretend it had never happened. This was to be just the same, if he pretended everything was all right it would all go away. It was so easy, that way he did not have to take any responsibility for his actions, it was no longer his fault. Annie was sure that he pretended so well that he convinced himself these things had never happened or at least they became so trivial that she would be made to feel guilty for making such a fuss. It was happening already, that slippery process whereby he became in control, and although she could feel it Annie had made her choice, and now she must learn to live with it.

Two hours later as she prepared his meal in her own kitchen, she realised that he had not even looked at, let alone held, Jamie. Her heart was cold, she must somehow bridge this gulf between them. Jamie must be loved at all costs, Joe must think that this was his own son if they had any chance of survival. As if on cue Jamie awoke and whimpered hungrily, stirring from where she had laid him on the chair.

'Joe, will yer nurse him for a moment,' she called airily as if it were the most natural request in the world.

Joe hesitated, he really did not want to pick up the child, but Annie still had to be won over. He had seen the look in that doctor's eyes and it was far more than just concern for a patient; he would have to be careful for a while, he didn't want her running back there. Steeling himself, he bent down and picked up the warm infant, the tiny face studied his and

246

then realising that this was a stranger let out a frightened wail. Joe held the baby closer to him and began to rock back and forth, until the noise abated.

The feel of the baby's skin against his was comforting and soft and Joe liked the warm special smell of his son. Strange feelings stirred within him, a warmth that spread across his body, he liked the contact with the innocent little body.

Annie, relieved that Jamie had stopped crying, watched tentatively, as Joe hummed a little tune to his son and stood with his back to her, swaying gently back and forth. Perhaps, she thought, things will be fine after all. She busied herself back in the kitchen and it almost seemed as if the past two months of nightmare had never happened. Now they would simply have to get on with life as best they could. Jamie had a home and her to love him and maybe even a father to care for him. The pans were his future, and that was what Annie must concentrate on now, she knew she must bury her own wishes and desires. Jamie's needs were all that mattered.

As the months passed and Jamie grew, Annie watched with relief as Joe played with and cared for her son. He was always willing to change and wash the baby, always the first to cuddle and kiss him when he cried. This was her only consolation, for her life was becoming once again a prison sentence. Joe's determination that she would never escape again made her existence unbearable. She was not allowed to go anywhere without him, he even went to the shops with her, he followed her from room to room in the house, threw out her best dresses and made her wear plain dowdy clothes; sometimes she felt she wasn't even allowed a thought that he had not first censored. But still he loved Jamie and that was all that mattered, she had made her choice and she would live with it, her life was devoted to her son and at twenty-eight years old she felt her own was over.

# Twenty-Six

**W**hen Jamie was five years old, there were two certainties in his young life. One was that his mother was the most important person in the whole world, and the second was that he hated his father. There were several reasons for this animosity. His father made his ma cry. He was always shouting and yelling at her and when he was really angry he would hit her. Whenever Jamie witnessed these attacks he would burn up inside, vowing that he would make his father pay one day. The second reason was that Jamie was afraid of him, for his father was always grabbing hold of him, pinching him and punching his arms. It was supposed to be a game and his father would laugh whilst Jamie yelled at having his hair pulled or bottom slapped. His father's breath was always stale upon his face, and the worst thing was when he held Jamie in his arms and kissed and cuddled him. Jamie would fight and struggle to get free as the thick lips slobbered towards his face. They were scary kisses, not like his ma's soft, gentle ones. His father's lips would stay pressed to his too long, and his breathing would come in short hot gasps, his eyes flashing frighteningly. Jamie knew it was wrong, but he wasn't sure why, it just felt bad, dirty somehow. He tried to avoid his father as much as he could and this had been quite easy until now, but life was beginning to change, suddenly people were saying he was a big boy now and big boys had to help with the work.

His father wanted him to go down to the sheds with him and help with the sacks, and this he hated too.

There was nothing unusual in Jamie helping in the sheds, the salt industry was a family affair, almost from birth children would spend their days alongside their parents in the pans for there was nowhere else for them to go. As soon as they could be useful they were expected to help if only with the sweeping up or filling the bags. There was no time for play, especially in his father's eyes.

Usually his ma came to the shed with him and that wasn't too bad but today she was in the big shed that was across the other side of town and he had been left with his father. He had never said anything to his ma about how he felt, she had enough to worry about and besides it would only cause another row between his parents and if his father lost his temper she would end up with a clout. So that day when she had kissed him goodbye, he had simply smiled and hugged her back and promised to be a good boy until she returned.

As soon as she had disappeared Jamie scurried to the far end of the shed and hid himself amongst the piles of salt bags, where he could work away filling the bags undisturbed and hopefully his father wouldn't even notice him. He preferred to be away from the steamy vats, all the hot vapours hanging in the air scared him, he could see strange shapes moving and the slap, slap of the rakes made eerie echoes above the brine. Here in the corner it felt safe. Surrounded by the solid sacks, Jamie imagined himself to be in a castle. His imagination took him to places that he and his ma found together in the books they looked at. He became an Arabian prince dressed in flowing silks or an Aztec warrior, face painted, and a magnificent war head-dress on his head. Ma's favourite picture was the Indian princess and she told him that she once had a dress just like the lady in the picture. He had pictured her with her long black hair swirling around her in the pretty dress, he thought she would make a good princess. But his best dream was to be the Russian tsar, dressed from head to toe in silver and blue furs, sparkling snow sticking to his eyelashes and hair and in his hand a huge sabre. The blade would gleam and the

249

handle be encrusted with rubies and diamonds. Jamie would sit and stare at the picture for hours willing himself to somehow be transformed into his hero. Today he was pretending to be the Arabian prince and the salt became sand blocks with which to build his pyramids.

He was so lost in his make-believe that at first he was not aware of the raised voices in the shed. It wasn't unusual for everyone to shout, for it was difficult to hear across the vat with the bubbling liquid and the steam that seemed to swallow the words. Jamie knew that as well as his father, his Uncle Jack was here and another man who was stoking the boilers. He didn't really like his uncle for he was gruff and bad tempered, but at least he felt safe from his father when other people were around.

It was only when the voices began to shout really loudly that Jamie poked his head from between the sacks to investigate. He could see the shapes of his father and Uncle Jack standing on the narrow wooden walkway that surrounded the vat. He wasn't allowed up there because it was too dangerous; he had heard lots of gory tales of workers slipping on the wet boards and falling into the brine to be boiled alive in the scorching liquid. He strained his ears to listen to the yelling noises.

'I've sent 'im over to the other shed an' that's all there is to it. I'm foreman 'ere, not you.' Jack's voice penetrated the air and Jamie could see him jabbing a finger at his father's chest.

'Yer've no right. I need 'im in 'ere, the salt needs rakin' off or it'll just lump. I can't manage it all, get 'im back now.' Joe's voice screamed.

'That just about sums you up, can't manage the pans, can't manage the loadin', can't even manage yer own wife.'

'What does that mean?' Joe roared.

Jamie could tell, without even looking, that his father's face would be stretched tightly now in anger. He knew too well the tone in his voice.

Jack laughed and Jamie saw him move as if he was going

to walk away, but then Joe grabbed him and pulled him back.

'I asked yer a question. What does that mean?' The words seemed to fire from his mouth like gun shots.

'It's common knowledge. You an' yer injuries yer can't even give me sister a good seein' to.'

Jamie wasn't sure what this meant, but if it was that his father didn't look after his ma, then Uncle Jack was right.

'Even the boy ain't yours, yer've only got to look at 'im to see that, but you're so stupid yer can't see what's under yer nose.'

What happened next was over in a flash so that Jamie could hardly take it in. His father grabbed Jack by his shirt and swung him around. His uncle seemed to fly through the air like a feather and then with a blood curdling cry his body splashed into the boiling brine. Jamie froze to the spot not daring to breathe, all his skin tingled and he felt as if his blood was gushing around in his head.

Within a few seconds the other worker had returned to the shed for his rake and as he entered the door, Jamie's father immediately cried out, 'There's been an accident, quick 'elp me get 'im out.'

Both men then fished around in the bubbling liquid with rakes in a vain attempt to recover the body but it was lost, sucked down to a salty grave.

'What 'appened?' asked the worker, shocked and upset.

'I'm not sure, he must have slipped, one minute he were 'ere an' the next I 'eard 'im shouting. If I hadn't been so far away I might've saved 'im.' Joe's voice sounded distraught as he feigned his sorrow.

'We'll never get 'im out of 'ere,' replied the worker shakily.

'Don't stoke the fire again, we'll just have to wait for the pan to cool, by the mornin' we should be able to reach 'im. You go back to the other shed, there's nothin' you can do 'ere, nothin' any of us can do.'

The man left, distressed and shaken. Jamie, still too afraid to move, watched his father as he began to rake off the

251

crystals. As he worked Joe muttered to himself. 'Shame, we'll have to lose a whole day's work now,' and he continued to slap the brine, as if nothing much had happened.

Jamie knew he had to get out of the shed. His father had obviously forgotten he was there. If he could just get to his ma he could tell her everything.

Easing his legs from where he had had them crossed beneath him, he slipped from between the salt bags, but he tripped and fell. He froze instantly to the floor, hardly daring to breathe, hoping he hadn't been noticed. His heart sank as Joe bellowed his name.

'Jamie, Jamie is that you, boy?'

'Yes, it's me,' Jamie whispered and dragged himself to his feet.

Within seconds his father was towering above him, his large hands bearing down on Jamie's shoulders.

''Ow long have you been there, boy?' Joe boomed.

'I'm sorry, I were bored in the shed so I went out to play,' Jamie stammered nervously.

'Outside, an' yer've only just come in this minute have yer?'

Jamie nodded frantically as the pressure of his father's fingers gouged into his neck.

'Well now, if yer tellin' the truth then you'll have to be punished for not doin' as you were told, an' if yer lyin' an' you've been spyin' on things yer shouldn't, then yer precious ma will have to be punished fer givin' me such a wicked child. D'yer understand, Jamie?'

Jamie understood only to well. If he told anyone what he had seen today then his ma would be the one to suffer, maybe his father would throw her in the salt pan with Uncle Jack. Jamie shivered as his father's eyes seemed to bore straight through him.

'Yes,' he mumbled feeling very close to tears.

'Well, which is it to be? Are yer tellin' the truth, mummy's boy?' Joe spitefully twisted Jamie's arm behind his back until the child cried out with pain.

'Yes, I'm tellin' yer the truth,' Jamie sobbed.

'Very well, bend over an' take yer punishment.'

Jamie bent over in front of his father and closed his eyes waiting for the pain. It was worth it if his ma would be all right. He heard the swishing sound as Joe removed his leather belt from his trousers and then the whoosh of the strap flying through the air. As it stung into his skin he bit his lip until he could taste the sweetness of his blood. One, two, three, four times it lashed across him viciously and then it stopped. He waited knowing that if he moved before he was told to he'd get another one for being cheeky and not waiting.

'Stand up boy, an' come 'ere.'

Jamie knew what was coming and he hated this next part more than the excruciating pain of the belt.

'Kiss yer father and tell 'im yer love 'im.'

Jamie screwed up his face as his lips came into contact with his father's, the wet slimy feel made him want to be sick. As Joe enclosed his son within his arms Jamie struggled to get free, he hated his father and the only thought in his mind was to run to his mother's safe arms.

'Say it.'

'I love yer,' Jamie whispered, with his fingers firmly crossed behind his back.

'Yer can go now, but remember if yer lied I'll have to punish yer ma.'

Jamie understood perfectly well and fleeing from the shed, he ran until his legs couldn't run any further, then he dropped to the ground and sobbed with fear and confusion.

'Whatever is the matter, lad?' The voice of the stranger seemed kind and Jamie tentatively opened an eye. 'Are yer 'urt?'

Jamie shook his head and took a long look at the speaker. She was an old lady, with white hair hanging loosely around her shoulders, her face although wrinkled was still pretty and Jamie immediately liked her. She extended her hand to him and without hesitation he let her help him up, scrubbing his fist across his face to wipe away the tears.

'Has someone 'urt yer, then?' she persisted in a quiet voice.

'Me father,' Jamie stated flatly.

'Oh I see. Well, perhaps it's best forgotten if yer'd done something you shouldn't.'

'No I hadn't done nothing wrong, he had,' Jamie said indignantly.

His little face was so full of childish honesty that the lady smiled to herself and sitting down on a nearby log she tapped the space beside her so that he perched alongside.

'D'yer want to tell me about this bad thing?'

Jamie's face fell and his voice took on an urgent tone as he replied. 'No I can't, I mustn't or he'll do something to me ma.'

The lady was anxious for him now, he was obviously afraid of whatever had happened. She took his hand in hers and squeezed it reassuringly. 'Well, perhaps yer can 'elp me instead.'

Jamie nodded enthusiastically, eyes wide at the thought of a challenge.

'Me name's Sarah. What's yours?'

'Jamie Jenkins, James Edward Jenkins really, but Ma calls me Jamie.'

'Well, James Edward Jenkins, I'm looking fer a lady, a very special lady an' maybe yer know her . . .'

But Jamie was off without waiting for Sarah to finish speaking as he spotted his ma approaching. 'Ma, Ma I'm here.

He flung himself at her nearly knocking her off balance and she swung him up into the air, planting a kiss on his cheek. 'What are yer doin' here, you should be at the shed with yer father.'

'I think they may have had a falling out, he was cryin' when I found him.'

Annie stopped in tracks as the familiar voice spoke to her.

'Ma, this lady's lookin' fer someone, can we 'elp her,' Jamie chattered, holding firmly onto his mother's hand.

Then to his amazement the lady and his ma began hugging and laughing and talking and crying all at once.

'Sarah, is it really you, after all this time. Where have yer been, how are yer?' Annie turned to her little son and kneeling down so that she was his height she drew him to her. 'Jamie, yer remember me tellin' yer about the lady who gave me the books we love, the one with the tsar an' the princess . . . the lady who lived on the barge. This is her, this is Sarah an' she's comin' home with us right now to tell us all her news an' where's she's been.'

Linking one arm with her long-lost friend and clasping Jamie's hand with the other Annie led them off towards the cottage. In all the excitement Jamie had forgotten about poor Uncle Jack, but then he suddenly remembered he couldn't tell his ma anyway. He bit his lip, wondering what he should do. His ma looked so pretty when she was smiling and she was smiling now. His father would have to tell her later and then she would probably cry again, but still that would be better than his father hurting her which was what would happen if Jamie told her the truth. Trouble was, Jamie was a boy who knew right from wrong, his ma had taught him that and as they walked along, she and the nice lady deep in conversation, Jamie kept hearing Uncle Jack's cry as he flew through the air. He knew his father had done something very bad and he knew he really ought to tell, but he just couldn't.

'Jamie, are yer daydreamin'?' Annie smiled fondly at her dark-haired son. As he gazed up at her with his piercing blue eyes, she was struck as always by his beauty and by his resemblance to his real father.

'No. Can I go to bed, please?'

'But it's so early, d'yer feel unwell?' Annie anxiously felt his forehead for fever.

'I'm really tired. Please Ma?' His voice was pleading.

Annie ushered him into the cottage and whilst Sarah seated herself by the warm kitchen range she fussed around her son whilst he scrambled into the safety of his bed.

'You call me if yer need me,' she whispered, stroking his hair.

Jamie nodded and threw in a yawn for good measure,

255

and then snuggling down into his bed he closed his eyes tightly until she left the room. He sighed in relief. He didn't want to see his father, not tonight, besides he had to work out what to do, to decide what was right and that was fairly hard when you were only five years old, even if you were a big boy.

'I don't think he has a fever,' said Annie anxiously as she returned to the kitchen.

'When I found 'im he was cryin', he said something about his father,' Sarah replied sipping her steaming tea.

'They probably had another set-to. Joe's so strict with him, he forgets he's still only little.'

'Joe? Yer married Joe from the shed?' Sarah sounded surprised.

'Yes I did.' Annie's reply was curt, almost defensive, but it did not hide her unhappiness from Sarah's wise eyes.

In haste to change the subject, Annie asked about Sarah's life over the last twenty years or so. It seemed that she had continued to sail her barge and transport salt and other goods but she had never returned to Lytwych, she had never felt she was able to until recently. This visit was a kind of crusade, she felt she had to come to Edward's grave at least once before she died herself to say her proper goodbyes. As she spoke of her life-long love her eyes filled with tears and her voice began to shake, Annie tenderly rushed to hold her in her arms and together they wept fresh tears for a lover and a father who was still so badly missed by them both. They were still comforting each other when Joe returned home, as he walked into his kitchen and saw the two weeping women his first thought was that Jamie had told them what had happened. He did not recognise Sarah for he had only ever seen her once or twice.

'Oh, Joe, this is Sarah. Remember? We were just gettin' all sentimental about Pa.' Annie sniffled, drying her eyes on her apron.

Joe's face lightened, perhaps the boy had been telling the truth after all and had seen nothing. Inwardly he breathed a sigh of relief.

'I'm afraid I've got some bad news fer yer, Annie. It's Jack. There's been an accident at the shed.' He paused as her face froze in expectation. 'He slipped an' fell into the vat. He's dead Annie, yer brother's dead.'

She stood rigidly as the news sank in. Jack dead, all her family gone now. She couldn't cry, for she had been afraid of him all her life, but she felt a strange emptiness. She was the only one left, and it was a lonely feeling.

Sarah sat watching but saying nothing. She thought a lot, though, and it seemed to her that Joe was far from sorry about this news he had imparted, in fact she would say he was almost smirking. Then there was Jamie, something had happened today that had upset him, and if she wasn't mistaken it was all to do with his father. There were a lot of bad things here, Sarah thought, and she sighed. She had hoped to find Edward's daughter happy but all she saw here was misery and if she wasn't mistaken ill doings as well.

# Twenty-Seven

'Why does she have to stay 'ere tonight?' Joe grunted irritably. He hated people here in his house.

'It's just one night, an' besides she's not just anyone, is she. I haven't seen her fer years an' she meant so much to Pa,' Annie reasoned, knowing that Joe was furious with her for making Sarah a bed up in the sitting room for the night.

'His tart, yer mean, everyone knew what she was,' he returned nastily.

'Don't say that. They loved each other. Why must yer always see the bad side of everyone.'

''Cos that's all most people have. Besides, I don't want her 'ere fillin' yer 'ead with ideas.' Irritably he flung himself into their bed, resenting anyone coming near his wife. 'She's interfering already, going on about finding Jamie all upset.' His voice began to rise in agitation.

'She only mentioned it,' Annie whispered, trying to appease the situation before it got out of control and before Sarah heard the conversation.

Joe sat up in bed, he wasn't going to have this woman telling him how to bring up his own son, planting ideas in Annie's head, turning her against her own husband. Within seconds as always, his mind rampaged along, clogging itself up with distorted imaginings.

'Get rid of her first thing in the mornin',' he yelled.

'I can't just tell her to go Joe . . .' Annie knew she was on dangerous territory now and that Joe was likely to explode at any minute.

258

'Do it, or I'll do it right now.' His face was distorted and the words spat from his twisted mouth. He stared at Annie for a few seconds, his wild eyes daring her to rebel, and then flinging himself over to his side, he closed his eyes and ignored her.

Annie slid down in the bed, at least he would not touch her now, but how on earth was she going to tell Sarah that she had to leave without hurting her?

In truth it was heaven for Annie to have someone here to talk to, she had forgotten how much she had missed Sarah. She was an ally, a friend, and Annie desperately needed that. She imagined what her pa would say if he could see her now, letting Joe treat her this way, and she despised herself. If only he were here, he would know what to do, how to help her, but there was no one she could turn to and now even Sarah was being sent away. Tears slid silently down her face and dripped onto the pillow, tears of self-pity, which only made her hate herself more. She didn't even pray any more, for she knew God had given up on her years ago; she didn't blame him, she was hardly worth the trouble.

Joe had gone the next morning before she arose, which was unusual, but then he had to get to the pan to remove Jack's body and make the arrangements for the burial. A doctor would have to come to certify his death, and Joe wanted to see to that himself. He was taking no chances that Annie might see that Doctor Ellis again, even though it was years ago, he had seen the look in the man's eyes. Besides, the sooner they got rid of Jack's body the sooner they could reheat the pan and start work again. Joe was feeling really quite pleased with himself. With Jack out of the way he would be in charge, he could make the rules. He liked the feeling of power, it made him feel important, it was almost as if the pans were his and not Annie's at all. Yes, things were definitely looking up, Annie did as she was told, most of the time. She spent too much time with Jamie, gave him far too much attention, but then he could deal with the child. Jamie was actually becoming more and more

259

attractive to him as he grew, he enjoyed the feeling he got when he hugged the boy to him and it would soon be time to teach the boy that his father was the most important thing in the world. He must learn about that special love that only he could give him. He licked his lips as he thought about Jamie's white smooth body. Still, he thought, mustn't rush these things, it had to be done slowly for that was half the pleasure, denying himself the physical act but letting his imagination run wild.

When Annie awoke a small cold hand slipped under the covers and brushed her skin.

'Ma are yer awake?' a little voice whispered.

'Yes. Jump in, yer freezin'. Has yer father gone?' she asked for Joe did not approve of Jamie getting into bed with his mother.

'Hours ago. I expect he's gone to get Uncle Jack out of the vat,' he said in child-like innocence.

'How d'yer know about Uncle Jack?' Annie asked, turning the small face towards hers.

Jamie bit his lip, he'd let it slip out when he shouldn't. Frantically his sharp brain sought an answer. 'I heard father tellin' you, I were listenin' on the stairs. Sorry,' he mumbled, hoping that she would believe him.

Annie frowned. There was something in Jamie's voice that didn't sound quite truthful, but then perhaps he was upset by the accident. She hugged him into her warmth and he squirmed in pleasure at the closeness.

'It would have been very quick Jamie, yer Uncle Jack wouldn't have suffered.' She knew she was lying. Jack's death was horrific as he boiled alive, but she didn't want Jamie having nightmares.

'What will 'appen to his 'ouse?' Jamie asked.

Annie hadn't even thought of the house. Of course she could sell it, but she probably wouldn't get much for it. Or she could rent it out. That would mean some more money coming in. Joe would approve of that idea. Whatever, she would have to go over to the place and sort out all Jack's things, and the thought filled her with dread. She had never been back there since her mother had died and by now she knew the place would be filthy for Jack had been completely idle. Still it would have to be done, and she steeled herself mentally to address the task tomorrow.

Jamie wriggled around impatiently when his mother did not answer him, he was hungry and wished she would suggest breakfast. Seeing him fidgeting Annie smiled and kissed his dark hair lovingly.

'Come on wriggle-breeches, time we were up and makin' some breakfast.'

Sarah had beaten both of them and the smell of warm sweet tea steaming in mugs and bubbling porridge sprinkled with sugar met them as they entered the warm room. 'Sarah you didn't have to do this,' Annie protested, as a mug of tea was thrust into her hand.

'The least I can do for a warm night's sleep,' Sarah replied to Annie's protest. 'It's so cold on that barge I'd forgotten what comfort was.' But in truth she was relishing the company as much as the warmth and food.

She didn't want to admit it but she was desperately lonely, and had been for years. Smudge her faithful dog had died long ago and then she had had no one. The barge was so old and dilapidated, no one would use her any more and besides Sarah could no longer heave and haul the heavy loads. For the last few years she had sailed along the rivers selling flowers and herb potions to the other river folk. It didn't bring her much and she was often hungry. Now she was really afraid, for soon the barge would not be fit to live in at all, it was draughty and damp, the wood was rotting. She could not afford to have it repaired and all that was left for Sarah was the workhouse.

She hadn't come to beg from Annie, her pride was too fierce for that, but she enjoyed the company and had hoped to stay for a short while. However, in spite of Annie's attempt to prevent her from hearing Joe last night, the walls in the cottage were thin and Sarah had overheard every word. She was sad, sad for Annie; the little girl she remembered with all that spirit and adventure had gone. What she

261

saw was a downtrodden wife, afraid of her bully of a husband. Something had killed Annie's very soul, and what was left was a pitiful creature with no self-respect, no pride, a shell with no life. Edward would be heartbroken to see her like this, but what could she do. If she stayed it would only cause Annie more trouble with Joe. She resolved to leave straight after breakfast and save Annie the embarrassment of having to ask her to.

'Can I come and see yer barge?' Jamie piped between mouthfuls of warm porridge.

'Yes of course, as long as that's all right with yer ma.' Sarah smiled and hesitated for a second before adding, 'Yer can both come to say goodbye and wave me off.' Annie's eyes met Sarah's and an understanding flashed between them. 'It's best. I can come and see you again, can't I.'

The two women hugged, and so much was said in that embrace that words were not necessary. Jamie pulled a face at what he called the kissy stuff, and jumping from his chair pulled on his boots eager to be off to explore the barge. Sarah and Annie laughed at his eagerness and wiping away their tears, they cleared the table as quickly as they could, under his continual insistence that they should hurry up.

As the three of them made their way down the river, the figure of Joe appeared strutting towards them. His whole manner was one of arrogance and he disdainfully ignored Sarah's presence, directing his speech directly at Annie as though she were an object, not a person.

'The undertaker's been, body's gone, buried in two days' time.'

There was no compassion in his voice, no understanding that this was, after all, Annie's brother, that she might just have feelings. Sarah seethed inwardly, she loathed everything about this man, and it took all her resolve to keep quiet.

'Yer'll be at shed soon, then,' he went on. It wasn't a request but a statement, and Annie nodded apologetically.

'We're just goin' to see Sarah off, Jamie wanted to see the

262

barge. I'll be there in a few minutes.' Her words rattled out and she put Sarah in mind of a nervous dormouse.

'Don't be long,' Joe boomed threateningly and then without acknowledging Sarah at all he strode off.

Sarah and Annie walked in silence as if a shadow had been cast across them. There was so much Sarah wanted to say to Annie, she wanted to get hold of her and shake her by the shoulders, mostly she wanted to scream at her, 'Remember who you are, Annie Hayes.' But in her heart she knew it was useless, she could see the fear in Annie's eyes as Joe spoke, she had no right to make Annie's life worse by causing trouble. This was none of her business and it would be best if she went away for good because she knew if she stayed she would certainly have to tell that evil man what she thought of him. She knew she couldn't just sit by and watch Edward's daughter and grandchild be treated so badly. She almost wished she had never come, for she knew that this would be difficult to put from her mind.

Jamie explored the barge, longing to go for a sail in her, and sulking when he was firmly told no, not this time. Sarah hugged him to her and told him he must look after his ma, to which he solemnly said he would.

'Where will yer go?' Annie whispered, knowing that tears weren't far away for either of them.

'Oh who knows, along the rivers, there an' back, I'll be fine. But what about you?' Sarah's eyes met Annie's but she dropped them immediately to the floor not wanting to expose her sorrow to the old woman.

'I'm fine, really. Jamie and I, we manage.' Her voice was forced and unnatural.

They embraced for the last time, and Sarah climbed aboard the tatty vessel.

'Goodbye Sarah, come back soon won't you,' Annie's voice sounded desperate.

The barge chugged into the centre of the river and the waving figure of Sarah began to shrink. Jamie leapt up and down waving and shouting and then he began to run along the bank to try and keep up with the boat.

263

'Not too far,' Annie called, though she too had a yearning to chase the barge and then sail away with it.

Sarah's voice was carried by the wind as the barge began to turn the smooth bend that would take her from view. 'Remember who yer are, Annie Hayes.'

In the next instant she was gone and Annie was filled with such an aching emptiness that it doubled her over for a second in agony. Jamie was racing back towards her anxiously thinking she was hurt, and she knew she mustn't cry in front of him. Straightening up she produced a smile and with arms outstretched swung him up into the air for a hug.

'Come on young man, we've got work to do at the shed.'

Her cheerfulness did not fool him, for he sensed his ma hated being near his father as much as he did. He knew he had to be brave for her, so squeezing her hand and giving her his most loving smile he pulled her along the path.

'Never mind, Ma, we've always got each other.'

'Yes Jamie, we have an' that's all that matters.'

The two of them pushed their misery aside and sang 'London Bridge is falling down' all the way along the towpath.

'I've got to go an' empty the house tomorrow, Joe, it's been over a week an' we must do somethin' with it,' Annie mentioned tentatively over supper.

Jack was buried and it seemed stupid to leave the house standing empty. There were always lots of people looking for cheaper properties to rent and Annie was sure they could find someone easily.

'Wait and I'll come with yer tomorrow night.'

Annie sighed, she wasn't allowed to do anything without him. 'I can manage, yer needn't waste yer time, Jamie can 'elp me.' She tried to make her voice sound casual but she knew it wouldn't work.

'I said I'd come.' Joe put down his mug and stared straight at her, his tone intimidating.

'Very well, I'll call an' put a notice in the grocer's window advertising the house, then.' She knew it was a slim chance but she kept trying to find any excuse, just to be free if only for an odd half hour or so. It never worked.

'I've already found someone. The new lad at the pan's lookin' fer somewhere.'

Her heart sank, she felt as though she were drowning and Joe was slowly pushing her under. If she took Jamie for a walk in the woods he would time them to see how long they were; it always caused a row. He went to the shops, the bank, the solicitor, everywhere with her. If she spoke to someone, whether it be man or woman, he would glare to silence her. He followed her from shed to shed, from room to room in the cottage, always suspicious and accusing. She could do nothing right for him, his meals were regularly thrown at the wall with demands that she make something else. His clothes were never washed properly and had to be re-done, or the house was never clean enough. Any excuse to persecute and punish her, to assert his authority and power over her, to keep her in fear.

Sometimes she thought she was going mad; just the sight of him, the sound of his voice sent shivers down her spine. When he touched her body, which he did whenever he felt like it, she froze, repulsed at the closeness of him. He took her more and more violently, beating her if she protested and then abusing her until she could sometimes hardly walk the next day. All this had somehow been made worse, if that were possible, by Sarah's visit. Some part of her which she thought had died was re-awakened and Sarah's parting words for her to remember who she was kept ringing in her ears.

Reality came in the shape of Jamie. She had to put him first. She tried to make his life as pleasant as possible, keeping him away from Joe and protecting him. She knew if she ever tried to leave home Joe would kill her, he had told her often enough, and then what would become of her darling son. Left in the clutches of his father, what would his life be? Annie could see no other choice, the pans were hers but Joe would never leave, and she was trapped with him forever.

In her mind, only when Jamie was grown and was able to look after himself would she be free and she knew she would have to run and keep running so that Joe would never find her, but it would be worth it. Until then she just had to put up with her miserable life, for Jamie's sake. She did have one other choice and when she was feeling really low she would allow the wicked thought to seep into her mind: if Joe were dead all her problems would be over, she and Jamie could live their lives without fear.

Even though she knew she would be punished for such ideas, when she watched Joe standing on the slippery walkway by the boiling vat, she wished many times he would simply slip and follow her brother to a salty grave. But it never happened.

# Twenty-Eight

The great Cheshire salt industry was in decline, overproduction had flooded the market and as the price of salt tumbled week by week, more and more salt pans went bankrupt. Hundreds of men lost their jobs and families their only means of income. In an attempt to stabilise the situation the manufacturers banded together to form the Salt Union. They could set stable prices, present a unified image to the buyers and by implementing rules and regulations they hoped to save the industry from complete destruction.

John Ellis, being a prominent member of the community, not to mention a very rich landowner with vast numbers of wych sheds under his control, naturally was chosen to head the new union. As chairman of the board he had the discretion to refuse membership to those pan owners he felt would not be beneficial to the group. It was virtually impossible to survive outside the closed ranks of the Union and one by one the ostracised sheds fell victim to the recession. Once foreclosed they were easy pickings for John Ellis, who simply added them to his empire for next to no cost.

Annie was one such exile, as there was no way that the mighty Mr Ellis would allow this upstart woman, who had irritated him for so long with her success, to be allowed into his group. At first things were not too bad. Annie had a good relationship with her buyers, even if she was never allowed to go and see them without Joe trailing along. But gradually the prices began to drop, so much that she was forced to close the big shed across town and three of the families who rented pans from her left, bankrupted. To make it worse, it was one of these families that rented her mother's house and they had to leave that too. Annie knew there was no way they would find another tenant, the whole town was full of to let and sale boards as people packed up and moved to other areas in despair, seeking new work. Times were hard for everyone and they were only going to get worse.

Having laid off all but two of the remaining workers, Annie and Joe worked the three sheds they had left between them. Jamie, who was by now seven and half years old, worked too, all day in the steamy sheds. He should really have been at school, but Joe didn't hold with that, 'Books won't put food in his belly', was his philosophy. Even though the school inspector was now regularly calling to see why Jamie was not attending school, Joe always found some excuse. Occasionally Jamie did go just for a day or two to appease the authorities but then he was soon absent again working in the shed.

At night, before Joe returned home, when Annie and Jamie relished one or two hours alone in the cottage and whilst she was cooking or cleaning, she helped Jamie to learn to read. Joe never knew about the secret lessons; if he had he would have given Jamie extra hours at the shed to work, instead of idling his time. Joe could read a little himself and he could certainly add and subtract his numbers, yet he saw no value in it for his son, believing it would give the lad ideas above his station; far easier to keep him under control if he were ignorant. That, he believed, was half of Annie's problem, she thought she was something she wasn't. He had to keep reminding her that she was worth nothing, that she was ugly and ignorant, just to keep her in her place. He certainly didn't want to have the same problems with Jamie, respect was what he demanded and they would show it if they knew what was good for them.

Annie was worried, more than she had been over the past few months, the sheds were stacked to the ceiling with sacks of salt that they could not sell and she believed they would soon have to let the fires out beneath two of the three remaining sheds. Her concern though was how to keep Jamie fed and warm. Winter was approaching, there was hardly any money left in the bank now and hardly any salt being sold. Joe was as always totally unreasonable about their sorry plight, he refused to acknowledge the seriousness of the whole situation and blindly carried on producing more and more unwanted salt. Any discussion she tried to have with him always ended in rowing; he insisted that the market would pick up, and when it did he would be ready.

Today Annie knew that there would be a huge argument, for without even asking him she had laid off the remaining two workers. There was simply not enough money left to pay them and even though this meant more work for herself and Joe, at least what money they had left would last a little longer and maybe they would make it through the winter months.

Purposely she sent Jamie to the grocer's so that he would not have to witness another rumpus, and steeling herself she went to deliver the news to Joe. Whenever she entered a room in which he was in, or came in close contact with him, the same heavy feeling descended over her. It was like a huge blanket that draped over her, pulling her down and blocking out the daylight. It made her feel old and weary and even sometimes as if she could hardly breathe, her lungs and heart having sunk somewhere in her chest. Today was no different and as she caught sight of him, limping along the shed, she knew she despised him. The arrogant way he held his head and the tight lines of his mean mouth made her shiver and she could not even remember now ever feeling any different about him.

'Where's Jamie?' he barked irritably at her.

'I've sent him to the shop. I wanted to talk to yer.'

Joe carried on walking away from her so that she had to follow behind him and shout above the noise in the shed.

'I've laid off the last workers today.'

The effect was immediate and he stopped dead in his tracks, swinging around to face her.

'Yer've done what?' he bellowed.

'I've laid them off, Joe, we can't afford them. We've got to be sensible.'

''Ow dare yer without askin' me.'

'I don't have to ask yer. These are my pans.'

Momentarily he was stunned, this was a new Annie, a defiant one, and for a second he was thrown.

'Your pans, your pans are they? A little piece of paper might say that, but who works them an' has done for years. I'm yer 'usband an' what's yours is mine. I make the rules 'ere, an' you just do as yer told.'

As he yelled, eyes bulging, face red and contorted, Annie was struck by how ugly he was. But he was right, this was a different Annie, an Annie so beaten and destroyed that the threat of further punishment meant nothing at all. She didn't care what he thought or what he did, it really didn't seem to matter any more. What she did care about was Jamie and her desire and need to care for her son overrode everything else now. She would protect him at no matter what cost to herself. She squared up to Joe in obvious provocation, and stared straight into his eyes as she spoke.

'I'm goin' to sell some of the pans Joe, you can't stop me, we need the money, an' there's only one person likely to buy them, we both know that.' Truthfully it was going to hurt Annie a lot more than she allowed herself to think to sell her precious sheds to John Ellis, but what choice did she have.

'Yer not sellin' them to that man, never, I'd sooner starve, I forbid it . . .' He continued to rant and rave, though Annie wasn't even listening, she had heard it all before.

Picking up a large wooden brush she began to sweep the floor. She would not say another word to Joe, it would be pointless anyway, and she could not stand any more arguing. She had made up her mind and she would to it, despite the consequences. When she thought about it, what could he do? Beat her, ignore her, abuse her? She was used to that anyway, so what did it matter?

She resolved to go and see Mr Ellis tomorrow before her

nerve failed and before things got any worse, though she wasn't sure yet how she could get away without Joe noticing her. All afternoon she schemed but it was not going to be easy. Joe watched her every move, he knew exactly how long it took her to do certain jobs and if she were a minute late he would be looking for her. By the next morning she had still not decided on a plan. Joe was particularly bad tempered and things were not going well. His breakfast was apparently not warm enough and he had left it, refusing to have it heated up again but stamping around in a temper because he was hungry. Jamie had received a sharp smack on the top of his head with the end of Joe's knife for making too much noise while he ate and Annie had to hold herself back from running to his protection. She knew this would only have made matters worse and so she watched in agony as her son gallantly tried to swallow his porridge and fight back sobs at the same time. When Joe was in these moods there was no stopping him and if he could find nothing wrong, he would invent it.

'Where are yer going?' he bellowed at Annie as she cleared the table of his untouched plate.

'To the shed of course,' she replied bluntly, but trying not to aggravate him.

'Dressed like that? Yer must think I'm stupid. Blouse half undone like a tart.'

'Joe, please.' Annie exclaimed, not wanting Jamie exposed to this talk.

He was obsessed about her going with other men. If she as much as spoke to one of the workers or smiled in their direction he would immediately accuse her of sleeping with them. If the whole thing had not been so sick Annie would have found it amusing, for as she was never allowed anywhere alone she wondered how, or where, Joe thought she actually conducted all these lurid affairs.

'What's wrong, yer don't want yer precious son to know what yer are, a slag, a cheap whore.' His eyes were wild now and he leaned across the table towards her, mouth foaming.

'Joe yer don't know what yer sayin', I don't even know

271

what I've done wrong. Please just stop,' she pleaded, knowing full well that if this turned into a full scale row he would never let her out of his sight all day.

Jamie sank lower and lower in his seat, eyes downcast, waiting for the explosion.

Annie hated Jamie listening to this, she hated Joe, and she hated herself for being so weak that she did nothing about it. Quickly wiping the table she nodded to Jamie to get his jacket and the three of them walked in single file to the sheds. Every step of the way Annie churned the same question over and over in her head, why couldn't he die, why couldn't he? Nobody would miss him, no one would be sad, and Jamie would be released from the nightmare world he had to live in. She knew she was becoming obsessed with the idea but she couldn't help it, it seemed the only answer. She believed that Joe was sick, ill in his head, he had to be, normal people didn't do such crazy things. Maybe it would be a release for him from his tortured brain, maybe it would be the kind thing. The seed was planted and it grew and grew silently; at every dreadful encounter she endured with him it strengthened, beckoning her like a dazzling light.

All morning she worked alongside her gaoler, her mind frantically seeking a reason to leave the shed for a while, but one just wouldn't come. Then fate stepped in and provided her with one. A young boy, one of the barge owner's sons, came racing up to the shed, to tell Annie that her last cargo had been brought back and it would have to be unloaded off his father's barge. It seemed that when they had arrived in Liverpool the usual warehouse had been all boarded up. The merchant buyer had also fallen victim to the rampaging recession and having already got a warehouse full to the brim with unsold salt, he could take no more and had closed up his shed. The barge men had no choice but to return the salt to the wych sheds.

Joe was livid, and yelling at the terrified boy, who was after all only a messenger, he set off to 'sort it out'. In his fury he never gave Annie a thought as he left the shed for the

272

quay-side. Annie couldn't believe her luck, she knew Joe would be gone for ages, arguing and yelling before he finally would have to accept that the salt would simply have to be unloaded and barrowed back to the shed. This was her chance. Quickly she grabbed her shawl and headed for the door.

'Jamie, I have to go somewhere fer a little while, be a good 'boy an' stay here in the shed.'

'Why can't I come?' Jamie did not want to be left alone to face his father or to have to try to explain where she had gone.

'I haven't got much time an' I can run without yer. I should be back before yer father but if not, just pretend yer don't know where I am an' stay out of his way. I'll be as quick as I can, I promise.' She kissed his angelic face and raced out of the shed.

As she ran she began to prepare a speech in her head, a speech to face John Ellis with. She knew how delighted he would be to have beaten her after all these years and she knew that he would offer her nothing like the true value of the sheds, for he would know that she had no choice but accept his price. Her only consolation was that she would never part with her pa's shed, even if she had to stop working it for a while, that was Jamie's for the future. One day the market would recover and then she would start all over again, and if only she could get rid of Joe, it would be just her and Jamie. She was puffing and panting as she approached the Manor, her face bright red from the exertion and sweat sticking her clothes to her body. Slowing down, she tried to regain her composure. Summoning all her courage and swallowing her disgust at what she had to do she hammered on the solid wooden door.

Her arrival had already been noted, for John Ellis, standing at his bedroom window, had watched the slight figure racing up the drive. At first he had not recognised her but as her face became clearer, a smile spread across his face. Annie Hayes. He had waited a long time for this day, and now she was here to beg for his help. He laughed to himself as he descended the ornate stairway to the grand hall below, beg she would have to, for he was going to enjoy this. As the butler turned to ask his master if he could see the woman at the door, John nodded.

'Ah yes, but put her in the kitchen for now, I'm busy for half an hour.'

He proceeded to the drawing room and sat down to read, smirking to himself as he imagined her discomfort at being made to wait with the servants.

When eventually she was shown into the grand drawing room, her stomach was a mass of knots, not so much from nerves but from anger at being deposited in the kitchen like a maid to wait for his convenience. Still she reasoned she must stay calm for she needed the money from the sheds desperately.

'Well Annie, so nice to see you, please sit down.' John Ellis graciously pointed to the plush embroidered cushion on the chair next to himself.

'I'll not waste yer time, Mr Ellis,' Annie began trying to disguise the desperation of her position from being conveyed in her voice. 'I'm 'ere to make yer a proposition.'

'Really? Well then, let's hear it, though if it has anything to do with the salt sheds, I have to tell you that the industry is in such a bad state now I doubt it will ever recover. I don't think I can offer you any advice on that subject.'

Annie knew he was playing games, he knew exactly why she was here and he was going to make this as difficult as possible. She hated having to do this and for one second she was tempted to simply get up and walk out away from this pompous man. But she knew she couldn't, she had to think of Jamie's future.

'I don't want yer advice, I'm 'ere to offer yer me sheds, if yer interested.' Her voice was flat, she was determined to give him no satisfaction here.

'All of them?' His eyes twinkled wickedly, this was better than he thought.

'Except Pa's, it's the smallest an' not much use to yer, but

I want it fer sentimental reasons.' Her eyes never left his, nor did her tone falter.

Looking at her now, he couldn't help but be struck with her determination. He knew full well that this must be tearing her apart inside, but she was showing nothing. He faltered for a moment, unsure whether to insist on having her father's pan or none. The stubborn shine in her dark eyes told him she would rather sell him none than lose that shed and so he relented, unable to do anything but admire her courage much though he despised it.

'It's not a good time, Annie, you know that. I don't know if we really need any more sheds, it's hard enough selling the salt we've got.'

'We both know the market'll pick up, but if yer don't want the sheds that's fine.' She rose to leave. 'I won't beg yer.'

'Very well, as long as you know I can't offer much for them. One hundred pounds a shed, that's all.'

Annie was stunned. She had expected much more than that, and she tried frantically to calculate how long she and Jamie could survive on the money, until she could find some other form of income.

'The machinery alone's worth more than that in each one. I can't just give them away.'

'Maybe in boom times, but what use is machinery when the salt won't sell. Seeing as we are old neighbours I'll go to one hundred and fifty, but that's the last offer.' His face was set now, he knew the victory was his, there was no one else in a position to buy the wych sheds from her. Even he knew she wouldn't let her stubbornness send her family to the workhouse.

'Can I think about it for a day or two?' Annie whispered, torn apart at having to let all her achievements go for so little money.

'The offer is now. Who knows, tomorrow the market may have fallen further and I may not be in a position to buy at all.'

She knew it was blackmail, she knew he was cheating her,

but despite that she knew she had to survive and there was no other way.

'Very well, I accept. Can we get it over and done with as quickly as possible?'

John Ellis was jubilant. At last they were his. Reaching for a sheet of paper and a pen he quickly scribbled the agreement down and handed it to her.

'Can you read?'

'Of course,' she said disdainfully and having checked the details reached for a pen to sign the paper.

'The solicitors will draw it up properly but in the meantime this will stand, in case you change your mind. It's a pleasure doing business with you Annie. I will see to it that the moneys are transferred to you as soon as possible. Now if you'll excuse me I have work to do, the butler will escort you out.'

His tone was arrogant and disdainful and Annie longed to slap his fat grotesque face. Trying to keep some pride at least she slowly rose and gathered herself together. She refused to meet his eyes, and without a word she walked from the room.

Only as she left the sweeping driveway did the emotion flood her body, she had lost it all, and to that obnoxious man. Tears streamed down her cheeks, tears of anger and frustration, but also relief. At least they could live and eat, they still had the cottage to live in, her mother's house to rent or sell and there was always Pa's shed. If the salt picked up again they could still sell some, enough maybe to keep them going. If not, Joe would just have to look for work elsewhere or accept the fact that she might have to.

Now there was a way forward again, even if it was a very narrow one.

She stumbled along the pathway, anxious now to get back to Jamie. As for Joe, it didn't really matter what he thought; it was all too late now, anyway. She fingered the sheet of paper in her pocket. She had changed their lives with one signature, and she knew she would have to pay the price when she got home.

276

# Twenty-Nine

**B**y the time the snow had begun to fall in November, John Ellis had fully taken over all of Annie's sheds, except of course her pa's. The river bank buzzed with activity again as his men worked the sheds, carts came and went each day, and the sky was filled once more with steam. In the tiny shed in the middle, Annie and Jamie worked side by side, between them they kept the pan going, producing enough salt to send a load once a fortnight to the docks. It wasn't much but it kept the pan running and Annie's contract with the merchant intact. Normally the buyer would not have been interested in such a small amount of salt but they had traded with Annie for years and her circumstances were well known, so out of loyalty and pity the trading continued.

The bruises had long since healed, from the beating Joe had given her the day she returned from John Ellis's, but the punishment continued. Joe knew he had lost, there was nothing he could do, for she had sold the sheds and the fact that she was obviously no longer afraid of him hurled him into total paranoia. He was now convinced that she was having an affair. He wasn't sure who with but with so many men working in close proximity, it could be any or all of them. He was convinced she was plotting against him, every conversation she had with others he imagined to be about him. If he overheard giggling between her and Jamie he would demand to know why they were laughing at him.

Even the wrong expression or gesture on their behalf sent him into a frenzy of rage.

He had decided that the best way to keep control of her was to never let her out of his sight, never let her talk to anyone without him being present; and so he began his guard duty. As punishment for her behaviour he refused to work, but sat in the shed or cottage or wherever she was and simply watched her. He rarely spoke except to criticise or yell at Jamie, but would sit staring at her for hours on end, glaring with animosity as his sick mind wove more and more elaborate webs.

Annie for her part was learning to ignore him, to shut herself off as if he didn't exist. His power seemed less these days and even though his presence made her miserable and still like a prisoner she was no longer afraid of him. If he threw his food against the wall and demanded more she would no longer rush to prepare something else, she just ignored him. If one of the men from the sheds spoke to her, she no long scurried away, afraid Joe might see her in conversation, but stopped and chatted. If she wanted to take Jamie for a walk in the woods or to town she would go and if he wished to trail behind, so be it. When he took her body, she would no longer disguise her hatred of it but turned her face abruptly away from his lips. She would lie limp and doll-like until he had finished. As he rolled off her body she would immediately rise from the bed and wash herself all over in front of him and then make sure no part of her skin touched his for the rest of the night. Her disgust began to disturb him, and he took her less and less frequently.

Her whole outlook on life was changing too. She realised she didn't need him at all, she could look after Jamie and work the pan alone. Her mind sought desperately for ways to get rid of him out of her life, but no answers came to that. He would not just go and she could not physically make him. In her darker moments she considered poisoning him, she even went as far as mixing a potion to slip into his food but at the last moment her nerve failed her. God's voice intervened, sternly and firmly reminding her even if she didn't get caught on earth for her sins, in which case she would lose Jamie for ever, she would certainly burn in hell for her endeavours. She begged him for other answers, pleaded for a fatal accident or terminal illness to remove Joe, it seemed so easy in her mind. But God would not bargain with others' lives, no matter how much misery they caused, so Annie knew she would have to find another way. Her other main worry was Jamie. She knew he needed to go to school but that too was causing huge problems. Firstly because Joe had kept him away for so long, not that she cared what Joe thought, she was already resigned to another argument with him over it. But because Jamie himself didn't want to go. He had no friends, and because of his isolated life he didn't know what to say to other children or even how to play with them. Beside which he wanted to stay and work with his mother in the shed, she needed him now that his father did nothing and he didn't want to leave her. Truthfully Annie did need his help but she knew his education was more important and so she determined to persuade him that he must go back. Tomorrow she would take him, no matter what.

'Where are yer going?' Joe bellowed after her as she headed for the kitchen door next morning, Jamie trailing miserably behind.

'Jamie's goin' to school today and every day from now on,' she replied firmly, ignoring her son's look of complete dejection.

'He's needed in the shed. Get those good clothes off, boy, right now.'

Jamie hovered nervously not sure what to do, but for once wanting to abide by his father's rules.

'Jamie, come along, we're goin' to be late,' Annie continued and steered Jamie in front of her through the open door.

The next thing she knew Joe was dragging her backwards. Flinging her up against the wall, he spat in her face.

279

'I'll not be defied, woman. Jamie, get to the shed now. I'm still master in this house.' Annie struggled to get free but her arm was pinned behind her back and Joe scrubbed her cheek against the wall viciously. 'Yer gettin' above yourself and it's goin' to stop.'

His hand crashed into her face. In an instant Jamie launched himself onto his back, kicking and screaming at him to leave his ma alone. Joe, demented with rage, turned on his son and grabbing him by the throat hoisted him high in the air, allowing Annie to break free. She grabbed for the kitchen knife that lay on the table and brandished it at Joe's throat as she screamed hysterically at him.

'Put 'im down yer hear, put 'im down or so 'elp me I'll kill yer.'

Joe dropped his son to the floor and lurched towards her instead.

'Jamie run, run an' don't stop,' Annie screamed.

They grappled for the knife, and Annie was easily overcome by Joe's strength. He knocked her to the floor and then, pressing the blade to her skin just enough so that it punctured it and a tiny drop of blood oozed out, he stared maniacally into her eyes.

'If yer ever threaten me again, Annie, I swear I'll kill yer, in front of the boy. Get to the shed an' no more talk of schools in this house.'

Slowly he rose and casually strode out of the door. Annie lay still for a few moments trying to regain her composure. Her heart was thumping in her chest, and the realisation that Joe was probably quite insane reinforced itself. She was terrified, not just of the fact that he was quite capable of killing her, but that in the moment when he held her son she knew she was quite capable of the same. She groaned. What was he turning her into? She was as bad as him. The sound of Jamie sobbing filtered into her troubled mind and she dragged herself up from the floor to find him.

Outside huddled against the wall, his hands over his face, her son shuddered as crying shook his entire body. Her heart twisted, this was all Jamie saw and heard, violence and anger. She trembled as she thought what they were doing to him; he was just a little boy, he wanted and deserved sunshine and happiness, not this nightmare he lived in.

'Jamie, Jamie, come 'ere, it's all right.' She beckoned him and he fled to her outstretched arms, where he collapsed in a fresh bout of weeping.

'I . . . I thought yer were goin' to die . . . Ma please stop fightin' with 'im . . . I don't have to go to school, it don't matter . . .' The words were interspersed with shakes and gasps.

'Stop, Jamie, calm down, everythin's all right now.' She stroked his head and kissed him.

'No it's not all right. I hate him. Why can't he go away an' leave us alone.'

'It's not that simple Jamie, I'm his wife, we live 'ere, he won't just go.' Annie knew that his was not an answer but it was all she could offer.

'I wish he were dead.' Jamie spoke with such vehemence that Annie gasped.

'Now yer mustn't say that, it's wrong, you mustn't. Come on, let's walk by the river an' see if the ice is thick enough slide on.'

She pulled him to his feet and hugged him to her. All this anger around him was making Jamie aggressive too, and that was the last thing Annie wanted for her son. This had to stop and she had to find a way, before Jamie's childhood was destroyed.

The morning light was beginning to fade, the sky was streaked with purple and black as in the distance snow clouds piled up in billowing heaps threatening to burst at any time. Annie and Jamie walked in silence, hand in hand along the crunchy towpath. They were in no hurry to get to the shed and have to see Joe, so they dawdled along trying to put off the agony. Jamie kicked the loose stones onto the ice where they skidded right out in the freezing water beyond the line of ice. Both deep in thought, both feeling safe in each other's company, the bond between them was solid and nothing could break it.

In the distance a lone barge was tied up to the bank, bobbing up and down almost as if it were dancing. The river was no longer the thriving busy place it used to be and it was not unusual to see only one or two boats here. As they got nearer it became apparent that this one was particularly old and dilapidated. The paint had faded and the wood looked rotten and decaying, there was no smoke coming from the chimney and it looked deserted. Neither Jamie nor Annie took much notice of it as they came up level to it, they were both so lost in their own thoughts. Then Jamie noticed the faded name on the side.

'Ma, look it's the *Mary-Rose*.'

Gingerly they climbed aboard the seemingly deserted vessel and began calling Sarah's name. The only reply was a tiny moaning sound from within the cabin. Racing through the door they found Sarah in heap at the bottom of the narrow wooden steps.

'Sarah, are yer all right?' Annie cried, gently trying to lift the old lady up.

'Thank God yer've come, Annie. I think I've got a fever or somethin', I just can't seem to get about.'

Between them Annie and Jamie managed to lift her onto her bunk. Her skin was burning and she wheezed chestily trying to catch her breath. All thoughts of Joe and the shed flew from Annie's mind as she sent Jamie to get a doctor.

It was only when Jamie had gone that Annie realised how cold and damp it was in the barge. There was no fire in the stove and so she couldn't even make Sarah a warm drink. Instead she wrapped her in a blanket and sat with her arm around her to try and generate some heat.

'Why on earth have yer got no fire?'

'I can't afford one all the time, so I save the fuel for at night. Times are a bit tough at the moment but it'll pick up in the spring.'

Annie had to smile. Sarah was the eternal optimist, she never changed.

'Yer can't stay 'ere, that's fer sure. Somehow we'll have to get yer home.'

'Oh no I don't want to cause any trouble, not between you an' Joe. I saw 'ow things were.'

'Sarah, believe me yer couldn't make things any worse. Besides it'll do Jamie good to have someone else in the house, as long as yer can ignore Joe. He hasn't changed; well, only to get worse.'

'I must admit the thought of gettin' out of 'ere for a day sounds grand.'

The sound of footsteps approached. Annie hoped secretly it might be Richard. She hadn't seen him for years, but he was never far from her thoughts, and whenever she thought there might be a chance of seeing him her hopes rose. Disappointment swept over her as the new young doctor, fresh from medical school, breezed down the steps.

'Well, well what have we here. Doctor Evans, pleased to meet you.' His enthusiasm brimmed over into his speech. Without waiting for anybody to answer he proceed to examine Sarah, tutting at her rattling chest and obvious temperature.

Soon he gave his verdict. Bronchitis at least, but if we don't get you somewhere it's warm you'll be getting pneumonia as well.' He looked expectantly at Annie, waiting for some offer of accommodation.

'Sarah's comin' home with me for a while, if we can get her there,' Annie replied.

'Is it far away?'

'No, just along the towpath, five minutes' walk at the most.'

Doctor Evans considered for a moment and then directing Annie to wrap the patient up well, he gave Jamie his leather bag to carry. 'I'm sure you're as light as feather, Sarah, all skin and bone, so I'll just have to carry you. But when this lady has fed you up in a few days, I don't want to carry you back.'

Sarah managed a smile at the thought of being carried by such a handsome young fellow, especially when he gave her a cheeky wink as he lifted her into his arms.

Within ten minutes she was safely deposited on the sofa

283

in Annie's cottage, in front of a roaring fire sipping a warm drink. The doctor promised to return later in the day with some medicine for Sarah's chest, and gave strict instructions that if she deteriorated he was to be sent for straight away. 'Keep an eye on her, we can't rule out pneumonia yet.'

As Annie showed him to the door, Joe marched in from the other side, nearly knocking the young man flying. He didn't apologise but gave the intruder a filthy look.

'This is Doctor Evans, he's very kindly brought Sarah 'ere,' Annie explained.

'Where, in our house?' Joe demanded, still ignoring the doctor's presence.

'An' she's stayin' till she's better.' Annie's voice was firm; trying not cause a scene in front of the stranger.

'Is she now. We'll see.' And with that Joe stamped off into the house.

Annie was embarrassed and she felt the colour flush her face. 'I'm sorry, please take no notice of me husband, he can't 'elp himself.'

Doctor Evans, though amazed at the display that had just taken place before him, said nothing and smiling reassuringly at Annie he nodded and left.

Annie seethed as she closed the front door. How could Joe be so rude and in front of the doctor? And now she knew there was going to be a scene about Sarah. After this morning's encounter with him she just didn't know how much more she could take.

She peeped in at Sarah. She was fast asleep, with Jamie sitting next to her watching her anxiously.

'I want 'er out of me house now.' His words hit Annie before she even entered the kitchen.

'She can't go anywhere Joe, she's ill. Even you can see that.' Exasperation filled Annie's voice.

'This is my house. I want 'er out, or do I have to teach yer another lesson like this mornin',' he grinned sadistically, twisting his lips.

There was something in that leer that snapped a cord in Annie's head and she knew that this was the limit of all she

284

could stand. For years she had taken his abuse, she had listened to him decrying her and intimidating her, making her feel worthless and useless, and now suddenly just the expression on his face flushed all that away and a voice in her head screamed out, no more.

'Just shut up Joe, d'yer know how stupid yer sound. Yer can threaten me all yer like, I don't care. This is *my* house, Sarah is my friend an' she's stayin', I don't care what you say or do. D'yer know why, Joe? Because yer are nothin' without me, yer have nothing an' yer are nothing.' Her voice was high-pitched, almost hysterical as she held his astonished eyes with hers. 'Go on hit me, do what yer want I don't care, go on,' she goaded him, taunting him with her words. 'I'll simply leave, Joe, I have another house to live in remember. You can't keep me here.'

For once Joe stood spellbound, he wasn't sure what to do. And then to Annie's sheer amazement he burst into tears and fell at her feet.

'Annie, please don't leave me. I'll die without yer, please, if yer go I'll kill meself, I swear.' His words were choked out amidst incoherent sobs and he pawed at her legs, the spit dribbling from his lips splattering her feet.

Far from being moved by this display of emotion, Annie was repulsed. She yanked her legs away from him, unable to stand the physical contact.

'Get up. Stop it. I'm not goin', but Sarah is stayin' an' I don't want to hear anythin' else about it.'

He pulled himself up her body and flung himself at her neck, sobbing still. In sheer disgust she unwound his arms from her and pushed him away.

'Stop it, stop right now, yer pitiful,' she cried angrily, and pushed past him to go and see her patient and hope that Jamie had not overheard them.

She felt no sense of victory, only that a whole new round of the battle had begun and these were simply Joe's latest tactics.

# Thirty

For the next three days Sarah tossed and turned as the fever rampaged through her. Jamie and Annie took turns sitting with her, wiping her brow and trying to get sips of liquid into her burning body. Every day Doctor Evans called and listened with growing concern to the ominous rattling in her chest. Sarah was for the most part delirious and she cried out for Edward and even Smudge her little dog from long ago. Just when everyone began to fear that the worst was about to happen she began to recover, her temperature fell and she woke up her usual bright self as if nothing had ever been wrong. The doctor said it was miraculous and Annie was overjoyed that her friend was on the mend again. She was still very weak and Annie would not allow her to get up for she had every intention of spoiling her until she was perfectly well again. Sarah for once did not protest. This whole incident had frightened her and made her realise that old age was creeping up on her no matter how unwelcome it was. Jamie too was delighted and sat with her for hours talking to her to keep her company. She loved her to tell him tales about Liverpool and the ships, just as she had done with Annie, when she was a little girl. Annie smiled to herself as she watched him, the same wide-eyed wonder in his eyes that she remembered experiencing. It was good for him to have someone new in the house, it diverted his mind from his father and made him see a world different from the narrow one he knew. The whole house took on a new feel, there was the sound of laughter again and Annie felt a confidence grow within her. The longer she sat and talked with Sarah, the better she felt. They relived all the treasured memories, the fun they'd had with her pa, all that love flooded back into her and made her feel alive again. Sarah's presence gave her courage to be herself. The time had come to make a stand, for Sarah once again had reminded her that she used to be Annie Hayes and it was time she was again.

Only Joe was miserable, pacing the cottage like a caged tiger, excluded from the joy the others had found in each other's company. He sat for hours staring into the fire, his mind a whirlpool of destruction. He was losing Annie, he could see her slipping away and he felt powerless to stop it. As with everything he felt incapable of dealing with, he ignored it, as if it didn't exist, so he hadn't spoken one word to Sarah since she had arrived. The only concession he gave to her presence was to flash her looks of hatred and contempt whenever he walked past her, which he avoided doing, spending most of the time in the kitchen. This was all her fault, intruding on their lives, he despised her. He knew she was tempting his Annie away from him, he'd overheard the whisperings that stopped whenever he came within earshot. Even Jamie was being taken in by the impostor and was spending all his time with her, ignoring him totally. Like a spoilt child Joe sulked, barely answering if Annie spoke to him, picking at his food and stamping and slamming around the cottage. Annie still continued to work the shed and although he followed her there every day, he refused to help but sat watching her, an accusing expression on his miserable face, in an attempt to somehow make her feel guilty for treating him so badly.

In fact it only made Annie angry; she seethed inside as she hauled the heavy rakes and sweated with the cumbersome sacks. All day long she could feel his eyes boring into her, weighing her down. She refused to ask for his help, for she knew that was what he was waiting for, that would be the trigger for an argument, and she was determined not to play this game with him. So she ignored his tantrums,

287

and spoke him to him as if everything was quite normal, despite the fact he did not answer her most of the time.

She cooked his meals and pretended not to see the look of disgust he feigned as he swirled the food around on his plate, and when he made some vile comment about her she smiled and carried on as if he had never uttered a word. The battle was now one of minds and Annie knew she was beginning to win, for Joe's emotions would never allow him to be rational enough to deal with this. The fury was building up in him again and try as he might he would not be able to control the inevitable explosion. The worm had grown and it squirmed in his head hungrily.

Annie had made a decision, and that was that Sarah could not return to the damp and draughty barge. That was why she was now working every spare moment in her mother's old house to get it spick and span. It was the ideal solution for Sarah to live there, and somehow it seemed only right that the woman Edward had idolised all his life should have his house. Annie knew he would have approved of the idea, for he had felt he had never given Sarah enough in his lifetime, and at last she would have some comfort in her old age. Annie was even more delighted with the idea, as it meant she could see her friend every day and, more to the point, so could Jamie. He was so much brighter now that Sarah was around. Annie saw this as a wonderful opportunity to get him away from Joe. She hummed to herself as she swept the dusty hall floor, opening the door to let out the musty smells. Things were definitely looking up and she was feeling so much better about her life already. The victories were happening all the time, for today when she had announced that she was going into town, Joe had not immediately followed her but merely made a grunting noise and continued poking the fire angrily.

As she whisked the brush out of the door onto the pavement, voices on the other side of the street caught her attention and looking up she saw a man leaving the house opposite. He wore a long heavy black coat and carried a

288

large leather bag, obviously a doctor's bag. Annie looked harder and her heart pounded; although he was older, greyer and a lot heavier, it was undoubtedly Richard.

Unable to contain herself she called his name across the street and as if he had seen and heard a ghost Richard stopped dead in his tracks, wondering if his imagination was playing tricks on him.

'Annie, Annie, is it you?' he cried, and rushed across the street.

'Yes, yes it is.' Her whole face was alight with pleasure at seeing him.

For a second an uncomfortable silence hung in the air as they both hoped they were not being too enthusiastic, and then realising the ridiculousness of their coyness, they hugged and Annie led him into the house.

'Come in it's freezin' out there. Have yer got five minutes to spare to talk to me?' she asked, suddenly desperate to share some time with him.

'Of course I have. Oh Annie, it's so good to see you. How are you? How's Jamie? Come on, I want all the news and a cup of tea.' His laugh was infectious and he suddenly felt carefree and alive in her presence.

They sat for an hour in the tiny scullery, warmed by the fire in the range and over several cups of tea they talked and talked. Annie had forgotten how easy he was to open up to, and she poured out her heart to him without hesitation. It felt so comfortable and safe, he was still the best friend she could ever have and she realised just how much she missed him.

'Annie, you must leave him, for Jamie's sake if not yours.' Richard's eyes were full of concern for her, he was still so angry with himself for letting her go back to Joe in the first place. He knew he had been a complete fool, he should never have simply let her go but should have told her just how he felt, and he had cursed himself ever since.

'It's not that simple, Richard. Joe's sick an' I'm not sure what he'll do. I have to be careful.' Annie could hardly believe she was having this conversation, but in doing so it made her so much stronger and sure of her mind. She had a plan now and at least she could see a way ahead.

'I'm goin' to move Sarah into this house first. Jamie'll have somewhere to go, a safe place. Sarah loves 'im an' I thought maybe he could gradually stay more with 'er here. That way Joe won't notice so much. I have to do this slowly Richard, I can't just run away, I tried that before an' it didn't work. Joe'll not just let me go an' no matter 'ow far I run he'll find me. Believe me this is the only way.'

Richard was not convinced, Joe was mentally unstable and that only meant one thing for Annie, danger, the whole time she was with him. But at least this was the old Annie he could see again, the one with life and fire in her, Joe had not destroyed her totally as he feared. Ever cautious not to scare her from his life he held back his emotions and offered his friendship instead, afraid of a rebuff if he went further.

'Can I come and visit you and Jamie here? Joe won't come here if he sees Sarah as some kind of threat.'

'Yes that would be wonderful. Jamie'd like it, he needs to see other people.' She didn't add that she would be delighted too, for she reminded herself that he was married and they could never be more than friends.

'Perhaps I could help him with his reading, and then when he felt more confident get him back to school.'

Annie nodded. She had explained her fears about Jamie's education to him earlier and the idea seemed brilliant to her. 'Let's hope he's a better pupil than I was,' she laughed reminding him of the secret lessons in the woods all those years ago.

'You were an excellent pupil, and if I remember learnt far more quickly than I could teach you. Don't undervalue yourself,' he chastised her playfully, making her blush at his praise. They talked for another half hour or so before Richard said he really must leave but promised to visit often as soon as Sarah was in residence. They laughed and teased each other and as he left he kissed her hand, sending shivers along her spine. As she closed the door and he disappeared, she hugged herself and smiled and smiled as she relived the afternoon again. When she walked back to the cottage, a new spring was in her step and a lightness in her spirit.

A week later, Sarah was up and about, she had even managed a short walk by the river in the pale afternoon sunlight. Annie thought that the time was right to tell her about the house, though she wasn't sure how Sarah would feel about leaving the barge that had been her home for so many years. Dilapidated it might be but it held all her cherished memories and it would not be easy to leave it behind.

That night when the meal had been eaten and Annie had sent Jamie off to bed, protesting as always that he was not at all tired yet, she sat with Sarah in front of the fire. Joe, no longer able to stand sitting alone in the kitchen, had started to sit with them at night, although he turned his chair almost into the fire and never spoke.

'Sarah, we have to talk about what yer goin' to do now yer better,' Annie began gently.

Joe immediately pricked up his ears, though pretending to be snoozing.

'I know it's time I moved on again,' Sarah sighed.

She knew this day was coming but she had been dreading it, and hoping she could have stayed a little longer. The thought of going back to her cold damp barge sent shivers through her, she had no money left and she wasn't quite sure how she was going to survive the winter months. Nobody wanted to hire her services any more and she had no flowers or herbs to sell in the winter. Still, she would think of something, maybe she could make pegs or baskets. But it wasn't just the fear of hunger and cold that was making her reluctant to go but also she would miss Annie and Jamie so much. She had grown to love the little boy dearly and it was always a joy to be with Edward's beloved daughter, whilst she had only loneliness and empty days to look forward to. But it was unfair to ask to stay any longer, Annie had enough trouble as it was. She cast her eyes over Joe. How she despised that man. She had heard the way he

291

spoke to Annie, she could see the fear in Jamie's eyes whenever his father was around. If Edward could see the way Annie was treated he would turn in his grave. She knew Joe hated her being here, he did not try to disguise it and she guessed that he must be putting pressure on Annie to get rid of her. It was only fair to Annie that she should go, and soon. Leaning forward she clasped Annie's hand within hers and squeezed it tenderly.

'It's time I got back to that old barge of mine, I know. Tomorrow seems as good a day as any.'

Joe's heart leapt, she was going, he opened his eyes in delight.

'Sarah, I don't think yer should go back to the barge. It's so wet an' cold there an' it's too much for yer to handle these days.' Out of the corner of her eye she saw Joe glaring in indignation, but she ploughed on. 'I think it would be far better if yer stayed in Lytwych. Jamie an' I could see more of yer an' you'd be safer.'

Sarah's eyes filled up with tears, she couldn't believe what she was hearing, for there was only one place to go when you had no money and the thought terrified her.

'I won't go to the workhouse, I'd rather die,' she cried.

Annie rushed to hug her. 'Yer don't understand. Yer really don't think I'd let yer go to the workhouse, do yer? I want yer to have Pa's old house. It's been empty for a time, but it will soon be cosy again. An' we can see each other more often. Pa loved yer an' he'd want yer to have it.'

Sarah cried, tears of joy and gratitude. Joe sat silently taking in the scene and thinking. At least Sarah would be out of his house and he would have Annie back for himself. There were other bonuses too, for he reasoned that if Sarah lived in 34 Union Street, Annie couldn't. She couldn't leave him, and what was more she couldn't have been planning to, not if she was giving the house away. He relaxed, soon things could get back to normal. All the nonsense would die down and Annie would be back under his control.

'I'll go an' light all the fires to warm the place through tomorrow,' he suddenly volunteered.

Annie smiled inwardly, it had worked, her plans were beginning to move. 'That'd be wonderful Joe,' she purred, and like a child he soaked up her attention greedily.

At first Jamie was cross when he knew Sarah was moving out of the cottage. He liked her around, she would always talk to him and play with him, and his pa kept well away when he was with her. The house had felt different since she had been there, for one thing there was no shouting or fighting, his ma hadn't cried and neither had he. Then his ma had taken him to one side and whispered to him that he would be able to go and see Sarah and maybe even stay there sometimes. Sarah had winked at him and pressed her finger to her lips, letting him know that it was a secret from his father. Now suddenly it all seemed very exciting and he couldn't wait to help move Sarah over there today. He couldn't quite see why his father was so keen on the idea, but what did it matter if it meant he wasn't shouting for once. He had actually gone and lit all the fires and was now coming back with a carriage to transport her across town. The atmosphere in the cottage was happy and carefree as everyone busied around packing blankets and food. Later Annie would go the barge to fetch some of Sarah's treasures.

The carriage drew up in front of the cottage and Joe alighted, for once looking calm. He loaded the parcels and boxes of food and even helped Sarah into the carriage. Watching the carriage drive out of sight, his heart soared. She was gone. Let Annie settle her in, he thought, and then when she came home things would be back to normal again. Closing the cottage door he headed for the shed – time he went back to work. He would show her how much he loved her and then she would never leave. She was his, and that was how it was staying.

# Thirty-One

**B**y the time the snowdrops were pushing their heads up through the unfriendly soil in February, Annie felt she was living two separate lives. One was a dark miserable one, where she was constantly under Joe's tyranny, and the other was a light, bright, free world where she could be herself and breathe.

By subjecting herself to Joe's torture, it guaranteed that Jamie could spend time with Sarah. She endured being punished for her regular visits to Union street. Joe soon took advantage of letting Jamie sleep there every now and then by taking his wife's body with extra force, to subject her to a little more humiliation, to remind her he made the rules.

For Annie it was a small price to pay for the carefree smile that lit up her son's face when he saw Sarah or Richard. In her mind it was not her body that Joe savagely raped or her mind that was so tortured with cruel words, it was just a shell, a pretend person. The real Annie Hayes lived somewhere else, she was safe from him and he couldn't hurt her no matter what he did. Her plans had worked perfectly: Sarah was comfortable and Jamie happy, and although he still worked in the shed it was for less and less time – as long as she stayed, Joe didn't stop him going off earlier and earlier. At least twice a week Richard called at Union Street in the evenings and helped Jamie with his reading and sums. The lad was a quick learner, like his mother, and was soon picking up everything Richard taught him. He knew he had to keep Richard's visits a secret from his father or they would stop and he certainly didn't want that, for Richard was kind and fun, and besides, he was hungry to learn.

Moreover, he enjoyed anything that involved getting one over on his father, whom he hated intensely. Joe had stepped up his verbal onslaughts, calling him stupid and a girl and a tart, and he constantly thumped his arms and legs, supposedly in fun. Jamie could ignore all this, knowing he could escape to Sarah and he slept at the house more and more. His only wish was that his ma could stay with them too, but she always smiled when he asked her and said, not yet. He saw the way his father treated her, although she never made a fuss, or talked about the bruises and hurt, he could feel it for her though. At night when he lay in bed he would try and plot ways they could all be together and ways to get rid of the monster, and sometimes when he really couldn't sleep he would creep into Sarah and cuddle up in her arms. She understood when he said he hated his father, she never told him it was wrong or that he had to try to be nicer, and that understanding brought its own comfort. One day, he told himself, his father would pay and his mother would be free, he'd see to that.

It was cold and rainy when Richard called that February night. He had some new books for Jamie and he was hoping as always that Annie would be there. It was such joy for him to be able to spend time with her. Sometimes instead of doing school work they would all play games, cards or dominoes, for Jamie loved them all being together, like one family. That was how it felt for Richard, one family; his life was more complete now than it had ever been. Tonight, however, she didn't come. He was disappointed and he understood, but it didn't prevent him from missing her.

Sarah watched him as he patiently explained the mathematical problems to Jamie. Sometimes it moved her to tears to see them together and she asked herself a thousand times why for once a miracle couldn't happen and make everyone happy. That Jamie and Richard loved one another was perfectly obvious, as obvious as it was to her that Richard felt the same way about Annie. It was written in his eyes every time he mentioned her name or spoke to her, so why didn't he just tell her. The whole thing was very frustrating for Sarah, she was a passionate person and expected everyone else to be the same. She could never have hidden her love from Edward, they were both too consumed with passion and that as far as she was concerned was how it should be.

'I think we've done enough for one night Jamie.' Richard stretched himself and finished the cup of tea that had gone cold in front of him.

'I could do some more,' Jamie eagerly volunteered, not wanting to end the session just yet, for that meant he had to go home.

'Are you staying tonight with Sarah?'

'No, I have to go home, Father said.' Jamie's voice saddened at the mention of Joe. 'He has been 'ere all week,' Sarah gently reminded them, knowing how he hated going back to the cottage at all.

'You'd best be gone then before it gets too late, or your ma will be worried,' Richard ruffled the boy's hair affectionately.

'I suppose,' muttered Jamie and stooping to kiss first Sarah and then Richard he sidled miserably out of the room.

'Put yer coat on, it's rainin',' yelled Sarah as the front door slammed.

'He really hates going back there, doesn't he.'

'Is it any wonder,' Sarah sighed. 'I wish he could stay 'ere all the time but Annie says, bit by bit, we must be patient. Why doesn't she just leave 'im, that's what I can't understand.'

'I don't think it's that easy, Sarah. She did it once before you know, and he found her again.' Sarah shook her head indicating that she didn't know and Richard told her of Jamie's birth and the happy few weeks they had all had.

'Why on earth d'yer ever let 'er go?' Sarah cried, incredulous at the story.

'I couldn't stop her, she is Joe's wife, she thought it was

296

the right thing to do. Besides her feelings for me are not the same as mine for her,' replied Richard, sadly shaking his head.

'How d'yer know that? Have yer ever asked 'er?'

'No, but I don't have to. I hurt her once before in the past and I don't think she would ever forgive me for that.' He pulled his fingers roughly through his hair in exasperation, 'At least I have some contact with her this way. If it's all I can have I won't do anything to jeopardise it. I know she's miserable, but she asked me not to interfere, to let her do it in her own way. I think she will. She won't be pushed, you know that, and as ridiculous as it seems she feels she owes that man something.' He rose to his feet and paced, agitated at his lack of power in this hopeless situation.

'If that's what she wants we must let 'er do things 'er own way. But I'm afraid fer her, Richard. I'm not sure what he might do an' there's things goin' on in that house that don't bear thinkin' about.'

Sarah felt as if Richard needed a good shaking, he was just too nice, too reasonable. She wanted him to sweep Annie off her feet, take her away from Joe and protect her. She had to face it, Richard just wasn't made of such fiery stuff, he was dependable and safe but he was no cavalier and that was what Annie needed. Besides, he was still married, and even though his wife had lived in London for years now Richard, being Richard, hadn't wanted to subject her to the disgrace of a divorce. The situation suited him, he lived his own life and she hers, and now he had the added bonus of seeing Annie. He felt it would be too much to ask for more, and his reserved nature reinforced Annie's belief that he was no more than a dear and good friend. Sarah shook her head; the situation which seemed so clear to her, was also so impossible.

When Jamie arrived back at the cottage, Joe was waiting for him.

'Where yer been till this time?' he boomed as soon as Jamie poked his head through the door.

Annie jumped in to rescue him. 'He's been at Sarah's. It's all right, Jamie, you get ready fer bed.'

'No it's not all right.' He turned on Jamie again. 'Yer spend too much time with that old hag. I should stop yer from goin'.'

Jamie stood biting his lip, fuming inside. How dare he call Sarah names. He held his tongue though, afraid that if he pushed his father too much his visits would be stopped and he couldn't bear the thought of that.

'As if yer aren't a mummy's boy already without spending all yer time with that slut,' Joe growled.

Jamie looked at his mother anxiously, hoping she would provide some means of escape for him.

'Go to bed, Jamie. I'll be up in a minute,' Annie whispered, running her hand along Jamie's cheek gently.

It was all the signal he needed and Jamie shot from the room like a scalded rabbit, trying to ignore the shouts from Joe that followed him up the stairs.

'Go on little girl, run off to bed an' have a good cry,' Joe laughed cruelly.

Annie leaned against the sink and closed her eyes, this made her so weary. Joe was in a mood, that was nothing new but it meant another night of agony ahead. Sometimes Annie just wanted to scream at him to shut up, to just stop for one minute, but it was useless; once Joe was set on a course of destruction, nothing could halt it. She dried her hands and, refusing to meet his glare, she slipped up stairs to Jamie to say goodnight.

'Are yer all tucked in sweetheart?'

'Richard missed yer tonight at Sarah's.'

'Ssh, Jamie, yer know we mustn't mention his name 'ere,' said Annie bending down to hug and kiss her son, though it always made her feel warm inside when she thought of Richard.

'Can I stay at Sarah's tomorrow, please?'

'We'll see. I can't promise. Now go to sleep.' Blowing kisses, she quietly left the room, making sure to latch the

298

wooden door so that he wouldn't hear any fracas which might come later.

She wished she could let Jamie stay at Sarah's all the time, even though she would miss him terribly. But she had to be careful. Joe was beginning to get agitated about the situation, so perhaps it would be best not to push things too fast. In the long term she had decided to use the excuse of Sarah's failing health as a reason for Jamie living with her. It was possible that Joe would tolerate that, especially if she said that if Jamie didn't sleep there, she would have to. Once Jamie was completely safe then she could relax and start to think about ways of leaving herself, but at the moment that seemed so far ahead it was impossible.

Her head ached tonight, thumping on each side of her brow and making her eyes sting intolerably. All she wanted to do was go to bed and sleep but from the look on Joe's face that was not going to be possible. Dragging herself back into the parlour she was met by an icy glare.

Joe's mind was becoming more and more warped, he was totally paranoid and imagined Annie to be plotting against him all the time. The demand for salt had continued to drop and the sacks were piling up in the shed. He saw this only as some kind of personal vendetta against him. He accused Annie of collaborating with John Ellis to try and close the shed completely so she could sell it to him. His fear of course was that she would leave him then and he constantly threatened that he would kill her if she tried to leave.

Like some kind of robotic maniac he kept on and on producing the unsaleable salt as if it somehow proved his worth. Annie pleaded with him to slow down, maybe even let the fires die under the pan once a week for a day or two, but he simply saw this as part of the plan against him and became more and more suspicious of her.

Today she had decided to stop saying anything but she refused to work all hours by his side when it was so pointless and had left the shed early that afternoon without saying a word to him. She knew that there would have to be a confrontation about it, but tonight she was just so weary she wanted him to disappear and give her some peace.

'What took yer so long up there then, whisperin' with 'im again?' Joe spat his words out accusingly.

'Don't be silly, I were just sayin' goodnight to 'im,' Annie retorted immediately, regretting her sharp tone.

'Don't speak to me like that. I know what's going on, I'm not stupid.'

When Joe began to get annoyed his lips shone with moisture and Annie could see the tell-tale signs of saliva now shining on his skin. Involuntarily she shivered, he repulsed her so.

'Where the 'ell did yer run off to this afternoon? To Ellis, plottin' again?' His voice was rising now with each syllable.

'No of course not. Yer know there's no point in makin' all this salt. Yer won't listen to reason. I'm not goin' to work all day at the shed when there's no need to. Why won't yer see sense?' Annie tried to sound calm, though inside she shook.

'Yer'll do as yer told, or else I'll stop the kid from goin' to Union Street an' have 'im back in the shed instead of you,' Joe bellowed.

'Leave Jamie out of it. You have me, isn't it enough to make one life miserable, without ruining another?' Annie felt the tears rise dangerously, and she fought to control her anger.

'Yer don't know what misery is yet,' Joe yelled. He leapt across the room and pushed her to the floor, and sitting astride her he scrubbed his fist viciously into her nose. 'Think yer can plot against me, d'yer? I'll kill yer before yer ever leave me, you bitch, an' him too.' Triumph shone in his wild eyes; he loved this.

'Don't worry, I can't leave, I'm a prisoner 'ere, but Jamie isn't. Do what yer want to to me, I don't care, I'll willingly die for his freedom.'

Joe's clenched fist smashed into her cheekbone, but she didn't seem to feel it. She was fuelled with such an intense anger tonight she was determined to say her piece in total.

300

'Jamie's goin' to live with Sarah an' yer can't stop it, Joe. You may own me but that's the limit of yer power, so make the most of it. You either let Jamie go or I go too. Yer don't frighten me any more.' Her eyes matched his now in fury, and struggling against his body weight she freed her pinned down arms. As she dragged at his hair, he was lost in his rage and slapped her face forcefully. Only when he saw the look of sheer contempt in her eyes did he stop and the other Joe, the one she hated more than this, emerged.

'Annie, please, I'm sorry I don't want to lose you. I'm nothing without you, you know that. What else can I do, I've given my whole life for you. I almost died for you and now look at me, limping everywhere, always in pain, but it was worth it for you.' Tears fell so easily from his little red eyes and he threw himself on her breast, slobbering and whimpering. 'Please don't leave me, remember yer promises on our weddin' day, till death do us part yer said. Please, Annie, please.'

He clawed at her breast, snivelling pathetically. Annie felt the guilt and repulsion within her well up and swirl around in her head. She couldn't bear this, it was worse than the violence and in disgust. She pushed him from her.

'I won't leave yer, Joe, but Jamie is goin'.' Determinedly she dragged herself to her feet, pushing him away from her.

He remained sitting on the floor and drawing his knees up to his chest he sat like a small child rocking back and forth. He felt no remorse for hitting Annie, but watched her bitterly as she pulled her clothes straight and moved away from him. When she winced with pain as she tentatively felt her bruised nose he smirked, served her right for being horrible to him and upsetting him. He knew just how to make her feel guilty and he continued to sob every now and then piteously. It was almost as if there were two separate people within him, each fighting to be supreme. The furious angry Joe, that he hated, and yet thrived on the power; and the lost little boy who was so afraid and scared, that he hated too. He despised himself totally, the dark demons still lurked in his sick brain and he knew that Annie was his only

301

salvation. He wanted to lock her into a glass box, sealed in from the rest of the world, so that he could take her out whenever he needed her. In there she would be uncorrupted by other people, then she would love him and serve him, and give him the total attention he needed. As he rocked back and forth getting comfort from the movement, his brain began to swim again and in the muddiness images appeared every now and then, to haunt and torment him. He reasoned that she wasn't a bad girl, but that other people tempted her to be disloyal to him, Sarah and Jamie, and now he was sure that John Ellis was somehow involved, and all those men that smiled at her and enticed her from him. He wouldn't let them, he'd keep her here all for himself and then he would be safe.

Let Jamie go, what did it matter, it was one less distraction. If he was honest things hadn't worked out as he wanted with the boy anyway. He hated the way Annie kissed and touched her son, she always gave him more attention, fussing and worrying over him. He was still attracted by the boy's young body, but he was so jealous of Jamie he had never done anything about it, the boy didn't deserve his attention. And besides, Annie made sure that they were never left alone together, protecting her precious son as ever. Let him go to Sarah and good riddance, all the more time for him to be alone with Annie.

Annie was splashing cold water on her face now and as she did so she flicked her ebony hair back from her eyes. He felt the surge of desire flood through his groin and all other emotions were quelled as the overwhelming urge to take her spread through him. Leaping to his feet he encircled her with his arms from behind thrusting himself against her, moaning in urgency.

Annie froze, she felt she couldn't bear this, not tonight, and she tried to push him from her. It was to no avail, her resistance only fuelled his ardour and he dragged up her skirts and forced himself roughly into her body. He was completely oblivious to her reactions and only when he was satisfied did he release her. Straightening up, he moved

302

away and in a thick gruff voice announced that he was going to bed.

Hot tears spurted from her eyes, she was angry and hurt and humiliated all in one. She did not move from the sink but stood holding on to it for support as all her emotion spilt from her. To say she hated him wasn't enough, she loathed and despised him, she prayed and prayed that he might die, that she might be released from this nightmare. Over and over she begged her God to show her a way, to help her before she went quite mad. No answers came, so she sobbed quietly and, not wishing to get into bed with him, she resolved to sleep on the chair in the parlour. If it was cold it didn't matter, anything would be better than being near him tonight. He wouldn't notice her absence, she knew he would be snoring loudly now, satisfied that he had won.

Jamie sat on the top step of the stairs. He had listened to all the night's activities. Now he could hear grunts from his father as he slept and occasional sobs from his ma downstairs. He had rejoiced inside when he heard that he was to live with Sarah and then immediately felt very guilty at leaving his ma behind. As he sat there he made a vow, a silent and yet solemn pledge that he would somehow rescue her from this house and get rid of this evil father once and for all.

# Thirty-Two

In the middle of the night Joe awoke and realised he was in bed alone. He was cold and like a child he felt lonely and in need of warm arms to comfort him. The events of the night came flooding back to him, the shouting and fighting and then Annie's words that Jamie was leaving. His head ached and confusion swirled around in his brain. Jamie was his, another possession, she had no right to take him. It was just another step in the destruction of his world, it was all falling away, crumbling around him and he couldn't control it. They were all in the plot to destroy him, and he knew he would have to fight to keep Annie, he would never let her leave. Of course if Jamie wasn't around it meant more time for him with Annie and so it wouldn't be so bad. He tossed and turned restlessly, he couldn't settle without her, and he was suddenly afraid. He didn't want his father's ghost dancing in his head and it was there now taunting him, he knew he had to find Annie.

Slipping quietly down the stairs, he crept into the parlour. She was asleep, huddled under a rug, she looked peaceful for once. For a few minutes he sat gazing at her in the half light, she was still very beautiful, her dark hair falling in a sea around her shoulders. If only she would understand that he only did all these things because he loved her so much, worshipped her. No one else would ever have her, he knew that, he would kill her first and himself at the same time. They would be together always then and no one could harm them or drive them apart. Annie shifted in her sleep and as she did, the rug slid to the floor. Joe carefully placed it over her body again. She momentarily opened her eyes and the look that flashed in them caused him to jolt backwards it was so powerful. Sheer hatred shone there and he felt the full force of her contempt. Within a second she was asleep again, though the touch of his hand brushing her skin made her shiver and she turned abruptly away from him.

Tears welled in Joe's eyes as he moved from her. She truly despised him, he knew that. But it didn't matter; she was his, and he would make sure it stayed that way. He longed for love and understanding, to see pleasure rather than disgust in her eyes. Slowly he wandered back up the narrow stairs, though he really didn't want to get back into the big cold bed by himself, for then the dreams would start and he couldn't bear that. Passing Jamie's door he saw it was ajar and he watched the boy slumbering. He was a pretty child, with his mother's dark hair and yet piercing blue eyes which made him so striking. Inch by inch Joe moved towards the bed as if drawn by a magnet. He could hear Jamie's soft breathing and see his small nostrils flaring rhythmically in and out. The urge to climb into the bed beside the boy was overwhelming and he succumbed to his desire, slipping silently under the covers.

Jamie stirred and Joe lay perfectly still, hardly daring to breathe, he didn't want to wake him yet. He waited until Jamie's breath had fallen back to a regular pattern before he allowed himself the delight of enjoying the feel of the small body beside him. His fingers slowly travelled along Jamie's arm and then traced his leg and thighs. Joe began to sweat as the excitement grew within him and as his body responded by stiffening with desire. Rubbing his hands across the boy's stomach in ever downward circular movements, Joe began to pant and nuzzled against Jamie's neck.

As the movements became more urgent Jamie began to be disturbed and awaken, though Joe was now too lost in his own sick desires to notice and he slobbered hungrily against his son's body. As he pushed Jamie's body over so that he would be lying on his stomach, Jamie jolted to life.

For a second he thought he was dreaming and then that maybe, his mother was in bed with him. Only as the hot hands pulled at his pyjama trousers did he realise that it was his father. Every nerve in his body tingled as he shot upright, struggling to free himself from the iron grip. He opened his mouth to scream but before the sound could escape, Joe's hand was clasped across his face, so that he could hardly breathe.

He struggled valiantly but the weight of his father's body was too much and now Joe had ripped away his clothes, burying his face in the pillow. Sickness churned in his stomach as Joe's stale breath wafted up his nostrils and drops of saliva dribbled on his neck.

'Quiet Jamie, this is our secret, 'cos I love yer so much, 'cos yer special an' yer ma is sending yer away from me. I want yer to remember this as our secret.'

Joe frantically tried to push himself into his son's delicate body but Jamie was squirming around so much it was impossible. Grabbing both arms with one hand he forced his son's legs wide apart with the other, cursing now in his frustration.

Once both of Joe's hands were occupied it allowed Jamie the freedom to move his head and he let out a piercing scream, which reverberated around the room. Crying hysterically Jamie wriggled to try and escape from the monster that was pinning him down.

'Stop it, stop it, please,' he sobbed, not aware fully of what his father was trying to do, but he was more frightened than he had ever been in his life, so much so that he thought he was going to die.

Joe, by now was completely lost in dementia, neither heard nor saw Jamie any more as he viciously tried to rape his son.

Downstairs, Annie sat bolt upright, she was sure she had heard Jamie cry out. A few seconds later she heard it again and she bounded up the stairs two at a time. At first she too failed to take in what was happening and thought that Joe was hitting Jamie. Only as she flung herself on his back, pulling back the bedclothes as she did so, did the full horror of it hit her. Jamie's pale naked body quivered in the approaching dawn light as Joe hung above him. She saw the rigid outline of his body and recognised only too well the slobbering lips and dilated eyes.

In that split second she wanted to kill him, and she launched herself against this beastly body in a vicious attack. She kicked and bit, scratched and tore at his skin until her fingers were soaked in his blood, she screamed abuse at him and cursed her weakness for not being able to tear him apart. In his initial surprise at the onslaught Joe released Jamie who scrambled from the bed pulling on his clothes as if to protect himself. He then slid to the floor in the corner of the room, sobbing hysterically as his mother continued to fight like a wild cat. Strangely Joe did not fight back, but merely covered his face with his hands in an attempt to protect himself. He too slowly fell to the floor as Annie kicked and hit him, crying as she did.

'Yer coward, yer bastard, yer animal,' she screeched, hardly able to get the words out.

Joe said nothing but curled up in a ball on the floor, whimpering like a wounded animal. Annie turned to her distraught son and, gathering him to her breast, she rocked him gently, as he sobbed uncontrollably.

'Come on Jamie, let's get yer things, yer goin' to Sarah and yer never coming back 'ere again.'

Swiftly she gathered a few things together and dressing her son in a warm jumper and coat she guided him out of the room. Jamie walked trance-like down the stairs and stood staring into space as Annie quickly put on her boots and coat.

The dawn had broken as they walked along the river towards town, the sun was strengthening and the birds sang noisily. They stumbled along, both of them stunned and shocked, but at least feeling safer now they were away from the house.

'Jamie, has he ever done anythin' like this to yer before?'

307

Annie asked gently, slipping her arm reassuringly around the boy's stooped shoulders.

Jamie shook his head violently and the look in his bewildered eyes told her that it was true. She sighed with relief, thank God for that at least. She thought she had managed to stop Joe today before he was able to penetrate Jamie's body but she wasn't sure; even if she had, God knows what damage had been done in Jamie's mind.

They approached Sarah's with relief and Annie let herself in with a key that she always kept for emergencies. Sarah was up as always at this time, sipping her warm tea by the kitchen fire. Her look of astonishment turned to despair as she saw the two distraught faces. She knew without asking that Joe had done something and from Jamie's pale complexion, she guessed it was something to do with him. She knew better than to ask questions, that would come in time, first they both needed looking after.

'Sit down both of yer and get warm by the fire, while I make yer a drink,' and she fussed around chatting about nothing to ease the strained atmosphere.

Annie held Jamie in her arms and rocked him quietly, whilst he stared silently into the flames, hatred of his father biting into him. Annie tried to coax him with a drink but he refused and clung to her instead lest she might disappear.

'Jamie's moving in with you now, if that's all right?' Annie said, trying to sound cheerful.

'Why that's wonderful, best news I've ever had. Yer room's all ready for yer anyway.' Sarah smiled and stroked Jamie's head.

He was oblivious to everything around him, and Sarah couldn't imagine what dreadful thing might have happened to cause this.

'What about some of Sarah's special potato cakes an' jam for breakfast?' she coaxed, knowing these were his favourite.

He shook his head and closed his eyes to shut out the whole world.

Annie and Sarah exchanged worried glances, and silently

Annie mouthed the name Richard, indicating with a nod of her head that she needed to go and fetch him.

'Jamie, d'yer think you would like to sleep fer a while, 'ere in front of the fire?'

Another shake of the head was the most reply she could get.

'I've got to go out fer a while but you'll be all right with Sarah,' Annie crooned, tenderly hugging him.

Panic swept through him and he clung to his ma desperately. 'No, yer mustn't go back there,' he stuttered.

'I'm not goin' there, Jamie. I need to get Richard to come an' see if yer hurt anywhere, that's all.'

'I'm not, I'm fine.' Jamie snapped clamming up again. He felt strangely dirty as if he had done something terrible and the last thing he wanted was Richard looking at him or having to talk about what had happened. All he wanted was for him and his ma to stay here where it was safe and where his father couldn't get them.

Annie sighed, torn inside. She really did not know what to do for the best. Richard would be at least able to tell her if Jamie had been raped, she had to know and her son was not going to be able to talk about it. Suddenly her need for Richard was overpowering, she wanted his calm reassurance, he would know what to do, she could rely on him.

The three of them sat in silence, Jamie burying his head on Annie's lap while she stroked his head soothingly. Suddenly he opened his eyes and sat up abruptly.

'Can I have a bath in front of the fire, please?' His eyes pleaded with Annie and in that second she knew just how he felt. She knew only too well that feeling of being soiled and dirty when Joe had touched her. Jamie was feeling that way too.

''Course you can, I'll boil the water right now an' you can have a good long soak,' she cried, gulping back the tears that threatened.

So whilst she and Sarah prepared the tub, Jamie lay on the chair wrapped in a blanket, staring blankly into space. Gratefully he stepped into the hot water and sinking down in the tin tub he closed his eyes and let the steam carry him away.

'Will yer be all right with Sarah now if I go an' fetch Richard?' she whispered to him.

He nodded his head. He felt better in the smooth water and Sarah would stay and talk with him and maybe then the pictures in his head would go away.

'I'll be back very soon.' Annie kissed his face. 'Yer safe now, nothin' can 'appen.'

His eyes so full of trust met hers and that special bond between them shone out above all the nightmare of events.

She slipped out of the kitchen, Sarah one step behind her, closing the door behind them.

'What in God's name has he done to that child?' Sarah whispered.

Annie also whispered. 'He tried to rape 'im. I can't believe it 'appened. I think I stopped it in time but I'm not sure. Oh Sarah, what have I done to Jamie, I should've got 'im away years ago. This is all my fault.' Annie choked on her tears as she fell into Sarah's arms. The old woman was stunned for a moment. Even she didn't expect this. How she wished Edward were here; none of this would have happened then, he would have taken Annie away years ago.

'Annie, Annie, listen to me, yer mustn't blame yourself. No one could be a better mother than you. Jamie's safe now, he never has to go back an' neither do you. It's over. Get Richard, he'll know what to do about Jamie. You have to be strong fer yer son now.' She hugged the sobbing body and then pushing her away wiped the tear stained face with her hands. 'I'll look after Jamie, go on, go and find Richard.'

By the time Richard and Annie returned, Jamie was sitting eating hot potato cakes and sipping warm milk. He looked much brighter and even found a smile for his ma as she walked into the room. He knew he was safe now, he felt clean again. He could no longer smell his father's stale sweat on his skin or taste his foul breath on his lips. His back hurt him, but he supposed that was just from the sheer weight that had been pressing down on him, otherwise he felt better. He tried not to think about his father at all, he didn't want to talk about it. He wanted to think about being free, of never going back to the cottage or the wych shed. Sarah had been telling a story about a kissing bush and how it made wishes come true. She said his ma had made one with his granddad and sure enough her wish for an Indian Princess dress had come true. She had told him that good things could happen if you made them and as soon as he was better she would go to the woods with him and make a bush. He was to think of a really special wish, maybe a day out in Liverpool or a new book he really wanted, and they would see if the bush could make it come true. It was an exciting thought and Jamie could think of little else now that the idea had been planted. He had already decided on his wish and the sooner he could make the bush the better.

Richard kept to himself all his anger and fury at what Annie had told him and showed only his usual calm manner. His first concern was to see that Jamie was all right, then he would consider what to do about Joe later when he had taken in the full extent of the horror. He was far from a violent man but the urge to rush over to the cottage and simply put everyone out of their misery by killing the monster overwhelmed him, and it took all his resolve to hide his emotions. Now having seen Jamie's pale innocent face a whole new gush of anger coursed through him and he swallowed it with difficulty.

'Well now, Jamie, shall we get rid of all these women while I see if there are any bumps and bruises?' he smiled kindly.

Annie and Sarah left the room silently, both dreading what he might find. Jamie was relaxed with Richard, mostly because he didn't ask awkward questions or push him into telling every detail of the incident. Instead he was very matter-of-fact, checking for bruises and breaks as if it were an everyday thing. They chatted about the new steamers on the river, and Richard promised to take him to the docks to see some of the big ships, and before they knew it the examination was over.

Richard was more relieved than he could express, as he related to Annie, that apart from a few bruises and sore ribs Jamie was untouched. For Annie too a huge black cloud lifted, she had got there in time, and she whispered a silent prayer of thanks.

'He will be fine, a few days' time and he'll be running around again and forgetting all about it.' Richard held her hand reassuringly. They both knew it wouldn't be quite that easy but at least the worst hadn't happened.

She was so grateful for Richard's support and she kissed him on the cheek in spontaneous gratitude.

'Now what about you, Annie Hayes, what are you going to do? You can't go back, you know that?' His eyes held hers, so full of love that it seemed incredible that she failed to notice it. She hadn't thought about what she was going to do, her mind being so full of concern for Jamie that she had looked no further than her duty to keep him safe. She didn't want to think about it for that meant thinking about Joe, and that was just too painful at the moment. But think about it she must, for the last thing she wanted was for him to come here looking for her and terrifying Jamie all over again.

'I have to go back an' sort things out,' she said quietly. 'He won't just go away, yer know that, Richard. I have to make 'im understand that I'm leavin' him for good or he'll always be looking for us. I just don't know 'ow to do it.'

Richard enfolded her in his arms, wishing he could just make all this right for her. 'I'm always here, Annie, you know that. You mustn't go back on your own, it's too dangerous. Take me with you and we'll sort it out once and for all.'

Richard, Richard, Annie thought, why did you leave me all those years ago. Why couldn't it be that you loved me as I loved you? Yet he was always here as a dear, dear friend whenever she needed him. It just wasn't enough. She sighed and pulled away from him.

'I will think about it, but not today, today I want to spend with Jamie,' and she led him back into the kitchen where

312

Jamie and Sarah sat huddled together lost in conversation. Annie smiled at the two of them, so content with one another.

'What're you two plottin' there?' she laughed, relieved to see her son smiling again.

'Sarah's told me about the kissin' bush an' we're goin' to make one.'

'The what bush?' put in Richard bemused.

They all laughed and proceeded to explain to him. Annie squeezed Sarah's arm and mouthed a silent thank you to her, as Jamie chattered on to an incredulous Richard about the wonderful, marvellous magic of the kissing bush.

# Thirty-Three

Annie spent the next two days at Sarah's house, whilst she churned in her head what would be the best thing to do. Her head ached with thinking as all the possible solutions flew round and round in her brain. She knew that she had to go back, that Joe would be waiting and if she didn't go soon, he would come looking for her.

She rehearsed the speeches countless times. It seemed so easy and logical this way, to simply tell him that she and Jamie were not coming back. She decided to let him stay in the cottage if he wanted it, for she was quite happy to live with Sarah, besides she didn't want Jamie to have to go back to the scene of his nightmares. The salt pan was another thing though, that was her pa's and it was Jamie's, she was determined that he wasn't having that. She decided the best thing would be to close it altogether for a while. That way if Joe had no means of support, he might just move away when he realised that she meant what she was saying. Of course she did not fool herself that things were going to be that straightforward, not with Joe. She wasn't really afraid, even though Richard and Sarah both kept telling her that she mustn't go back to the cottage or shed alone. She knew Joe; he would be distraught by now and would be begging her to stay when she came home.

The hard part would be to convince him that she was going for good, that it wouldn't matter how much he pleaded or threatened, nothing would change her mind. She kept trying to put the picture of him lying over Jamie

314

in his bed from her mind, for whenever she thought about it she was filled with such loathing and contempt that she didn't feel she would ever be able to look at Joe again, let alone talk to him. Her feelings towards him were so violent that it scared her, for she could not control the raging hatred that wanted to see the monster pay for what he had done to her son. She knew that she had to get this under control before she went to see him or she would not be responsible for her actions. She had thought quite coldly about killing him and ridding them of his presence for ever, it seemed such an easy solution. She had even worked out several ways of doing it. Two things stopped her each time her tortured mind wandered along these dangerous alleys. Firstly, she knew that she would not be able to hide his murder from the world and so she would have to pay the penalty. If there had been no Jamie she would have done it, but the thought of being taken away from her son was too painful to contemplate. Secondly, there was the ever present voice of God in her head, reminding her constantly that her soul would burn in hell and then she would be separated in the next life from her loved ones. The price was too great to pay, and she knew her conscience would weigh too heavily. What frightened her most was that she knew she was quite capable of taking his life if he provoked her enough and she prayed for strength to control her anger.

She had also decided that she must go alone to see him. It would be far too dangerous to take Richard, his presence would only aggravate Joe and there would be more trouble. Besides, she didn't want Richard involved in anything that might damage his reputation or position, it wasn't fair, he had already done enough for her. She knew she had to do this alone, and the sooner the better. That however was easier said than done, for Sarah and Richard were so determined that she should not put herself in danger that one or other of them was with her constantly. She could see too in Jamie's eyes a fear lurking in case his ma went back to the cottage, and he stuck close to her constantly as if he

315

were afraid she would disappear if he closed his eyes for a second. Despite the careful watch of those around her Annie knew that she could put it off no longer and today was the day. It was just after lunch and Richard had called in whilst on his morning rounds but had now gone again and wouldn't be back until the evening. She had persuaded Sarah to walk down to the woods with Jamie to make the wonderful kissing bush that he had never stopped talking about for the past two days. He had already chattered so incessantly to Richard about wanting to go the docks at Liverpool and see all the sights that they all imagined that this was the thing he would wish for, and so Richard had determined to fulfil this dream the very next week, even taking him on a ferry boat for a ride.

She feigned a headache and said she would go and try and have a sleep while they were out. Fortunately Jamie was in such a rush to get out that he didn't give Sarah a chance to argue and soon Annie was left alone.

She waited for ten minutes to allow them time to be well away from the house and then she slipped out along the street. The weather was unusually mild for February and the sun shone to warm up the cold pavements, certainly enough to dry them out from previous weeks of rain. By the time she could see the cottage ahead of her, she could feel the sweat prickling in the middle of her back. She slowed her pace, suddenly her home look forbidding and she had the urge to turn and run away again back to the safety of Union Street. She steeled herself, reprimanding her weakness and with determined step she walked to the door.

It was open and Annie pushed it gingerly, cringing as it squeaked noisily. Tentatively she poked her head around the doorway, not sure what she was expecting to see. A sigh of relief flooded through her, the kitchen was empty, in fact it looked exactly as she had left it. Creeping as quietly as she could she surveyed the parlour. That too was untouched.

Annie stood at the bottom of the stairs, head cocked to one side listening; there was no sound, Joe was not here. Suddenly the thought crossed her mind of him threatening to kill himself if she left him. Maybe he had done it. Her heart soared at the prospect, but she knew he was far too much of a coward. As she mounted the stairs, the events of three nights ago replayed themselves before her eyes, churning up the anger within her and firing her courage. She would tell him, and that would be an end to it all.

She was not expecting the sight that met her as she pushed open her bedroom door and she gasped as she took it all in.

The bedroom was almost a shrine, a shrine to her. The bed was made and tidy and spread all over it were her clothes, not tossed anywhere but laid out neatly. The room was filled with crocus and daffodils whose buds had not yet opened. Strewn around the chair and dresser were all her belongings, jewellery and ribbons, underwear and night-gowns. Her precious books and the treasured Indian dress took centre place on the chest of drawers and there with it was the little wicker mirror that Joe had given her for her sixteenth birthday and the white dress she had worn when she married him. She shivered as she looked around, it was as if her whole life was spread before her. The ghostly reminders of her past made her shudder and she quickly slammed the door shut, not wanting any reminder of her life with Joe. Hastily she checked Jamie's room, this had not been touched and the bed clothes lay in a heap on the floor where they had fallen in the struggle. Perhaps this room had been too painful for Joe to face.

He must be at the shed, so she hurried across the field to it. Sure enough, steam billowed out from the roof, drawing wispy pictures as it rose. Her heart began to pound as she entered the misty shed, not knowing what she would find but accepting that there was no way back now; she had to go through with this.

It was so difficult to see in the vapours that swirled in the air, her ears heard the bubbling of the vat but no other sounds, just an eerie silence that hung in the atmosphere.

'Joe? Joe are yer here? It's Annie. Joe, answer me.'

Stumbling against the bench, she banged her shin hard

317

and this caused her to cry out sharply. 'Joe, yer have to talk to me, Joe.' She knew he was in here, she could sense him. She groped her way along the wall and as her eyes slowly focused in the steam, she squinted trying to see him, listening for any movement. Then she spotted a bulky shape ahead of her and she moved forward thinking this was him. Reaching out with her hands, she grabbed a sack of salt. She sighed and turned on her heel to make her back towards the door, perhaps he wasn't in here after all.

From out of nowhere two hands grabbed her from behind and dragged her back against the wall. An arm slipped around her throat while the other twisted one of her arms viciously up behind her back.

'Joe,' she screamed, terrified by this sudden attack.

'Yes, Annie, Joe. Yer husband, the one yer betrayed.' His voice sounded thick and the words squeezed themselves out from twisted bitter lips.

'I came to talk to yer, Joe, I have to talk to yer. Jamie and I aren't coming back.' She stumbled on the words, frantic to get them out now she had started. 'It's over Joe. Let me go.'

He laughed and swinging her around to face him, grabbed her shoulders savagely so that she could not escape. She could see him clearly now and she was shocked at his grotesque appearance. His whole face had taken on a wild stare, his eyes shone wickedly, red and narrow and his thick lips glistened with saliva. He looked totally insane as he laughed in a manic, high-pitched tone.

'It's over is it, Annie? I don't think so. You aren't leaving me, not now, not ever. Yer belong to me Annie, I can't let yer go.' As he spoke he began removing her clothes, deliberately at first but then tearing at them violently.

'What are yer doing?,' she cried. She knew she had to try and stay calm, otherwise she would make him worse.

'Yer've been a naughty girl, Annie, an' now yer have to be punished.'

She saw his eyes widen in lust as he revealed her naked body bit by bit, and she knew that as soon as he had taken all her clothes he was going to rape her. Fighting back would only make it more painful so she stood perfectly still and let him continue.

He licked his lips as the last article of clothing fell to the floor and Annie closed her eyes and cringed waiting for the dreadful feel of his hot hands groping her body. But the next thing she knew he was roughly binding her ankles and wrists together with rough rope.

'What are yer doin', Joe, stop this please, yer hurting me, stop.'

Her pleas fell of deaf ears and when she was bound, hands behind her back, feet together, he stood back to look at her.

'Now Annie, I'm goin' to teach yer to be good. I know yer can't help bein' bad, that other people take yer away from me, but not any more.' He patted her head and disappeared into the steam.

Annie struggled and pulled at the ropes that bound her but that only served to tighten the knots and the rope ripped into her skin, until her blood was soaking the fibre. She tried to hop but the ropes at her ankles made this impossible and she fell forward hitting her head on the floor as she did. It stunned her for a second and then she became aware of Joe singing, she couldn't make out the words but the sound was getting closer and closer. She trembled as her mind plunged into total panic.

He appeared over her like demon, in his hand a whip, which he cracked in the air, laughing hysterically at the sheer terror in her face. He didn't even hear her begging him to stop as he began to wield the leather thong again and again against her soft bare skin.

After the first two or three agonising slices Annie lost consciousness. Yet he continued his onslaught until he thought she would have learnt her lesson sufficiently. Then he stopped.

When she awoke the first thing she was aware of was the agonising stinging all over her body. She moved slowly but every part of her seemed to hurt, her legs, back, chest, stomach. Then she looked down at her naked body and gasped in horror, her skin was a criss-cross of red weals that oozed blood which was now congealing in lumps all over her. Her hands and feet were no longer bound together but the ropes had left deep circular cuts. She knew she had to get out of there before he started again and she frantically tried to sit up, grimacing at the pain.

'Annie, yer awake. Would yer like a drink?' Joe was hovering over her grinning, as if nothing had happened.

'Let me go.' Annie sobbed as she pulled herself up to an agonising sitting position.

'Yer still don't understand, do yer. You aren't goin' anywhere me love, yer belong to me.' He grabbed her hair and yanking her head forward pressed a beaker of water to her lips forcing her to drink. His pleasant expression of a second ago changed instantly to anger and Annie could see he was quite insane.

He threw her a blanket and rose to his feet towering above her.

'Cover yourself up, whore, we've got work to do, the salt needs raking.'

Annie was convinced now that she was going to die, he had gone mad, completely mad and she could do nothing to save herself. In complete terror she pulled the horsehair blanket around her chest, tucking one end in to keep it up. It rubbed her wounds and she cried in pain and agony as she shuffled across the shed, led by Joe's gripping hand.

'Here. Rake,' he yelled and throwing her the heavy wooden tool he stood to one side watching her.

'Yer've brought this on yerself yer know, Annie. Now perhaps yer'll behave, an' we can get the shed workin' properly again. It's going to be so good, Annie, just me an' you, like it used to be. No more Jamie or Sarah. I can't let them ever see yer again, they're just too much of a temptation for you. This is how it should be, just you an' me.'

He sat grinning like an imbecile. As she hauled the rake over the brine the salty spray bit into her open wounds and tears streamed down her face. She continued for what seemed to her like hours, for her arms ached intolerably

320

from the heavy weight. Every time she begged to stop Joe would strike her face and tell her she was an ungrateful wife and to carry on until he told her.

Looking up through the open louvered roof Annie could see that the light was beginning to fail outside. Sarah and Jamie must be back from their walk now, surely someone would notice she was missing soon. She cursed herself for her stupidity, hadn't Richard and Sarah warned her not to come here alone. She prayed frantically now for some help, she didn't want to die, she didn't want to leave Jamie, she wanted to survive.

As it turned out, it was several hours before anyone noticed that Annie was not at home. Jamie and Sarah, having solemnly performed the ritual of the kissing bush, had meandered home at a leisurely pace. They had settled themselves comfortably in the kitchen with cakes and hot drinks, leaving Annie, as they thought, to have a rest in peace upstairs. It wasn't until the daylight began to fail and tea time approached that Sarah suggested it might be a good idea to wake Annie or she would never sleep tonight.

Jamie bounded up the stairs eager to tell his ma all about the excursion to the woods, but had found the bedroom empty. His heart pounding with fear he had raced down again, and jabbering out a garbled tale of his ma being missing, he had grabbed his coat and fled towards the cottage. Poor Sarah was left in a state of agitation, she knew her legs wouldn't make it all the way to the cottage, especially after this afternoon's walk. Cursing old age and her fading health she paced the kitchen anxiously praying that Richard would come soon and he at least could follow Jamie and see what had happened.

In the hot shed Annie shovelled salt into the canvas sacks whilst Joe sat watching her. He was feeling very satisfied with the day's work. First he had Annie back and they had produced a good load of salt. Things would be back to normal quicker than he thought, he smiled to himself; all

321

she needed was putting in her place and everything was fine. The worm in his head had eaten his brain, he knew that, but the feel of its tail thrashing around inside his skull was comforting. He wasn't even sure if he was Joe any more or whether he had become his father. He giggled at the thought of it. It was a pleasing idea, he remembered that his father had a big hard dick and he wanted to feel it steel-like pushing into him right now. His father had loved him, Annie would love him, or he would let the worm eat her too.

Annie felt as if she couldn't lift another shovel, she was in so much pain now especially as the cuts on her body had stopped bleeding in the salty air and begun to congeal together. Each bend and stretch tore open wounds afresh and the agonising process began all over again. Her back and arms ached cruelly and she felt so faint in the intense heat she thought she was going to pass out.

One thing kept her going, and that was the knife that lay on the sacks just by Joe's side. He had used it to cut off her ropes and then slung it carelessly to one side. Although he sat right next to it, it was temptingly close.

She kept watching it out of the corner of her eye, it was her chance, her only chance if she could just get it. Joe's moods changed swiftly throughout the afternoon, one minute he was laughing and behaving as if nothing had happened, the next he could be hitting her and calling her names, wild eyed and uncontrollable; he was like a volcano, totally unpredictable and volatile. Throughout it all he never took his eyes from her. They were evil, wicked eyes that bored into her like a hot blade.

When Jamie reached the wych shed, he hesitated outside before creeping silently in. He slipped quietly amongst the salt sacks from where he could see without being observed. His eyes widened with horror as he saw his ma bent over the salt, a blanket draped around her, which did not hide all the cuts on her body. Her face was ashen and he had to stop himself from running straight out into the shed to try to rescue her. Then he saw his father, sitting watching her work. Every now and then he would hit her for no apparent reason and Jamie would cringe for her, as pain shot through her body. He racked his brains frantically for a solution, every nerve in his body jangling with hatred for his father. Annie fell to her knees, the heat and pain too much for her to bear any more. Instantly he was up dragging her to her feet, yelling and screaming at her to work. They struggled, the glinting knife blade tantalisingly close to Annie's hands. She scratched at his face with her nails gouging great lumps of skin out and as he cried out she kicked and hit him in the groin. In his state of insanity, Joe found supreme strength and leaping up he placed his hands around her throat and began to squeeze.

Harder and harder he pushed his fingers together, enjoying seeing Annie's eyes bulge and the last wisps of breath being forced out of her. She continued to fight, arms flailing, feet kicking, her will to live urging her onward.

Joe laughed raucously, spitting his saliva in her face. 'Die, die, Annie. Then no one can have yer except me. I can't let yer live, you're a bitch, nothin' but a whoring bitch.'

Black shadows began to swirl in Annie's head, her lungs felt as if they were about to explode and her eyes as if they would burst from her head any minute. She was dying, he was murdering her. No, no, no, she screamed the words in her head, she wanted to live.

The crazed expression on Joe's face changed, first to one of surprise and then shock, before he released his grip and slid unceremoniously to the floor. Blood spurted from him where the knife had punctured his skin and he died with his eyes wide open staring accusingly at Annie. She stood rooted to the spot, crying hysterically, Jamie in her arms and Joe at her feet. It was over, the monster was dead, she was alive, the nightmare had ended and she was free. Mother and son stood clinging on to one another as sobs of relief shook their bodies.

That was how Richard found them when he burst into the shed a few moments later.

# Thirty-Four

Annie sat on the wooden seat underneath the blossoming roses that twined around the trellis arched above her head. The smell was intoxicating, and the greedy bees buzzed drunkenly around in an ecstatic frenzy. Closing her eyes against the hot August sunshine she happily soaked up the fierce rays on her face. She was at peace for the first time in her life and the feeling brought her such joy that she felt she must be smiling continually. She wanted to sing and dance and run and feel the soft breeze in her hair, she wanted to shout out how lucky she was, how grateful to have been given a second chance in her life. She was totally in love with being alive, and she blossomed in her discovery.

It would be at least another hour before Richard and Jamie returned from their shopping trip and so she was in no hurry to interrupt this indulgent solitude of afternoon bliss. Squinting against the sunlight she happily gazed around the garden. It was beautiful, cascading with fragrant flowers and undulating emerald lawns. Beyond the hedges, blue skies and poppy-filled meadows stretched as far as she could see. There was no smog, no skyline of dirty roofs or billowing steam, just wide open spaces. Behind her the square Georgian house, blinking with its symmetrical windows, warm red bricks and straight white columns, stood solidly. It was not a particularly large house but it was hers, hers and Richard's, and it exuded safety and strength, it was their fortress.

A figure waved from a downstairs window and then reappeared at the door carrying a tray with tea and scones on.

'I thought yer might fancy these,' Sarah smiled as she tottered across the lawn on her arthritic legs.

'Yer spoil me, I should be lookin' after you.' Annie moved along the seat to make room for her friend. 'I can't sit in this heat, thanks. It'll wrinkle my skin and spoil me looks,' grinned Sarah, carefully placing the tray down.

'This is real, Sarah, isn't it? I want yer to pinch me to make sure. I'm so scared that I'm goin' to wake up an' find it's all a dream an' I'm back in the cottage.'

Sarah perched for a moment beside her, stroking her shining hair lovingly. 'Yes it's real Annie, an' it's only what yer deserve. Enjoy it, Richard loves yer, always has and Jamie's happy and free. The demons've gone, don't let them spoil this, Annie. Besides, I 'ope it's not a dream or I'll have to go back and live on that draughty barge an' I like 'ere thank you.' Sarah laughed and bending forward she kissed Annie's head lovingly.

After the nightmare in the shed, Annie had fallen apart completely and without Richard's love and strength she didn't know how she would have survived. The physical wounds had healed quickly but as always the mental ones took longer, still reappearing every now and then to remind her who she really was.

During the trial that had followed Joe's death, Annie had put herself completely in Richard's hands. She knew she could have hung for the crime but she was resigned to that, and as long as Jamie was free, it was a price she considered worth paying.

Richard had shone. No longer reserved and careful, he had embarked on a crusade for her freedom. She had listened in awe to his eloquent speeches about her life. He delivered with such passion the story of her miserable existence with Joe, illustrating the persecutions and cruelty so vividly that the judge was almost moved to tears. All the hidden truths had come out, how Joe had murdered Jack, all the miseries he had inflicted. By the time the story had

325

reached the actual climax of Joe's death both judge and jury were quite happy to accept that it was self-defence, that if Joe had not been killed then Annie most certainly would have been. To her utter amazement she had walked free from the court to the open arms of her hero, the Richard she had fallen in love with all those years ago.

The later decisions were made so easily, to leave Cheshire and start a new life together. Within weeks they had all moved miles away to another part of the country where no one knew of their sorry past. Her only connection now with Lytwych was the pan. Annie couldn't bring herself to sell her pa's shed to Richard's father, it seemed so disloyal. However, she found a young enthusiastic couple anxious to start out on their own, and she rented it to them, along with the cottage. She hoped that all their joy and zest for life would wipe out the misery that surrounded the place and infuse it with new hope. She doubted that Jamie would ever be able to face going back but if he changed his mind in the future it was always there for him.

Richard was still married to Dorothy but they decided to leave things as they were. They made the rules in this brave new world they had etched out for themselves, and the villagers in Richard's new practice all thought what a pretty young wife he had, and complimented him on that very point. He did not contradict it.

Voices interrupted Annie's daydreams and she smiled as Jamie raced across to her, wielding two large brown parcels in the air joyously.

'We've got them Ma, all of them. Shoes, trousers, jacket everythin'. His face was animated and happy and it made Annie feel so good to see him like this.

Richard had taken him shopping for his new school clothes, for Jamie was enrolled at the local school. They had already been to see the headmaster and Jamie met some of the other boys. For the first time in his life he had a friend who lived in the next house along the lane, and the two of them would go off to play for hours at a time. The transformation in him was incredible and Annie glowed when she saw the happiness shining in his eyes.

'Can I go an' try them all on?' he pestered eagerly.

'Yes, go on in an' come out an' show us when yer dressed.'

He scampered off, yelling as he went for Sarah to come and look. Richard sat down beside her planting a loving kiss on her cheek which she returned with a fervent hug.

'What's that for, my Annie Hayes?' he laughed.

'Just to say I love you,' she said, with such complete honesty that he melted against her. 'I don't deserve yer, Richard, but I'm so thankful that yer here.'

Richard sighed. He hated when she allowed that sad look to veil her beautiful eyes, she was so hard on herself. He knew that there were still many dark secrets that she kept locked within her tortured soul. Bit by bit they emerged as she felt ready and able to let them go. He didn't rush her. In time she would believe his love was true and that she was safe, in the meantime he was quite happy to reassure her whenever she needed it. Perhaps there were things that she would never share with him, things so terrible that she must lock them away for ever; so be it. He was determined that he would make her happy, the love he felt for her was so strong that it could defeat any demon that still lurked.

He cradled her head against his chest now, gently as if she were made of porcelain, so precious was she to him. If they could have read each others' mind at that moment they would have laughed, for they were each thanking God for the other one.

Annie closed her eyes in contentment. She could want for nothing more in her life, she felt she had more than she deserved. She thought about Joe quite a lot, but the thoughts were becoming more and more controlled now. The events took on a logical sequence, she found reasons and explanations, and the more she did this the easier it became to accept that many of the dreadful events in her life had not been her fault. She could see now that Joe could no longer hurt her, she was free, and his face could pass in front of her memory without causing her to shudder.

Her feelings of hate turned to pity and these she neatly placed in a dark cupboard in her mind that had its door firmly closed. It would be wrong to forget, but she would remember only when she chose to. Her life was better now than she had ever dreamt possible. Only Jamie concerned her. Outwardly he seemed so happy, but she wondered if it were possible that in so short a time he could have come to terms with the events of his life.

Up in his bedroom, especially painted for him by Richard, Jamie tried on his new clothes. He knew he was very lucky and he tried very hard to forget his other life, though it wasn't easy. So many things seemed distorted and confused in his head. He and his ma had talked about that day in the shed only once since it happened, and that was just before her trial. Jamie had been distraught that she should take the blame for his father's death, when he knew it was the kissing bush that had done it. Hadn't he wished for that very thing when he and Sarah had made the bush, that day? He was confused when she had insisted that she had killed his father, she had held him tightly as she said it, her eyes burning into his. 'Remember Jamie, it's very important. I killed him, you saw me do it, promise me.' She had said it over and over again, until he had promised.

The events in the shed all became a kind of blur in his mind, it was all very complicated but if that was what his ma said, then it must be true. He didn't want to make things worse for her and so in the court he repeated what she had told him to. As he spoke, her smiling eyes had held his, encouraging his words and when he had finished she had blown him a kiss, so he knew he had done well.

Jamie didn't tell anyone about his nightmares or how he sometimes woke up crying and terrified in the middle of the night, imagining his father's hot hands on his skin. He didn't want to spoil his new life by remembering his old one. So he plunged himself into this new world with enthusiasm and he fooled everyone – except his ma. Sometimes at night she would come into his room and give him an extra hug or kiss and reassure him that everything was all right now. They shared a secret, nursed a pain, and that special unbreakable bond they possessed shone out, as they held each other's eyes, a private thing between the two of them. No one need ever know that it was Jamie's hand that had held the knife that plunged into his father's back that day. It was Jamie who had slain the dragon and rescued the damsel, just as he had vowed he would, and that secret would remain theirs as long as they lived.